KT-478-038

Love

OTHER BOOKS BY THE AUTHOR

Must Love Otters

Hollie Porter Builds a Raft

Neurotica

To Dwayne "The Rock" Johnson,
who helps us believe in the power
of hard work;
and to all my ducklings, for whom
I have never worked harder.

PROLOGUE

March 28, 1997

Dear Dwayne Johnson,

Hi, my name is Danielle Steele. (Yes. Like the romance novelist. Except I have an e on the end of my name and the writer lady doesn't.) You can call me Dani. I am ten years old and in the fifth grade in Portland, Oregon. We are doing a school project about our favorite celebrity, and we have to write them a letter. I picked you because my dad has been a huge fan since you played college football.

He loves the University of Miami because he had a wild spring break there one year, even though when he talks about it, my mom gets really mad. I play soccer because they don't have football for girls, and I picked my jersey number—it's 94 because that was the number you wore for the Hurricanes when they won the national championship in 1991.

And even after you were drafted by the Calgary Stampeders way up in Canada, but then they cut you, it doesn't matter because my dad says Canadian football is weird with its bigger field and three downs instead of four. Did you like Calgary? Was there a lot of snow when you were there?

My dad says you are half Canadian so it makes sense that you wanted to play in the CFL.

My dad also says you were the best defensive lineman the University of Miami had ever seen and that Warren Sapp is overrated.

I have two annoying older sisters named Georgette and Jacqueline. We are all named after romance writers because my mom loves to read romance novels with tons of kissing and women being rescued all the time. This drives my dad crazy. I love that your wrestling name is Rocky Maivia after your dad and your grandfather. What is it like having a high chief as a grandfather? There is a girl in my homeroom whose mom was born in Hawaii, and she tells everyone that means she's Hawaiian, even though she's never been to Hawaii and she's afraid of the sun so I think she makes a terrible Hawaiian because Hawaii always has sun, right?

My dad says he's the chief in our house and that's why he gets control of the remote.

It rains a lot in Portland. Do you have alligators in Miami? Do they really come up through the toilets? A kid in my math class went to Tampa once and he says that alligators live in the sewers. He also eats his own boogers, so I don't believe everything he says.

So maybe if you can write back to me, you can tell me about what life is like as a wrestler. Good luck at the next big wrestling match. I will try to watch it on TV, but it depends if it's a school night or if my mom gets mad at my dad because he is exposing me to "trash TV." I don't think wrestling is trash, but it does look like it hurts a lot.

Sincerely yours,
Danielle Steele with an e

⌐∾

On September 27, 1998, Dwayne Douglas Johnson, by this time officially known as "The Rock," was in a Triple Threat Match as part of a huge pay-per-view event called "Breakdown: In Your House." The Rock pinned another wrestler named Ken Shamrock, won the match, and became the number one contender in the World Wrestling Federation Championship.

I know this because I watched it.

At my house, the weather had been in the seventies, the summer refusing to let go despite the fact that "she'd" been excused from duty six days prior with the official equinox. My sisters were out with Mommy buying school shoes, so it was just me and Dad, Gerald Robert Steele, sharing in the reverie of watching our favorite superhero via the magic of cable pay-per-view television.

When The Rock won his match, Gerald Robert Steele swallowed the last of his Budweiser, clicked off the TV before the entire event concluded, patted me on the head, and got out of the squeaky, plaid knockoff La-Z-Boy my mother had threatened a thousand times to set ablaze.

He then picked up an old, fat duffel bag sitting next to his chair, its bloated side decorated with a crackled silk screen from some gym he used to go to. I hadn't noticed the bag until that moment. He held a finger against the mustache-topped lips that always tickled when he kissed me good night and said, "Sssshhhh."

He opened the front door, stepped out, and never looked back.

The child psychologist Mommy dragged us to said that journaling, in whatever form we found most helpful, was an effective way to handle our abandonment issues. I didn't know I was going to have abandonment issues until they told me I would. I sort of figured Gerald Robert Steele would come home eventually.

Apparently my sisters felt abandoned, though, and they liked the cookies the therapist fed us (oatmeal-raisin that tasted like feet). In her therapy sessions, Georgette, the middle child, started painting. On everything. She now has a degree in studio art, emphasis on the anti–Industrial Revolution Arts and Crafts Movement, with a minor in early childhood education that she uses to homeschool her three very excitable, very sticky offspring, all of whom are named after well-known Arts and Crafts artists.

Jacqueline, my oldest sister, decided that the therapist's profession was noble, asked how to become a doctor, and then followed said steps by throwing herself into her studies. Except now she's a plastic surgeon who specializes in cosmetic enhancement, not a shrink. (Also: It's beyond apropos that she's a plastic surgeon—with a name like Jacqueline Collins [Steele]? You remember what the romance novelist Jackie Collins looked like, right? I'm guessing she kept her own plastic surgeon in a.testoni oxfords and winter holidays in Zurich.)

Georgette painted. Jackie studied bloody things. I doodled and wrote in my diary—mostly entries in the form of letters, every single one addressed to Dwayne "The Rock" Johnson, none of them ever sent.

I know what you're thinking: Why spend so much time and energy talking to someone who doesn't know I exist?

Because he listens, without judgment or comment or disapproval. He doesn't tease, snicker, reprimand, pooh-pooh, or shake his head quietly.

The Rock is always there, and I'm sure his girls, when he has a duffel bag sitting next to his La-Z-Boy, don't worry if he's going to come home at the end of the day.

Because he always does.

ONE

PUBLISH   SAVE   PREVIEW   CLOSE

March 15, 2016

Dear Dwayne Johnson,

He's doing it again, DJ. Trevor. I'm not even kidding.

It's so far beyond toilet seats and not closing the toothpaste (these tubes don't even have lids! How hard is it to not blob friggin' toothpaste all over the top of the tube??). THIS is why we can't live together. THIS is why I keep my own tiny, overpriced apartment that smells like pot all the time thanks to the neighbor's glaucoma.

I know guys fart. That's what Febreze is for.

I know guys don't usually notice the pink and/or black mold growing in the tub. That's what bleach is for.

But seriously, seriously, I cannot handle it when he clips his toenails in the living room.

WHO DOES THIS? You would never do this, right? God, tell me you would never do this.

He plays Frisbee golf with his stinky friends and asks me to meet him at his apartment so we can go out for a "nice dinner" (read: Red Lobster) and then he comes home, strips off his socks, and clips his toenails in the living room because he says his nails are nice and soft from being sweaty.

It probably wouldn't bother me to such an extent if the nail clippings didn't get lodged in the CARPET and then in my flesh. Soft, my ass! It feels like glass, stepping on those dead toenails. Like, I had to pull one out of the squishy part of my foot and then use Neosporin so I didn't get a Staph infection from his sweat.

Why am I even with this guy???

Mommy keeps reminding me that Timothy (his name is Trevor) doesn't have a good aura, that something is off with his terrestrial vibrations or some whackadoo thing—"Just like Gerald Robert Steele, your father, Danielle, and look how that worked out. Don't be impulsive. You're just like your father that way. Impulsive. I think this Timothy character has nefarious energy, I really do. One of these days you'll come home and find that he's packed a bag and left. Mark my words."

No, Mommy, Gerald Robert Steele probably did what he did so he didn't throw a toaster in with you while you soaked in your tub of "magic space leaves." (Yeah, it was marijuana. A lot of marijuana.)

I am considering a move to Port-aux-Français, French Southern and Antarctic Lands, which is the farthest point I can get from Portland, Oregon. (I googled it.) It only has an average population of about 80 (45 in winter, up to 120 in summer), and they're mostly scientists so I'll need to learn something sciencey to make myself relevant. At least I'd have an excuse when I told Mommy I had bad reception for her unceasing faxes.

Anyway, I think the fact that I'm not living under a bridge means I'm doing all right. I just need a boyfriend who doesn't shed his body parts in common living areas.

Seriously.

Disgusted in Derpville,
Dani Borderline-Podophobic Steele

P.S. I finally binged that HBO show where you play the financial manager guy to all those hot football players, and sir, you certainly know how to wear a suit. But why so many boobies? So many beautiful buns? Are there women who really look like that? I really need to stop eating so much sugar if I ever want pretty boobies and buns. Speaking of buns, I'm going out for a cheeseburger. Can I get you anything? Man, I miss In-N-Out. I wonder if they have cheeseburgers in Antarctica . . .

SAVE
CLOSE

TWO

From: Jacqueline Collins Steele, MD, FACS <DoctorJacqueline@
JCSMed.com>
To: Danielle E. Steele <DS.May21972@gmail.com>
Subject: Your lab results, et cetera . . .

From the Desk of Jacqueline Collins Steele, MD, FACS

Hi, Dani,

My secretary called you about your blood work, but she said your voicemail is full and that your message sounds like you're growling? Maybe look into that?

I wanted to let you know that your iron is a little low, so it would be good if you could cut out the sweets and Diet Cokes (diet soda is poison!). Mild anemia would explain the dark circles under your eyes too—weren't you talking to Mommy about how your hair feels like it's thinning? Take naps when you can—so good for you!

Technically your BMI is just above normal limits, but at 5'5", every pound counts. Your LDL cholesterol is a little concerning—less meat, more greens! You know heart disease runs in our family. Our father's father had several serious cardiac events (yes, he smoked two packs a day and ate cow liver regularly), but you remember him—he was a beanpole when he died. And I think it would help your acting endeavors if you took better care of yourself. Healthy body, healthy mind, and all that, right?

Even though you tend to be a bit sturdier than Georgette and me, you still must be mindful of developing osteoporosis. Have you considered buying a juicer? I juice cruciferous vegetables every day and drink it with a protein mix to keep me going between patients. At the very least, eat a Tums (calcium carbonate) every night before bed. Some calcium is better than what you're getting from the daily lattes, although calcium citrate is better absorbed by the body. Ask the pharmacist to help you find this.

I know your job is quite sedentary, but your body will change in your thirties, so it's time to start thinking about your future self. Speaking of, did you call my guy about setting up savings and retirement accounts? He said he'd give you a family referral discount because I've been such a loyal customer since medical school.

Mommy needs us to talk about her 60th birthday dinner/party. Maybe bring that guy you've been seeing?

Your loving sister,
Jacqueline Steele, MD, FACS
Board Certified, American Board of Cosmetic Surgeons

THREE

Thomas the Singing Barista holds the song, adds extra whip (thanks to Jerky Jackie, a.k.a. my sister the doctor, I want all the whipped cream in the world), but gives me a longer glance than usual.

"So either you've changed professions since I saw you last week," he says, eyeing my ripped fishnet tights under an almost-too-tight plaid miniskirt, the chunky late-nineties-era black platforms, and my boobs flashing what is most definitely forced cleavage thanks to a push-up bra and those silicone enhancers, "or you have an audition."

"If these auditions would actually *work*, I could definitively say, 'Yes, Thomas, I have changed professions.'"

"You should go back to LA, Dani."

Mm-hmm, 'cause that experiment worked out so well. "Can I borrow a magic carpet?"

"That's super racist, you know," he says, sprinkling cinnamon on my latte's poufy whipped-cream hat. "You're saying that because I look like Aladdin."

"Dream on. You're so Polish. And you want to *marry* Aladdin."

"Who wouldn't? Look at that bone structure."

"And I say it because your grandfather sells Persian rugs."

"You know too much about my life, Danielle Steele."

"Doesn't everyone know what their favorite singing barista-slash-acting-class-snark-buddy's grandfather does?"

"If you want to be svelte when Hollywood calls, maybe cut back on the whip."

Hmmph. "I'll take one of those scones too."

He lifts an eyebrow so blond it's almost invisible but slides the glazed maple scone into a small paper bag for me anyway.

"Is this one for you, or is it your contribution to the Cluckers?"

"All mine, baby. For a job well done."

"What job? You haven't even gone to the audition yet."

"I'm out of bed, aren't I?"

"And playing hooky, I might add. Today's excuse?"

I hand him my money. "My tire was flat?"

"I thought you used that one last month."

"I have old tires?"

"Joan the Crone's gonna have your head on a pike if you're not careful."

"You should get a job there, Thomas. You and Joan could compare plans for world domination."

"Tempting. But sitting in a room where estrogen is pumped through the ventilation ducts, listening to people whine on the phone about their genital herpes? I'll pass."

"It's not all herpes. We get warts and crabs too. Plus, health and a 401(k)," I say, tearing a piece off the scone. "I can put in a word with the Crone." The maple glaze melts on my tongue.

"I'd rather sell Grandpa's rugs."

Imagine the witch who gives Snow White the apple. Make her more than six feet tall. Braid the hairs growing from the mole. Give her the personality of Miss Gulch, the mean lady on the bike who yells at Dorothy's aunt and uncle about little Toto.

Boom. My boss. Joan the Crone.

Eliza Gordon

Thomas moves to hand me my change, but I nod toward the tip jar. "You could always start writing romance novels—you've got the perfect name for it," he says, mouth poised as if he's about to segue into yet another song.

"Thanks, but I'm pretty sure my whole existence is copyright infringement at this point." I wave and shuffle toward the door, praying I won't sprain anything before I get where I need to be.

"Break a leg!" Thomas says, the last word overwritten by the jingle of the coffee shop's door as it closes behind me.

FOUR

Text conversation outside of coffee shop:

Trevor: Hey hot stuf. Don't 4get it's Monday. My place? Bring the black thigh-hi's. My favrite!

Me: FavOrite.

Trevor: Wha?

Me: You spelled favorite wrong.

Trevor: Ur correcting my spelling?

Me: Can't talk. Going in to audition.

Trevor: Break a leg. Or don't b/c then you can't wear the thigh-hi's. Mmmm sexy.

Me: Sorry. Unexpected plans tonight. Will have to rain check.

Trevor: Ur blue-balling me again? ☹☹☹

Me: If I made you an appointment for a pedicure, would you go?

Trevor: What R U talking about?

I set my phone to vibrate.

FIVE

The audition is, luckily, not far from here. A few blocks over at a repurposed school. Something about a music video. No lines to learn, but apparently, I have to dance. My agent—and I use that term loosely because Portland's acting scene isn't exactly lighting up the phone lines of the Oscars' voting membership—said that it's for a local band with money from some big LA producer. They're going all out with the video for their debut album, despite the fact that MTV is more concerned with pregnant teenagers and catfishing humans than filling the airwaves with actual *music*.

Whatever. I need the résumé credit. Plus, day rate on a union shoot would be awesome. Craft service? Hot musicians? Hair and makeup? What better way to spend a day or two?

I park up the street, cram one quick bite of the maple scone into my face, and check the rearview mirror—freshen lips, wipe off offending crumbs. My phone buzzes against the side of the plastic cup holder and scares the crap out of me.

Text, from Viv, one of the few human beings with a soul at Imperial Health and Wellness:

Where R U? Cluckers meeting 12 PM, moved to Conf Rm
B. DON'T BE LATE.

Even though I'm living in Fancy Actor Dreamland for the next
forty-five minutes, dressed like a grunge Rockette from the Cobain
days and not a "professional" twenty-nine-year-old woman, I do have
to go back to work today. There, properly attired in my cubicle that
is shamelessly decorated with Dwayne Johnson's face and stunning
muscles, I shall resume processing medical claims and smiling through
the phone when someone screams at me about how we refuse to cover
her boob job. (Although, between you and me, much of my time is
spent hunched over the billing-code book with my back turned away
from the wider viewing public, my forehead resting on my fingers so
it looks like I'm searching for some obscure code—perhaps hypertri-
chosis: "werewolf syndrome"—so I can just take a quick nap. Naps are
good for you. Jerky Jackie said so.)

Being a part-time actress and full-time sister/daughter/auntie/
worker chicken/substandard girlfriend can be very exhausting.

So is staying out late after acting workshops. Like last night. Every
Sunday, I swear I won't follow the other budding stars and starlets to
the bar, but I do it because I'm stupid and weak and I really like drinking things that make my lips tingle.

And Trevor and I have reached that point in our on-again, off-
again relationship of convenience where we schedule sex: Mondays,
Wednesdays, usually Saturdays if he doesn't have a Frisbee golf thing or
if I'm not babysitting a member of my family.

Truth: I don't have plans tonight. I just don't want to wear black
thigh-highs to play Hide the Sausage. Can't we just bone and then binge
on two-bite brownies and Netflix like normal friends with benefits?

Truth number two: I can't stop thinking about those toenails.

But today, lingering hangover and canceled sex date aside, there *is* something magical to look forward to. The MotherCluckers meet up every two weeks in an available conference room and feast on whatever desserty decadence the assigned Bringer of the Treats has found while we dish on the latest gossip, celebrity news, TV/movies, and books. Management agreed to let us do it when some European study convinced them that productivity spikes in employees who are granted a slice of time during their workday for book clubs, yoga, Zumba, or healthy walks around the neighborhood. (Thank you, Europeans.)

Since none of us own yoga pants that have ever seen a single downward dog, we get away with calling the MotherCluckers a "book club." Someone brings in a few books to have on the table, and then we slather our faces in processed sugar.

What will it be this week? Éclair? Cream puff? Napoleon? A simple but always delicious maple bar?

It's sort of awesome.

What is not awesome are the forty-two stairs I am going to have to climb to get into this Jurassic-era brick building. Honestly, what happened to equal access for all? Including women in ridiculous chunky heels that could probably support a car's weight should she *really* need to change a tire?

Though I do manage to make it into the building, and just in time as a fat gray spring cloud has decided to pour her overburdened heart out on the outdoors, my stomach sinks when I walk into the holding area and see this is a cattle call. Overriding the stale smell of old building is the virtual tidal wave of body spray and perfumes worn by two dozen other girls in various states of dress, some more goth than grunge, way more black fishnets than red flannel, and all of them younger, tighter, prettier, likely dressed in outfits they had to borrow from the back part of Mom's closet, that space where you keep stuff you're just not ready to get rid of because you can feel your youth draining away like the last few drops of Irish cream from the Bailey's bottle.

I really need to go back to LA.

I sign in and hand over the obligatory headshot and résumé, my stomach settling a little when I recognize the casting assistant. Show business in this town is a tight-knit group. Any talent who spends more than a month in the audition trenches gets to know the casting assistants and casting directors on a first-name basis. This one—Brittany, as bubbly and bonny as her name suggests—asks about my family, if my sister has room for new patients and if I can get her a discount *ha ha ha* (everyone wants a nose job on the cheap), how she hasn't seen me around a lot so where have I been hiding?

"Ask my agent," I say.

"Still with Lady Macbeth?" My agent, Janice, is a former child actress. Did a lot of commercials in LA as a kid, made the transition to Disney programming, and then after college she did one season with the Oregon Shakespeare Festival as the conniving wife of the doomed Macbeth. Then she had an affair with the (married) director and high-tailed it out of town swollen with their alleged love child, landed in Portland, and decreed herself the city's best agent. Janice is a woman of many fictions, but she's treated me very well, so who am I to question where she stands in the agent hierarchy?

"Hey, is your email still the same?" I nod. She lowers her voice. "I'm running a new improv group on Thursday nights, if you're interested."

"That would be awesome . . ." I've done a few of Brittany's improv classes. She's hilarious, and the crew she runs with is super talented—whenever she offers me a spot, I accept. Always time well spent. But she keeps it on the down-low, an invite-only sort of thing, so we don't have to babysit all the teenagers looking for a venue to make dick jokes. Such jokes should be left to the professionals.

"I'll send you the details. And they should call you in about twenty minutes," she says, leaning closer. "I hope you're ready to shake your ass. The lead singer is in there, and he's about twelve and a total perv."

"Awesome." I give her a weak thumbs-up and pick a seat off to the side. Yeah, I'm lucky because I look younger than my real age, but seriously, I still look way older than any of the girls here. Why the hell did Janice send me out on this? Where are the *real* gigs, you know? Like tampon or feminine deodorant commercials? The residuals on those can be nuts—I knew a woman in LA who bought a house in the Hollywood Hills just from the residuals she earned on Massengill Douche ads. Sure, she was known as the Douche Lady, but she has an infinity pool *and* a pool boy named Sven. A clean vagina is no laughing matter.

Man, I miss my LA people. I'm not gonna lie. Friends who talked about acting, friends who went to the movies with me when we weren't talking about acting, friends who shared a plate of sweet potato fries after the movie so we could dissect what we'd just watched, friends who let you practice your monologue the night before class so you'd really nail the pathos, friends who would read your lame first attempt at writing a screenplay and offer constructive feedback, friends who would let you raid their wardrobe so you wouldn't have to buy a new outfit for an audition . . .

Portland's great, but it's not LA.

Fifteen credits short of a bachelor of fine arts, I used the last of my student loan money to put new tires and brakes on Flex Kavana (my Honda, named after Dwayne Johnson's first wrestling name) so I could blast into Hollywood because *obviously*, after doing years of theater in junior high, high school, and college, I must've had a talent they'd never seen before.

They had seen it before.

On a million other eager beavers who had no idea that Los Angeles was ready with her gaping maw. If the chronic swarm of LAPD helicopters had infrared for lost dreams, said corpses would be splattered over every paved inch of that city.

I lived in a shitty three-bedroom, fourth-floor apartment with three other very smelly actors in the sizzling, overcrowded San Fernando

Valley. Fun fact: A severed head was found in the dumpster of a pizza place just around the block. One of my roommates took a picture of it. (She was really weird, actually.)

It was basically the best time of my life.

Two years, three months, nine days in the City of Angels. That was it. Tons of unpaid gigs, necessary to build a résumé, as well as some paid "acting" jobs—hand modeling for a medical-device company where I just had to pretend I was pushing buttons on an EEG machine, two weeks as a zombie (so much fun, except for the 5:00 a.m. call time to spend three hours in makeup) on a low-budget film, as a day player (that means the actor gets a few lines) who then dies on camera for a now-canceled CBS show. It was down to me and one other girl for a pilot that went on to a full-season order for NBC. Booking this gig would've been a real coup—not only would it have changed my life, but I'm also a size 10, which is pretty much huge by LA standards, so landing a lead role on a network television show where I wouldn't have been playing a frazzled mom but rather a powerful, single CEO in search of love in the cutthroat world of online sex-toy sales?

I mentioned it was a comedy, right?

That loss led to a bottle of Black Label, a dozen or two Krispy Kremes quietly delivered by sympathetic roommates, and a week spent under my covers bingeing *Gilmore Girls* on DVD. Not one of my prouder moments.

When actors aren't acting, though, we wait tables and froth nonfat, organic milk for overpriced coffee drinks, spending more than we earn on headshots and acting classes and teeth whitening and movies and plays (because we can write those off!). Acting is the greatest job in the world, if you can stand the constant rejection and recurrent bouts of self-doubt without becoming addicted to some hazardous substance. (Like sugar.)

But it only took a single phone call from my sister, Dr. Jacqueline Collins Steele, for it all to come to a screeching halt: "Mommy is sick. We need you to come home."

So I did.

And once surgery and a little radiation took care of Mommy's very pissed-off thyroid, and she was well enough to resume normal nagging duties while stroking a rather frightening bright-pink scar at her neck (she now tells people it happened when she was abducted by aliens and transported outside our galaxy on their ship), it didn't seem right to leave and go back to LA. Plus, I was broke. The move back to the Pacific Northwest ate the bulk of my savings.

Of course, there was plenty to spend in the Guilt Bank: "You should stay. Mommy misses you too much when you're so far away," and "Mommy sure worried about you down in that dirty, scary place," my sisters and well-meaning family friends would drone. Note: LA isn't that dirty. Hollywood sort of is, and maybe some spots in the Valley, but the beaches are nice.* And it's not scary. Unless you find yourself in the wrong neighborhood after dark. But that's true of any city.

(Oh, and before you think it's weird that we call my mother "Mommy"—everyone calls her that. That's just who she *is*. Everyone's mom. It's how she introduces herself to new people, in her long broom skirts circa 1974 and the beads and the no-bra policy and her Margaret Atwood hair. I'd tell you that she's eccentric but given that her daughters are named after women who've made fortunes spinning yarns about throbbing manhoods and bursting cleavage . . .)

Even finding an acting community in Portland wasn't enough to safeguard my sanity during the time I had to cohabit with Mommy. When it got to the point where I was considering living in my car, I had to make a change, or as Jerky Jackie said, "Find a respectable, grown-up occupation with benefits and a retirement savings plan, Danielle."

---

*   Except the beach at the Santa Monica Pier—thanks to a huge storm drain that empties untreated gunk into the ocean, this area always ranks as one of the most polluted beaches in the state of California. Don't say I didn't warn you.

So I went to a job fair. And Imperial Health and Wellness hired me.

Six blissful years later, here I am, sitting in an abandoned school with aspiring actresses who likely still wait outside convenience stores and bribe hobos to buy them shitty beer.

That was one thing my dad did manage to impart before disappearing: If some poor kid from Hayward, California, can become the next greatest thing in the World Wrestling Federation (rebranded as World Wrestling Entertainment in 2002), then I can do whatever the hell I wanna do too.

Although it's fair to say that poor kid from Hayward has done a smidge better than I have. Hey, at my age, The Rock was still finding his sea legs, though his sea legs probably weren't adorned in ripped fishnets, but yeah . . . I can't panic yet.

My phone chimes again. A text from my middle sister, Georgette. Another inquiry about Mommy's birthday fête. It's in what, two months? We have plenty of time to order a carrot cake. Sheesh. **Mommy wants you to bring a date to her sixtieth so you don't feel left out. Are you still dating that one guy?**

My family's inability—unwillingness?—to even attempt to remember Trevor's name is blindingly annoying, even though, to be honest, I don't know what the deal is with *us* most of the time, either; we call each other "carnal companions." I think we're both at that age where a partner free of STDs is enough, as is having someone to call "boyfriend" or "girlfriend" to keep nagging relatives off our backs ("Aren't you *ever* going to settle down?"), but we're both a little fickle, and though we have our moments where we coo at each other, we also have those moments where we say stuff like "If I ever do get married, my partner will be into _____," and we fill in the blank with something we know the other person isn't really into. Which says a lot about how we're probably not going to commit to each other in any real, legal capacity anytime soon.

Our unofficial treaty has one important caveat: If we want to date someone else or swipe right or whatever, we have to be honest. No one has time for chlamydia these days.

So I can't totally blame my family for their condescension. Before Trevor, there was a string of failed relationships, both before and after LA. Love is mercurial in the acting world—you work very closely with a set group of people for an intense, concentrated amount of time. You learn to trust these people—you *have* to, or else you won't give your best performance—plus you're working insane hours and they see you when you're not at your best. When that kind of vulnerability is laid bare, the heart can't help but respond. These "showmances" are basically the reason so many Hollywood marriages end in divorce after just a few years.

But being a member of Clan Steele does not make this process any easier. Pretty much as soon as I introduce a guy to my family, he bails. I tried to tell my sisters that our family jinxes every relationship I've ever had, but then they both reminded me how they're engaged and/or married and their respective partners haven't run away scared.

"You date losers, Danielle," Jerky Jackie said. "Face facts."

And, lord knows, Jerky Jackie is *all* about facts. It's why she signs every email and letter to me with her full name and all those stupid initials to remind me of all the brainiac things she's done: Jacqueline Collins Steele, MD, FACS. I think FACS stands for "Fabulous at Condescending [to my] Sisters."

She's very good at it.

INT. ODD-SMELLING AUDITION WAITING ROOM –
DAY

          DWAYNE "THE ROCK" JOHNSON
     (pushes librarian glasses up his
     nose)

Kid, I hate to break it to ya, but it's not always about you.

DANIELLE
Sure it is. Didn't you get the memo? Poor me, my daddy left so I have abandonment issues and a total lack of follow-through in pretty much everything I touch.

DWAYNE "THE ROCK" JOHNSON
You should call that therapist Jerky Jackie recommended. She has a wait list.

DANIELLE
I'd rather talk to the FedEx driver than any shrink Jackie recommends.

DWAYNE "THE ROCK" JOHNSON
Your sister is a doctor. She just wants to help.

DANIELLE
You clearly know nothing about Jacqueline Collins Steele, MD, FACS.

DWAYNE "THE ROCK" JOHNSON
Talk therapy can do wonders, Danielle.

DANIELLE

Eliza Gordon

I'm talking to you. Is that not
enough?

DWAYNE "THE ROCK" JOHNSON
I'm a figment of your very active imagination. This is sort of unhealthy,
as are your feelings of inferiority
in light of your older sisters' suc-
cesses. If I let everyone who was
better than me rule my life, I'd
still be walking around with seven
bucks in my pocket.

DANIELLE
With your seven bucks and my gift card
to Baja Fresh, we could get lunch
after this audition. I'm starving.

A girl a few seats over stands and plants herself next to me, interrupting my imaginary conversation, one hand holding the spaghetti
straps of a very sheer triangle-shaped top. "Excuse me—I know this is
super weird, but can you help me tie this?"

"Oh. Yeah. Sure," I say, shoving my phone into my bag.

"Thank you. I wasn't sure who to ask, but I figured asking a
mom would be safe," she says, flashing her perfectly white teeth as
I tie the strands in a bow. "Are you waiting for your daughter? Is she
auditioning?"

A mom? I look like a mom?

"Oh, uh, no. I don't have children. I'm auditioning today."

She turns in her chair, eyes wide, her very perky breasts now even
perkier that her newly secured top is tighter around her torso. "Really?

Oh, cool! That's so funny—I saw your bag and my little brother has one just like it so I just assumed . . ."

I look at the seat next to me, at the bag with Dwayne The Rock Johnson's face screen-printed across the front.

"I'm just a fan."

"That's so cute! Well, thanks! You look like you'd be such a great mom. Break a leg!" she says, and bounces away, leaving me to question my reason for living.

Based on how bloody slow everything is going, that pervy twelve-year-old rock star must be really enjoying this show. I pull out my phone, ignore the billion texts from Trevor about his blue balls, and log in to the "diary" where I write all my letters to Darling Dwayne. Hey, it's the safest place to keep these missives. In ninth grade, I sort of came home really drunk and puked all over Jerky Jackie's brand-new senior prom dress that was hanging in our shared bedroom, so in pursuit of vengeance, Jackie read all my diaries filled with the letters to Mr. Johnson, and then she told Mommy a bunch of secrets that were only ever supposed to be between me and my hero.

(I told you she was a big fat jerk.)

In the aftermath, as this was still in the days before cloud computing, I created a password-protected diary in the form of an unpublished blog where I could write my letters. Jackie is smart, but she's no tech head—no way she could reach under my mattress and hack my private correspondence ever again. (I nicknamed it "Operation Rock Solid"—get it? Rock Solid, as in unhackable by stupid sisters?)

This system worked. She's not read a diary entry since. And the prom date was totally cheating on her with a junior, so that was almost as unfortunate as the dress she chose. At least the wine cooler–infused vomit gave it some color.

PUBLISH   SAVE   PREVIEW   CLOSE

March 21, 2016

Dear Dwayne Johnson,

This audition—what was Lady Macbeth thinking? Thomas says I should go back to LA. The evergreen question: What would Dwayne do?

Is it considered pedophilia if the pervert lead singer of this band is underage and I'm supposed to dance for him? I should leave. This feels weird. And the waif next to me just asked if I'm here waiting for my daughter. I can tell you, I'd never let my daughter dance for some prepubescent, bonered-up musical wunderkind.

You're right. I should go. Thanks.

Also, Jerky Jackie emailed with medical crap and I want to believe that she really cares about my LDL cholesterol, but mostly, I end up feeling like I want to run to Dunkin' Donuts so my heart will explode for real and then I can come back as a ghost and haunt her office. I wonder if all her patients would think she's so great if they knew she won the senior class president election because she sent an Ex-Lax cake to her competitor on speech day or that she actually cheated on her SAT by hiring an impostor to take the test for her. See? Even Jerky Jackie is human.

Yours in chocolate-glazed bliss,
Danielle Elizabeth Steele, H.D. (Human Disaster)

P.S. The email she followed up with? A self-help article about children of parents who walk out on them, complete with a quiz: "Do You Have Daddy Issues?" Come ON, you guys—Gerald Robert Steele left, like, a million years ago, because his family is batshit crazy. Do I love the guy for doing it? No. Do I blame him? Double no. Am I serious about moving to Port-aux-Français? TOTALLY. I'm on Amazon looking at this dope faux-fur-trimmed parka as we speak.

SAVE
CLOSE

Before crossing my name off the sign-in sheet, I text Lady Macbeth: A girl auditioning just asked me if I'm waiting for my daughter. Maybe something less boy band next time? ☺

The smiley face says *I hate you, but I love you.* I've learned with Lady Macbeth that passive aggressive works best; who knows if her latest nanny has quit or if the wife of the father of her child is still cyberstalking her. Honestly, Janice has earned every inch of her widely known nickname.

Without explanation to Brittany, who is now on her phone, I draw a line through my name and shuffle to the door, avoiding eye contact with the pretty young things tittering with nervous energy. Let them worry about ass-shaking and booby-jiggling.

I'll shake my ass for the other half of this maple scone.

SIX

"Your eyeliner is a bit dark for the office, don't you think?" Viv says, doing her best impression of the Crone. She even wags her finger at me from her spot at the edge of my cubicle.

"It's grease and rubber. From changing my tire."

"How'd that tire-changing go?"

"I left early. Not my kind of tire," I say, stashing my bag in the oversize drawer of my boring gray metal desk.

"Shame on you! This could've been your big break!" Viv leans over and caresses a well-loved photo of The Rock. "What would *he* say if he knew you skipped out on an audition?"

"I didn't skip out. I went. But it was for a music video, and I was a granny compared to the other girls there, and *he* wouldn't have stuck around, either."

Viv tsks me. "You're never going to get your Oscar if you behave like this."

"I'm never going to get my Oscar prancing my wares in front of twelve-year-old rock stars."

"*Eww.* That does seem borderline illegal."

"Thank you."

Lydia canters by and yes, she canters because she's six two and all legs and has a mane of chestnut hair that would make an Appaloosa jealous, and we've threatened multiple times that we're going to steal her DNA to clone her metabolism so we can all eat as much as a linebacker and not gain an ounce. "Nine minutes, ladies! Don't be late!"

"I think I'm going to become an actor," Viv says, grabbing my coffee cup from the chaos that is my desk, grimacing when she realizes the cup still has last week's coffee in it. "That way I can skip work to play dress-up."

If anyone else said this, it would piss me off. But Viv lacks the Mean Bone.

"You missed the big drama this morning, though," she says close to my head as we step into the long gray aisle that divides the seemingly endless room in half. "Lisa's boyfriend sent her another dick pic, and somehow she managed to attach it to a company-wide email instead of a memo intended for her little circle of horny friends."

"Lisa's boyfriend is always sending dick pics. And his dick isn't that impressive. I see everything that pops up on her screen."

"Yeah, but management hadn't seen her dick pics before," she says. "Although I'm sure Elliott the IT Guy probably has. That dude creeps everyone's computers."

Note to self: Change password so Elliott the IT Guy doesn't hack into my blog.

I push the heavy door open that separates the henhouse from the cafeteria. Someone's burned popcorn again.

The cavernous room buzzes, filled with the conversations of the cliquish claims processors who have been released from their cages for their respective coffee and/or lunch breaks.

"Did they fire her?"

Viv hands me the coffee cup, and I dump the brown gelatinous goo into the sink. "She's in with the Crone right now."

Ah. That explains why the Crone hasn't yet perched on my desk edge.

I scrape the slimy residue off the cup's insides. My phone buzzes in the pocket of my work- and age-appropriate black cotton slacks. It can wait.

"Seriously, PMS has made me its bitch this month, so I hope the Bringer of the Treats has something chocolate stashed in that pink box," Viv says, nodding at the huge pastry carton on the opposite counter.

"So . . . no preggo, then?" I ask quietly, pausing my scrubbing for a beat. Poor Viv. She and her adorable husband, Ben, have been trying to get knocked up for the last two years. She's been known to rush home on lunch hours because her "temperature is perfect for baby-making," but alas, still no bun.

It's so weird to me that I have friends—younger friends—who are actively trying to make babies. I think I'd rather have open-heart surgery performed by John Cena. Me? With a kid? I spend hours worrying if Hobbs the Goldfish is depressed.

Viv grabs her lunch-size insulated bag out of the fridge while I refill my mug with fresh coffee. I sniff deeply—gourmet it's not, but at least the caffeine-laced steam is a salve to the persistent gin-infused ache behind my eyeballs.

"My mother keeps sending me meal plans she finds online, designed specifically for people trying to conceive," Viv says, opening the lid of her squishy lunch box. "I am really, really tired of beans and spinach. And I feel sorry for the other women sitting around me. So much farting."

"We'll get you an air freshener." I pinch her cheek playfully. "And today, after you eat your beans and spinach, you get a treat. Then go home with frosting on your face, and tell your man to put a baby in you."

"Such a classy broad, Steele." She laughs.

A box set in the corner is overflowing with soda cans and other recyclables. While Viv microwaves her lunch—likely killing any and all nutritional value in her beans and spinach   I gather the bag, tie it off, and carry it out the back door to set along the brick wall.

As I'm installing a new bag, I feel Viv's eyes on me. "You're a nice person, ya know."

"You've eaten too many beans. They're making you delirious."

"Howie the Pop-Can Man thinks you're nice."

"I've paid him off," I say, folding the plastic bag over the bin's edges.

"Don't worry. I won't tell anyone."

Howie the Pop-Can Man is a local transient who washes the front windows of our building in exchange for all our recyclables. The Crone kept chasing him away, but I sat down one day and talked to him. Turns out, he has a PhD in English lit with emphasis on the English Renaissance as well as lesser degrees in linguistics. As he says it, "I also earned a PhD in alcohol," which is why he lives the way he does. "This career track," he says, kicking his cart full of soda cans, "is almost as competitive as academia. But I like setting my own hours."

He recommends books to me—and says that my mother's fixation on romance novelists is actually charming, that "love transcends time. Look at Shakespeare's most successful plays." He's right. But most of the books he recommends, I'm not smart enough to get through— until he explains them. Sometimes, weather permitting, I order take- out and doughnuts and we sit at the picnic table behind the building, or we meet at a coffee shop down the street where it's warm, and Howie the Professor delivers a literature lecture some students would pay big bucks for. His brain is an impressive thing.

When I explained to the Crone that we could set up a symbiotic relationship with Howie and save the company a few dollars a month for window washing, she reluctantly agreed. So now Howie gets soda cans, Imperial Health and Wellness gets clean front windows, and I get books that will allegedly make me smarter.

When Viv has her Tupperware meals all warmed up and ready to go, I loop my arm through hers. "Let the clucking begin."

We move through the crowded room and head west, through two more long buildings filled with hen hutches. There has been much discussion among the Cluckers of whether referring to ourselves as chickens is misogynistic or wildly antifeminist. In our defense, if you saw these buildings—if you saw how we're set up in here, cubicles upon cubicles, and the stacks of paper we have to get through every day in order to fulfill the managerial numbers written on whiteboards on the back wall of every corridor—you'd see why we refer to ourselves as chickens. At least those of us with enough sense to find the humor so we don't chase a whole bottle of Tylenol PM with boxed wine to end the misery.

Inside Conference Room B, Lydia is already setting out plates and napkins. I know it's weird and maybe even creepy, but I love watching Lydia move—she was a dancer from kindergarten through college, and if it weren't for her obnoxious braying laugh, we wouldn't like her because she would be too perfect for us.

My phone buzzes again in my pocket. I don't want to look. Probably Jerky Jackie emailing me the number to her financial planner, or Georgette, who needs me to babysit so she can teach her dog-painting class. Who knew you could sign up for classes to teach your dog to paint?

With just moments to spare, the MotherCluckers file in, the door swiftly closed and locked so no intruders can impede our gathering. The vertical blinds along the three windows that overlook the rest of the building are flattened, preventing outsiders from looking in. We are locked and loaded.

The Bringer of the Treats—Charlene, this week—stands at the front of the oblong table, the pastry box settled before her. She flicks her coarse gray-but-maybe-blond hair over her shoulders; a teasing smile, a sparkle in her eye, she straightens her sweater, the one with the giant calico cat face stitched into the front, joins her hands, and stretches her fingers with the cat face–painted nails before her to crack her knuckles in preparation for the big reveal.

We hold our collective bated breath as Charlene lifts the lid of the bubble gum–colored box and turns it slowly around for us to see . . .

And the crowd goes wild. "Cupcakes!" Viv declares.

But not just any cupcakes. These are premium-grade numbers, wearing frosted plumes in every shade, some adorned with chocolate buttons, others festooned with chocolate-dipped berries, and still others with sprinkles. My LDL cholesterol just punctured a hole in my heart.

The coolest thing about the MotherCluckers, beyond the decadent sugary goodness? In this room, there is no such thing as vitamins and minerals or calories or cholesterol or gluten or high-fructose corn syrup. There is only deliciousness. We had one member for a while—Melinda something—at every meeting, she'd insist on an ingredient list for whatever treat had been offered. Then she'd take all the fun out of everything by reminding us of all the diseases our insurance policies cover, diseases caused by the ingredients included in the treats we were all trying to enjoy.

Thankfully, Melinda got a job with the IRS, so she's left us to go annoy unwitting taxpayers.

And in her memory, we instituted a zero-tolerance policy for healthy bullshit.

Lydia's elegant arm slides a chocolate-sprinkle and vanilla-frosted cupcake in front of me. She smells like gardenias.

"That's, like, three inches of frosting," Viv says, eyes wide.

"Best three inches she's had in a while," Shelly says from across the table, still awaiting delivery of her own treat.

I raise my coffee cup to her. "Amen to that."

My phone buzzes again in my pocket. This is three times in ten minutes. I should check.

But I can't. The MotherCluckers secretary, Simone, bangs her tiny gavel on the tabletop. She smooths her severe-cut black bob and sits up straight, looking very much like a mime in her black leggings and white-and-black-striped top.

She calls the meeting to order. This week's agenda is no different from any other week. Since management thinks we're a book club, at least one among us will have read something worth chatting about.

And then we catch up on movies and binge-worthy TV.

Followed by gossip, today's hot topic being Lisa's Dick-Pic Fiasco.

And then Charlene updates us on fund-raising efforts for the feral cat and kitten rescue (twice a year the Cluckers help her with a lunch-hour bake sale out in front of the office, which the whole of our business-centric city block looks forward to because cool people like kittens and baked goods, and we always sell out) and shares a slideshow on her iPad of her latest group of foster cats, all of which are really cute, but they are also why Charlene kinda always smells like cat litter.

Phone buzzes. And buzzes. And buzzes. Which means it's a call and not a text.

Someone really wants to talk to me.

"You guys, my phone has gone off four times in twenty minutes. I gotta . . ." I hold it up in front of me. We have a no-phone policy while we're in here, except in the event of kid or cat emergencies. I have neither kid nor cat, but now I'm worried Mommy left the stove on and burned down her kitchen again, or maybe one of my derpy sisters botched a rhinoplasty or the other lost her Bob Ross DVDs.

I step out of the sealed room. The three text messages and missed calls are all from Lady Macbeth. Awesome. She's probably pissed I didn't stay for the audition.

First text: **Sorry about that cattle call. U busy? Very cool news.**

Second text: **Srsly call me.**

Third text: **WHERE R U DANI I have an amz'g opp for you.**

And a voicemail, her voice breathy and excited: "Danielle Elizabeth Steele, you'd better get off the toilet or wherever you are and call me immediately! You're going to love me forever!"

I dial. "Janice, it's Dani. Should I be worried?"

"Oh sweet Jesus, I thought you'd dropped off the planet. Are you sitting down?"

"No, not really—"

"So there's a charity event coming up in August—for some children's hospital—and they're doing this thing, this Ironman-like thing with racing or swimming or whatever, and the event organizers have put word out to all the agencies in the city to let their performers know."

"Okayyyy . . . And this applies to me how?" The last time I stepped on a treadmill, I think *Friends* was still on in prime time.

"Well, the winners of each of the four age divisions win a walk-on role, possibly with lines, to a major motion picture being filmed here this fall."

"And?" While I did a lot of feature-film auditions in LA, the Portland scene is a bit thin on major films. But why would I want to compete in a physical contest for a walk-on role where I'm on and then off the screen in the amount of time it takes you to shovel a handful of popcorn into your face?

"Danielle . . . your Moon and Stars, the man who makes your heart go pitter-pat—Dwayne 'The Rock' Johnson—is sponsoring the contest, and he's starring in the film."

"Wait. What?"

"*The Rock* is sponsoring this event—called Rock the Tots—and you'd get to spend a day on set with Mr. Dreamy Muscle Pants, and you guys could hang out and do push-ups and eat protein bars or whatever."

My brain buzzes. Not sure if it's sugar or excitement or sugar-fueled excitement, but *Oh happy day The Rock is coming to Portland to make a movie and I could be in that movie and maybe he'll want to be BFFs and then he'd put me in all his future movies as that hip, cool, undercover cop/spy/sex goddess and we could make funny Instagram videos together about all the fun we're having on set and . . .*

I might pass out.

"Dani? You there?"

"Yeah. Yes. I'm—shit, this is amazing. Wait—how come you can't just submit me for a role? Why do I have to compete to get one?"

"They're not casting locally, or I totally would try."

"Not even on tape?"

"Nope. Everyone's being cast out of LA," she says.

Of course they are. "Couldn't you get me in as an extra?"

"Maybe—but we won't know that until they get closer to filming, and even then, you know the chances of actually *meeting* the stars is little to none." She's right. They call background performers "props that eat." Plus, we're not supposed to talk to the talent. And although Dwayne Johnson has been known to take selfies with extras and crew working on his films, there's no guarantee, especially if the extras' wrangler takes his or her job a little too seriously.

"Okay, so what's this competition?" I ask, hoping there is *some* way to do this that doesn't involve sweat. Or sore muscles. Or pain. Or exercise, basically.

"The whole gig sounds more like a souped-up obstacle course/road race/endurance thing, but only for amateur athletes—no professionals allowed. Whatever that means," she says.

It means I could have a fighting chance if there are other fluffy pastry-loving competitors on the course with me.

"Participants are split into four qualifying divisions: two youth classes for the under eighteens, adult, and senior, which is fifty-five-plus. Too bad you aren't older. You could take that division easily."

"Gee, thanks."

"You know what I mean. People get slower when they get older." The Rock is in his forties. He definitely has not gotten slower.

"Any idea how many people will be competing?"

"It's open to whoever wants to do it, because it's a fund-raising thing, but seriously, Dani, *The Rock.* How long have you been pining over this man?" *Nineteen-ish years?* I don't tell her that part. "Tonight, you leave that pit of damnation where you work and you go to the mall and get some shoes, and then proceed to the nearest gym and pay your fifty bucks to join."

Shit.

"You are not allowed to doubt yourself. This minute—commit to your dream, Danielle. You can do this. From this moment on, you are a living, breathing Nike advertisement. Got it?"

Athletic prowess? Gulp.

The fund-raising part will be easy. I work with seventy-five other women who love charities and causes, especially if cats or children are involved.

And The Rock. *I could actually meet him in real life, in all his glorious flesh and blood. The man I've been pouring my heart out to since forever—he wouldn't be just the Perfect Man Creature of my dreams. He'd be a real human, standing right there in front of me and what will I wear and what are we gonna talk about and what if I fart in front of him because I'm so nervous—*

"Dani?"

"Okay. Okay. I'll do it."

She cheers and I jump up and down until another hen sitting at the desk ten feet away flashes me the some-people-are-working look.

"I will email you everything you need. Go to the website to register. Make sure you tell them who sent you—"

"Danielle." Joan the Crone's voice behind me makes me jump for a wholly different reason.

"Janice, I'll call you later." I hang up before Lady Macbeth is done talking and turn to face my boss. "Hi, Joan. How are you? I love your blouse. Is that new?"

"I thought you were to be in your 'book-club meeting.'" She air-quotes with her long, bony, witchy fingers.

"Oh, I was. I just had a call. An important call so I—"

"You're disrupting the employees of this building. Either finish your book-club meeting or return to your own building."

"Right. Sorry about that. I got some good news and I—" She stops me with her veined hand flattened in the air between us.

"Also, another fax arrived for you. From your mother. Please tell her to stop using the company fax machine."

"I am so sorry about that. She really just does not like email—"

"I'll leave it to you to handle before I have to send her an official notice from Imperial Health and Wellness along with an invoice for paper and toner."

"Right. Okay." Joan doesn't linger for my response. I'd tell you that she jumped atop her broomstick and flew away, but that would be insulting to those among us who are really good on broomsticks.

Every time I have an encounter with this woman, I expect someone to call "Cut!" and a makeup artist to come over and peel off the scary mask that doubles as Joan's face, thereby revealing something more human underneath.

My insides crackle like an Independence Day sparkler. I could go back into the meeting, but we've only got fifteen minutes left, and I've already finished my cupcakes.

I skitter back to my desk—sure enough, a fax from Mommy. It can wait.

I double-check my surroundings to be sure no spies are on the prowl, then open my browser and log in.

PUBLISH   SAVE   PREVIEW   CLOSE

March 21, 2016

Dear Dwayne Johnson,
    Oh man.
    You're coming to Portland. To make a movie.
    And I am going to be in it. I AM.

When I win this competition, you'd better be ready for the hug to end all hugs. In fact, we should probably record it for your YouTube channel so the whole world meets the other Danielle Steele, not the one who writes romance novels, but the one who ran faster and jumped higher because she's YOUR BIGGEST FAN and she wanted to make you proud.

And then when that's done, we should probably have pizza and brownies, because that's what champions do.

Love,
Danielle The Champ Steele

SAVE
CLOSE

SEVEN

FAX
From: PENELOPE "MOMMY" STEELE
To: Danielle E. Steele, Building 4

Danielle,

Hi. It's your mother. I need you to do me a favor because Jacqueline is in surgery all week, and then she's babysitting residents over at OHSU, and Georgette, well, she's just so busy with the kids, and little William Morris has developed some pesky rash from the soy milk and your sister is freaking out that he has polio. You're the only one who works normal hours with free evenings (although that could change if you'd go back to school to finish your degree and maybe consider a graduate program—I can't emphasize enough the dire straits you could be left in if you lose your job, especially if you marry Travis and he impregnates you. Remember, I was a single mother for years after Gerald Robert Steele left. It is a very difficult way to live one's life, Danielle!).

I'm trying to get my hands on a signed first edition of Georgette Heyer's *Cousin Kate*, and Niles over at Longfellows (on SF Division) said he has one and will hold it for me until the weekend. Also, Vintage Books across the river in Vancouver has a signed first-edition of *44 Charles Street* by Danielle Steel (aren't I a great mother for giving you such a prestigious name?), and Candace said she will keep it until Sunday at close.

You can pop over to Washington this weekend, right? I know your job doesn't require you to work weekends. I would go, but my astrologer told me I shouldn't operate a motor vehicle until Uranus is out of retrograde because chaos, chaos, chaos. Plus, I know you still want to pay me back for allowing you to live here rent-free after that little Los Angeles situation.

Also, if you bring Timothy to my 60th birthday, I'm not making anything with meat. I recall he likes a lot of meat, but you know how I feel about that. I'll sage the house before you arrive to make sure our energy fields have a level playing field from which to interact.

Love and light,
Mommy

P.S. Dante changed the font on my computer. He says all grandmothers love this font. I think it says FUN, don't you?

EIGHT

You'd think the Crone would take pity on me—all she has to do is read my mother's dispatches. Shouldn't I get a pass on compassionate grounds? Or at least a hug?

The guy I'm seeing—his name is *Trevor*, Mommy. Not *Timothy*. I've never dated a Timothy or a Travis.

And every time I walk into one of these bookstores to pick up these damn books, as soon as they find out I'm Penelope "Mommy" Steele's daughter . . . *Oh, your mom is so amazing and funny. I'll bet you just had the greatest childhood.*

Sure. The greatest. Should we recap the time my homecoming date stood me up because my mother had interrogated him the night before about why he didn't believe in the Greys? (From Wikipedia: *Grey aliens, also referred to as "Alien Greys," "Greys," "Grays," "Roswell Greys," and "Zeta Reticulans," are alleged extraterrestrial beings whose existence is promoted in ufological, paranormal, and New Age communities, and who are named for their unique skin color. Forty-three percent of all reported alien encounters in the United States describe Grey aliens.*)

On the following Monday, my locker was covered in Xeroxed pictures of ET.

Fine. Whatever. I'll pick up Mommy's books. It's not like I hate bookstores. The opposite, actually. And I do love romance novels, though in my teenage years I would only read comic books around my mother because it drove her crazy, considering I'd been named after one of *the* most prolific and popular romance novelists of the twentieth century. Between you and me, though . . . I read all her romance books. But I'm a devotee of Diana Gabaldon. The woman was a professor. *She has a PhD in behavioral ecology.* Yeah, she writes superheated love scenes, but she is also a historical and botanical genius. I like my romance to have substance. And a kilt.

I suppose I should be happy Mommy doesn't collect really weird stuff like rhinestone-encrusted dildos or petrified mammoth poop.

But it's not about that. It's about my mother reminding me that I don't have a life, and therefore, I'm available for everyone else, whenever they need me. Jacqueline has her medical practice, Georgie has her kids and husband. These Very Grown-Up Occupations appear to rate higher than my prior commitments to acting classes, my theater group, auditions. Obviously if I can take off work to go audition for a music video, I must be available to pick up another of Mommy's books. Right?

I fold my mother's fax and slip it into my bag, returning my attention to the very exciting email that Lady Macbeth has just sent me. Everyone in my building is half-comatose with their postlunch lull, so I quietly read over the info sheet—Rock the Tots sounds like boot camp. We have to run and swim (in a pool)—so far, no mention of mud. Last year we had a bunch of insureds in the Gresham area get sick from *E. coli* after ingesting poop-laced mud. I don't do poop or mud.

Apparently, there's an obstacle course: "a program designed to push you to your limits, the ultimate test of endurance, stamina, strength, and mental fortitude."

Okay, I have none of those things. Can you buy that stuff at the sports store at the mall? Is there some pill I can take?

And while I'd love to leave immediately and head straight for the store where you buy fitness-y things, I missed the whole morning because of the nonaudition, so I have to at least make it look like I'm being productive. The Crone is likely still occupied with the dick-pic scandal, if the whispers from the cubicle ahead of me are any indication, though I'm wondering if she's actually punishing Lisa or if she's sitting in her office really examining the photos, you know, forensically. It's probably been a while since Joan has seen a real, live penis. Although, what do I know? Maybe Joan's not even into penises. Which is cool. Whatever. Penises can cause a lot of trouble. Maybe Joan's a mature adult who doesn't think about penises at work except when her juvenile underlings send dick pics to the entire company.

Man, I think that cupcake was made with meth. I can't stop bouncing. Which Viv notices.

But it's not because of the meth cupcake.

I don't wanna tell her about the competition, at least not yet. I love Viv, but she wears sensible shoes and cotton cardigans that match her skirts and she never takes sick days and she's already saving for her not-even-conceived child's college fund. And while she pats me on the head and says, "Oh, you're so cute" with regard to my love of all things Rock, she, like many other people in my life, questions my grip on reality. What can I say . . . in the cult of celebrity, I am but a mere disciple.

My in-box dings with a follow-up email:

P.S. Go to the Hollywood Fitness over on Sandy Blvd. Be there by 7:30 PM. Ask for Trish. She's the manager, and she'll introduce you to your new trainer, who you'll work with after tonight—Trish will give you the tour and then have you do something easy tonight before you go full bore. I got you a discount for the first two months. It's all about who you know, baby.

Awwww, Lady Macbeth, that was so not murderous of you.

I click through to the website's registration page. The fee isn't too bad—seventy-five bucks to participate in Rock the Tots, and you get a T-shirt and water bottle, and the money after costs goes to the charity. The Rock has promised to match the total entry fees from his own pocket.

Of course he did. Because he's awesome that way.

I enter my info and credit card, telling myself that I can always close the browser if I change my mind in the next forty-five seconds.

Maybe I should just go and cheer for the other competitors. Maybe I should just raise money for this charity. Maybe I should wait and see if they're hiring extras or if maybe they decide to open up casting for the Portland talent market too—

INT. IMPERIAL HEALTH & WELLNESS - DAY

THE ROCK is wearing his trademark Bull tank top, muscles glistening from a workout, beautiful tribal tattoo a beacon of hope for all. His voice whispers in my ear.

DWAYNE "THE ROCK" JOHNSON
Come on, Dani, you know this isn't about the charity. This is about winning. This is about being in a movie with me, DWAYNE JOHNSON, your favorite human ever, remember? We could have so much fun . . .

DANIELLE
Right, I hear you, DJ, but have you seen me lately? Like, really looked? I'm short of breath walking up the

```
three stairs that lead to my favor-
ite bakery.
```

```
    DWAYNE "THE ROCK" JOHNSON
What did your agent say on the phone?
"From this moment on, you are a liv-
ing, breathing Nike advertisement?"
Channel that. Do you think I quit
when I lost the WWF title to Stone
Cold Steve Austin at WrestleMania
XV? Hell, no. Or how about when the
Stampeders cut me? No, dammit. I had
to commit at that moment to becom-
ing The Best. I had to work harder
than everyone else in the room. You
can too.
```

```
I ain't no candy-ass, and neither are
you. Be the Dani you're meant to be.
Join up, and I promise to do the Pec
Pop of Love when we're on set.
```

My finger hovers over the "Submit" button.
I close my eyes, and click. I'm in.
I'm doing this.
I am a living, breathing Nike advertisement from here on out.

NINE

I cannot believe I'm actually walking into a sporting-goods store. On purpose.

At least now I feel less guilty about lying to Trevor that I had plans tonight. Because I do have plans. Here I am. Enacting my Very Important Plans.

"Welcome to Dick's. Can I help you find something today?"

My inner fourth grader just giggled. It did. I'm immature and stupid when I'm nervous.

"Yeah." I clear my throat, smile at the nice-looking young girl standing before me whose name tag I swear reads SUSIE LOVES DICK'S and almost giggle again, "I need some shoes. And some clothes to wear to exercise in. Like pants and maybe a sports bra and some shirts I can sweat in. I actually don't even know what I need. I just know I can't wear jeans to do exercising."

She flashes that I-work-on-commission-follow-me-into-my-lair grin. She can't be more than eighteen. "So, what kind of 'exercising' are you going to be doing?"

Eliza Gordon

She air-quoted. Why did she air-quote?

Do I tell her what I'm really doing? What if she laughs at me?

"Um, well, I'm thinking I might join a gym? You know, running, lifting weights, treadmill, that sort of thing." I sound like a total moron.

"Awesome, okay, well, maybe we should start with proper footwear."

Good. Yes. Let's do that.

I follow her to the Great Wall of Shoes. Dear lord, why do exercising humans need so many different kinds of shoes?

After forty-five awkward minutes and several pointed comments about how I'm actually really lucky because my options are so much greater since "not very many women wear a shoe size 10 or 11," Susie talks me into two pairs: a zero-drop shoe for the gym ("It will help you keep your balance, like being barefoot, when you're squatting and deadlifting"—I have no idea what either of those things involve, but I'm guessing one might be for pooping and the other might be for carrying a corpse), and for cardio activities, a higher-profile shoe with good arch and ankle support "because your ankles look a little puffy."

Oh, sweet Susie, you're so cute. Just wait until life catches up to your nubile form and you have to sit for a million hours processing medical claims for people who make bad life choices. Then tell me how *not* puffy *your* ankles are.

Susie then introduces me to the wild world of activewear, pointing to a circular rack of leggings. "We have everything you might need to start your gym adventure. This line here," she picks up a pair of blue-and-pink capri-style pants that look like they would fit a Keebler Elf, "comes in different levels of fit. You can get 'em loose, semifitted, fitted, or even compression, which are super tight." She leans closer. "Some women like the compression because it really sucks everything in. My mom calls it her sausage casing."

Wow, probably not the best sales approach, Susie.

"Do you know what size you might be?" Before I can answer, Susie steps back and looks up and down my body. "Let's start with a large and work our way from there."

A tight smile drags itself across my face, if only to hold back the caustic comeback burning a hole in my tongue.

The humiliation continues when we get to the rack of sports bras. Apparently, I'm at least a large there too—"Maybe not cup size, but you don't want the band to be too tight or else it's uncomfortable. The goal is to keep the girls from bouncing up and hitting you in the face!"

Susie laughs. I do not laugh.

Thank all the gods that the T-shirts are just normal, loose-fitting cotton sweeties sent to make me feel human again.

By the time I get to the dressing room, arms laden with enough elastane to squeeze the life from an elephant seal, the doubt is so loud in my ears that it overrides the grating in-store music.

"Make sure to wear your panties and bra when trying everything on. I'll put your shoe purchases up at the front counter for you, mm-kay?" She slams the dressing room door behind me. I dump everything onto the padded bench and slump next to it.

What am I even doing here . . .?

I should've told Viv about this. She'd give me a pep talk. Or she'd talk some sense into me.

I pull out my phone, my finger hovering over her number. But it's dinnertime at her house. She's probably eating her beans and spinach and taking her temperature or practicing baby-making.

Instead, I open the earlier email from Lady Macbeth and reread her added comments:

You can DO this. Whatever you need from me, let me know. And send me pictures of all the cute workout shit you buy. OH, and also—get some bikini, or better yet, thong underwear. No one at the gym wants to see your granny panties through your workout pants. XO from the Lady.

What's wrong with my Hanes Her Way?

I didn't notice this earlier, but in the attachments, she's included a recent photo of The Rock on the set of his latest *Fast & Furious* film, his beautiful bare chest shining in all its muscular glory. She's crudely photoshopped an arrow pointing at his tattooed half with the words "You want to lick this in real life so go do push-ups."

I laugh under my breath. She's right. I would do push-ups to lick that, but I'm pretty sure that would be super weird. "Hey, Dwayne, nice to meet you. Can I lick your tattooed pectoral musculature?"

Phone tucked away, I take a deep breath, stand, and strip to my undergarments, trying *very* hard not to throw shade at the pudgy, dimpled body staring back at me. For courage, I run my finger over the tattooed 94 on my left rib cage—Dwayne Johnson's jersey number when he played college football. I'd tell you that I did this one drunken night in the Valley with my acting friends, but to be honest, it was one very sober night in the Valley with my acting friends, and I'd been saving for it for a year. While my thespian comrades weren't hard-core Rock fans, they understood. We all had our talismans— a lucky ring or T-shirt or a small tattoo with personal symbolism. (They did razz me because my tattoo is not small but rather six-by-six inches of embellished black-and-orange numbering.) When you hear *no* as often as an actor does, you search for tokens of luck and courage everywhere you can.

But this stack of pants isn't going to get any smaller with me standing here staring at my reflection. One after the other, I yank and tug them on. Susie, the little imp, was right—the large pants fit best. And I do feel like I'm stuffing sausage into its casing, but whatever. In a few short months, I will be partying with my buddy DJ, and Susie will still be here hoping she gets enough likes on her latest selfie.

INT. DICK'S CHANGING ROOM - EVENING

          DWAYNE "THE ROCK" JOHNSON
You're being kind of a brat, Danielle.
Susie's trying to give you a hand.
She seems to know her activewear.

          DANIELLE
Seriously?

          DWAYNE "THE ROCK" JOHNSON
I'm just saying, you don't have to
be rude to people who're trying to
do their job.

          DANIELLE
Yeah? Well, where were you earlier
when that angry woman in Tigard
yelled at me because Imperial H&W
won't pay for her labiaplasty? I was
just trying to do my job too, but she
was super rude and kept screaming
at me about how her labia "flap in a
strong breeze because she birthed a
child the size of Godzilla," and we
should pay to have this fixed.

```
        DWAYNE "THE ROCK" JOHNSON
    That   image   will   never   leave   me.
    Thanks so much.


                DANIELLE
    I do what I can.
```

I find two pairs of pants that will work and then start on the bras, but I've managed to work up a wee sweat from all the grunting and stuffing and pulling and arguing with DJ.

First lesson in workout gear: If there is any form of moisture on your upper body while putting on a sports bra, the difficulty level of situating said paraphernalia over the boobage increases by a factor of twelve.

And then it somehow gets caught on your regular stretched-out bra with the torn lace over one cup because you bought it four years ago at a Victoria's Secret "Black Friday" sale, and yeah, you should've replaced it, but everyone knows that bra shopping ranks up there with Pap smears performed by young male doctors fresh out of medical school who say stuff like, "Wow, I've never seen such a friable cervix. Does it hurt when I do *this?*"

Shit.

I'm stuck.

Like, my left arm is stuck over my head and I . . . cannot . . . move . . . it. And then there is a tearing noise, which cannot be great because this sports bra is expensive, and I'm not sure if there's a you-break-it-you-buy-it rule at Dick's, but . . . if I can just get my left arm through the hole . . .

"Everything okay in there?" Susie's chipper voice sings through the crack in the door.

I almost say yes, but I realize I am super stuck, and my wallet cringes with every popped stitch.

"Actually . . ." I scoot over to open the door with my free right hand, thanking myself that I at least put my slacks back on so I'm not standing here completely exposed. "Somehow, Susie," I laugh nervously, "I've managed to get myself a little bit tangled."

She comes into the changing room but leaves the door open. Before I can ask her to close it, she's all hands and fingers and she's pulling and twisting. "Wow, I've never seen anyone do this before. It's somehow tangled up with your regular bra. Like, I think it's snagged on a bent hook or something."

"Okay, let's just ease the sports bra up and over because my arm is sort of falling asleep."

"Hang on, I need to get someone to help us, or maybe find some scissors—" And then she's gone again, and I'm *really* tangled because whatever she did made it worse.

In less than a minute, there are two Susies in my changing room, tugging and pulling and tee-heeing about how "this is definitely a first," and then they pull me into the main area just outside the wee boxy cubicle "because the light is better and we need more space" and all I can think about is how this is a unisex changing area and how my very white belly is jiggling around and my boobs are about to pop free as these teenagers yank on me and how hard everyone is going to laugh at the Dick's Christmas Party when they review the security footage of the half-naked chick who got herself entangled in a sports bra.

I should really get a discount.

Instead, I end up buying the sports bra because they have to cut my regular bra right up the back to untangle it, and I am not comfortable with the girls footloose and fancy-free under my rather sheer blouse when I still have to walk through the mall to my car. I also end up spending half a month's rent on athletic wear that I may or may not be able to commit to using because it's ten to seven, and as I bid the Susies adieu, all I can think about is a Quarter Pounder with extra pickles.

Nope. Dwayne would never eat that before a workout. Only on a cheat day. And even then, he'd rip into two deep-dish pizzas and a stack of pancakes that reaches the ceiling.

I might need to google some diet plans.

In the food court, there's a smoothie place. Aha! A smoothie—perfect. I've seen the late-night infomercials for those expensive blenders that turn spinach and kale into liquid gold. That's what I'll do. Kale is supposed to be super good for you.

And as I stand gaping at the overwhelming menu, a dreadlocked kid named Brandon with ear gauges big enough to drive through happily tells me they can add whatever extra stuff I want, like protein or echinacea and flax or ginseng or chia or creatine or hemp or even organic chocolate syrup.

Okay, I know what chocolate syrup is.

I tell him I need something healthy and with lots of energy and bravery in it.

Eight bucks later, I'm holding a plastic cup with more vegetables in it than I've eaten in a decade. The first sip is okay—chocolatey, not greasy like carob but properly chocolate. It's thick like a milkshake but sorta grainy too, and the aftertaste—you know when you're pulling weeds and you inhale and you get that dirt taste on your teeth and tongue? Like that. With each successive sip, I realize there's more chewing involved than I would've expected—is that from the protein powder or maybe the kale?

It's a little weird for me to be drinking something without whipped cream slobbering down the side of the cup, but Dwayne would approve of this.

Take that, Dr. Jerky Jackie.

She can't hear you. She's reconstructing the face of a gunshot victim right now.

So what? I'm drinking kale.

Bags stashed in the trunk, I pull up the GPS app on my phone to find the quickest route between here and Hollywood Fitness. My heart skitters in my chest at the thought of walking into an actual gym with hard bodies and beautiful people, but before turning the key in the ignition, I stare at The Rock's face (the wallpaper on my phone, naturally) to Steele myself. (Get it? Steele?)

I can do this.

I can do this.

I can do this.

Time for a smackdown.

TEN

March 21, 2016

Dear Dwayne Johnson,

Darling DJ, I don't know how you do this. This gym thing. You do it every single day, like some sort of mythical beast fueled by lactic acid and virgin tears. And kale.

I went to Dick's (tee-hee-hee) and bought the activewear. Shoes, pants, bras, a couple of shirts long enough to hide my butt.

I bought the smoothie that Dreadlocked Brandon said would make me feel brave and strong.

I ate an antigas tablet like Lady Macbeth advised so I don't fart when I'm on the treadmill.

I drove to Hollywood Fitness and even parallel parked on the second try. (A record!)

I changed my clothes in their air-freshener-enhanced locker room and didn't make eye contact with the sweaty, fit bodies walking around half-naked talking about the best ways to soak chia seeds. (Did you know that chia means "strength" in the Mayan language? I did not know this.)

I checked in with Trish (the club manager who has muscles growing out of her muscles)—as Lady Macbeth promised, she showed me around with the agreement she'd introduce me to my new trainer as soon as he (He! He?) was done with his current client. Then Trish talked really fast and used words like "free weights" and "cable machines" and "interval training," but I will take these things up with Google later.

Then she cut me loose after she showed me how to operate the very confusing digital panel on the treadmill. Of course, there was this miraculously beautiful man a few machines over, a clipboard in hand as he stood monitoring another human, this one a male with basically the same fluffy attributes as me, but this guy's beet-red face looked like he was close to needing an ambulance. It was a little worrisome, actually. I think my CPR card is expired.

That's not important, though.

I was just trying to look cool and look like I knew what I was doing in my $250 worth of new activewear while Clipboard Guy looked down, made notes, and looked back up, smiling—he had loose, dark, slightly curled hair about chin length that would've looked over-the-top on any other dude, but on him it accentuated the rich coffee of his irises and the brilliant, infectious smile and the five-o'clock shadow and the eyebrows that even you would envy. And he was wearing these shorts—let's just say he has really impressive knees. (You know I have a thing for nice knees.)

And then I realized that Clipboard Guy is a trainer, and please don't let him be my trainer because I don't want to embarrass myself in front of someone that pretty.

As we hadn't properly met yet, this is how I imagined our introduction going:

INT. HOLLYWOOD FITNESS - EVENING

CLIPBOARD GUY
Wow, that is some impressive activewear you've got on tonight.

ME
What, this old thing?

CLIPBOARD GUY
I've not seen you here before. In
fact, I've never seen anyone like
you here before. Honestly, your hair
is like something out of a shampoo
commercial.

ME
I eat a lot of carbs. It helps.

CLIPBOARD GUY
Well, whatever you're doing, it's
working. Keep it up. (Clipboard Guy
blushes) Something about you . . .
do you want to grab coffee after you
finish your bruising workout?

ME
I'd need to shower and freshen up
first . . .

CLIPBOARD GUY

I'll gladly wait. Something tells
me I just have to get to know you
better.

Clipboard Guy winks and moves back
to his client, but he looks over his
shoulder more than once, ensnared in
the meteoric power of my feminine
charms.

Sadly, this is not how it went.

The treadmill I mentioned—I do think it had a mind of its own. Because it started going faster.

And faster.

And faster.

And I was keeping up, even though I was having a hard time catching my breath, but then the thing started to slow down again so I was okay, but it only slowed down for about a minute and then, holy Jesus, here we go again, going a million miles an hour and my legs were absolutely on fire and my lungs were burning like that time at the year-end bonfire when I smoked weed laced with something bad, and then I couldn't breathe properly for a week, and then that smoothie, that smoothie was bouncing in my gut and tickling my esophagus not in a that-feels-good-do-it-again sort of way but rather in that I-might-revisit-the-oral-cavity sort of way—

ANYWAY.

This treadmill.

Did I mention the last time I participated in strenuous physical activity was that semester in college where I had a lady-boner for one of the English department TAs who happened to be a marathoner? Yeah, I went jogging with him once. I threw up.

Which sort of happened tonight.

And Clipboard Guy—whose name is Marco, by the way—he's a trainer—in fact, HE'S MY TRAINER—he left his beet-faced client for a few minutes to hold my ponytail as I introduced the garbage can to the healthy shit that Dreadlocked Brandon fed me just forty minutes earlier.

And then Marco says, "It happens all the time, dahling." Did I mention Miraculously Beautiful Marco with the great hair and delicious knees has a fetching British accent?

Well, he does.

And I can never show my face there again.

Pass the Pepto,
Danielle Barf-Queen Steele

P.S. KALE IS THE DEVIL. Jesus, these farts are so toxic that Hobbs just covered his tank with tinfoil. No more kale. Ever. Again.

P.P.S. I did that quiz Jerky Jackie sent me. Remember, the one about daddy issues? Apparently, there's an 87 percent chance I have daddy issues. The quiz app then recommended another quiz after I finished: "Is Your Mother an Extraterrestrial?" I SCORED 100 percent.

SAVE
CLOSE

ELEVEN

"Hiya, I'm hoping I have the right number. This is Marco Turner from Hollywood Fitness calling to follow up with Danielle Steele with an e— great name, by the way. My mum loves your books"—he laughs into the phone—"no, but seriously, I'm calling to check on how you're feeling after last night. I hope everything's all right. You'd be shocked to learn how often that happens with folks coming in for their first time, so don't you worry a moment about it.

"So I'll see you tonight at half past six, Ms. Steele, and be sure to bring runners and water to rehydrate. Oh, and eat one hour prior—a light meal with carbs would be great. Maybe no more smoothies? Cheers!"

TWELVE

Half past six.

Half past six *tonight*.

But the Great Smoothie Debacle—how can I possibly look him in the eye?

I should find and self-diagnose some obscure medical condition from my hulking ICD-10/CPT—it's a huge reference book filled with medical diagnoses and procedures codes. I can find something that fits before six thirty. Right?

I'm sweating. Why am I sweating? I'm just sitting here. Did someone turn up the heat?

Is this a hot flash? Oh lord, maybe this sweat is menopause. Maybe I'm entering early menopause at twenty-nine, the youngest person ever, and I shouldn't exert myself or I will expel an ovary on the gym floor.

That could work.

INT. IMPERIAL HEALTH & WELLNESS - DAY

DWAYNE "THE ROCK" JOHNSON

```
Dani . . . don't you want to win and
hang out with me and swap gym stories
while we admire my muscles?


          DANIELLE
Yes, Dwayne. I do. But I barfed. In
front of that trainer, who is appar-
ently MY trainer now, Miraculously
Beautiful Marco.


     DWAYNE "THE ROCK" JOHNSON
I've barfed tons of times. Get over
yourself. Winners barf. Losers quit
and hide in their apartments watch-
ing Netflix.


          DANIELLE
But . . . but . . . I like Netflix.
```

My buzzing phone skitters on my cluttered desktop. From Lady Macbeth: **Don't be a chickenshit.**

I look around, at the ceiling, behind me, around my cubicle. Is she spying on me?

Perhaps I'll get lucky and a zombie apocalypse will infect the world between now and six thirty. Or a meteor. Viv's husband, Ben, is an astronomy guy—maybe he knows of some meteors that are on a collision course with the planet. I could ask . . . but then I'd have to explain why I'd very much appreciate Earth's timely destruction in T minus seven hours.

I'm not getting out of this.

I will need something to eat that isn't deep-fried dough drizzled with heavenly icing.

The first half of the morning I've wasted pretending to read the stack of memos management gave birth to overnight regarding personal correspondence at work in the wake of the ongoing dick-pic scandal; now I'm looking over my shoulder to time when I can print recipes for kale-free smoothies without getting caught using the company printer for personal reasons.

Who knew smoothies were such serious business?

Broccoli and raw egg? These people have lost their damn minds.

Common themes: bananas × infinity, protein powder, spinach, kale *(no no no)*, avocado, blueberries, natural peanut butter, Greek yogurt, almond milk.

I did not know you could milk an almond.

Nowhere on any of the healthy-smoothie-recipes-to-supercharge-your-workout web pages did I find a single mention of adding a croissant or maple bar to the smoothie.

This is concerning.

My desk phone rings—an interoffice call, from Viv's extension.

"So, did you make a baby last night?" I ask.

"Man, I hope so. If not that, we probably made a bladder infection," she says. "Hey, Trevor is at the front desk."

"Oh. What? Why?"

"Dunno. Didn't ask him. Were you not expecting him?"

Was I? Oh god, is he here wanting a lunchtime quickie in his car to make up for me missing Sex Night?

"He's talking to Lisa, and she's leaning. A lot. You might want to intervene."

Lisa "Dick-Pic" Rogers wears notoriously low-cut shirts. She thinks the whole world loves her cleavage. Yes, that is my jealous voice speaking because I lack great cleavage, so when I get pulled over for speeding, I leave with a ticket. Lisa (allegedly) never gets tickets.

"Thanks for the tip." I hang up, stand, and straighten the pants I hope the Crone doesn't notice are a little too wrinkled, a little too tight, and hurry through my building to the front counter in the reception area.

Sure enough, Trevor is red-cheeked and enjoying the view.

"Trevor," I say, sliding in a little harder than necessary next to Lisa and her envy-inducing cleavage. "Thanks, Lisa." Tight smile. She pushes back, flips her impossibly perfect bouncy chocolate curls, and waves with flirty fingers before disappearing into our building. "What's up?"

"Can't I come see my second-favorite actress and whisk her away for lunch?"

"I'm guessing Angelina Jolie isn't returning your calls again," I say. "Trevor, it's a little early for lunch. You should've texted—could've saved you a trip."

"Actually, I left my Frisbee bag in your trunk last weekend, and we've got practice tonight, so I thought I'd pop by while I was between runs." Despite a degree in theater arts with an emphasis on stagecraft and lighting, Trevor manages his father's auto parts store. He hates his job, but he loves his dad, which means I listen to him whine about carburetors and solenoids and other car bits when he really just wants to be sitting in a booth over some stage, designing complex light and sound arrangements for live theater.

The thing that keeps him from driving his dad's '68 Cadillac Fleetwood Brougham off a cliff is Stage III, the community theater where we met—he was running the light board for a show I was in. There, they think he's a lighting genius, whereas his dad thinks he needs to work longer hours and stop putting dents in the company van.

That first night, he said my bone structure was a pleasure to light. I quipped that all the lighting gods tell me that. Fast-forward three months to too many consecutive nights spent in rehearsals and at the pub our kind tends to frequent, and poof. Coitus.

"Let me get my keys, and I'll meet you in the back lot."

Except as I'm moving toward my desk, I remember that the motherlode of activewear is still in my trunk—I'm superstitious when I spend a lot of money on stuff that maybe I shouldn't have spent money on, so I leave it in my car until I'm sure I'm keeping it.

How am I going to explain this? It's not often—ever—that I'm found with overflowing bags from Dick's Sporting Goods.

Do I tell him? If I do, he'll make fun of me. He already gives me a ton of shit about my "unhealthy obsession" with The Rock. (Thank goodness he doesn't know about the blog.) If I tell him I just decided to get in shape, he'll check my head for fever and insist on drawing up an exercise plan for me that'll involve a great deal of Frisbee golf, which—no offense—is really, really lame.

Then again, if I tell him I want to exercise, but I don't tell him about the competition—because at my core, I am extremely competitive and this is something he might want to get in on, and he's already in good shape so he could win his division, and then he'll blow everything with me and DJ . . . I can't tell him. I can't let Trevor get in the way of my meeting Mr. Johnson.

I feel like an Avril Lavigne song—everything's so complicated—standing with my keys in my hand, The Rock's unlawfully handsome, slightly sweaty face staring back at me from my cubicle wall.

Text from Trevor: At UR car. Chop chop, gotta make more delivries.

I start to correct his spelling again but hold off. My mother says that just because I won the middle school spelling bee every year for three years running, I don't have to be a jerk about it.

(Deliveries.)

Yeah, so I'm a jerk.

I hustle through the as-yet mostly empty cafeteria and out through the back door, checking to make sure the Crone isn't lying in wait as I am doing something personal when I should be working. Trevor is leaning against Flex Kavana's trunk, positioned so there's not even an opportunity for me to surreptitiously stow the bags before he gets a good look at 'em.

As I unlock the trunk, he moves in behind me and whispers in my ear. "We could grab a quickie in the delivery van."

I don't let him see the wan smile his offer inspires. I ease the trunk open and reach in for his bag as quick as I can, hoping he won't see my purchases.

"Hey—what's all that?"

"Oh, nothing. I just picked up a few things."

"From Dick's? What, are you sick?" He starts to grab at the bags, but I step in.

Lie, Danielle. "Umm . . ." Lie *faster*. "Viv and I are going to start walking a few times a week after work, now that the weather is getting nice again."

"Oh—yeah, that would be good. Although you know I like a little junk in your flesh trunk," he says, eyebrows quirking in what I think is supposed to be a seductive expression but mostly looks a little like a petit mal seizure. I turn to squish the bags down nice and flat as he grabs a handful of my butt.

I slap his hand away, reminding him that there are CCTV cameras all over this lot.

"So? You hate your job."

"I also hate being homeless." I slam the trunk, relieved the bags are out of view.

"My roommate is moving out end of the month. You could have his room—we could split the rent," he says, his voice husky, "and then every night could be Sex Night."

"Mmm. Tempting." I try to slide out from under him, as I'm pinned between Trevor and the back end of my car, but he puts an arm in my way.

"Dani . . . you okay, girl?" A voice from across the lot. Howie moves toward us tentatively, his cart momentarily abandoned, a short-haired tabby kitten with giant green eyes trotting happily beside him in a black harness and neon-pink leash. Even though he lives outside, Howie's jeans and the black duster he wears year-round are always clean. He says it doesn't take much to use a Laundromat. He hasn't shaved in a while, and his gray-white hair floofs out under the sides of his knitted cap. If I didn't know him, his lanky six-three frame might freak me out a little.

"It's okay, Howie. He's a friend."

Trevor's head whips toward me. "A friend?"

I clear my throat as Howie stops about five feet away. "Howie, this is Trevor. Trevor, this is Howie and his sweet little girl, Aldous."

Howie picks up the kitten, cradles her atop his arm.

"Isn't Aldous a boy's name?" Trevor says, but as soon as he touches the kitten, his smart-ass demeanor disappears. Trevor loves animals. He runs a hand down Aldous's tiny back and smiles—a real smile, no pretense. "She's got quite the little motor, doesn't she?" Why can't that boyish smile be the Trevor I see all the time? It's those rare glimpses of the Trevor under all the bullshit—that's the guy I started hanging out with. That's the Trevor who pets puppies and feeds feral cats and babysits his nephews and changes the oil on Mommy's car because she doesn't trust Jiffy Lube. It's that softer side of his personality that has kept me from walking away for good. Unfortunately, that softer side only makes the occasional appearance.

"She's gotten so much bigger since I last saw her!" I say.

"She likes your friend, Dani." Howie smiles, his eyes crinkling at the corners.

"So, you're the window-washer guy?" Trevor says. Aaaaand we're back to jerky Trevor.

I smack his arm. I've told him about Howie, about how freaking smart he is. And Trevor chooses to lead with that?

Howie snorts under his breath, a subtle shake of his head. "As long as you're okay, Dani." He gives Trevor a look that says so much—I might have confided in Howie at one point the lack of roots extending from this relationship. I'm glad he doesn't mention it.

"Oh, I finished *Titus Andronicus*," I say. "You're right. Titus got the shaft. And I'm never eating potpie again."

"Well, as long as you don't make the pies with the flesh of your enemy's sons, it could be tasty," Howie teases.

I give Aldous a final cheek rub. Howie waves and walks back toward his cart.

"You didn't have to belittle him like that. Dude is smarter than both of us put together."

"Which is why he lives out of a stolen Whole Foods cart?"

"You're so compassionate," I say, pushing his arm away so I can go back inside.

"I hope he's at least feeding that poor cat." He reaches down for a kiss, but I turn my head and offer him a cheek. He smells like motor oil.

"Have fun tonight with your Frisbees. Gotta run. Lots of claims to process."

"Are we still on for tomorrow night?" That eyebrow waggle was cute, like, for the first three months. Now I want to shave them off while he's sleeping. Really, the only man alive who should do the eyebrow thing is . . . yeah, you know. (But seriously, he's so *good* at it.)

"I might do some overtime. We're really backed up in there, so I'll text you and let you know what the plan is." He opens his mouth to protest, his face edging toward crestfallen, but I have to get inside before he reminds me about how blue his testicles get when I cancel our carnal collaborations. ("It's a bona fide medical condition, Danielle," he says to the girl who spends her days processing claims for bona fide medical conditions. He's not exactly wrong; it's called epididymal hypertension and can most often be relieved with one's dominant hand, some lube, and a magazine of choice.)

"I'll call you later—"

The heavy fire door clicks closed before he can finish.

What is wrong with me?

Why am I being such a dick? Trevor isn't a bad guy. He brings me soup when I'm sick and feeds Hobbs when I forget; he's friendly to my mother and sisters and educates himself about politics and current events; he has a soft spot for critters; he understands the weird acting life; he has a stable family background and isn't into anything kinkier than the occasional whipped cream or ice cubes; and he sometimes buys Girl Scout Cookies from first graders who set up in front of Target . . .

Maybe it's how condescending he can be with people who are situated differently from him.

Or how he says that certain costumes I wear onstage make me look heavier than I am.

Or how he says my love for Dwayne Johnson is unhealthy and unrealistic, that "no man is that perfect."

Or how sometimes he wants me to call him "Daddy," even though that totally creeps me out.

Or how he tries to give me acting advice when he's working a play I'm in, even though he's a lighting tech and I'm the actor.

And the toenails. Oh my god, the toenails.

Why do I get into unfulfilling relationships with men who don't make my heart race? Georgette said she knew Samuel was the one on their first date. She said he's all she could think about. He still does romantic things for her—a flower on her pillow, Starbucks runs on Saturday mornings, takes the kids so she can have a hot bath, has dinner sent to the house when he works late . . . She says by my age, she'd long since found her Prince Charming. And she's not shy about telling me why I haven't found mine. Apparently, I fear being alone.

INT. IMPERIAL HEALTH & WELLNESS - AFTER-
NOON

DWAYNE "THE ROCK" JOHNSON

Aw, come on, Dani. You do realize that Trevor probably has his own list for you. Why do you stay with the guy if he's so annoying?

DANIELLE
Didn't you hear what Georgette said?

DWAYNE "THE ROCK" JOHNSON
Are you afraid of being alone?

DANIELLE
No. I can be alone. I like spending time alone. Besides, it's not like Trevor is down on one knee professing his undying love for me either.

DWAYNE "THE ROCK" JOHNSON
Would you want that?

DANIELLE
No . . .

DWAYNE "THE ROCK" JOHNSON
Then why not cut the guy loose?

DANIELLE
(feeling cornered)

Seriously, what is the point of a relationship anyway? You find someone you don't want to murder, and

71

you marry them because you're afraid
your biological clock is going to
leak battery acid all over the stash
of eggs you were born with? Isn't my
mother enough of an example for you?
The odds aren't in my favor here.

Plus, I don't even want kids. Georgette
has three, and all she talks about is
how her hair is falling out and she
can't poop alone and how her vagina
has lost its pep. I don't want my
vagina to lose her pep. I have it on
good authority my group health insurance won't cover fixing that.

DWAYNE "THE ROCK" JOHNSON
Well, your vagina and its pep are
your own business, but it seems to
me you're wrestling with some pretty
strong insecurities here, both within
your own development as a responsible adult and as a willing partner
in an intimate relationship. This is
likely stemming from your father's
departure when you were at an impres-
sionable age.

DANIELLE
I like how you worked the word *wrestling* into that. Also, you sound like
a self-help book.

Dear Dwayne, With Love

DWAYNE "THE ROCK" JOHNSON
I listen to audiobooks when I'm trav-
eling. I'm all about self-improvement, ya know. Plus, kids are awesome.
You don't want kids?

DANIELLE
(bites into a warm Krispy Kreme doughnut)

Rock, it's like you don't know me at
all.

THIRTEEN

From: Georgette H. Steele-Preston <pupperspaintwithGeorgie@gmail.com>
To: Danielle E. Steele <DS.May21972@gmail.com>
Subject: Worr*ed about Mommy . . .

Hey, Dan* . . .

F*rst—the aster*sks are *n place of the m*ss*ng vowel (A-E-*-O-U) because Dante sp*lled pomegranate ju*ce on the computer keyboard th*s morn*ng and now the * won't work and * am not r*sk*ng another tr*p to the Apple Store w*th these three *n tow. You should see what Dante d*d to the d*splay *Pads last t*me. Samuel sa*d he'd p*ck up a new one for me, but you know how much he works . . . * would call you but the house phone has gone m*ss*ng aga*n and my cell phone *s currently *n a Tupperware of r*ce. Don't ask.

Thank baby Jesus your ema*l *s saved *n my address book. ;)

Anyway, * saw Jack*e yesterday to get a ref*ll of my b*rth control p*lls (she gets them for me from her off*ce drug rep—saves me a ton!) and *t seems Mommy *s aga*n *nvolved *n some mult*level market*ng scheme. Mrs. Jenk*ns from next door called Jack*e at her off*ce because Mommy's mak*ng her way around the ne*ghborhood try*ng to sell some sort of mag*c "wand" allegedly *nfused w*th moon dust, granulated crystals, and other chopped-up rocks and m*nerals that are supposed to cure *llness and *ncrease the nutr*t*onal value of food. She really upset Mrs. Jenk*ns, whose husband *s f*ght*ng cancer, so we have to step *n. S*gh.

We're meet*ng th*s weekend for d*nner at Mommy's— Saturday, *f you're not busy—under the gu*se of talk*ng about her 60th, but really Jack*e and * th*nk she needs another *ntervent*on. Maybe don't br*ng the boyfr*end du jour? Could get ugly.

Gotta go. Mary May just fed the dog her yogurt and the dog *s lactose *ntolerant so now he's puk*ng on the carpet.

* love my l*fe.

* love my l*fe.

* love my l*fe.

See you soon,
Georg*e

P.S. St*ck w*th goldf*sh.

FOURTEEN

By the time I pull up to the curb in front of Hollywood Fitness, I'm shaking so hard I forget to put the car in park. Thankfully, I realize this before I get out and the car rolls down Sandy Boulevard.

God, I stink already, and I haven't even done a single sit-up.

What am I doing here?

My phone buzzes: It's 6:20 PM. U'd better be at H'wood Fitness or I'm firing U as a client.

My reply: What if I fail miserably?

Lady Macbeth: U will. And then U'll get up and try again. THE ROCK DOES NOT QUIT. NEITHER WILL DANIELLE STEELE.

I grab my shiny new water bottle and gym bag and step out into yet another chilly spring cloudburst. My heart leaps into my throat the second I open the front door, a heady cocktail of sweat and feet and air freshener washing over me. Marco the trainer is standing at the counter, talking to a shiny-faced middle-aged woman, and she's smiling and chuckling at whatever he's saying. This is good. No one in here, at least that I can see, is crying. Solid start. Unless they have a separate room with the crying people.

Marco lifts a pleasantly sculpted arm, bare to the shoulder in his white-and-black tank top, and waves hello. I'm not sure what to do—do I grab a locker, or do I wait, now that he's seen me?

He makes the decision for me. "Excellent to see you again, Ms. Steele," he says.

"Please. Dani." I offer a clammy hand to shake.

"Excellent. All right, well, go and pop your things in a locker, and I'll meet you back here. Janice explained a little about your unique goals, so I'll show you the fitness plan I propose and we can discuss. As I understand, you have a rather short time line?"

I nod, because my voice box is now quaking with fear behind my tonsils.

"Not a problem. We're going to jump right in and get you fit as a fiddle. Meet me back here in two minutes, yes?"

He offers his fist for a bump, and I try not to notice how his chin-length, naturally curly dark brown hair is sort of perfect, and how when he smiles it is a full-mouth smile revealing really nice white teeth, despite the old saying about British people having shoddy dental care, and I just can't help but wonder how this pretty man who speaks the Queen's English ended up in rainy Portland, Oregon, helping insecure, over-BMI almost-thirtysomethings chase unreasonable fitness goals that really have nothing to do with fitness, or where that little scar above his right eyebrow came from. Probably from playing polo with Princes William and Henry and—

"You all right, Dani?"

"Yes. Sorry. I'm just sorta freaked out. And embarrassed. About last night—"

"Not another word about it." He leans closer. "It might not be the last time it happens, but we're going to work on that."

"Great. Awesome. I didn't have kale tonight, so that's good."

He smiles and turns to the sweaty lady who has sidled up beside him. "A new victim for you, Marco?" she says, winking at me. "Don't worry, kiddo. You're in good hands. Except for the part where he makes you cry, but you'll thank him later."

She pats Marco's arm and moves toward the exit. I swear she's limping.

I move toward the women's locker room before Marco can see how nervous I am. Against the painted cinder block wall, a guy in silky, loose-fitting, blue-and-white shorts that almost reveal too much, his tank top shoved into their front and his silvery hair succumbing to gravity, is doing a handstand—though not well. He almost crumples into a heap as he smiles at me when I pass. I'm not sure if he's being friendly or if he's in pain.

I almost collide with Trish with Muscles, a basket of used towels under one impossibly perfect arm. "Hey, glad to see you came back!" she says.

⟨~⟩

On wobbly legs, I walk out of the locker room and look over my shoulder to see if Handstand Man is still there. He is. Only he's managed to get his legs against the wall this time, his eyes looking at the floor, his skinny, wrinkly arms quaking with the task of supporting his body weight. This does not look at all safe.

I find the way back to the treadmills, where Marco stands with a clipboard in hand; he points to a bench he's pulled up. "Have a seat. We're going to chat a bit first, if that's all right with you."

Over the next half hour or so, Marco's affable nature calms the storm raging in my guts. He asks about everything—from dietary habits to my exercise routine (he doesn't even laugh when I tell him it involves running the stairs to the Dunkin' Donuts as fast as I can) to food allergies and preexisting medical conditions. He has me complete a health inventory that covers everything he hasn't asked from medications to my last period to if I think I could be pregnant.

"Question: Do I have to do handstands?"

"I beg your pardon?"

"That guy over there—by the women's locker room. Handstand Man?"

Marco laughs. "You do not have to do handstands. That's Walter. And he gets all his fitness advice from YouTube. He claims it's good for circulation."

I look over at Walter just as he smiles at two other women walking past to go change. "Mm-hmm. Which is why he's doing it near the women's locker room? I think it has more to do with those very fancy, very *loose* silk shorts."

"It's the only brick wall that isn't covered with a mirror. He already broke one. That wall was our compromise," Marco says. "But if you need to know anything about American history, and I mean *anything*, Walter's your guy."

He again turns to his trusty clipboard. Once the formalities are out of the way—to cover the club's liability in case I drop dead of a cardiac event on the elliptical—he invites me onto the treadmill.

"Slow and steady. You walk, I'll talk."

"Okay." I mostly know how to do that.

"Before we get started, Dani, you should know everyone in this gym is here for a different reason. No one is staring at you. No one is laughing at you. We're all just happy you're here. This is a safe place. We all lift each other up. All right?"

I nod. Although this sounds a little airy-fairy, my eyes sting.

"So"—he clicks the treadmill up another notch—"Janice tells me you're looking to enter a competition that involves a range of athletic tasks." He reads from his clipboard. "You will be completing an obstacle course with crawling and scaling, balance beam, hurdles, stairs, and a sandbag carry, followed by a hundred-meter swim in a five-foot-deep pool and two full laps around a track, which is the equivalent of approximately one-half mile."

I'm already short of breath at 0.12 treadmill miles, at level 2 incline on walking speed. How the hell am I going to do all that stuff he just listed?

"Is it too late to admit . . . that I didn't really . . . look at everything involved?" I ask, sheepish grin firmly affixed.

"Well, if I'm going to get you in shape to be the victor, we've got our work cut out for us, haven't we?" He smiles again. "Janice says the winner gets to be in a film with Dwayne Johnson, who I understand you might fancy a bit." He nods at my T-shirt. Which has The Rock's face on it.

I blush. "You could say I'm a fan."

"Whatever it takes to motivate you. And he seems like a decent fellow, though I was more partial to John Cena myself," he says.

"Blasphemer!" I say a little too loudly.

"When you're done walking, we can address any concerns you might have before I take you through the beginner's program I've designed."

Once I've finished the ten-minute treadmill warm-up, I follow like a drunk lemming with broken legs as he walks me through the gym, demonstrating the exercises on each piece of equipment.

Rowing machine for extra cardio to burn fat. Squats on a thing called the Smith Machine, great for legs and buns. Cables for glutes, hamstrings, triceps, and back muscles. Medicine balls for shoulders and upper back. Lunges for hamstrings and glutes. Dumbbells versus barbells and the fun things we can do with both to benefit multiple muscle groups. Four different kinds of sit-ups.

Marco demonstrates—his very fit body putting on quite a show and making all this shit look super easy—and then has me do the specific exercise once through for five or six repetitions, and I realize that I could very well die in here.

INT. HOLLYWOOD FITNESS - EVENING

Miraculously Beautiful Marco, his luscious brown locks just dusting his jawbone, stands beside a quiet treadmill, phone in hand, other arm draped deliciously over the tread-mill's handrail.

MIRACULOUSLY BEAUTIFUL MARCO
Hello, yes, my name is Marco and I'm phoning from Hollywood Fitness. It has unfortunately become necessary for me to contact the next of kin for Danielle Steele with an e. Have I reached an appropriate number?

ANY MEMBER OF MY CIRCLE OF
FAMILY OR FRIENDS
Uh, where did you say you're call-ing from?

MIRACULOUSLY BEAUTIFUL MARCO
Hollywood Fitness, on Sandy Boulevard. We've had an unfortunate evening, and Danielle is, in fact, dead. It was the treadmill that got her.

ANY MEMBER OF MY CIRCLE OF
FAMILY OR FRIENDS
Well, the Danielle that I know wouldn't be caught dead in a gym.

MIRACULOUSLY BEAUTIFUL MARCO

```
Sadly, that is exactly what has hap-
pened. We will need someone to col-
lect the body. There's quite a queue
for the treadmill.
```

"Though we will be meeting once a week, when you're on your own, the idea will be to work up to four sets, with at least eight to ten repetitions for each exercise. That will take some time, so for now, one to two sets with four to six repetitions for each. Ten minutes on the treadmill to warm up, two minutes on the rowing machine to cool down at the end of your workout."

When he points us to a vacant bench, I almost sob with gratitude. My muscle fibers are already weeping such copious quantities of lactic acid that I fear my legs will burst open and I will have to be wrapped in a giant maxi pad to soak up all the pain.

"I'm going to give you this," he says, handing me a journal-size, spiral-bound notebook, "and in it I want you to record everything you eat. I mean *every little thing*. I've included a printed list of foods you'll want to phase out of your diet, as well as a list of complex carbohydrates, proteins, good fats versus bad fats, and how much of each you should be consuming based on your height and weight—even if weight loss is a goal, we want to focus on exchanging fat for muscle. Strong, not skinny. To be successful in this competition, we need to make you a powerhouse."

I'm nodding my head, even though I'm barely surfing above this tsunami of panic as I look through his food recommendations. Pretty much everything on the this-is-bad-for-you list is a staple of my daily or weekly diet.

"The look on your face tells me you might have a question or concern."

"Um . . . no. Well, a little. I have a lot of dietary issues, it seems."

"Think of it as flexible dieting. Don't allow yourself to get into a trap where, if you have a pastry or latte, you need to be punished by spending extra time on the treadmill. As I tell all my clients, visualize your goal. See yourself taking each small step to get there, and by the time you look up again, you've reached that first milestone."

"Really? You think I can do this?"

"Absolutely. You can do anything you set your mind to."

I smirk. "You sound like one of those motivational posters they put in conference rooms, with soaring eagles or majestic landscapes."

"Only if I get to be the soaring eagle," he says. That million-watt grin competes with the glaring fluorescents overhead. "I absolutely believe that if this competition means that much to you—and according to your T-shirt it does—then we can get you ready. It's going to be hard—I'm not gonna lie to you. We are working with a short time frame, and there will be loads of folks who'll have a leg up with their training. But that doesn't mean you can't throw yourself into your own program. Be here five days a week, six if you can swing it.

"We can modify your workouts so you're not overdoing it, as that too is counterproductive. Your body requires rest days for sure. But follow the diet. Make the changes. And if you win, I will take the photograph of you and The Rock at the finish line so I can brag to all my future clients that I trained you—you know, when you're rich and famous and you dust this town off your sleeve like yesterday's crumbs."

"And then will you forswear your allegiance to John Cena and come into the light?"

Marco's rich brown eyes squint with his laugh, a confident sound that echoes off the high ceiling. "I will consider it, Ms. Steele with an *e*."

I look over his list of exercises once again, knowing I will likely have to ask a dozen more times how to do each of these things. "I'm really gonna do this, huh . . ."

"You really are." He offers his hand to shake. "Your fans are counting on you."

FIFTEEN

PUBLISH   SAVE   PREVIEW   CLOSE

March 27, 2016

Dear Dwayne Johnson,

FIRST OF ALL: OWWWWWW. Ow. Just so much ow. Dear gods, the pain.

Second: I am the worst daughter and sister ever. I have the texts and voicemails to prove it. Jerky Jackie is probably going to have her secretary transcribe a scathing letter, and once Georgette regains use of the letter "I," there will be emails. Did I mention this "intervention" they wanted to do? Because Mommy is trying to sell these ridiculous healing wands to her retired neighbors whose primary income is Social Security? I probably didn't tell you. I know I'm behind with entries . . .

This is the end of my first week at the gym, and per the aforementioned, I didn't know I had muscles in the weird places where I have pain. In fact, I woke up in the middle of the night to some pathetic whimpering—I thought maybe there was a kitten stuck in my wall and then I could record myself digging the baby cat out from behind the sheetrock and then the video would go viral because I'm nothing if not an attention whore and saving baby cats IS noble—

But really, the sound was just me. I woke myself up, moaning in my sleep. And not the good kind of moaning that involves you putting your hands on secret places on my body but the kind of moaning where, if anyone were near, they might think a person was actively dying.

ANYWAY. Those first-edition books Mommy had on hold—I raced out Saturday morning and stopped at the two different bookstores (including the one across the damn bridge in Vancouver) and got her dumb books before I hobbled into the gym. I called to let her know I had them, but then she blindsided me: She said she was canceling Saturday dinner AND her sixtieth birthday party because her daughters are "micromanaging and impinging upon her freedoms to exercise her rights as a capitalist," which is so weird because Mommy hates capitalism, or so she says, and yet here she is, trying to swindle her neighbors out of $69.95 in two easy payments so they can have some useless acrylic tube full of sand and broken dreams to cure their arthritis.

(Although, if the wands really DO work, I could so use one right now. I could come up with two easy payments of $69.95 if it stops the heartbeat in my calves.)

So Mommy nixed dinner, which I was all too glad for because I really just wanted to rub Betty Crocker Whipped fluffy white frosting all over my arms and legs and then roll in sprinkles while rethinking my life choices and sucking back ibuprofen-infused gin and tonics, but nooooooo, Jerky Jackie and Georgette demanded Mommy let them into her house (I'm going to guess that Georgette again threatened to call the cops about the weed Mommy grows among the hothouse tomatoes in her basement), so when I ignored Jerky Jackie's texts and didn't pop right over to Mommy's to join in on the anti–healing-wand smackdown . . .

You get the gist. I'm obviously the worst.

But I'm so tiiiiiiired. And Trevor showed up last night just before midnight, and he smelled like beer and didn't have his car, which means one of his Frisbee-golf nerd friends doubling as designated driver dropped him off here, and he was all about making up for the missed Sex Nights this week. So whatever, I went along with it, although again with the moaning—pretty sure he thought I was super into his drunken fumblings, but mostly, my body aches so much, I was just trying to get through it so I could go to sleep and visualize the sinewy fibers in all my major muscle groups stitching themselves back together like good little knitters. Knit one, purl two, knit one, purl two . . .

Side note: When Trevor is drunk, his penis curves funny. I mean, I think it always curves funny when it's flaccid—but when he's boozed up and his tumescence is less than 100 percent, his wiener curves to the right, as if it's leaning over to tell his testicles a secret. Is that normal? I should ask Jerky Jackie about this. Maybe she's performed penoplasties and will therefore have some excellent firsthand advice. Firsthand . . . get it? Like, her hand and a penis . . . okay, never mind. I'm not funny. I'M DROWNING IN LACTIC ACID, DWAYNE.

(Except: I googled it. It's not lactic acid at all that is making me wish for death. That's a myth. Apparently, the soreness is from actual muscle cell damage and elevated amounts of various metabolites in the muscle. I am counteracting this tonight with a maple bar AND a Boston cream. Please do not tell Miraculously Beautiful Marco.)

Trevor was pretty proud of himself this morning, hangover aside, that I was sore. He thought it was his doing. As I haven't told him about the gym and the competition, et cetera, I let him gloat.

I should tell him—right? I'll tell him.

Maybe.

I don't want him to sign up, though. And it's the kind of thing he might do, not because he particularly cares about meeting you or raising money for the children's hospital, but because if he wins and I don't,

I'll never hear the end of it. That's just the way he is—I'm still hearing about his team's Pictionary victory at the theater Christmas party three months ago. Plus if I tell him, Mr. Frisbee Golf Team Captain will insist on training me himself, even though he's not a trainer, and if I don't end up injured, I won't get in the best shape ever. I need someone with legit skills to show me how to do this stuff—and to motivate without me wanting to punch his lights out.

I've managed to make it to the gym every day except today (Tues through Sat). I'm too bloody sore AND I had acting class tonight, after which, I'll have you know, I did not go drinking with the other miscreants, thank you very much. But I'm doing the program Marco gave me, and I've discovered that banana + yogurt + almond milk smoothies keep the toxic farts to a manageable level, so I call that progress.

Speaking of which, Miraculously Beautiful Marco remains miraculously beautiful, moving about the gym with those perfect knees, training his clients, sharing that smile I'm guessing he paid a lot of money for. I really do owe Janice a beer. Or a protein shake.

Oh, and Viv wanted to know why I was drinking a smoothie during coffee break instead of my usual Diet Coke. Man, I hope Trevor doesn't show up at work again and ask Viv about our walking dates we're totally not having.

Oh, tangled is my web of lies.

I should tell Viv. It might give us something to talk about other than the consistency of her vaginal discharge and where she is on her ovulatory cycle. TMI, Viv, TMI. Although we did have an interesting conversation about the elasticity of a vagina. Did you know that the vaginal canal is actually flat? Like, yeah, it stretches—duh—but we don't walk around with this open tube down there. I told Viv that if we did, women would whistle as they moved. Can you imagine how noisy that would be in a public place with lots of women? All that whistling? Like a vagina chorus.

I'm trying to figure out what my song would be. "The Imperial March"? Maybe that song you sang from that Disney movie! Oh my god, that would be perfect! Every time I walked by a dude, my vagina would sing, "You're welcome!"

I just ruined that song for you, didn't I? Sorry, Maui.

Okay, this entry is too long, but I had to catch you up. And now I have.

Wish me luck. Audition tomorrow morning for some new holistic brand of family shampoo. Or something. Still waiting for that magical tampon gig to come through . . .

Yours forever,
Danielle Noodle-Arms Steele

P.S. GYM UPDATE: I managed to work up to fifteen minutes on the treadmill, and I haven't barfed again! Well, I almost did once, but it was because I drank a Diet Coke before I went in and that was just me being dumb. I'm doing all the exercises now and I'm learning how to squat AND I learned how to use the bench press, and even if I can only do the weight of the lightest bar in the gym, I STILL DID IT. (Handstand Man even applauded me!)

But I absolutely dread when my bladder/bowels tell me it's potty time because no one warned me that sitting down/standing up and basic personal hygiene would be so effing PAINFUL. To remedy this: I taped a photo of you on the bathroom mirror so every time I think I can't do this anymore, I will see your face staring at me to remind me that we're gonna hang out in a few months and my muscles won't be so sore by then.

Right? RIGHT? It gets better, less painful, doesn't it?

Also: Handstand Man is probably a total perv with his large collection of 1970s-era silk shorts, but he brings in a new crop of Dad Jokes pretty much every day and cheers for the gym patrons when he sees one of us doing something hard or new. And here's the craziest part: After he saw me wearing T-shirts with your face on them (multiple days in a row), he brought me a trading card with YOU on it, when you were with the Miami Hurricanes—he said it's from the 1994 Bumble Bee Seafoods set that was given away at the stadium after you guys won the national championship. He apologized for it not being in mint condition (he had it in a Ziploc)—it was part of his son's football and baseball card collection, but his son works in New York City now (something about the stock exchange) and told his dad to donate whatever he left in his old room, so Walter thought I'd appreciate such a collectible. I am so stoked. These are super rare!

What Gerald Robert Steele would've given to see this.

Gotta go. Epsom salts and a gin & 7 calling my name.

SAVE

CLOSE

SIXTEEN

I hear notes from "Defying Gravity," of the Broadway hit *Wicked*, before I even have the coffee shop door open. How Thomas the Singing Barista hits those high notes, I'll never understand—this man truly does sing for his supper. When he's not slinging iced coffees and flat whites for Portland's caffeine addicts, he busks at the Saturday Market, which has led to regular gigs at nightclubs and bars all over the city—plus, he's a blast at karaoke nights. He's talented enough that he could've made a real go of it, as he proves regularly in the Sunday night acting workshop we both attend, but his family needs him: a widowed mother with very traditional views who maybe hasn't quite accepted that Thomas will marry a He and not a She, a grandfather who will live forever selling his rugs, a sister with a bunch of kids . . .

When he finishes the chorus and slides an Americano across the marble counter, splashing nary a drop over the white porcelain cup's side, the patrons gift him with applause. "Thomas the Singing Barista, everyone," his coworker announces. "Tip jar is to the left!"

"My beautiful Danielle—no fishnets today?"

"A shampoo commercial. I'm supposed to look like a 'fresh, happy housewife.'"

"That would explain the chinos."

"I'm wearing black lace undergarments to quell my urge to buy a minivan."

Thomas grabs a paper cup and starts writing the little codes that list the ingredients for my caffeine hit.

"Wait—I need to change my order."

He stops and looks up at me. "I have some very nice dark chocolate syrup that just came in, if you're looking to shake things up. Eighty percent cocoa so it's better for your heart. Wink wink."

"Um . . ." I lean in. I cannot believe I am going to be one of *those* people who orders a skinny. With no whip and sugar-free syrup. And nothing from the treat case today.

But I do.

And Thomas gasps mightily.

When the drink is done, he whispers to a coworker that he's taking his fifteen and slides out from behind the bar. He gets to do that because he's the boss.

"Follow." He leads me to a vacant table in the corner. "Sit."

I do.

"Spill. Did you and Frisbee Golf break up? Is Jerky Jackie being mean to you again? Oh god, are you turning into your mother? All organic and sourced from other worlds?"

I should tell him. I need to tell someone.

As I've only got a few minutes before the audition and then I have to race to work, I give him the long and short of it.

When I'm done, Thomas sits back against his wooden chair, arms over his chest. And launches into "I Will Survive."

"Gloria Gaynor's heart would skip a beat if she heard you sing," I say, above the applause I add to everyone else's.

"A boy can dream," he says. "Girl, this is gonna be good for you. You need this. You love The Rock. And he's gonna love you right back."

"I'm totally freaked out. And so sore I can hardly breathe. You're the only person I've told . . . and you should see all the crazy things I have to do to win."

"One crazy thing at a time. You got crazy in your blood, Dani. This won't be any big thing." He reaches into his apron and pulls out free-drink coupons. "And for the next little while, we're gonna keep you fueled with large skinny vanilla lattes made with almond or soy milk. And the egg white and goat cheese quiches. Good protein, low fat. Your trainer will approve."

"I think you would approve of my trainer," I say.

"Do tell." He smooths his eyebrows theatrically.

Instead of trying to do justice to Miraculously Beautiful Marco, I pull out my phone and show Thomas a photo I sort of sneaked in the other day when Marco was talking to the Limping Lady.

"I think I just decided to join your gym," Thomas says, licking his lips.

"He's a bit mean, though, always talking about one more set and one more mile, so gird thy loins."

"I'd gird anything he asked me to."

My phone alarm chimes. I have to go. Thomas scoots out from the tiny table and wraps me in a hug. He smells like cinnamon rolls and expensive hair product. "Whatever I can do, Dani, you let me know. And when you're rich and famous and hanging out with The Rock, hire me to be your manservant and I will sing-and-sling for you every single day." He smooches my cheek.

"I'm off to sell shampoo. Do I look like a happy housewife?"

"You look like the dirty housewife who whips her man into submission while wearing her PTA president T-shirt. *Rooowwwwwrrrr.*"

Parking in this city can be a total pain in the ass—just as I'm making my third attempt at squeezing in between a Subaru and delivery truck on a side street (my parallel parking continues to be an issue), my phone jingles with a message.

I jack the rear end of Flex Kavana up onto the curb, but whatever. Cars are waiting to pass, and their horns tell me they've lost patience with my ineptitude.

From Trevor. And he's sent a photo: U said I should get a peti-cure. LOOK WI IAT I DID.

I look closely at the photo, biting my lip over his spelling mistake. Are those his feet?

Me: Your toenails are *orange*?

Trevor: Go Beavers! I love beaver. LOL.

Me [*ignoring his innuendo*]: That's some school spirit if I ever saw it. Well done.

Trevor: Was actually nice. They soaked my feet & used lotion. Super-hot TBH.

Me: I hope you tipped well.

Trevor: Shit. Was I supposed to tip?

Me: GTG. Audition. See you later.

Trevor: It's Monday . . . can't wait 4 2night 2 show U nothin but my curling toes.

Me: I'll text you.

Ugh. No. We just had Sex Night. Orange toenails or not, he's gonna have to make alternate arrangements. I have a hot date with a treadmill and some kettlebells.

Inside the casting office, I sign in—different casting assistant I've never seen before, so I hand over my headshot and résumé and take a seat, relieved when I look around and see actual women and not scantily clad teenagers.

A woman across the way—a beautiful blond, thin, with a jawbone and slim nose that could've been hand-sculpted—is talking on her phone.

I steal another glance. I think I've seen her before—either at other auditions or maybe on TV. Or did we do an acting class together? I'd probably remember a face and body that intimidating. In fact, if we workshopped together, I'd probably pick her to focus all my years of insecurity on as I emoted through a heartrending scene of loss and betrayal. (Because my favorite scenes are about loss and betrayal.)

I don't want to eavesdrop on her conversation—I should be going over these sides one last time so I don't screw up the few lines I have to read on camera—but it's sort of impossible because she's talking loudly enough that everyone in the room is involuntarily privy to her grand revelations. Something about taking time off from work to train like she did for the last triathlon. She's wearing a skirt that is above knee length, and man, her legs—yeah, those could definitely pull off a triathlon.

"Oh, this event won't be a problem. I still have my amateur status. My trainer and agent and I think it'll be a great way to get noticed, to get some screen time. If nothing else, it's for a good cause. You know the twins spent some time there in the NICU—so the fund-raising is important to me."

Wait. Her trainer? Her agent? And what will be a great way to get noticed?

Twins? NICU? NICUs are in children's hospitals.

A chill washes over me. Shit. She's an athlete; she's talking about fund-raising for a children's hospital; she does triathlons.

She's talking about Rock the Tots.

When she giggles about meeting Dwayne Johnson in person, I'm a puddle on the floor. I mean, just *look* at her. I could work out for ten straight years and never look that amazing.

"Dani Steele?" The casting assistant stands in the doorframe with my headshot in her hand. Why am I up already? These other actresses have been here longer . . . And I wanna hear more of the triathlete's conversation.

The assistant looks harried, pulling her messy Little Mermaid–red ponytail over her shoulder and pushing black cat-eye glasses up her nose. I gotta move.

"Hi, I'm Natasha," she says, not offering a hand to shake as we hustle down the narrow hallway. "Your agent sent you the sides?" I nod yes. "Great. Okay, so what we're doing today—it's a line of organic family hygiene products manufactured here in Oregon. This will be a regional campaign, and what we need from you today is pleasant, fresh-faced wife and mother. We are pairing you up by skin and hair color—"

"Oh, I have a scene partner?"

Before she can answer, we turn the corner into the room, and she walks over to a woman holding a baby. Natasha scoops up the baby and starts back to me.

"Dani, this little cherub is Hazel. She's seven months old. She's a little cranky because it's naptime, but I just need you to balance Hazel on your hip, deliver your lines, and give her a loving look once or twice. Like a mom would, okay?"

Like a mom would?

"Sure! I have a niece and nephews," I say, pasting on my fakest smile. I leave off the part about how Georgie doesn't ask me to babysit said niece and nephews very often because last time Dante chewed all the gum in my purse and then smooshed it into Mary May's baby-fine hair while I was trying to figure out how the hell to operate William Morris's fancy organic cloth diaper and wrap.

Natasha nods at the gaffer tape X on the floor that tells me where to stand. I curl the printed sides and shove the pages into my bag, kicking it out of the camera's frame. Stand tall, shoulders back, flip hair.

Baby deposited in arms.

"Okay, whenever you're ready, Dani," Natasha says. "Go ahead and slate."

"Hello, my name is Danielle Steele with an *e*. I'm with Janice Sterling and Associates." Smile confidently, just as Hazel grabs a wad of my hair and shoves it into her mouth.

I gently unwind the hair from her chubby little fingers, which are, not surprisingly, covered in some sort of baby-biscuity-slobbery concoction that she lovingly shares with me. Natasha nods for me to begin.

"Pacific Heart shampoo gives my hair that lustrous, just-washed feel, even when I don't have time to wash it every day." Smile sweetly at baby, then back at camera. "Made with organic, humanely sourced products"—Hazel yanks again—"I trust the entire Pacific Heart product line"—yank-yank-squeal—"for the needs of my whole—"

Baby Hazel screams, and an explosion rattles my right arm, followed by a strange warming sensation against my arm, on my left hand resting on her lower back, and across the front of my blouse.

"I'll stop you there for a sec, Dani."

Of course, Natasha says this because little Hazel has just shat herself, and the tsunami of pea-colored poop has burst the borders of her diaper and her cute white onesie and is gooping across my front and both appendages.

Which, of course, is marvelous.

Ask me again why I have yet to breed.

"Oh, now that's a nice smile, Hazel-bear! Is that why you were so grumpy?" Hazel's mom coos as she extracts her shit-covered spawn from my arms.

One of Natasha's young minions offers me some water bottle–dampened paper towels. We do what we can to clean off the poop, with the added help of baby wipes mined from the depths of Hazel's enormous diaper bag, and then Natasha asks me to run through the lines Hazel-free.

Super fun to do when I smell like a public toilet, but this is Hollywood, baby.

When I'm done, Natasha apologizes and offers me a free bottle of Pacific Heart shampoo. "Sorry about your shirt, Dani. It should wash out. Just soak it in cold when you get home."

[*Director yells, "Cut!"*]

SEVENTEEN

I cannot go to work like this. Obviously.

My apartment is too far in the other direction—I'm going to be later than I told the Crone I'd be, and she's already on my case about going over my banked vacation hours.

I have gym gear in the trunk, but that's not work appropriate.

What's between here and the office . . . ?

Target! I can stop at Target and buy something to throw on to get me through the day so I don't give the Crone any more reasons to stab pins into my voodoo doll.

Traffic is light because all the other responsible worker bees are already at their respective hives, so I make good time getting to Target even though it's raining again and I have to drive with all the windows down because I smell, well, like something shit on me.

I run into the store, not bothering to cover the shirt because at this point, the rain might wash away some of the stink. Straight to the women's department I go, looking for a shirt, a blouse, anything that will match these awful mom chinos.

I finally find a suitable shirt, explain to the fitting-room clerk what has happened, and she helps by cutting the tags off if I "promise to go straight to the checkout." I do, mostly because I'm just so grateful to not smell like a ruptured diaper. The shirt Hazel defiled? Goes into the garbage. I know—I'm wasteful—but I have at least six hours of work to get through, and this will just sit in my humid car and fester.

Feeling remarkably cleaner, I head toward the front of the store to pay. An employee is walking toward me, pulling a tall cart full of merchandise—huge guy, like muscles thrusting out of his tight short-sleeve T-shirt under his red Target vest, glasses, close-cropped hair, smiling and nodding at customers as he moves down the wide aisle. We make eye contact and he stops.

"I know you."

"I know you too," I say.

"You're from the gym. Working with my man Marco?"

"Oh yeah—right!" I look at his name tag. "Minotaur? Is that your real name?"

"Nope, but if I told you my real name, I'd have to kill you." He laughs. I think he's kidding about the murder part.

"Okay, then. I'm Danielle. Nice to meet you."

"You too. How's it going with Marco?"

"He's great." I rub my tender neck and shoulder muscles. "He's tough, which is good. I'm sorta new to all this fitness stuff."

"You've not trained before?"

"Nahhhh. Just curls, and by curls, I mean lifting a heavy bear claw to my mouth." I mime curling a doughnut to my face.

He chuckles. "Well, you're in the best hands. Marco's a stud. Super guy. He used to be a stunt coordinator—did he tell you that?"

"Like, for the movies?"

"Yeah. Crazy, huh?" Minotaur's warm laugh echoes through the store. "So—are you the one who's doing that thing with The Rock in August?"

Gulp. How does he know? "Did Marco tell you that?"

"Yeah—he's only been in Portland for a year or two. And since I do a lot of trail running, he was asking me about good spots around the city to practice that outdoor stuff. Looks like you'll be doing an obstacle course for this event?"

"That's the rumor."

"You're gonna kill it," he says, offering his fist for a bump. "Come with me. I'll show you some great protein bars, cheap, so you don't get bullied into buying crap that tastes like sawdust at the health-food store."

I follow Minotaur and his huge cart to the pharmacy/healthy-foods area of the store. There he introduces me to a whole bunch of supplements, vitamins, protein bars, and drink additives. "You can get good stuff at the supplement stores—some of those brands are better quality, sure—but to start out, try these. See what you think. The price is right. I use a lot of these products and then splurge on the other things I like from GNC or the Sports Nutrition Center."

"This is awesome. And whatever you're doing seems to be working," I say. He flexes and kisses a bulging biceps. "Thank you again."

I pick up a protein shake mix and another powder that is filled with vegetables because I cannot choke down the recommended daily allowance of asparagus, no matter what's at stake.

"You going to the gym after work?" Minotaur asks, his hand on the wheeled rack again.

"Barring any unforeseen natural disasters or acts of god, yes, I will be there."

"Then I shall see you tonight, Lady Danielle, where we shall proceed to crusheth the weights." He bows deeply, winks, and heads back to work.

I watch him move down the aisle, a small smile creeping across my face.

I may not be a triathlete, but . . . I have a gym buddy.

EIGHTEEN

From: Charlene Moyers <feralcatsneedlove2@gmail.com>
To: Danielle E. Steele <DS.May21972@gmail.com>
Subject: A sneaky little feline left me a present . . .

Hi there, Dani,

You cheeky monkey, I found the Target gift cards you left on my desk while I was away at lunch. Thank you—and I know you don't like me mentioning this in front of the other Cluckers, but the kitties thank you for thinking of them. Every little bit helps—even if you think it's not much. Feeding these buggers and buying so much cat litter gets expensive!!!

Better go. The Crone is making her rounds. Hiss hiss scratch!!!

Love and pussycats,
Char M.

P.S. Your mother sent another fax—I grabbed it and tucked it away in the back of your codes book before Joan saw it. Penelope Steele sure is a character! The UFO convention sounds like a hoot!!! ☺

NINETEEN

FAX
From: PENELOPE "MOMMY" STEELE
To: Danielle E. Steele, Building 4

Hello, Danielle,

It's your mother. Thank you for leaving the books on the porch for me in that terrific insulated cooler. Very smart girl, you are. (Chip off the old Mommy block!) Now I can use the cooler to house my "special tomatoes" when I'm making deliveries—unless you want it back? It might smell a little like my friend "Mary Jane" now, but I can soak it for you. L-O-L (Dante says that's how we write that we're laughing in messages.)

I'm sorry I wasn't home when you stopped by. I was doing a wand consultation for a few members of my "Greys (Alien) Anatomy" study and research group before our monthly meeting. Despite your sisters' rather vehement protestations regarding my new business venture, I am doing quite well with these healing wands. The folks who've bought them from me are very satisfied with their results. If you would like a consultation, I can certainly arrange it.

For now, the plans for my upcoming 60th party are on hold until your sisters can be more reasonable. (Honestly, when Gerald Robert Steele told me he was infertile, I should not have believed him. All three times.)

However, in lieu of my grand birthday celebration, I have a different proposal: The annual UFO convention is the first weekend in August, and this one's a biggie so I'd very much like to go. I think it would be great if you would accompany me—it could be my belated birthday present from you? It's at the Oregon Coast this year, and I know how much you like it there. We could go halfsies on the motel, unless you wanted to pay for me too, considering I'm turning 60 and I'm on a limited income. I know your sisters won't go—Jacqueline can never take off time from her surgery schedule, and between you and me and the fence post, I don't think I could handle three full days with Georgette's kids running amok. (That Dante—I think Georgie's restrictive diet is going to turn him into a serial killer. I really do, Danielle. Not even I was cruel enough to feed you girls carob.) This year's convention has a lot of important speakers too—very big stuff going on out there beyond the stars, and therefore no place for young kids.

I thought if I mentioned it to you now, you could get the Thursday and Friday off so I could be there for all three days of the conference (Friday through Sunday). Of course, I would need you to drive. And as a bonus, I could introduce you to a nice young man in our UFO group—we have some very smart, promising young men in our ranks, Dani Beth!

Talk to your boss and let me know posthaste. First weekend in August.

Now for a joke I heard at this week's meeting:

How do you debunk an alien?
(Throw him out of bed.)

Love and light,
Mommy

P.S. This first-edition Danielle Steel has a coffee stain on the dedication page. Did you not look before you paid for it? I have a call in to Candace to remedy the situation, so I might need you to go back to Vancouver to pick up another one if she can find it. Honestly, who spills coffee on a first edition?

TWENTY

First weekend in August?

My palms are clammy as I look up the email from Lady Macbeth to confirm dates.

Rock the Tots—the thing I have restructured my entire life for—is the first weekend in August.

I cannot take Mommy to a UFO convention at the beach for her sixtieth birthday.

And the fallout from this—it will be nuclear. I mean, she called me Dani Beth. That only happens when she's pulling out the big guns.

How can I possibly get out of playing chauffeur and babysitter, not to mention financier, for her weekend away? I'll have to tell her about the competition, and then she'll lecture me about having my priorities in the wrong place, about how she only turns sixty once, how if I were like so-and-so's daughter/son, I would know that family comes first, that it's ludicrous to put all this effort into something that holds only the remotest possibility for me to meet my idol. (Note the irony of this last guilt ribbon, tied by a woman who named her children after her own idols in the hopes that she'd one day get to meet them.)

What the hell am I going to do . . . ?

If I stand up to her, she'll never let it go. It will become one of those Topics of Conversation—she stockpiles and catalogs our perceived wrongs against her, and then finds ways to weave them into the most benign exchanges whenever we're gathered. Example:

"Oh, did you hear that the *Farmer's Almanac* is predicting a colder winter this year?" says any one of the Steele daughters.

"Well, I will have to buy all-weather tires and not those cheap snow tires Georgie's husband talked me into in 2014. I almost died driving with those on." For the record, Georgie's husband was working a second job at a tire shop to finish his last year of law school, so yeah, he sold Mommy some tires she didn't like, and now . . . we hear about it. Like I said: Topics of Conversation.

INT. IMPERIAL HEALTH & WELLNESS - MIDDAY

    DWAYNE "THE ROCK" JOHNSON enters wearing an alien costume, carrying an odd-shaped acrylic wand filled with . . . sand?

           DWAYNE "THE ROCK" JOHNSON
Dani, girl, you really need to stand up to your mom. Dig deep and find that empowerment you engage and deploy when you are at an audition. Don't be a--

           DANIELLE
Please . . . don't call me a candy-ass.

           DWAYNE "THE ROCK" JOHNSON
Well, if the shoe fits . . .

                    DANIELLE
You know my mother. If I stand up to
her, she'll send me a million blis-
tering faxes and burn through all the
toner left in the office, and then
the Crone will make me clean out the
cafeteria refrigerators to atone.
You do know there are anthrax-level
contaminants in that fridge, right?

Wait . . . is that one of Mommy's
healing wands?

          DWAYNE "THE ROCK" JOHNSON
Yeah, I have a sore elbow. She gave
me a good deal.

And don't change the subject. You
have to stand up for yourself!

                    DANIELLE
This is going to come back to haunt me.

          DWAYNE "THE ROCK" JOHNSON
So is dropping out of my incredibly
awesome fund-raiser so you can drive
your mother to the beach to talk
about crop circles and anal probes.

                    DANIELLE
Says the man who's dressed up like a
seven-foot extraterrestrial.

DWAYNE "THE ROCK" JOHNSON
Protection from accidental probing
in case of alien invasion.

I cannot think about making this phone call right now. I also cannot think about the fact that my mother is likely making regular deliveries of a controlled substance to her hippie friends in *my* lunch cooler. Good god, I hope my name's not on it. Just what I need—a felony.

Rather than contending with doom shaped like my mother, I work double-speed, ignoring the flashing light on my phone that tells me there are voicemails (the caller ID reflects that those voicemails will belong to at least one sister), so none of the other hens in my building flash me dirty looks because they think I've been off playing about town while they're here toiling away. Among my coworkers are a few who regard my morning and/or afternoon auditions as inappropriate, and they're not shy with pointed glares to express their petty jealousies.

Which is why there are two boxes of Dunkin' Donuts on the back counter with a love note: "Sweets for sweeties . . . xoxo Dani in Bldg. 4."

Yeah, I'm not above kissing a little ass now and then.

Thing is, the auditions are done on my vacation time, in small bites here and there. It's why I never take a week off to do a real vacation.

And precisely the reason I cannot take two days off for UFO Fest.

My stomach growls—and since I am not allowed to eat the doughnuts I brought for everyone else [*insert sad face*], I dig out a protein bar that Minotaur sold me. This one says it's chocolate and peanut butter, but I'm still scared—what if it tastes like chocolate-peanut-butter-dirt kale?

With the first bite squished gingerly between my front teeth—not bad, actually—I check around the area for evidence of spies . . .

and navigate to IMDB.com, the Internet Movie Database. Minotaur says Miraculously Beautiful Marco was a stunt coordinator. If that's the case, he'll have a page listing the films he's done.

I type in his name one-handed so I can continue to shove the protein bar into my face, and sure enough, he pops up.

Marco Turner has worked on a ton of films and TV shows, big stuff I've actually seen. Weird that he didn't mention this—weirder yet, why is he now working as a personal trainer at some gym in Portland, Oregon?

Maybe he fell in love and followed the Object of His Affection to our fair metropolis?

Maybe he got bored with all those beautiful LA hotties and wanted to come find himself a web-footed Oregon beauty?

Or maybe he's a bank robber, on the lam from his native England, hiding out in America and building muscles while he plans his first big heist in the good ol' U-S-of-A.

```
INT. HOLLYWOOD FITNESS - NIGHTTIME


            DANIELLE
    That's it, Miraculously Beautiful
    Marco. The jig is up. I'm here to
    stop you before you empty another
    vault.


            MARCO
    (sips tea but not daintily)


    Danielle, darling, whatever are you
    talking about?


            DANIELLE
```

Where do you keep it? All the money you've stolen? Let me guess: under your mattress.

                    MARCO
            (looks around, whispers)

How--how did you discover my secret? Please, whatever you want, tell me. I am at your humblest disposal. Please don't tell the Queen. She'll throw me in the Tower of London, and . . . it's haunted.

                    DANIELLE
You can rob banks, but you're afraid of a few ghosts?

                    MARCO
I saw *Ghostbusters*. Twice. And I am quite sure I am allergic to ectoplasm.

                    DANIELLE
But why? You're so Miraculously Beautiful. You could be anything you want to be. Why a bank robber?

                    MARCO
Think of me as Robin Hood. I was born in Sherwood Forest, so it makes sense.

```
MARCO leans closer. He smells de-
liriously delicious, a cross between
maple glaze and sweat.

              MARCO (CONT'D)
Do you want to see my biceps?
```

I scroll through to the Personal Details section—it says my trainer was born in Dublin, Ireland, but his father accepted a new position when Marco was a kid, so his family moved to the Royal Borough of Greenwich. One younger brother is listed—and then links to a collection of articles. I click the first one.

Oh man. Marco Turner is in Portland because he coordinated a stunt that killed an actor—who happened to be his best friend. The article from the *LA Times* details that after the incident, the film was shelved, never to be released, and "Turner turned in his union card, packed his bags, and left the City of Angels in his rearview, off to seek an impossible absolution."

Shit, this is heavy stuff.

Poor Marco. Not only is he Miraculously Beautiful, but he's got a tragic story. And he's not a bank robber, which is probably good.

I close the browser window so no busybodies see what I'm staring at.

With an impressive stack of processed claims in hand to be filed, I ease out of my chair—I don't know what Marco did to my legs, but I think they might be actively trying to separate from the rest of my body—and walk up the center aisle between the gray cubicles shaped by those industrial fabric-and-steel half walls. The good hens of my building are busy busy *busy* on the phone, fingernails ticking on keyboards, papers shuffling.

As I approach Lisa "Dick-Pic" Rogers's cubicle, why am I not surprised at what I see on the screen.

Does this woman never learn?

Except—except wait a second.

In the photo on her screen, some jackass is holding his semi-erect penis in his palm, and I wouldn't care, I wouldn't feel like throwing up right this second if that dick wasn't curved to the right, if there weren't evidence of orange toenails just hovering along the periphery of the photo's framing of the crooked penis.

Orange toenails? Crooked dong?

Sometimes my mouth moves faster than my brain, unfortunately. Like now.

"You bitch! That's Trevor's dick!"

[*A thick stack of completed medical claims explodes from my hands and flies upward, gently returning to Earth like oversize snowflakes of ruination, somehow beautiful, like the floating plastic bag from* American Beauty, *if not for my hands around Lisa's stupid, skinny, fake-tan-coated, boyfriend-stealing neck.*]

TWENTY-ONE

From: Jacqueline Collins Steele, MD, FACS <DoctorJacqueline@ JCSAssocMed.com>
To: Danielle E. Steele <DS.May21972@gmail.com>
Subject: I just got off the phone with Georgie

Danielle,

Did you really attack someone at work? Physically attack someone? Georgette said it had something to do with your boyfriend sending pictures of his anatomy to another woman?

I have a call in to my lawyer to see if the length of the suspension is legal. A month seems excessive, even if a managerial and corporate-level review is necessary. There has to be some middle ground here where we can perhaps negotiate to get you back to work sooner, taking into consideration these exceptional circumstances. I'm guessing you don't have adequate finances saved to sustain a long unemployment?

Make sure your fax machine is on. Mommy refuses to plug in her phone

Is it true the police are involved?

Sincerely,

Jacqueline Collins Steele, MD, FACS

Board Certified, American Board of Cosmetic Surgeons

TWENTY-TWO

"Oh, hello, Danielle. This is Marco from Hollywood Fitness just calling to check in with you, as you've missed the last two nights, and I'm worried that you might have pulled a muscle. Can you phone me back to check in? Hoping to see you again soon. Do let me know if I can be of assistance. All right, take care, then. Cheers."

TWENTY-THREE

PUBLISH   SAVE   PREVIEW   CLOSE

March 30, 2016

Dear Dwayne Johnson,

Don't be mad at me. I know this was not my shiniest moment, and if you were here, you'd be coolly unimpressed like everyone else, although maybe not—you might be sorta proud of me for standing up for myself? Maybe? Aren't you always harping at me about that?

It was like my own personal WWE moment. I know, I know, WWE has no place in the health insurance workplace, but there she was, sitting at her desk, staring at Trevor's crooked wiener, and before I even knew what I was doing, my hand went around her neck and the other hand pulled her stupid ponytail and I flipped her back in her wheeled office chair—my own version of "spine to the pine"—and she screamed and clawed at me, but I'm stronger than I look, so she didn't get a good hit because I managed to take her by surprise and yeah . . . yeah, I may have given her The People's Elbow.

I'm sorry I borrowed your trademark move.

But it's a good move, Rock. Thanks for inventing it.

Secret, though . . . I did hurt my back a little. There's concrete under the thin gray industrial carpet. We don't have to tell this bit to anyone else. Well, I might have to tell Miraculously Beautiful Marco, because he's going to want to know why I can't move when I finally get back to the gym.

And naturally, everyone in my family is freaking the hell out.

Full disclosure—I'm kinda freaking the hell out too. It's not great the police were called, and I'm so lucky I didn't get arrested. That part shocked me the most—when Joan the Crone stepped in on my behalf. I've never seen that side of her. She was almost . . . nice?

But seriously. Why did I go mental like that? I think it's safe to conclude that I don't love Trevor. We both know that we're not The One for the other person. SO WHY DID I FREAK? I guess seeing his dick on someone else's screen—first of all, who takes pictures like that? In real life? Other than creepy congressmen from New York? Please tell me you've never done this. Next, I have no idea how long this has been going on or how involved he and Lisa Rogers are—Lisa and I WORK together! How could she look me in the eye and smile at me and eat the damn doughnuts I bring in for the whole staff, knowing what she's doing with MY boyfriend? Or un-boyfriend. Or whatever he is. WE HAD A DEAL, Trevor and me. When we're actively engaged with one another's body parts we are exclusive. He's totally violated the treaty.

This wasn't love. It was carnal companionship. I'm a modern woman—I can do what I want.

Including committing battery and assault, it seems.

They just met a few days ago. Could she have worked that quickly? Why wouldn't he just fess up and tell me he was into someone else?

God, I don't even care. It's so gross. All of it.

Viv called this morning to whisper that there were so many inappropriate photos on Lisa's hard drive (tee-hee-hee . . . hard drive . . .), they've called in the IT security team from corporate to deal with it, to see what laws she's broken. I'm suspended for four weeks, but she's fired, and likely in some big-time legal trouble.

And Jerky Jackie is wrong. I do have a few months' expenses saved, and I'll be fine until either they fire me for good or until I can get back to work. Maybe in the meantime I'll find a sweet new job or I'll finally land that elusive tampon commercial. (I called Lady Macbeth. Told her to submit me for everything that doesn't involve babies with explosive diarrhea.)

Trevor was just here, looking as sad-puppy as he could muster while picking up his crap. He honestly would not look me in the eye. And I'm not even bummed about the relationship ending—it's kind of a relief because now I don't have to deal with his toenails or his constant judgy BS—but it's such a betrayal that he handled it the way he did. *shudder* Still gross.

Anyway.

This month off will be good.

No, it will.

I have to keep telling myself this every few minutes so I don't have a panic attack. I've eaten a lot of doughnuts in the last forty-eight hours because CRISIS, plus Viv brought éclairs last night and we had a sleepover and watched *Fast & Furious 7* and *San Andreas* because she's awesome and knows how watching your movies makes me feel better. Who can resist you running around California to save your beautiful daughter and wife? If we have a series of massive earthquakes, promise you'll carry me out of one of the crumbling buildings just like that. I know my fellow feminists would roll their eyes at me for that, but I don't even care. Alexandra Daddario is LUCKY she has a movie dad like you, and when you finally kissed Carla Gugino in that stolen boat, my heart squeezed with envy.

Viv obviously doesn't share my love for heroic leading men, since she slept through most of the carnage, but it was nice of her to hang out. She also brought me a new book from Howie the Pop-Can Man. Geez, word travels fast.

Here's some irony—the book he's given me? *Brave New World*, by Aldous Huxley. Very funny, Howie. Also, now I know where he got the name for his cat.

And no, I haven't told Mommy about the weekend of the competition. I WILL. Just . . . not yet. I told you she wants me to take her to this UFO conference, right? Yeah, at the Oregon Coast—and she wants ME to take a million days off work and pay for the whole shebang because it's her birthday. Last year on MY birthday? She gave me a bowl of her tomatoes and a (used!) *Chicken Soup for the Soul on Dating Over Thirty*.

Yeah. I was turning 29.

Anyway . . . I've had to set up my fax here at the house because she's convinced the phone lines are bugged, so she's faxing every few hours to make sure I'm okay. I don't think I've ever seen so much Comic Sans in my life. I really need to get her a new font, Dante be damned. What does he know. He's five, and like Mommy said, probably a future serial killer. Only serial killers like the font Comic Sans.

(This month off will be good.)

And OMG, I forgot to tell you that Miraculously Beautiful Marco was a stunt coordinator and one of his stunts killed an actor—his best friend, no less! Whoa. I should offer him my breast—or shoulder—to cry on. That would be really kind of me, don't you think? AND I can do that now that I'm officially UNATTACHED.

shudder

Okay, I'm feeling panicky again so I'm going to get dressed and at least walk around the block before I lose the battle and smear these éclairs all over my face. I should go to the gym. Maybe my new gym buddy, Minotaur, will be there (you'd love Minotaur), and I can find some self-worth on the dumbbell rack.

Wish me luck.

Single and temporarily unemployed and hoping I'm not terminally pathetic,

Danielle Candy-Ass Steele

SAVE
CLOSE

TWENTY-FOUR

"Did all of this really happen, or are you having a laugh?"

"It really happened. I got into a fight at work. But in my defense, I was provoked," I say, already breathless, not even through the first mile. "Did you know . . . that the treadmill was invented in 1818 . . . by one of your countrymen . . . an engineer by the name of Sir William Cubitt . . . as a means of punishment . . . for idle prisoners?"

Marco flashes that winning smile. "We Britons believe in the power of industry and the sin of sloth."

"And I, Danielle Steele with an *e*, believe in the power of knowing thy enemy."

"The treadmill is not your enemy! Say it with me: *The treadmill is my friend!*"

I don't.

"Miss Danielle, I shouldn't applaud your sordid behavior, but in this case I will say you do offer a convincing argument. I don't think I would love it if I saw my girlfriend's assets on someone else's computer screen."

"He wasn't technically my *boyfriend*. We had an agreement." A treaty.

"Ah. An un-boyfriend. I get it."

Does he have a girlfriend? Or an un-girlfriend? What is that weird emotion when I think of him with a girlfriend? IMDB didn't list a significant other. And I hardly know Marco, even if he is Miraculously Beautiful. Would it be easier to grunt and wheeze like a geriatric pug if he were gay? Yes. Definitely. If he were gay, I wouldn't care about the sweat pouring down my thighs and soaking my underarms and my squishy stomach.

"That's why . . . I missed a few days . . . I was a little . . . upside down."

"And by a few days, you mean a week," Marco looks at me with one eyebrow raised. "Well, now we have extra time to get you caught up. The clock is ticking." Marco bounces a pen off his clipboard and then pushes the little button on the treadmill that makes it go faster. I really hate that button.

And even though Marco looks good enough to eat, he's not my favorite person right now. He made me weigh in (I've gained four pounds—I'm hoping it's water and poop), and he made me do the fitness assessment again (a dastardly set of step-ups and push-ups and a lot of other things involving the word *up* that suck a whole bunch), and he's trying to get me excited about this training stuff, but I can't stop thinking about Bionic Barbie from the shampoo audition and how there's no way I stand a chance against her . . .

When I've finished the required minutes on the Instrument of Infernal Torture, I follow Marco through the gym as he corrects my form on things I've already learned and introduces a few new exercises. He explains his plan for the next four weeks—which includes twice-daily gym visits while I'm off work—and notes that once we've reached the six-week mark, we will be going outside for trail and street running to build cardio and endurance.

Man, I'm tired already.

As I'm thanking him for the help, a familiar face drifts into my peripheral vision.

And I cough, choking on my own spit, nearly dropping a kettlebell on Marco's foot.

"You all right? Did you hurt something—"

By now Trevor has closed the distance between us.

"What the hell are you doing here?" I ask, probably louder than necessary.

Trevor gives Marco a sheepish look and offers his hand to shake. "Hi, I'm Trevor, Dani's boyfriend."

"Seriously, you are not this stupid."

"Can we talk?" he says, lowering his voice.

"Dani, should I give you a moment?" Marco asks. Before I can beg him not to leave, Trevor steps in.

"I'm sorry, who are you?"

"Trevor, this person . . . this whole place"—I gesture theatrically at the area around us—"none of this is your business. I don't even know how you found me."

"I'll give you a moment," Marco says, sliding away.

Trevor stands in front of me, pulling an envelope out of his back pocket. "When you gave me my stuff from your apartment, somehow this found its way into the box." He holds it up in front of me—the logo on the envelope says everything. It's from Rock the Tots. "Is that why you're here, at a gym? Because I am super shocked. I didn't think you had it in you, to be honest."

"Don't use the word *honest*, Trevor. It sounds so dirty coming out of your mouth." I snap the envelope from his fingers. "Oh, and I see you've helped yourself and opened it. Wow, thanks."

"I was curious."

"My business no longer concerns you. Thank you for bringing me my *opened* mail. Now kindly leave before I have you escorted out."

He chuckles under his breath. "By who, your new boyfriend?" He nods in Marco's direction where he stands talking to Limping Lady near the rack of exercise balls.

"That's Marco, and he's a *trainer.*"

"Wow, so you can afford a trainer, being unemployed?"

I step closer. "My temporary suspension is your fucking fault. So back off"

"I will take responsibility for my portion of this situation, but I did not physically attack a coworker in my workplace. *You* did." He waggles his eyebrows and places a hand over his heart. "I am touched that you were so jealous as to resort to violence, though."

"You're disgusting," I hiss. I wish I could physically attack him with this kettlebell, but I think that might kill him, and that would definitely be a felony. "Wait—how did you even find me?"

He pauses, a teasing smile curling his face that I would've once considered cute. Instead, I'm nauseated. "I followed you."

I take a step back. "Oh—my god. You've gone full creeper."

"Come on, Dani, don't be like that. Let's talk this out."

"Why are you even here?"

"Well, your mail, for one. It looked important." He digs into his pocket. "And your apartment key. I didn't want you to feel like you had to change the locks." Now that he's said that, I feel like I should change the locks.

"You followed me here to give me a letter and a key? You could've mailed 'em."

"This was faster," he says. "Come on, Dani, we're gonna have shows together in the future, and it'll be weird if we're not friends."

"You should've thought about that before you violated the treaty."

"I didn't *sleep* with her, if that's what you're mad about."

"No, because emailing someone a picture of your penis is so much less offensive. If you're willing to do that, what the hell else are you doing that you're not telling me about?" I lower my voice and step closer. "We had a deal. *No* STDs, remember?"

"I'm clean! Is that what you're worried about?"

"This is pointless. Can you leave now, please?"

"Dani . . ." He reaches for my wrist and I yank away.

"*Don't* touch me." It's loud enough that we draw the attention of other gymgoers.

At that moment, Minotaur sidles up on my side of the weight bench. "Hey, Danielle, how's things?"

"She's busy right now, dude," Trevor says, straightening his shoulders and puffing out his chest. Which is super funny because Minotaur still outweighs Trevor by at least a hundred pounds. It's like The Rock standing next to Christian Bale when Bale lost all that weight for that movie he did when he . . . lost all that weight.

"I'm thinking that Danielle is not interested in talking to you right now. So, you can either leave, or I can show you the door," Minotaur says. His eyes don't look friendly anymore.

Trevor's brief laugh indicates that he's scared—I know his tell—I also know that he knows his limits. He won't go up against someone so much bigger . . . or will he? "Is this your new meathead gym boyfriend, Dani? Damn, you move quick."

Minotaur grins, but it's not the hey-man-that-was-funny-*ha-ha* grin; it's more like the grin of a chimpanzee who's showing aggression right before he rips off your arms and beats you to death with the bloodied ends.

Trevor doesn't seem to get that he is toying with his own mortality. "Here's the best part," he says, digging into his jacket pocket. He flashes a newly printed ID card—for Hollywood Fitness. "I've joined up. In fact, I've not only joined this gym, I'm competing in this big event that your movie boyfriend is sponsoring. That way, when I win that walk-on role, I can be sure to let The Rock know that you're a freaky, obsessed fan and he should be restraining-order-level afraid of you."

"Why? Why are you doing this?" I know why he's doing it. Because he can't stand it for me to do something better than he can. And since he's already in better shape, if he beats me, he can rub it in my face every time I see him, which will be often if I continue performing at Stage III. (This is why the directors always warn us not to get involved with other theater people. Sigh.)

"Why not? I love sick children just as much as the next guy."
Minotaur raises a confused eyebrow.

"You never did have an original thought in your head," I say. But before Trevor can snipe back, Minotaur hops over the weight bench—very nimble for a body the size of a silverback—and gets so close to Trevor's nose that he flinches like a kindergartner who's about to lose his jar of bubbles.

"Listen, little man, I don't care what the fuck you do when you're in your car jerking off outside a Chuck E. Cheese, but Danielle is my friend, and no—one—fucks—with—my— friends." Every beat in that bit is punctuated by Minotaur's meaty finger jabbing into Trevor's scrawny chest. That's definitely gonna leave a mark. "Stay away from her, and stay away from me. Got it?"

Marco reappears like magic, easing between Minotaur and Trevor, who's only now stepping back, a smug look on his face as he straightens his jacket, his pale face blotchy with fear.

"Have we got a problem, gentlemen?" Marco says. "Dani, you all right?"

"Trevor was just leaving. He's harassing me, and Minotaur stepped in to defuse the situation."

Trevor looks at Marco and sizes him up. "Hope you're the best trainer money can buy. You've got your work cut out for you with *that* one," he snipes, nodding at me. "Better cut back on the maple bars, Dani. See you on the course."

He spins on his heel and heads toward the door, probably just in time. Anger shimmers off Minotaur like heat above lit birthday candles.

As soon as the front door has closed behind him, I collapse onto the weight bench. Minotaur's heavy hand rests on my shoulder for a beat. When I look up at him and mouth "Thanks," my eyes burn as he offers his broad fist for a bump and then returns to his workout.

Marco, however, sits down next to me, lightly placing an arm over my hunched shoulders. "I take it that's the un-boyfriend?"

I nod. My throat is too tight to talk.

"If his presence in the gym will make you uncomfortable, we can absolutely revoke his membership. You were here first, and we have a strict no-stalker policy at Hollywood Fitness," he says. I think he's kidding? "In all seriousness, if he comes in and says another word to you, we'll boot him out. He can train elsewhere."

Marco stands and thoughtfully tears some paper towel from the roll on the nearest stanchion—my nose is running. "And don't listen to that gobshite. Honestly, the guy's a total wanker. You, however, are doing great." He sits again and nudges his shoulder into mine. "We're going to keep training hard, and then you can prove to yourself that you are worth more—that you're far better than that tosser. Because you are—you know that, right?" He smiles, and I have to look at him, despite the fact that my nose is gross and my Maybelline is probably running in black-brown rivulets down each cheek.

"Thanks. Sorry," I say.

"Not at all. My ex is far enough away that I don't have to worry about her coming in and running her mouth off." He winks.

"I'm glad Minotaur stepped in," I whisper. "I really appreciate that."

"Well, you can tell him. He's a great fellow. Plus, due to insurance, we can't have you practicing any of those WWE moves in here."

"I could've shown him the Rock Bottom," I say.

He laughs. It's a melodious sound. "One of The Rock's signature moves?"

I smile. "I've been practicing on my sisters since I was ten."

"I don't doubt it."

Marco stands, his glorious knees the first thing I see when I look up, and he offers me a hand. "I think you have a workout to finish, yes?"

He's right. I do.

Especially now that Shithead Trevor is going to be on that course with me.

TWENTY-FIVE

From: Marco Turner <MasterKenobi@HWood_Fit.com>
To: Danielle E. Steele <DS.May21972@gmail.com>
Subject: Your trusty trainer, checking in . . .

Hey, Danielle Steele with an *e*,

I wanted to drop a quick note to make sure you're in good shape after the incident at the gym the other night. I have spoken to Trish and the other manager as well as Sayeed, our security guard, about Trevor's membership, and we wanted you to know that this is a SAFE zone, that if you ever feel threatened or intimidated by his presence, we will have him removed posthaste. Unless, of course, Minotaur beats us to it. ☺

I'm also putting together your new program, and I look forward to sending it along. With your unexpected time off work, I mentioned twice-daily sessions—yes, twice!—because I know you can handle it. You know what you're doing now, so you can handle this, even when I'm not at the gym to holler at you. Cardio in the morning, and weight training and endurance in the afternoon or early evening session, depending on your schedule, of course.

Listen to that voice in your head that tells you you're going to be brilliant. And if that doesn't work, listen to MY voice, telling you you're brilliant. And if THAT doesn't work, look at the meme I've attached with your hunky movie stud The Rock flexing his godlike muscles and yelling at you about being a "candy-ass" on leg day.

You've got this. #nocandyassesallowed

See you soon,
Marco

From: Danielle E. Steele <DS.May21972@gmail.com>
To: Marco Turner <MasterKenobi@HWood_Fit.com>
Subject: RE: Your trusty trainer, checking in . . .

Master Kenobi?

Really? That's your email address?

If you're a *Star Wars* enthusiast, it's okay—we can still be friends. I'm more of a DC Comics girl myself, but there is room in the universe for Jedis. (Also: Check out Piewalker's downtown. Best cherry turnovers in Portland, and they have *Star Wars* stuff EVERYWHERE in the restaurant! Even if you don't eat that sort of thing because you're, well, a Jedi. What do Jedis eat, actually? Other than protein and quinoa? Do you guys eat Ewoks? I knew it. That explains so much.)

(Also, why do they call delicious chocolate cake "devil's food" when the REAL devil's food is kale? I feel like the chocolate cake is getting a bum rap.)

Thanks for the meme. Printed and glued it to the fridge for those moments when I'm feeling sorry for the above-mentioned chocolate cake.

RE: Trevor—he's a wiener. No offense to wieners, of course. I'm sure there are some rather nice wieners in the world. His is not one of them.

This conversation just got really weird.

OKAY, I gotta go drink something involving protein so I can get my not-candy-ass to the gym TWICE today. Although we may need to chat about this—not sure I can afford two sessions a day.

Also: You've heard of the Marquis de Sade? That is reportedly where the word *sadist* came from—nineteenth century, from the French "sadisme," taken directly from the Comte's name. So, your name is Marco, which sounds a bit like Marquis, and you like inflicting pain, which is like Mr. de Sade, so maybe instead of an Ewok-eating Jedi, you're really a sadist?

Food for thought. Mmmm, food . . .

Yours in pain,
Dani

From: Marco Turner <MasterKenobi@HWood_Fit.com>
To: Danielle E. Steele <DS.May21972@gmail.com>
Subject: RE: Your trusty trainer, checking in . . .

My ex-girlfriend used to call me Marco de Sade. I think you two might get along well. I can put you in touch?

:)

Jedi Marco

P.S. RE: The cost—you're not hiring me twice a day, just working your program on your own. No additional expense, so don't fret. Also, now you have no excuses.

From: Danielle E. Steele <DS.May21972@gmail.com>
To: Marco Turner <MasterKenobi@HWood_Fit.com>
Subject: RE: Your trusty trainer, checking in . . .

Oh. Dude. Sorry. I didn't mean offense. Was your ex-GF a wiener too? Maybe we should put her in touch with Trevor instead.
;)

Candy-ass Steele

P.S. I'm sure I can come up with at least one excuse that doesn't involve money.

From: Marco Turner <MasterKenobi@HWood_Fit.com>
To: Danielle E. Steele <DS.May21972@gmail.com>
Subject: RE: Your trusty trainer, checking in . . .

My ex-girlfriend was a lovely woman with a singular problem: monogamy.

From: Danielle E. Steele <DS.May21972@gmail.com>
To: Marco Turner <MasterKenobi@HWood_Fit.com>
Subject: RE: Your trusty trainer, checking in . . .

Silly you, expecting loyalty and devotion and freedom from sexually transmitted diseases in your relationship. YOU ARE A BARBARIAN.

From: Marco Turner <MasterKenobi@HWood_Fit.com>
To: Danielle E. Steele <DS.May21972@gmail.com>
Subject: RE: Your trusty trainer, checking in . . .

Drat. The secret's out. Better wear your chastity belt tonight to keep yourself safe from the sadisme.

Light a candle for me. First client of the day is in 10—she says she needs to lose a full stone for the cruise she's going on in a fortnight (impossible), but she doesn't want to sweat because "sweating isn't feminine. Also, I don't want muscles because then I will look like a man."

Oy.

See you tonight, Steele,
Muscles Malone

From: Danielle E. Steele <DS.May21972@gmail.com>
To: Marco Turner <MasterKenobi@HWood_Fit.com>
Subject: RE: Your trusty trainer, checking in . . .

Stone? Fortnight?

Geez, Shakespeare. I need a translator just to speak English to you.

Also: Can a person safely lose 14 lb. in two weeks without donating a major organ?

See you after tea,
Mistress Danielle

P.S. Was Muscles Malone your wrestling name when you were getting your ass handed to you by that jabroni John Cena? ☺

From: Marco Turner <MasterKenobi@HWood_Fit.com>
To: Danielle E. Steele <DS.May21972@gmail.com>
Subject: RE: Your trusty trainer, checking in . . .

Jabroni? I had to google that one. And for the record, Mr. Cena is an outstanding gentleman and budding thespian, not unlike your Boulder Boy.

Just for that: Tomorrow night? Bring shoes to run. We're going outside.

Marco de Sade

TWENTY-SIX

"Thanks, you guys, for including me. I never thought I'd say I miss work, but I totally miss your dumb faces," I say. The MotherCluckers have been kind enough to move the meeting to a restaurant near the office under the guise that it's a birthday party, and yes, we'll order off your greasy lunch menu if you let us bring in our own "birthday cake."

The Bringer of the Treats for this emergency meeting: Lydia. It's only been ten days since I've seen everyone, but she's gotten auburn highlights in her lustrous hair, and she's wearing a gauzy pink dress that makes her look like she should be in a Tolkien book.

We're in a banquet room adjacent to the main restaurant, sectioned off by floor-length windows adorned in tired red drapes with unfortunate stains. This place is hardly a step above Denny's, but the spinach salad and whole-grain garlic bread they served weren't too shabby. The menu also had enough things on my Marco-Approved Food List that, in four minutes, I'll be able to exercise a little self-control when every last Clucker, including me, has her pastry in front of her.

This week's delight: tiramisu drizzled with a Kahlua glaze. I know, right? [*mouth waters*] A quick google under the table tells me that this little slice of heaven is 492 calories and 49 percent fat, which is two hours on the treadmill at 3.5 mph, something I cannot share widely because it is strictly forbidden to discuss such ridiculousness in the presence of the Cluckers. I'm the worst.

But I'm also starting to see some subtle changes—looser pants, looser sleeves on my shirts—important because Shithead Trevor has been at the gym and continues to give me the side-eye. Okay, he did it once, and then Minotaur reminded him that he could cause significant pain "and make it look like an accident." This Minotaur fellow is really kind of awesome—and I have a trunkful of discounted cat litter and kitten chow from Target for Charlene's rescue mission, thanks to my ginormous gym buddy. Even Handstand Man got in on the action and brought in a bag of cat toys and catnip. And Trish offered the use of a cat tree left behind by her ex-girlfriend. My faith in humanity is slowly being restored by a group of people I never expected to be friends with.

Once the cake slices have been passed around on their pretty white paper doilies, Viv calls the meeting to order. This session, however, lacks the usual subterfuge, the fake-book-club chitchat, to keep Joan the Crone in the dark. Instead, Viv launches into the heart of the day's gossip:

Lisa "Dick-Pic" Rogers doesn't exist.

Like, she does, but not really. "They don't know who she is. After you were suspended and she was fired and corporate moved in, there was talk that they'd be filing federal charges because whatever she's involved with, it's about way more than dick pics. So then they start pulling us into the conference room one at a time, questioning us about her activities. This name she's been using—the name we all knew her as—it was a false identity. Lisa Rogers isn't a real person. Everything was faked, down to her driver's license and Social Security card. They even went to her condo—"

"You know, the fancy one with the indoor heated pool she wouldn't stop talking about—" Shelly interjects.

"Yeah, her place was totally cleaned out. If she was really living there, she isn't now," Viv says.

"Where'd she go?" I ask.

The group answers, their theories layering atop one another like the ladyfingers on this cake staring me in the face. "No one knows. / Skipped town. / Total sham job. / Probably a cyborg."

"The freaking FBI is involved! They're even going through our PCs," Charlene adds. "A waste of time, if you ask me. They won't find anything but cat pictures on my personal drive."

"What, no *kitty* porn for you, Char?" Shelly says. The room loses it. Someone meows hungrily.

"Anyway," Viv continues, "there is some talk that whoever Lisa Rogers is, she has something to do with a global hacker group. Which is why the FBI is here. My cousin works in IT for a company Imperial has called in to consult—don't tell anyone that, you guys—and she said that this dick-pic scandal is just a cover-up for whatever else Lisa Rogers was doing. They're throwing around words like *corporate espionage*," she says.

"What the hell would there be to steal?" Shelly asks. "Other than medical records, which is terrible enough."

"Are you kidding? Health insurance is a nearly $900-billion-a-year industry. There is much to be stolen—corporate and trade secrets, market intelligence, dirty secrets on company executives making back-door deals with doctors and big pharma and medical organizations, massive data theft leading to widespread identity compromises for our thousands of payees and payors that almost always leads to Medicare fraud," Lydia says as she scoops a healthy bite of tiramisu into her mouth. All ten of us look at her like she's grown a second head. "No, I'm not helping her. I'm just saying, it's a huge problem."

"When she left that day, though, after your beatdown," Shelly adds, "she'd put on her whiplash collar."

"Who keeps a whiplash collar in their desk?" Char says. "Who does that?"

"She said it prevents double chins," Shelly says, licking the last of the glaze off her doily.

"Not eating this cake prevents double chins," I say under my breath, staring longingly at my sad slice.

"Nonsense. I happen to like my double chins. I earned them." Charlene pats the extra flesh around her neck.

"Well, whatever you did to her, Dani," Viv says, "you did it well. The Rock would approve." Everyone raises their forks and claps the table with their free hands. I blush. I should not be enjoying the accolades stemming from my physical attack on another human being, but if she is a corporate spy, maybe I'll get reinstated, and then the FBI will bestow upon me some sort of humanitarian-slash-civilian-superhero award for protecting the company from further damage.

INT. SHRINE AUDITORIUM - EVENING

JOAN THE CRONE
Ladies and gentlemen, we are here
tonight to honor a very special young
woman with above-average hair and a
winning smile, a young woman with a
fierce love for the greatness that is
Dwayne "The Rock" Johnson, a young
woman with a tireless devotion to the
theatrical arts and bipolar goldfish
and homeless cats and disillusioned,
PhD-wielding bums who collect recycling, a young woman with a love for
her fellow man--unless that fellow
man is a woman and also a conniving

corporate spy with a penchant for
penis pictures . . .

The sold-out crowd laughs; Joan waits
for the early applause to die down.

JOAN THE CRONE (CONT'D)
Help me welcome the reason for this
evening, our very "own" shining star
and the apple of the FBI's cyber-
crimes division eye, Miss Danielle
Elizabeth Steele.

Deafening applause as JOAN hands off
a shimmering statuette to Danielle.

DANIELLE
Wow, thank you so much. Holy cow . . .

Dani stares at trophy that looks sort
of like an Oscar but not as anatomi-
cally ambiguous. She then looks into
audience; the camera pans to front
row, following her view.

DANIELLE (CONT'D)
Dwayne, is that you?

Applause as The Rock stands and
greets the people.

DANIELLE (CONT'D)

```
Oh man, I can't believe you guys
pulled this off.

Applause settles.

          DANIELLE (CONT'D)
Thank you so much. I don't even
know where to begin or who to thank
first . . . You know, I didn't set out
to be a hero, to save the company
from ruin at the hands of that phal-
lus-obsessed evildoer. But thanks to
the People's Elbow, we did just that.

Dani points at The Rock; The Rock
points back at Dani; the crowd
erupts.

          DANIELLE (CONT'D)
This one's for you, DJ!

Dani thrusts trophy in hand into the
air in a victory salute; everyone's
on their feet.
```

"What I don't get, though," Charlene says with a mouthful, "is why she'd collect pictures of penises on her work computer."

"Because they're infected with viruses," Lydia says.

"The files or the penises?" Shelly asks, followed by a chorus of *ewww gross.*

"You're like a fifth-grade boy, you know that?" Lydia scolds. "The files are more apt to be spread if they're of a sexual nature. Those photos are more likely to go viral in an interoffice setting, whereas pictures of cats might not."

"What's wrong with cat pictures?" Charlene asks.

"Even if the photos don't get shared by staff members, they're already in the system, so whatever malware or bots she installed, it's already doing the dirty deed she needed it to do. Pun intended."

"Just goes to show that the ones who look the dumbest are probably the smartest of the lot," Shelly says. "Can't trust anyone these days. Especially women who like infected penises."

"The penises weren't infected," Lydia says, throwing a plastic spoon across the table at Shelly.

"Humans are perverts," Charlene adds.

"Thank god," Shelly teases. "You do know it's illegal in most states to marry a cat, right?"

The conversation continues, eventually diverting off infected penises and Lisa Rogers Who Isn't Really Lisa Rogers and along the normal course of our gossip river, and while I'm grateful they included me today, I am having a hard time not eating this cake. I take a couple of bites so Viv doesn't question me, and also because it's really freaking delicious. Come on. I'm only human.

My phone vibrates in my pocket.

I slide it under the linen tablecloth that was probably white when the first Bush was in office, and check to see who's bugging me.

Miraculously Beautiful Marco (yes, I may have programmed his name this way in my phone, so what?): Hi, Dani! Don't forget your runners for tonight.

Me: Runners? As in running shoes? You were serious? We really have to run?

Miraculously Beautiful Marco: Quite serious. Running is part of the competition. You're going to need to be able to do it without vomiting.

Me: That happened once. Now you're just being mean.

Miraculously Beautiful Marco: It comes naturally.

Me: What if it's raining?

Miraculously Beautiful Marco: Are you made of sugar?

Me: Maybe I'm the Wicked Witch and I'll melt.

Miraculously Beautiful Marco: I'll bring you a mac.

Me: How the hell am I going to run carrying a computer? Is this some weird new training technique?

Miraculously Beautiful Marco: Not a Mac, a mackintosh. A raincoat.

Me: I don't know if I'm smart enough to be your friend.

Miraculously Beautiful Marco: I will endeavor to speak Yankee English. Many apologies.

(Ohhhhh, this man is such a good speller.)

Me: Technically, a Yankee is someone from New England or the northern states along the Eastern seaboard, above the Mason-Dixon Line, and as I'm a native Oregonian—

"Dani?" A distant voice interrupts my flying fingers just as Viv's elbow jabs me in the arm. My upper arm that is sore from triceps exercises.

I wince and look up, meeting the eyes of everyone around the table. "Uh—yeah?"

"Charlene was asking if you've heard anything about your suspension being shortened." Viv looks up at everyone. "She's texting," Viv says to the entire table, tsk-ing me.

"No texting! Put your phone away! Rule breaker!" the group chides, lobbing their crumpled napkins in my direction.

I slide my phone back into the pocket of my sweater. "As far as I know, it's still the whole month. So, if I'm not fired first, I'm back in two weeks, I think? I've lost count."

"Enjoying the freedom to spend with whomever it is you're texting, I'll bet," Viv teases, peppering the air with loud smooches.

"Do you have a new beau? Already? Wow, you modern girls move fast," Charlene says, polishing off the last of her dessert. "And why aren't you eating your cake? Oh dear, it's because she's in love. Now you're watching your weight like one of those *Cosmo*-reading bimbos."

"God, no. No new boyfriend. I just got rid of the last one." But I feel my cheeks burning, not because this harmless flirtation with Marco *means* anything—he's just my friend! He's not even that—he's my *trainer*.

"What's wrong with *Cosmo*?" Shelly asks. I'm so grateful for her diversion. "They publish good articles about how to improve your orgasm. I read it religiously."

"Please don't use the words *orgasm* and *religious* in the same sentence," Charlene says.

"Why not? Every orgasm should be a religious experience," Shelly says, cackling. She and Lydia high-five.

The two waitresses who've been handling our "birthday party" return to clear plates and remind us that the next party booked for the room is starting to arrive. I again thank the whole group for moving the meeting, for the bizarre gossip, for the cake ("But you hardly touched it!"). Charlene and Viv follow me out to my car so we can transfer the load of cat supplies. When Charlene asks me where so much stuff came from, I realize I can't lie—my new friends deserve the credit, and most assuredly Minotaur for such a great deal on all this stuff.

"A friend of mine works at Target. He used his employee discount—"

"He? I knew it," Viv says.

"No, it's not like that at all, seriously."

"Well, whoever *he* is, tell him thank you so much," Charlene says. "You girls catch up. I need to get back to the office so I can poop in peace before everyone takes their second coffee break."

"Thanks for that visual, Char. Oh—and can you leave this smaller bag of Friskies out back with a Post-it for Howie?" She gives me a thumbs-up as she loads the last bag of dry cat food into her trunk. I hug her goodbye, but Viv shows no sign of leaving.

"What is going on?" she asks.

"What are you talking about?"

"You look different. You're walking taller. Have you lost weight? You have a new male friend at Target, just days after you dumped Trevor. You didn't eat the cake today. You ate a salad with actual green vegetables in it for lunch. I've known you for six years and have never seen you eat anything green unless it was a Shamrock Shake from McDonald's. And you were texting under the table. Something is definitely up, and I'm not leaving until you come clean."

Crap.

So I tell her the whole delightful story, talking as fast as I can because she has eighteen minutes before she needs to get back to work. When the sky opens up, we duck into my car that now smells like my gym bag.

"Dani, you should tell everyone about this competition so we can sponsor you! Don't you have to raise money for the children's hospital?"

"Probably. I think that's the point?" I say.

"You know how these women love their charities. We could raise a small fortune."

"They don't love Howie the Pop-Can Man. He's a charity."

"They're afraid of Howie the Pop-Can Man," she says. "Also, did you read that book he gave me to give you? Because he's gonna ask if I've seen you."

"Tell him I'm only a couple of chapters in and really freaked out about how this fictional society promotes promiscuity. Although if it were a real place, I'd move there yesterday."

"You guys read weird books," she says, checking the time on her phone. "Anyway—you absolutely need to make an announcement when you come back so we can all start fund-raising and supporting you. Can you imagine? If you got to meet The Rock? That would be like your whole life's dream come true!"

"I know . . . I *know*! But I'm afraid to even think about it. And I don't win by raising the most money—I win by winning my age group on this insane course. Plus, Shithead Trevor found out about it, so now he's signed up, and he's at the same gym, and thank heavens I have some new gym friends who've got my back—"

"Is that who you were texting? The new *gym friend?*" she air-quotes.

This time my face heats up. "He's just the trainer."

"*Just* the trainer. Mm-hmm."

"Don't! It's not like that!"

"And this is different from the Target guy?"

"Yeah. Target guy is named Minotaur."

"Like the mythical beast? Is that his real name?"

"You should see him. And I don't know what his real name is. He's just Minotaur."

"But he's not romance material?"

"He has a long-term girlfriend. Plus, he's huge. I'd actually be afraid of what a Minotaur penis looks like if everything else on his body is super size."

"You could google it, but then you'd be Lisa Rogers. Or whoever Lisa Rogers is," Viv says, cackling at herself. "Okay, but the trainer isn't married? Otherwise entangled? Oh man, is he gay?"

"Shut up, Viv," I say, my face aching from smiling so hard.

"His name?"

"Marco. Please don't tell anyone else."

"You know I'll tell Ben. But no one else, pinky swear. Wait—how can you afford a trainer right now?"

"My agent got me a deal for the first two months. And then after that . . . I guess I'll start looking into plasma donation?"

"Holy smokes, you're in love."

"I am *not*. I just really, *really* want to win this competition. I really want the walk-on role in a film. I *really* want to meet The Rock."

"Okay, Danielle Steele. Whatever you say."

"Don't tell anyone yet."

"Fine. But you're wasting precious time." Viv smiles and leans back against the seat. "I won't say anything if you promise to keep my secret too." She giggles.

I follow her hand down to her midsection, her palm now resting flat against where her uterus might be hiding under her tasteful, well-matched work attire.

"No. *No*. Are you serious? But—I've only been gone two weeks. You did the preggo test when I was still there. I thought it was negative!"

"The doctor said it could've been too early for the at-home test."

"A baby? Viv!" I reach across and give her a big squeeze. "Is Ben so excited?"

"I don't know if there's a word to describe what Ben is right now."

"So all the beans and spinach and farting worked," I say. "Oh my lord, you're gonna be a mommy."

"That's the plan."

"Whoa." While Viv talks about how it's still early in the pregnancy, barely seven weeks, and there's so much potential for things to go wrong and they're not telling anyone but close family and friends until the first trimester passes and more about vitamins and the beginnings of morning sickness, et cetera, talking long past her eighteen minutes . . . a disconcerting dread settles over me.

My friend, two years younger than I am, is going to have a baby. A baby she desperately wants. If I got pregnant right now, I'd likely consider jumping off the Fremont Bridge. Which is the second-largest tied-arch bridge in the world—i.e., it's super tall, in case you've never been to Portland.

I'd be terrified to be a mother. I'd either be as crazy as Mommy or run away in terror like Gerald Robert Steele did.

Speaking of parenting: I need to stop by the pet store and get gold-fish food for Hobbs.

See? I can't even remember to feed my depressed goldfish. Probably why he's depressed. Maybe he needs a girlfriend? No. Like I've told him before, relationships are complicated. Plus, he'd probably try to eat the other fish.

As Viv and I finally cheek-kiss and part ways, my secret suddenly feels really . . . unimportant. In the bigger scheme of things, you know?

Before I can get to wallowing too much, my phone buzzes again, my heart fluttering at the immediate (and unsettling) hope that it's Marco.

The caller ID says otherwise. "Hi, Georgie."

[*breathless, frazzled, as per usual*] "Are you busy? You're still off work, right?"

"Yup."

"I need a favor—just for a couple of hours."

These conversations never end well. "You always say a couple of hours, and then it turns into an overnighter. I have plans tonight."

"I thought you dumped your boyfriend."

"What favor do you need, Georgette?"

"Dante shoved a pencil eraser up William Morris's nose, and I need to go to the pediatrician first to see if they can extract it before I go to the ER. Our medical insurance deductible right now is ridiculous, and if the pediatrician can do it in his office—I just need you to watch Mary May and Dante until Samuel gets off work."

"When will that be?"

"He's in court right now or I'd have him come home. I called his assistant, and she said he's expected back at the office by four. So could you stay until then?"

Exhale slowly. "Fine. I'll be right over."

"You're a lifesaver, Dani. Seriously." [*screaming in background*] "Okay, drive fast, wherever you are now."

I never thought I'd say it, but I really miss Joan the Crone. At least when *she* screams at me, it doesn't involve handfuls of food or feces.

Pray for me.

Better yet, pray for Georgie's chimpanzee children in my care for the next three hours.

TWENTY-SEVEN

PUBLISH   SAVE   PREVIEW   CLOSE

April 7, 2016

Dear Dwayne Johnson,

The next time Georgie says IT WILL ONLY BE A COUPLE OF HOURS, please, please remind me that she's a liar-liar-pants-on-fire.

It's two o'clock in the morning. I did not make it to the gym tonight, and Marco said that means we're running double tomorrow night (er, tonight?), and I'd be scared, but I'm too tired to be anything but tired at this very moment.

My darling sister and her husband are at the hospital with their youngest child because the pediatrician could not remove the pencil eraser shoved into his face by Dante the Future Serial Killer, so poor little William Morris is having surgery right now to remove the rubber chunk from his sinus cavity. LET'S HAVE KIDS ALL THE KIDS AREN'T KIDS GREAT LET'S HAVE MORE KIDS. My sister is a moron. Maybe while she's at the hospital, she can get a two-for-one and have her tubes tied, you know, to save on that "ridiculous deductible."

So I'm on my old crappy laptop because Georgie's letter "I" is still not functioning, and I just managed to get Dante off the ceiling fan (you totally think I'm kidding, don't you? REFER TO EXHIBIT A BELOW—yes, that is a human child hanging from a ceiling fan!) and into bed, and I may have given him a dose of Dimetapp because Jesus, that kid never stops moving. (I never step foot in this house without my own stash of Dimetapp. Secrets!) At eleven I was bribing him off the refrigerator with Twix Bites dredged from the depths of my purse because he wouldn't listen to me, and poor little Mary May was conked out on the couch after a long crying jag because she thinks Dante killed William Morris, so I found some kids' show that makes the Teletubbies look normal and Operation Dimetapp went into effect because I was afraid Dante would wake her up again and renew the earlier anxiety attack brought on by the fact that her mother is still not home and she thinks her baby brother is dead.

Anyway, if Georgie asks, we're going to say that Dante was just extra sleepy. That's the story and we're sticking to it.

Oh, and Viv's pregnant. She's super happy. I think I should've invited her and Ben over to babysit Georgette's kids so they could instead make an appointment for a hysterectomy and vasectomy, just to be double sure. Then they could take all the money and sanity they'd save and travel the world.

The big news of the day should be the Lisa Rogers situation— she's some sort of super-secret hacker chick involved with an alleged global corporate espionage operation. It sounds a bit Jason Bourne to me—the Lisa Rogers *I* knew hardly seemed smart enough to open a mayonnaise jar on her own, but I guess that's part of her false persona?

I'm still glad I punched her lights out. She deserved it. Jerk.

This is all top-secret shit, though—like, apparently Homeland Security might even be involved. This is so exciting!

It was nice seeing everyone at the MotherCluckers' meeting. It really was. Except I didn't want to eat the tiramisu because now that I've been trying to cut out fattening stuff, I can't stop googling caloric contents, and seriously, that one slice of heaven was almost five hundred calories, bro! I know, right? I broke the Clucker rules, but I couldn't eat it because I knew Miraculously Beautiful Marco would make me do a thousand extra sit-ups.

And I never thought I'd miss working in the hen hutch, but I've spent the better part of the afternoon thinking about stuff . . .

I don't want to be these women.

I don't want Imperial Health and Wellness to be the only thing that defines me. I don't want to spend the next twenty-five years growing my ass and decorating my cubicle with photos of places I'll never get to visit and/or counting down the days to my one week of paid vacation wherein I will take an all-you-can-eat cruise down to Mexico and end up with norovirus so I can spend the entire trip puking and shitting my guts out in a cabin the size of walk-in closet while the poor maid sneaks around me dressed in a full hazmat suit to leave clean towels and Mexican Pepto-Bismol.

I cannot see myself doing the same mind-numbing job day in and day out, hoping that the company doesn't go under, thereby ruining my chances of a decent retirement, during which I can join a real book club where we giggle about mommy porn and cross-stitch naughty sayings while we pass around plastic plates of Triscuits topped with canned cheese product and pimientos for color as the party host fills our glasses with Costco boxed wine and I sip surreptitiously from my flask that reads "Vodka never disappoints."

It may be okay for these women, but I can't do it.

I want more. (Although I do want that flask, so keep your eyes peeled in your travels, yeah?)

Does that make me a jerk?

I called Lady Macbeth while I was waiting for Pizza Hut to arrive and asked her again what's available to submit me on, even if I have to drive to Seattle for auditions. (Yeah, maybe don't tell Georgie I fed her kids Pizza Hut. She'll figure it out once they get diarrhea from all the grease.) DJ, I need to rethink basically my whole life. Am I too young for a midlife crisis? If it is in fact happening, does that mean I'll only live to be, like, 58? Is that how this works?

I think I need to move back to Los Angeles if I'm going to make a go of this acting thing, especially now that the waters of Stage III have been sullied by the Trevor fiasco; plus, I've had to pull back on some of the evening acting classes for now, until ROCK THE TOTS is done . . .

～

Okay, that was a pause in the conversation because Mary May woke up. The aforementioned Pizza Hut just came out of her butt. That's what I get for breaking the magic Georgie diet.

She drank a cup of warm almond milk with some cinnamon as per Georgie's "Instructions for Babysitters" and then willingly returned to bed and curled up with her stuffed Canada goose named Ice Cream. There's hope for Georgie's offspring yet if little Mary May has anything to do with it. (Thank GOD she woke up to poo in the potty.)

Anyway . . . funny story: It's spring in Portland, so this house is freezing at night, and the thermostat is preprogrammed on the app on Samuel's phone, which happens to be in his pocket at the hospital, so I can't turn up the heat. Thus, I go into Georgie's closet looking for a sweater and some thicker socks, and guess what I find?

Ooh la la, Georgette, I didn't know you had it in you. You little vixen.

I didn't want to touch anything because EWWW, but I might have snapped a photo [EXHIBIT B BELOW]. You never know when you might need ammunition against a sister. Hey, growing up in a house full of angry estrogen makes you forever a strategist, as per the Strategy of Sisterhood, modeled after Niccolò Machiavelli's *The Art of War*, only with girl shit.

There's a studded collar and a riding crop and a chain leash and a whip thingie with these long tassels and two vibrators (okay, shut up, I have one too—what modern woman doesn't?) and then stuff I've never seen before and I'm pret-ty sure I don't want to know what it is, but this is hilarious because Georgette plays like she's pure as the driven snow and she pooh-poohs Mommy's romance novels and she behaves like the perfect mother and wife with her carob cookies and her organic diapers and responsibly sourced coffee beans and ha ha ha ha ha, Georgette Heyer Steele is a SEX GODDESS!

(Judging by the size of this studded collar, she's the dominatrix. Samuel's the submissive one. Oh. My. God. This is priceless!)

Way to go, sis. If I knew you wouldn't kill me for finding your impressive collection of very naughty toys, I'd give you a fist bump. But only if you washed your hands first because . . . gross.

God, no wonder they have so many kids. If the house is rockin', don't bother knockin'! (Now I need to bathe in bleach. Gerald Robert Steele used to say that and we didn't know what it meant when we were little, but now it's just icky and I feel stained in every possible way.)

ANYWAY, it is seriously 3:30, in the morning and Miraculously Beautiful Marco is expecting me at the gym twice at some point in the next 18 hours . . .

Devotedly yours,
Danielle Spy-Stopping-Baby-Watching-Dimetapp-Dosing-Sex-Toy-Sleuthing Steele

SAVE
CLOSE

TWENTY-EIGHT

"Hello, Danielle. It's Joan. I'm going to assume that Viv has updated you about the recent goings-on here in the office, as I know you ladies had your book-club meeting.

"In accordance with the ongoing investigation regarding the incident at work involving former employee Lisa Rogers, it has been requested that you come in and submit to questioning by the authorities handling the case. It should only take about an hour, and you will be paid your normal hourly rate for your time.

"As for your adjudication, your sister has had her attorney call me no fewer than six times. Your suspension remains intact for the full duration of the month, but you will not be fired at its conclusion. Please tell Dr. Steele to call off her attorney so I don't have to get corporate involved.

"Also, let me know if coming in today midafternoon will work for you. Thank you, Danielle."

TWENTY-NINE

FAX

From: PENELOPE "MOMMY" STEELE

Hello, Danielle,

It's your mother. I would very much like to talk about the UFO conference with you—we need to solidify our plans. It would be great if I could confirm with my Greys (Alien) Anatomy group that I will attend as our representative. Is there any way you could come over for dinner tonight? If not tonight, then it must wait until the weekend, as I have wand consultations booked for the next two evenings.

Even though your sisters don't like my business enterprise, I am pleased that it's going so well. Considering this, I am again offering to go halfsies for our trip, given your dangerous financial circumstances (you really should finish your degree, Danielle!). Any word on if you're going to have a job to go back to? I am not telling any of my friends what happened because physical violence goes against everything I believe in—which is why I do not understand your fixation with that wrestler fellow. Really, did you have to hit your coworker? What did she do that was so bad? Jacqueline said something about a penis picture—are you sending illicit materials over the Internet? This is exactly why I do not trust the World Wide Web. Malfeasance on every corner. Honestly, why would you need to see a picture of a penis in your email? Gerald Robert Steele used to keep *Hustler* under the bed, as if I didn't know it was there, and it would make me so angry, the objectification of those poor girls. I do hope you're not objectifying some young man by sharing these photos, Danielle. I raised you better than that.

Jacqueline also said her attorney is trying to get you your job back? This is all very confusing to me, and frankly, I'm embarrassed that you felt violence was the answer. This is definitely your father's influence. Nature versus nurture, I suppose.

And because you might be looking for a new job, I was thinking that we could go into business together with these wands. We could also look at doing a first-edition book resale business on eBay. I have friends who make several hundred dollars a month doing this.

I'm worried about you being holed up in your apartment by yourself. Are you still doing your acting thing? You know, me and another fellow from my UFO group have started writing a play about a couple who are abducted by aliens, but no one will believe them. Maybe you would want to help us with it? You're the one with the Hollywood experience.

I hope Timothy is getting you out of the house so you don't turn into a hermit. You could always join me and the UFO ladies—we walk the mall before it opens three days a week to keep in shape and talk about developments in our ongoing efforts to prove the government is lying about Roswell. I don't want to be nitpicky, but you don't have the same metabolism as Jacqueline—you have my predisposition to bulking up in your legs and bottom—so you'd better take care of yourself or you'll find a man like Gerald Robert Steele who calls you "thunder thighs."

I am so glad that little William Morris is going to be okay. That was a welcome fax to receive this morning. Thank you for going over to sit with Dante and Mary May, although perhaps next time, don't feed the children that terrible fast food. I think it's safe to say, based on the angry handwriting in her earlier fax, Georgette is not pleased with you about that, but she's too polite to say so to your face.

Okay, please fax me back with updates so I know how to proceed with my life.

Also, if you have time this weekend, Candace at Vintage in Vancouver found another signed first edition of *44 Charles Street*, this one without a coffee stain, and she said she'd throw in a signed first edition of Judith McNaught's *Until You* if I could get over there. Can you make that happen sometime soon? Will you need gas money?

Love and light,
Mommy

THIRTY

I cannot handle any more suckage right now.

Thanks to getting home at nine this morning after basically no sleep, only to find Mommy's fax on the floor waiting for me and Joan the Crone's voicemail, I think I'm already done with today.

Except I'm not.

After another missed workout, a brief nap, a smoothie, and a shower, I'm on my way to the office to "submit to questioning" regarding the Lisa Rogers scandal. I think Miraculously Beautiful Marco is losing patience with me—which is why he's meeting me at five outside the office so we can *run*. "No excuses!" was his last text. Me running? Oh man, I hope he's in the mood for some laughs.

At least I don't have to worry about seeing Shithead Trevor tonight, though. Yeah, that's his new name. I know. Real mature. Hey, it's better than my family who can't remember his name *at all*.

Whatever. I'm crabby and tired of my mother thinking I'm a total screwup and that I have no life.

INT. FLEX KAVANA (DANI'S CAR) - MIDAFTERNOON

DWAYNE "THE ROCK" JOHNSON
You know, if pity parties could
build muscles and prep you for that
course . . .

DANIELLE
Really? You're going to give me
shit for feeling a little sorry for
myself? Did you read Mommy's fax?

DWAYNE "THE ROCK" JOHNSON
Blood, sweat, and respect—

DANIELLE
Yes, I know. The first two you give,
the last one you earn. But how can I
earn my mother's respect when everything I do is less important than
what everyone else is doing, according to some bizarre set of expectations I cannot possibly reach?

DWAYNE "THE ROCK" JOHNSON
Maybe you need to stop measuring
yourself by your mother's ruler. Stop
comparing yourself to your sisters.

DANIELLE
Are you--is that pizza? Are you seriously eating pizza right now?

DWAYNE "THE ROCK" JOHNSON

What? Georgie was gonna throw it out.
It's deep dish, babe.

DANIELLE
You're not helping. You're not supposed to be eating stuff like that
except on cheat days. You're sending
me mixed messages.

DWAYNE "THE ROCK" JOHNSON
Here's the difference: I've been
doing this for thirty-four years.
You've been doing this for thirty-
four days. There is no mix in my
message. Get your ass to the office
so you can get your ass to the gym,
and stop whining about your family.
Their suck isn't your suck.

DANIELLE
Did you at least save me a breadstick?

I'm wearing slacks and a blouse, but under it I have on my work-out gear—I don't want to change in the office bathroom postinterview and then pop out in activewear; that would lead people to question what I'm doing. Not yet.

But as I sit down in the conference room across from the impos-ing, gray-suit-wearing federal agent with Superman hair and the shiny badge hooked on his pocket, I realize that so many layers of clothing make me look suspicious, secondary to the perspiration beading on my upper lip and forehead. And before he utters so much as a how-do-you-do, he slides a rather lengthy nondisclosure agreement in front of me and offers a weighted black metal pen so I can sign it.

Once I do, we're off to the races: "How long did you know Lisa Rogers? / Did you ever notice anything unusual about her behavior, other than her affinity for inappropriate pictures? / Did she ever allude to the fact that she was dissatisfied with her employment with Imperial Health and Wellness? With her coworkers? / Did she have any noncoworker friends visit her here at the office? / Did she ever express any political opinions or affiliations? / Are you familiar with the term *dark web*? / Have you ever visited any sites on the dark web? / Given that she was found with a picture of your male friend's penis on her computer, which led to the assault incident and subsequent suspension, it's clear that one Trevor Kurzmann had some level of familiarity with Lisa Rogers. Can you give us any insight into the extent of his involvement with her? / Can you provide us with contact information for Trevor Kurzmann?"

Ohhhhhh, finally the interview delivers on something other than making me sweat like a pig in a hot dog shop!

Trevor is *busted*.

How much did he know? Holy shit, is he part of this whole thing?

When the questioning turns to how much I might have observed, even in passing, during my "romantic relationship" with Trevor, I tell the investigator, from the depths of my nervous stomach, that my relationship with Trevor was only occasionally romantic and we weren't serious enough to live together or anything and I doubt Trevor is smart enough to have learned the skills necessary to become a hacker. Farting around with Photoshop Elements to make crappy logos for his dad's business is one thing, but he's way too lazy to go much beyond that, and his mom still does his taxes because he doesn't want to learn the software.

His eyes droop the longer and faster I talk. I don't know if this is a good thing, but I've never been interrogated by a federal agent before, so I want it to be *very* clear that I don't know anything more than what I've told him. Especially about Trevor.

"We will get to the bottom of that with Mr. Kurzmann. Thank you for your time."

That earlier fantasy that I would be rewarded for saving the company loads of money and embarrassment? Yeah, that evaporates. [*Dani returns ball gown, hands statuette back to Joan.*]

⁓

I am done earlier than expected, so I text Marco and tell him I will meet him at the gym instead of his coming to the office.

The interview with Agent Superman, lack of sleep secondary to dealing with Georgie's kids, and general anxiety from being temporarily unemployed, et cetera, means I'm already wiped. And although I had a momentary pick-me-up as I handed over Trevor's contact information to the agent, my mother's fax is again weighing heavily. I need to tell her about the competition, how there's no way I can take her to the beach for her UFO convention. I need to follow Imaginary Rock's advice and stand up to her.

But first, pain.

Miraculously Beautiful Marco recaps our plan for upcoming training as we inch closer to the Big Event—three months to go—and reviews my workout journal. I'm sheepish as he reads through the diet; I'm still struggling with assigning certain foods to the Not-Right-Now pile. But he doesn't nag. He reminds me that this is a process, that I'm new, and that things take time to adjust to.

Then he listens patiently while I rattle off my excuses for missing the last two days. I can't help getting a little weepy about how mean my mother is and she keeps comparing me to my deadbeat dad and Trevor is a huge jerk but he's involved with the dick-pic scandal and my older sisters are so accomplished and I'm not and I feel so betrayed and I'm just feeling doughy and unimportant—

"I'm sorry, can I interrupt?"

I look up at Marco, the moisture in my eyes clouding my vision enough to give him a brief halo.

"I need you to listen, and not stop me as I speak. I ask that you be serious for a moment. I've known you for just shy of three weeks now, and already I'm noticing a pattern. So this is going to sound cruel, which I don't mean it to—I give this speech to all my new clients. I do think, however, you need to hear some tough love."

I sniff and nod. *Shit. Tough love?*

"Look around the gym. Every person in this place has a story. You are not the only one with a sad tale. And sitting there on the bench feeling sorry for yourself because you think you can't push a little harder— that is not the attitude that will get you a photo opportunity with your hero. What would The Rock say if he saw you sitting here sniffling because you're tired or because your subpar un-boyfriend has again done something subpar or because your dad walked out when you were a kid? We've all got tales of woe, Dani. Every single one of us. It's what makes us strong. It's what propels us to get out of bed every day and do better than we did the day before."

I think of the *LA Times* story I read about Marco's best friend dying on that movie set . . .

"You see Handstand Man? Walter? You know why he always wears a 'F*ck Cancer' tank top? He had non-Hodgkin's lymphoma. Lifelong athlete, master's degree in history, qualified for the Olympics in track and field. Then he almost died at fifty. But he fought. He fought so hard, and he's been coming here, fighting, every single day for the last decade."

I'm floored. I've worked so many cancer cases at IH&W where the survivors never return to their former quality of life.

"Or that woman over there, the one who always smiles at you when you come in?" I look over to where he's pointing—the Limping Lady. "Esther's son was killed by a guy who had just robbed a convenience store and was driving the wrong way down I-84. She limps because she was in the car with her son at the time of the crash. The cute guy you sometimes stare at who spends a lot of time on the bench press—he's a veteran of the war in Afghanistan. An IED went off under his rig, and his driver was killed. Now Alex has a 60 percent injury in his spine for life. He's *twenty-four years old*."

The more he talks, the dumber I feel. Though I don't think that's his intent, I have nothing to complain about here.

"And our hulking friend—do you know why we call him the Minotaur? Because he was walking down the street, minding his own business, when a drunk slammed into and propelled him fifteen feet, headfirst, into a concrete wall. He died twice, and he should be dead now, or at least in a vegetative state. Instead, he has come into this gym every single day since his discharge from the rehab hospital, two years now. He's gone from shuffling through the door with a walker, and then double canes, and now he's squatting and bench-pressing three times your body weight."

Wow. Okay. I'm a whiny ass. If Marco hadn't told me, I would've never guessed that Minotaur had experienced something so horrific. His strength is so far beyond his muscles.

"So you need to make a commitment, right here, right now. Everyone has a story. You just have to decide how you want the next chapter to be written. If listening to your naysaying friends or family who tell you that you're a silly girl for not meeting their expectations is how you want to spend your time, then I think your being here is not in anyone's best interest.

"You must commit. I cannot run this race for you, and you certainly won't win with this defeatist, the-world-is-against-me mentality you cannot seem to let go of."

By this time, I'm sobbing and snotty and I don't care who sees because I'm exhausted and every bone and muscle in my body hurts . . . Even though—Marco's right.

He's fucking right.

"You have three months left until the race. We can still do this, but you must stop cheating your meals. You must stop cheating the reps and sets I give you. You must stop cheating *yourself.*"

He hands me some paper towels. I blow my nose, the sound like an angry goose.

His voice softens a little, and he sits on the bench next to me. "You can do this. You're smart and funny and beautiful and strong and brave and determined. You can *do* this. You only have to prove it to yourself—no one else matters."

Marco puts a warm hand on my back, rubbing in slow circles.

"You're good at tough love," I say, laughing and sniffing. But he said so many nice things about me too. Should I feel special? Because while I feel a bit scolded, I also want to believe that he doesn't say this to every sad sack who comes to him for help.

"Tough love is an added perk, free of charge," he says. "But only because I know you can do this."

I nod.

"You have to say it out loud. It's not enough to bob your head simply to please me."

"Okay."

"Okay, *what?*"

"I can do this."

He leans forward and cups a hand around his ear. "I'm sorry, what did you say? I'm a little deaf from all the whingeing."

"I said, I can do this."

He smiles widely, the brown of his eyes sparkling under the bright gym lights. "I know you can. Because you're a mighty warrior. You're Danielle Fucking Steele."

I laugh—and I feel freer for a moment. Empowered, like a rush of adrenaline is whispering that I can lift a car above my head if I wanted to.

Marco nudges my chin and then stands before me, his broad hand out. "Now go wash your face. And then let's go run. You have a Rock to catch."

THIRTY-ONE

I wish I could tattoo Marco's words on my forehead, so when I look in the mirror I'd be reminded of everything he said. But since I cannot, as that would look really weird, especially since I'd have to have it tattooed backward so I could read it in the mirror's reflection, I will just tattoo it to the inside of my head.

I can do this because Miraculously Beautiful Marco said I could.

Even if he's being paid to be nice to me, it's refreshing to have someone so *positive* in my life. I know, he doesn't know what a jerk I can be or how I was to grow up with or what I look like in the morning or any of those things that only the people closest to us are ever exposed to—but he says he believes in me, and that's just going to have to be good enough.

It's these words I'm playing over and over in my head with every pounding step along the concrete.

We jog along busy NE Sandy Boulevard, heavy with rush-hour traffic, and down Brazee, a quieter side street, with its tasteful Portland-style houses—gable entry, bungalow, Craftsman, the occasional Tudor—kids playing on the sidewalk and street with scooters and bikes, people tending yards that are slowly awakening, drivers pulling

into driveways and loosening their ties or carrying in bags of groceries after a long day at their respective workplaces, stopping just long
enough to chat with the old lady with the rake or the guy with the
rambunctious golden retriever. There is life again, once the winter rains
slow and we can emerge from our cocoons without fear of drowning.

Marco and I continue down Brazee to Grant High School, around
the back to the adjacent Grant Park where they have a proper running
track. He says it's only a mile each way from the gym to here, but by
the time we hit the bouncy, rubberized red track, my legs and feet and
lungs are aflame.

I can do this.

The late-afternoon/early-evening weather is perfect—as we reach
the midpoint of spring, the days are getting a little longer, though the
rain continues to be temperamental, typical of Portland, and the chill
in the air lingers on exposed skin moving at our slow jog. Marco's
breathing is even and measured, each step precise and confident—
I'm just trying to match his cadence without falling face-first onto the
track, only to be trampled by the other joggers out here in their matching reflective coats and expensive shoes. My hands get so sweaty I drop
my shiny new water bottle, denting it. Hey, battle scars, baby. Look at
me run!

"Four times around the track is one mile. You think you can handle that?"

"I . . . think . . . so," I say between pounding steps. But I'm already
doing the math: one mile to get here, one mile around the track, one
mile back to the gym—that's three miles. The only time I've ever
purposely moved three miles without the aid of a vehicle was after a
concert, when my friend's shitty truck broke down in the middle of
nowhere and we had to walk to a Denny's up the road just to get cell
service, but I was seventeen and stupid drunk, so I just laughed as the
blisters formed on my heels and toes because I was young and dumb

and with my insane friends, and what are a few blisters in the face of youth and memories?

"Are . . . you . . . wearing . . . a fanny pack?" I say. Marco has a red zippered pouch installed backward so it bounces above his butt.

"Insurance requires me to carry a first aid kit if we train offsite."

"The Rock . . . would be . . . so impressed."

Marco's laugh bounces with his steps. "He did have an affinity for bum bags at one time, didn't he?"

"He calls it . . . his buff lesbian look." Man, when did breathing get so hard?

"Appropriately so," Marco says. "So in consideration of how much time we have left before the event, I'd like to do this run two to three more times in the next ten days, so we can get a good measure on your stamina and really get your body used to this sort of activity. Then I would like to move to Forest Park over off Thurman—there is much variety to be had there in terms of pathways and terrain. This will provide excellent preparation for the obstacle course, I think." Marco speaks as if he's standing still and not forcing his heart rate into the red zone. That must just be me, then. If I were a car, my rpm gauge would be spewing puffs of warning smoke.

We slow to a walk after completion of the final lap, and while I'm exhausted, I'm also exhilarated. Finally, those endorphins everyone screams about on the Internet!

"Anything sore? How are you feeling?" Marco says, taking my wrist in one hand and pinching at the joint with the other to count my pulse. Shivers race up my arms, and not because I'm cold.

He has lovely, very warm hands.

I take a deep drink and wipe the sheet of sweat off my forehead with the back of my free hand, not even caring that I probably look like a red uakari monkey right about now. (No. Seriously. Google it. That's likely what I look like right this second. Especially because he's still touching me.)

"Uh, I'm good. There are sore bits, and I probably won't be able to move tomorrow, but I feel good."

He releases my wrist and takes a sip from his water bottle, and I try not to notice how handsome he is with his hair tucked behind his ears, his deep-brown curls damp with exertion, or how his cheeks have pinked from the brisk air under the ever-present five-o'clock shadow.

There is no doubt about it: Miraculously Beautiful Marco's name suits him. I hope he decides to take my pulse again.

"Shall we walk a lap before we head back?" He takes the first step before I answer.

We're quiet for the first half lap, and I'm grateful—gives me time to catch my breath.

"Was I too hard on you? At the gym?"

I smile and fix my ponytail. "Nah. I need to be kicked in the ass. You're right. Everything you said—you're right. I spend too much time in my own head, I guess. Especially lately."

"It sounds like your family puts a lot on you. Do they know about the race yet?"

"Noooo. And they're just . . . my family. My sisters are both slaying their way through life, and I keep getting a little lost."

"What makes you say that?"

"Well, I'm a failed actress working at an insurance company with an unfinished college degree and a string of not-great relationships probably stemming from my overwhelming daddy issues and resultant fear of commitment?"

"Okay, I'm going to stop you right there: Everything you just said is editorialized and likely untrue."

"Meaning?"

"You are *not* a failed actress. I've lived in Los Angeles. I've played the Hollywood game. I know a failed actress when I see one."

"But you also haven't seen me in any major motion pictures, and I'm supporting myself by processing medical claims and not vacationing in Bermuda with Ryan Gosling and Jennifer Lawrence."

"Do they vacation together? Also, Bermuda? With all that triangle business and planes that disappear?" he teases. "You're missing a key point in what you just said, Dani: You *are* supporting yourself. Most actors have day jobs until they hit the Big One. You're still waiting for the right movie to find you."

I laugh under my breath. "I think I might be in the wrong city for that."

"Didn't you mention you once lived in LA?"

"Yeah, but only for just shy of three years. I really miss it, though. I'm busy here with the theater group and classes and whatever auditions Janice can get me, but it's not the same. The energy is so different—down there, everything feels so frenetic and *so* much of the city is focused around the entertainment industry—you know how it is, right? There's live theater everywhere, and you always have a friend or two doing a short film, and everyone just wants to get involved because *why not*. And it's crazy, long hours, most of the time with no pay, but it's so fun. Here it's just . . . different. Everyone's cautious and projects are slower to get going—we used to go to free invite-only screenings where we'd watch the film, and then after, we'd have live Q&As with famous actors and directors. It was insane. Nothing like that here."

"Portland is certainly quieter. But even in LA, three years is hardly long enough to build a career."

"Right?" I say.

"So why'd you come home?" He looks at me with that question, and before I can speak, he sees the answer on my face. "Your family. They called you back."

"Five points for Gryffindor."

"I didn't mind LA," he says. "Terrific parties, fun people, the great variety of food—fresh fish tacos with mango salsa, Thai spicy coconut soup, the Armenian chicken kebabs and rice pilaf. My mouth, it waters!" He flattens a hand over his heart.

"Portland's getting better, though . . ."

"Yes," he chuckles, "but I could do with less rain."

"Says the lad from Jolly Old England?"

"Oh, and the beaches. I do miss the beaches."

"The beaches, yesssss! So much flesh, so little time!" I say. He laughs. "What did you do down there?" I ask, hoping my face doesn't betray that I've already IMDB'd him.

"I worked as a stunt coordinator, so it really was a great deal of fun going to work every day." He takes another drink from his water, his eyes darkening a bit.

"What brought you to the City of Roses?" I say tentatively, hoping I'm not overstepping. "Wait—let me guess: You love food trucks, microbreweries, and hipsters."

He chuckles. "I had some LA friends who moved here after the '08 recession, and they raved about it. Seemed like a good place to land, given my state of mind at the time. And I didn't want to go back to the UK. Nothing really there for me anymore." He pauses. "There was a horrible accident on the last film I worked on—my best friend was killed, on a stunt I put together."

"Oh man, I'm so sorry. We don't have to talk about this, Marco."

"No, no, it's all right. As my therapist says, 'It's good to talk about these things.'" He smiles, but it doesn't reach his eyes. "It was a freak accident—I had performed the stunt myself once before to make sure everything was exactly right. A cable locked up, and the driver on the car rig wasn't going fast enough, so when the actor—my friend—jumped from the moving car onto this other green-screened flatbed truck, he fell short, the cable jerked him sideways, and the car ran over him." Marco takes another drink and clears his throat. When he speaks again, his voice is rough. "The workplace investigators concluded it wasn't my fault—it had something to do with the cable mechanism that locked when it should've released and the speed of the car, but that doesn't mean I'm absolved of my guilt."

Now it's my turn to put a gentle hand on his shoulder. "I'm sorry. For you, and for your friend."

His face is painted with momentary melancholy, and then it's gone. "We're not talking about me right now, though, are we, Ms. Steele. I think you are diverting our course."

"Me? Never."

"So we've determined that you are not a failed actor, and you *are* supporting yourself. Who cares about the university degree—I know lots of blowhards with degrees who can't scramble their own eggs."

"Hold up—you mean *you* can?" I say, winking. Miraculously Beautiful Marco has a great laugh, and it's quickly becoming one of My Most Favorite Things.

"As far as your string of *not-great* relationships, we're supposed to go through all that, aren't we? As humans?" he says. "Aren't we supposed to test out different people as we work to uncover who we really are? I think we need to do that before we can be of any value in a committed relationship."

"Wow, someone's been watching too much *Oprah*."

He places his hand over his heart. "I cannot tell a lie."

"Maybe that's what I've been doing, then. Testing out different people. I think maybe I need to come up with new testing parameters, though. This latest calamity—"

"Trevor?"

"Yeah. What a dick. Pun intended."

"But he wasn't a dick when you were dating him."

"Oh, he sort of was. He's *very* competitive—as evidenced by him joining the gym and signing up for the race. He was quite critical too . . . I think we both were of each other. We knew it wasn't a long-term thing, but we did have an agreement to at least be honest. That pisses me off more than anything. Betrayal. I don't like being lied to or misled."

"Yes, it's never pleasant."

"You've been the recipient of such behavior?" I ask. But he left that door wide open.

"Of course. And if I'm being candid, I wasn't so well behaved in my younger days. I'm sure there are a few girls back home who would tell you I'm a proper arsehole."

"You'll notice my halo is only slightly tarnished, so no judgment here," I say. "I don't even know what I want in a relationship. Someone who doesn't trim his toenails in the living room would be a good start."

Marco laughs again and swallows the last of his water. "Darling, you really do need to rewrite those parameters."

I love the way the word *darling* sounds coming out of his British mouth.

"As for the daddy issues, I don't think any child comes out of childhood without some degree of scarring from their parents," he says.

"I think I just pick the wrong guys. And you've not met my mother. She's completely mental." And though I don't say it to Marco—it's a little early in our friendship to bare my scars—I'm not in denial over the gouge that Gerald Robert Steele's departure left on my skin. I do miss him. I've always missed him, even when I've hated him. Georgie and Jacqueline moved on better than I have. They were older, and they weren't into the same stuff as Gerald Robert Steele. Hell, maybe the family therapy worked for them where it failed for me. And I was a Daddy's girl from the very beginning—sometimes I feel like I'm still that bony, scab-kneed kid sitting out front on the curb, waiting for my father's truck to rumble up the street, only going in when the mosquitoes had made mincemeat out of my exposed flesh and it was obvious Gerald wasn't coming back that night, or any night.

How could he have left me to navigate the waters of adolescence with Penelope Steele at the helm of the USS *Crazy Town*? But I like to think that if Gerald reappeared one day, we'd go have a beer and he'd explain his side of things, and I'd listen and probably yell a little, and then we'd go watch some wrestling and he'd try to convince me it wasn't at all fake, and I'd laugh and order us another round and bite back all the questions I had about what he'd been doing all these years while I was turning into a grown-up without him.

The sun by now has pulled on a sweater, ready to dip into the cold ocean as she paints the sky hues of purple and pink. My legs feel rubbery, and the sweat coating pretty much every surface of my body has cooled.

Just in time for us to jog back. "You ready to get moving?"

I am, but I'm not. I like being out here, having Marco all to myself.

Marco sets out at a slow jog, off the track, along the Grant Park Path, through trees that are slowly regaining the coats they shed just a few months ago, past the Beverly Cleary Sculpture Garden, past the tennis courts and pool, and around through the parking lot adjacent to the high school.

In the dim light, I hear—a meow? I glance around to see if there's a stray following us. Nah, I'm just hearing things.

"Meow!" I'm not imagining the sound—there is a hungry or hurt feline nearby.

From next to the building, a midsize kitten with a harness comes bounding toward us, dragging her bright-pink leash behind her.

"Aldous?"

I stop and hold my hand out. She bumps into my fingertips, gives me a gentle bite, and starts purring.

"You know this cat?" Marco says.

"Yeah, which is weird—" If Aldous is here running around with her leash still attached, where the hell is Howie? "She belongs to a . . ." What is Howie? "She belongs to a friend who collects the recycling at our office. But if Aldous is here . . ." Was she kittenapped? Did she run away?

I scoop up the cat and backtrack toward where she came from. As I'm rounding the corner, Howie's Whole Foods cart comes into view— but he's not near it. Something's not right.

Between the two bigger buildings and a smaller outbuilding, a beat-up tennis shoe sticks out from the building's end.

I run down to it, and the shoe isn't empty. Oh dear god—"Howie? Howie, it's Dani. Howie, look at me," I say, dropping hard to my knees, Aldous beside me, Marco looking over my shoulder. I shake Howie's shoulders. "Howie, come on, man, wake up. Howie!" I yell, shaking him harder.

I yank his black duster apart and drop an ear to his chest. He's not breathing.

"Marco, call 911!"

I launch into chest compressions, forgetting how sore I am as I throw my body weight into his barrel chest. Before I can put my mouth over Howie's, Marco pulls a plastic CPR mouth guard from the pack around his waist. "Never thought I'd have to use this in real life," he says quietly, his cell phone against his ear.

I'm pounding on Howie's chest, breathing for him, murmuring over and over that he can't leave the planet yet because I'm still trying to finish *Brave New World* and I have a lot of questions and he's the only one who can answer them. And who else is going to sit outside the office at that rickety, splinter-giving picnic table and eat Voodoo Doughnuts with me on my birthday and tell me about morphology and syntax and diphthongs and other smarty-pants stuff I have yet to learn?

The little cat wails beside me, clawing at my sweatshirt, and it adds to my panic because she's probably hungry. I really need her dad to wake up.

But his color isn't right. The only time I've ever seen a dead body, it was the neighbor lady's. Mommy would buy groceries for her once a week. That night when we let ourselves in to drop off her canned soup and Wonder Bread and six-pack of Ensure, we were greeted by Mrs. Jaffrey's pale-gray, half-lidded stare, the usual pink of her cheeks long gone. I stared at her until the ambulance arrived, waiting for her to wake up, worried they would bury her when she wasn't really dead.

Howie is near the same waxy color as Mrs. Jaffrey was that night.

Which means I need to pump harder.

"Come on, Howie!" I yell at him between breaths. Aldous wails alongside me. I'm not naive enough to believe the cat found me specifically. She needed a human, and for whatever bizarre reason, I happened to be the first human she came across or who listened to her.

"Do you want to trade off?" Marco kneels beside me.

"No. No, I got it. Just make sure the ambulance can find us." I have to save him. *He's my friend.*

As I'm throwing my terrified energy into reviving him, I notice his hair is wet. He mentioned once that the head of the Grant High School athletic department is an old college buddy. He lets Howie use the facilities twice a week to shower and run a load of clothes while they talk about old times and good books and if the Portland Trailblazers will ever see an NBA playoff again. He must've had his shower and then . . .

Suddenly Howie's chest rises on its own, and he starts coughing.

"Roll him sideways," Marco says, helping me do just that as Howie vomits onto the damp gray concrete.

Marco digs through the Whole Foods basket, extracting a T-shirt that he uses to wipe Howie's mouth and bearded chin. Howie blinks a few times and tries to speak, but whatever's going on, it's robbed him of his voice.

"Hey, Howie. Hey, big guy, you're okay. It's Dani. We've called for an ambulance. You stay awake and talk to me, okay? Don't close your eyes again because I have a lot of unanswered questions about that Bernard Marx fellow," I choke out, trying to hide the fear in my voice behind a strained smile as I watch his eyes flutter and his chest rise and fall.

My best guess: a stroke.

I stay with Howie, whispering how we've got everything covered, petting the back of his limp hand and his damp white hair while Marco runs around the end of the buildings and waits for the ambulance. Aldous climbs on top of Howie's chest, sniffing around his face. "You're a good girl, aren't you, Aldous? We'll take care of your dad." I pet her and she reaches a paw, claws out, toward my face, purring like a Porsche. "Howie, does anything hurt? So I can tell the paramedics?"

He points at his head with his left hand. I ask him to squeeze my fingers with his right hand; he cannot. And the right side of his face is drooping—his eye, his mouth. This is not good. I hope the medics get here soon.

I continue asking yes-or-no questions—do you have food for Aldous, is it in the cart, did you hit your head—until he seems too tired to answer. I talk about my progress reading *Brave New World*, how Bernard Marx and his overwhelming discontent is so eye-opening that I feel like an Epsilon in an Alpha world, and that I know now why he wanted me to read it.

Howie manages a lopsided smile.

Sirens scream down the side street, growing closer.

All at once they stop, and Marco leads the fire department to where we're tucked between these two buildings. Immediately the medics set to work on Howie, taking vitals, asking questions, cutting apart his beloved flannel shirt to attach chest leads, Howie's eyes on me. With his still-functioning left hand, he points at the cat in my arms.

"I'll take Aldous. Don't worry. And if you promise me you'll get better, I'll read Chaucer—I swear I won't fake it this time."

He winks with his good eye.

"Don't worry about your girl. I'll take good care of her. She can babysit Hobbs the Depressed Goldfish until you're back on your feet."

One of the medics, a young woman with a gorgeous mahogany braid snaking down her back, asks me a few questions about Howie, though my answers are not at all helpful because I don't know how to reach his next of kin, if he even has next of kin. He was never forthcoming about family stuff.

"Howie, we're going to look in your basket for your wallet, okay?" He attempts a nod, and the redhead hands me and Marco each a pair of blue medical gloves. I don't want to be a jerk and look like a germophobe—Howie is my *friend*—but I put the gloves on, just in case.

Digging through his prized possessions doesn't reveal much: changes of clothing, a lot of books in black plastic bags, a metal box full of what must be family pictures (I pull this out and ask Marco to tuck it under Howie's arm to take to the hospital), cans of pork and beans, the bag of cat food for Aldous, a few blankets, the sleeping bag I gave him for Christmas last year.

"No alcohol or evidence of drugs in here—do you know if Howie is taking any medication or if he's a drinker or street-drug user?" the redhead asks. Her name tag reads MAHONEY.

"I'm not sure about medications. I don't think he sees a doctor very often. He used to drink, but he's recovering."

"A lot of these guys are."

"He has a PhD in English lit and other degrees in linguistics," I say. I feel defensive. I don't want this young Mahoney maligning my friend with her preconceived notions.

"That would explain the books," Mahoney says. She finishes going through her side of the cart and reseats the plastic bag over the top of Howie's stuff.

"What hospital are you guys going to?"

"Emanuel," she says, pulling off her gloves, only to replace them with a new pair. She then pulls out her notebook and its tiny pen and jots down our names and contact info.

Mahoney walks over to rejoin her two male partners, grabbing a gear bag as they hoist the gurney atop its wheels in preparation for loading it into the rig.

"What do I do with this stuff?" I ask.

"We can't take it with us," Mahoney says. *No shit, Sherlock.* "Thanks for calling us, guys." The door to the back of the ambulance slams shut, and Howie & Co. speed away, lights and siren.

Aldous mewls in my arms and bites down on the blue glove covering my finger.

The sob that had been choking me for the last half hour escapes; heartbroken tears spill down my face.

Marco wraps me in a hug, the smell of exertion and his cologne or aftershave comforting given the events of the last fifteen minutes. I so appreciate this.

The cat squeals between us. "Your friend will be all right, Dani. He's in good hands," he says quietly as he rubs my back and cups the back of my head for a beat.

But Aldous will have none of this, squirming in my arms, claws unsheathed.

Marco lets go and moves back to the cart, reaches in, and pulls out the cat food, spilling a small heap onto the pavement.

The kitten bounds from my grasp, nearly hanging herself when I grab for her leash. She opens her mouth so wide for that first crunchy bite, she looks more lion than domestic housecat.

"What are we to do with his things? It doesn't feel right to leave them here," Marco says.

I'm kneeling next to this cat who's eating like she's never seen food, and I look up at Marco. "Would it be weird if we pushed it back to the gym, and then I could unload it into my trunk? He'd lose the cart, but his books and stuff I could keep for him."

The side of Marco's mouth rises in a half smile. "You're a good person, Steele with an *e*."

"Howie's my friend. To everyone else, he's just this bum who washes windows and recycles pop cans. But if you listen to him, if you listen to some of his stories . . ." My throat tightens again, cutting off my words, and I think of just a couple of hours ago when Mr. Tough Love was feeding me a dish of truths on the weight bench: *Everybody has a story.*

"The lengths you will go to just to get out of your program are really quite remarkable," Marco teases, pushing the cart free of the puddle it's been resting in.

When Aldous has eaten her fill, I scoop her up and she nuzzles into me, her purrs quickly leading to sleep now that her belly is full. When my voice feels a little stronger, I nod at Marco pushing Howie's shopping cart down the quiet residential street. "You've got a gym full of regular people doing regular exercises. I thought I'd come shake things up a little."

"Well, suffice it to say you have definitely done that."

THIRTY-TWO

Upon returning to the gym, I quickly retrieve my phone from my locker, the dozing cat still in my arms, only to find four missed calls from Viv, as well as text messages galore from both my sisters and even Trevor. I cannot look at these right now—I'm sad, and exhausted, and I need to get Aldous settled and stash Howie's stuff in my car.

Under a renewed rainfall—so glad it waited until we got back here instead of while we were pushing the cart—Marco helps me unload Howie's things into the trunk of Flex Kavana. Aldous curls up on a sweatshirt on the front passenger seat, oblivious to the world and probably just glad to be warm and fed. I'm weirdly jealous of that kitten.

My phone goes off again in my pocket. Could it be the hospital calling with an update for Howie already?

Marco pushes the cart around back, says he'll slide it in next to the dumpster for now until we figure out what's happening with Howie.

The caller ID tells me it's Viv. Again. Oh no, I hope she's not having a miscarriage.

I brace myself for the worst and answer the phone.

"Hey, Viv, you okay?"

"Dani, where have you been? I've been trying to reach you for two hours."

"I'm at the gym. Or I was. We were jogging over at Grant Park, and then we came across Howie, and I think he had a stroke and so we had to call the ambulance. Viv, are you okay? Is everything okay with the baby?"

"Dani . . . are you near a computer?"

"What? No. I'm—we're just wrapping up." Too much to explain what I'm actually doing right now.

"You need to get to a computer."

"Okay. Why?"

"Can you get to one? Right now?"

"What the hell is going on, Viv? You're scaring me."

"Just *go,* Danielle."

"Okay, okay—hang on for a sec." Marco's walking toward me from around back. "Hey, can I use your computer in the office real quick? My girlfriend is on the phone, and it sounds like an emergency."

"Oh dear, another one?"

We hustle out of the rain and into the manager's office of Hollywood Fitness. Marco logs on to the desktop and then offers me the chair.

"Viv, what am I looking for?"

"Dani . . . go to www.deardwaynewithlove.com."

"What?"

"Just do it."

"This is super weird, Viv—" I navigate to the address she's provided, and once the page loads, my stomach falls out of my body and runs for the hills to start a new life free of me and my dramas.

"What the fuck is this, Viv . . . What is this . . .?" But I don't need her to answer because I know exactly what it is.

It's my blog. My private, unpublished, super-secret, super-safe-from-stupid-prying-sisters blog-as-a-diary, up there on the World Wide Web for every human person to see.

Viv's voice buzzes in my ear. "I got an email earlier with this link—I think everyone in your address book got the email because the sender didn't use a BCC. Dani, you've been hacked. I didn't know what it was at first, but then I started reading it, and I realized it's you. It's your diary, isn't it?"

"I . . . I gotta go. I'll call you back."

I can't take my eyes off the screen as I scroll. Oh my dear baby Jesus, it's all here. Every single entry. Every single confession, complaint, secret, divulgence it's all here.

My phone lights up again, making me jump as it buzzes against the IKEA-veneered desktop.

It's a text message—on top of the other dozens of text messages. I scroll through. The email icon on the phone's home screen shows a little red circle with white numerals inside: 42. There are forty-two emails waiting for me.

Ding. Nope. Forty-three.

Ding. Forty-four.

Seems there are a lot of people who are trying to reach me right now.

I click open one email—it's from Shelly, one of the Cluckers. "Dani, is this you? Dude, you've been hacked! Everyone in the company got this email. You have to take this blog down before everyone reads through *everything!*"

Holy. Fucking. Shit.

Marco walks back into the office, his phone in his hand. "Hey, I got an email from you earlier," he says, smiling. "You didn't mention it."

"*No!* No, don't open it."

His smile retreats. "Why do you look like you're going to faint?"

Oh god, how—what—how—I can't think straight. Twinkly lights in my peripheral vision. Train roaring in my ears . . .

Marco moves quick around the desk and shoves my head between my knees. "Deep breaths. In and out. Too much running and excitement for you tonight, methinks."

I take a few cleansing breaths, and once the roar in my ears has subsided, I sit back slowly and point a finger to the screen.

"I've been hacked. Someone hacked me."

He leans across my weak body still seated in the manager's chair and squints at the screen. "What is this? Dear Dwayne Johnson?" He reads a few lines and then kneels before the screen. I don't want him to read another word—shit, what did I say about *him* in my latest entries?

"This is your diary . . ."

I nod. And then the tears, piggybacked with panic, and then I'm near hyperventilating as I push him away from the screen and try to log out of Blogger, but the logout won't work, and whatever the hacker has done, he or she has wrested control of my life's most intimate missives from me. How am I going to take this down before it does damage I will never be able to repair?

"It was supposed to be safe," I sob. "It was supposed to be *safe*."

Marco closes the browser tab and, for the second time tonight, pulls me against him. I wish I could enjoy this, but everything is ruined and my life is over.

"I have a friend," he says. "We'll get to the bottom of this. Let me make a call."

"How did this even happen? Who would want to hack me? Who would even know about this blog?" I push back against the faux leather chair. Marco stands and scrolls through his phone.

"Is someone mad at you? Someone with an ax to grind? Could it have been Trevor?" Marco asks.

"No, I seriously doubt it. I mean, unless he was lying to me about being computer illiterate, but I doubt it—"

Wait.

Dick pics.

Trevor's dick pic.

Trevor's dick pic on Lisa Rogers's computer monitor.

Lisa Rogers's ponytail in my hand as I slam her to the floor.

Lisa Rogers in trouble with the FBI and Homeland Security and everyone else whose name involves acronyms and long prison sentences and black-op sites.

"Shit. *Shit.*"

"What?"

"I need to call the FBI."

Marco chuckles. "Dani, I know this is an embarrassment for you, but I don't think—"

"I gotta go." I stand and push past him, not stopping as he calls my name, asking me to wait until he can get ahold of his friend.

The door of Hollywood Fitness shushes closed behind me, and the hiss of car tires on the wet asphalt of Sandy Boulevard underscores the alarm screaming in my head.

You've really done it this time, Steele.

THIRTY-THREE

On the drive home, I'm serenaded alternately by my phone and Aldous. I think she needs to pee.

What in the actual hell is going on?

It had to be Lisa Rogers. This is payback for what happened at the office, right? Does she know we've all been talking to Agent Superman? Does she know the feds are involved and they're looking for her?

Of course she does, genius. You straight-up blabbed about it to DJ in one of your posts. Now the whole world *knows the US government is after her!*

I check my mirrors obsessively—am I being watched? Oh god, is she going to find me and put one of those dark pillowcases over my head and zip-tie my hands and then take me somewhere to be tortured until I tell her everything I know? Because I will be super terrible at torture. They'll pour one jug of water on my towel-covered face, and I will sell my soul to make it stop.

When a car that looks like Trevor's slides in behind me, my heart thuds against my damp sports bra, now uncomfortably cold from the abrupt end of exercise. When the car passes, I exhale so loudly, Aldous answers me with a mewl of her own.

"I know, sweetie. We're almost home."

Shit, she's going to need a cat box, litter, food, some toys—I have no idea how long Howie will be out of commission, and I can't have Aldous peeing in my piles of laundry or eating Hobbs. But I *must* get home and deal with this—this—hacking . . . Jesus, I've become one of those people on the news who I used to shake my head at because they were hacked after using *QWERTY* or their birth year as their one password for all their accounts.

I'm too long at a stoplight, the driver behind me courteously lets me know with the soulful stylings of his Ford F-150's horn.

I don't have time for a proper pet store. Grocery store it is.

Oh man, I didn't write anything awful about anyone at the grocery store, did I?

What *did* I write? If the ever-increasing number of text messages and emails is any indication . . . I wrote a lot.

I have to focus.

Into the store. Kitten chow. Cat litter. Cat litter pan and poop scoop. Fluffy mouse-shaped catnip toy to keep Aldous out of the fishbowl.

Home. Everything inside. Litter poured, food in the bowl, fresh water.

Open my laptop. Eighty-two emails waiting for me.

My phone battery's at 11 percent, a response to the jump in activity. I plug it in, open a beer, put a second beer on standby, and one at a time, I scroll through.

Ohhhhhh boy . . .

You are the worst sister ever. CALL MY OFFICE IMMEDIATELY.

Did u really right about my dick on the INTERNET? Expect to hear from my atterney!

YOU FOUND MY SEX TOYS—AND PUT IT ONLINE? OMG, Dani! You took a picture? I'm the PRESIDENT OF THE KINDERGARTEN PTA!!!

Seriously, Danielle, you need to take down the post where it says I cheated on my SATs. And the Ex-Lax cake—DANI, that girl is a patient of mine now! This is extremely grave. And if the authorities read that Mommy has pot growing in her basement . . .

Mommy's heart is going to be broken when she hears about this. I still cannot BELIEVE you fed my son CANDY? YOU WILL NEVER BABYSIT FOR ME AGAIN.

U faked the groaning when we were doing it? Bitch!

You gave them PIZZA HUT *and* DRUGGED THEM? I should call the police.

Dani, call me. Unless you don't want to talk about my ANNOYING FERTILITY ISSUES.

And Dante is NOT a serial killer. HE'S FIVE.

Whut the hell is wrong w/ Red Lobster? I thot U liked shrimp scampi. U ate enough for 5 people!

Is this payback for me reading your diaries when we were in high school? We were KIDS, Danielle!

I can't believe U told the whole world my penis is curved. I hope Lisa got a good punch in 2.

Gosh, I hope U don't end up like us poor LOSER HENS who are happy to have JOBS.

You get the idea.

And the emails—some were just from ladies at the office who clearly had not yet read anything but were inquiring to know what this was all about—but more were from really, *really* pissed-off people who must've received the link from my hacked address book and spent time reading the entries.

By the look of things, whoever hacked me—it *has* to be Lisa Rogers—was very thorough. No private stone left unturned.

The only email that doesn't shave off a layer of skin: Charlene the cat lady, telling me how sorry she is that she read a few of my "stories," but they're "nice and honest, and honesty is rare these days, but I might want to delete some of them so folks don't get upset" *(I would love to, Charlene, and folks are plenty upset already)* and "My daddy left me when I was little too, so if you ever want to talk about it, I'm always available." (Why does everyone keep harping on my daddy issues?) Also, she will donate money "for your race so you can meet The Rock because I know how much you admire him." (Okay. That part's cool.)

After two hours of tears and beers, I cannot get control of anything related to my very private online diary. The hacker has changed the password, and none of the safety protocols are working for me to wrestle it back. I can't redirect the URL because I can't get into the dashboard. Blogger is owned by Google, and there's only an online Help Center and Help Forum, but there is no one to *call* to talk to in real time to help me save my own ass.

I can't tell how many hits it's getting or how widely it's been spread—I can only gauge this by the comments section, which grows nearly every time I refresh the page.

Very little of it is friendly.

I gotta call Agent Superman. As embarrassing as this is, maybe he has the tools to get the blog back under my control. Maybe I can redeem myself by leading the feds right to Lisa Rogers and then the hens won't peck my eyes out when I return to IH&W.

He gave me his card—I dump my purse out all over the couch, coins rolling off the cushions, immediately catching Aldous's attention.

I dial. Voicemail. Not surprising—it *is* after nine o'clock.

"Hello—hi—this is Danielle Steele, one of the employees at Imperial Health and Wellness. We talked about the Lisa Rogers case? Yeah, well, it seems I've been hacked, pretty severely, actually, and I am in desperate need of help . . ." I give him the URL and explain about the blog and the info online and how horribly embarrassing this is and the damage it's doing and that it has to be her and please, *please* call me back at your earliest convenience. "Also, if you could just not read the diary? That would be great."

Awesome. I just called an FBI agent, and of course he's going to read the diary, and then my mother will be arrested for manufacture of, and intent to traffic, a controlled substance.

Just in case, I text Jerky Jackie: Obviously I've been hacked. Tell Mommy to destroy her plants. The feds are involved in this hacking situation through work. Thanks. Sorry. About everything.

Aldous, tired of chasing pennies, jumps onto my lap and curls up, her long nails in need of a trim and her whole self in need of a bath. Which reminds me—I need to call the hospital and see what's happening with Howie.

Except when I do, they won't tell me anything because I'm not family. The woman on the line at least confirms that he's still *alive* and gives me the visiting hours for tomorrow.

My phone won't stop dinging with texts from my annoyed friends and family—Trevor's messages are getting meaner, his spelling more atrocious. I'd turn the phone off, but I need to talk to Agent Superman if he calls back—

Knock at the door.

Oh Jesus, Lisa's come for me. This is it. Black pillowcases and zip ties.

I scoop Aldous into a purring heap and situate her on another cushion so I can pull the curtain apart and see whose car is out front.

It's not Trevor's. Which is good.

And there's no black windowless van or huge SUV with tinted, bulletproof windows.

Another knock.

I tiptoe to the door and risk a look through the peephole.

Marco waves from the other side, takeout bags resting atop his opposite hand and arm.

Oh god. I look like a drowned rat who has had time to dry off but still looks mostly drowned. How did he find where I live? I'm equal parts thrilled to see him and relieved it's not someone coming to take me away.

I undo the dead bolt and open the door. "Hey . . ."

"Am I interrupting? I brought pho."

"Wow—no, just me and Aldous trying to figure out the fastest way out of town without anyone seeing us." I invite him in. As he passes, I throw my arm up and quick-sniff my underarm. Seriously, I need a shower.

"I hope it's all right that I looked up your address from the gym computer. Total privacy violation. Could get fired for it. Will you tell on me?"

"Marco, after tonight, I have no secrets. I appreciate the company. Especially because you brought food." I lock the door behind him, just in case.

My apartment is small enough that he finds the kitchen himself. He sets to unpacking the takeout containers. "This one's chicken noodle, this one's brisket—wasn't sure if you're eating beef—and this is a hot-and-sour seafood. After our rather cold adventures outdoors, I thought this would be a pleasant way to settle our stomachs for the evening."

My eyes threaten tears again. Maybe it's the two beers. Maybe it's the hacking. Maybe it's Howie's medical emergency.

Maybe it's because this person who hardly knows me is standing in my kitchen looking delicious, and he's brought me food when, based on the manic chiming of my phone, it feels like the entire world is stabbing my voodoo doll with the pins I inadvertently provided for them.

"Oh dear, no need to get emotional. It's only soup."

My laugh is choked off. "I really like soup," I say.

Without saying anything else, I pull out bowls and utensils. We dish up our own servings, and I lead Marco to the table, pausing to clean off the recent purchases for Aldous. Hobbs the Depressed Goldfish perks up when he sees me reach for his flake shaker.

And speaking of Aldous, as soon as she gets a whiff of the human food—which does smell divine—she's off her cushion and mounting an expedition up the leg of my very thin workout pants.

"I called the hospital," I say, pinching in half a chunk of chicken for the voracious kitten. "They won't tell me much."

"Will you go see him?"

"Yeah. Tomorrow. He doesn't have any local family that I know of . . ."

The subsequent moments are filled with quiet slurps, spoons against the IKEA bowls, the crinkling of paper napkins as we wipe dribbles off our respective chins. The soup indeed warms the earlier chill, plus it dulls the buzz left from the beers I consumed on an empty stomach.

"When I was a lad—twelve years old—I fell head over heels. Her name was Nicola, and she was the love of my life. Well, up to that moment. I didn't think any other human had ever experienced a love quite like mine. Sadly, it was unrequited. Nicola had eyes for the very dapper Jonathan whose father owned a chain of minimarts. The family had loads of money, and they lived in a huge house down the block, and Jonathan had terrific hair and his nanny would bring in these amazing sweets whenever it was a holiday. I was a bit of a swot—I liked studying—and my glasses were too thick and I had acne before the other kids, so compared to Jonathan, I was a nobody."

Looking at him now? It's impossible to picture it.

"Yet I was undeterred. Every night, I would write ardent letters to Nicola, pouring my heart out to her in the way only a besotted twelve-year-old boy could."

So glad I'm not the only preteen who did this. The preblog, paper-and-pen Dear Dwayne diaries have tons of letters to the Objects of My Unrequited Middle School Affection.

"I compiled the letters in an old rectangular tobacco tin my gran gave me, but worried that my brother would find my correspondence, I kept the tin with me at all times. We only had cubbies at our school—no proper lockers with locks—but I'd never had an incident of theft at school before, and my brother was constantly stealing my pocket money and comic books, so I felt the letters were safer *with* me, in my knapsack, away from the house."

"At this juncture, it's fair to postulate that even on the other side of the world, siblings are demons," I say. He laughs quietly. About this time in the story, Aldous discovers Hobbs. Marco and I take turns feeding her leftover chunks of meat from our soup bowls to keep her from murdering the goldfish.

"One day I'd been called to the headmaster's office to discuss my results on a district-wide test in which our school had competed with other schools. While I was gone, someone helped themselves to my knapsack."

"Noooooo . . ."

"When I came back into the classroom, at first I didn't pay any mind to the giggles and funny looks the other students were giving me, or to the pieces of folded paper they were passing about when the teacher's back was turned. Until the student in front of me opened one of these folded pages, and I recognized the handwriting."

I feel mildly sick for him—I remember in vivid color when I discovered Jackie with my journals, the embarrassment, followed by rage. And again now, with the blog, only this time it's not my sister's evildoing . . .

"Across the room, Jonathan was watching me, his face purple with the laughter behind his cupped hand, his other hand resting comfortably atop my tobacco tin."

I sit back against my chair, shaking my head in empathy, cradling Aldous so she'll settle down.

"They read the letters. All of them. Nicola read all of them as well. Jonathan made sure of it."

Marco runs a hand through his curly hair and leans his elbows on the table, a small smile tugging at his mouth.

"After seeing what a jerk Jonathan was by breaching your privacy, did Nicola run into your waiting arms?"

The small smile blossoms. "Not even close. But when I ran home bawling and told my Irish grandmother what had happened, she made me some soup and fresh biscuits—cookies, for you Yankees—and she gave me another empty tobacco tin."

Marco stands, goes to the kitchen, and returns with a plastic box of chocolate chip cookies as well as—a book?

He sits across from me again, opens the cookies (they smell *soooo* good), and slides a leather-bound blank journal across the table. "This will keep the Internet out of your thoughts." He pats the closed book. I pick it up with my Aldous-free hand. It's heavy. Quality paper, smooth, brown cover embossed with a Celtic design.

Beautiful. Expensive.

"Marco . . . you didn't have to do this." I can't remember the last time someone bought me such a meaningful gift. Seriously, for my last birthday, Trevor gave me a Frisbee, "top of the line, Dani," so I could learn Frisbee golf—his team was short a player. Gosh, so thoughtful!

I don't know what to say, so I default to a heartfelt thank you. Why would Marco go to such trouble, such expense, for me?

He shrugs playfully and continues. "Later that night, after Gran nursed my bruised feelings, she went out for her evening walk with her dog, Spartacus. I sat in the front window and watched her go, like I often did—only her route deviated. She crossed the street, walked down the way, and stopped in front of Jonathan's house. She climbed the three steps, placed a small paper bag I hadn't seen her carrying, lit it on fire, and rang the doorbell.

"Then she and the dog scurried off the porch and resumed their walk, like every other normal late-spring evening. Only when the person at Jonathan's house answered the door—it happened to be Jonathan himself—he was greeted with a flaming bag. Upon Jonathan stomping on it to put out the flames, I quickly learned that Gran had filled that paper bag with shit from her beloved Spartacus. And he was a big dog."

I laugh so loud and so hard, Aldous meows and digs her claws into my chest, eyes wide open.

"I am *so* stealing this! Can I?"

When Marco's laughs subside, he wipes clean the cookie crumbs from his fingertips and leans back on two chair legs. "I'm just saying that if your phone keeps doing what it's doing tonight, a little fire-shit might be in order."

I transfer the kitten back to the couch, retrieve two glasses of almond milk, and we quietly polish off two more cookies apiece. "Promise you won't tell my trainer, yeah?"

He winks. "Your secret is safe with me."

Marco helps me clean up the dishes, few words passing between us, a surge of warmth rushing through me when our shoulders occasionally brush. Everything he's done tonight has been extraordinarily kind—from helping with Howie to bringing dinner and dessert and the journal. Where everyone else is screaming at me, he's doing exactly the opposite. It's gotta be because he's a good guy who takes care of his clients . . . right?

Maybe it's more?

When he pulls on his Gore-Tex Hollywood Fitness jacket, my stomach drops. I like having him here. He brings such a quiet peace.

And as soon as he leaves, it'll just be me and the emails and text messages again. Plus, a hobo's smelly cat.

I walk him to the door. "Thank you. For this. For tonight. For being my friend."

He offers his fist for a bump. What I really want, though, is a hug. I abstain. I don't want to read more into this than I should. "I'll see you tomorrow. We can do two sessions, right? You can go to the hospital in between to see Howie?"

I nod. "Solid plan."

"Bring your runners. Maybe during tomorrow's jog, you can save a stranded whale or rescue a child from a burning building." With a final wink of his beautiful, long-lashed eyeball, he's out the door.

I lock up, turn to glare at my phone, and find Aldous with one paw in the fishbowl, a bloodthirsty look on her kittenish face.

Oy.

THIRTY-FOUR

"Hello, Ms. Steele, this is Agent [Superman] *returning your call. Per the information you provided in your voicemail, we have looked into your hacking incident, and we're fairly certain it's tied to the case we discussed at your place of employment. We are in the process of following the breadcrumb trail, so to speak, and as soon as we're able to break through so we can return the blog to your safekeeping, I'll let you know.*

"I know this isn't an excellent time to bring this up, but I did read through your entries, and because they address the Lisa Rogers' case directly, you are in violation of the nondisclosure agreement you signed. I understand these are extenuating circumstances, so I will talk to my superiors about this, but do expect a call from another agency representative.

"Thank you for your cooperation."

THIRTY-FIVE

FAX
From: PENELOPE "MOMMY" STEELE

Hello, Danielle,

This is your mother. What have you done? I TOLD you the World Wide Web was a gateway to malfeasance and intrusion from the outside, and now you have all of our dirty laundry out there for the entire planet to read!

Georgette and Jacqueline were just here—they made me chop and bag up all but four of my marijuana plants per Oregon State law for fear that federal agents were going to break down my door. You know I rely on those plants to help my friends! How could you tell the government about them? They're already watching me because of my involvement with Greys (Alien) Anatomy, so this is just the icing on the cake.

I tried to respect your privacy and not read the articles you've posted—your sister says that you were hacked and that's why the stories are out there in the light of day. That does sound really terrible, Danielle, but I am not feeling sorry for you right now because your tirades about your family are quite cruel.

And if you'd rather spend your weekend in some inane competition I don't even understand instead of spending time with your mother at the beach, the least you could've done is been honest with me. You know that I won't live forever, right? You know that it's important to spend time with your family while they are still here. Or maybe that isn't as enticing to you as spending time with your fantasy wrestler friend. I know that your obsession with that man started with Gerald Robert Steele, but you really should put all of this childishness behind you. Your father's influence has clearly been very unhealthy.

I hope no one in my UFO family hears about your online diary. I could be kicked out—the NSA and Homeland Security people are already sniffing around our extended membership, which is why NO INTERNET! This is just too much, Danielle. Too much. You've always been the child who needed to be the center of attention—just like Gerald Robert Steele. Well, congratulations. You've finally gotten your wish.

If you decide to come to my house, please leave your electronics at home and check your vehicle for a GPS tracking device. I don't need you to lead them right to me.

Love and light,
Mommy

THIRTY-SIX

Random sampling of blog comments so far:

Hey, if you decide to move to Port-aux-Français, I'd totally go with you. Might be a good time to consider that move *now*—your blog is pretty harsh! LOL . . .

Your boyfriend, Trevor, should put that thing about his soft toenails on Tinder. Bet that would help him get dates! Ha ha ha ha ha . . .

I know you think your trainer is hot, but you made him sound like a total airhead and that's super sexist. Just sayin'. It goes both ways. Don't be that girl.

Treadmills ARE the devil! I almost died on one once! Not even kidding!

Where did you go to school? The TAs in our English department were pompous jerks.

If your sisters don't disown you, they be crazy.

Girrrrl, you have a picture of The Rock in your bathroom? He watches you POO?

You really shouldn't drink. Alcohol undermines your training. Doesn't sound like you're very serious about this at all TBH.

Your boyfriend is probably going to sue you for talking about his dick like that. I wouldn't blame the guy. And it's normal for penises to have a curvature. I'm sure your anatomy is PERFECT, right? #bitch

THE ROCK IS SO HOT OMGGGGGGGG

Girl don't be sad about your BF showing his peen to that other girl just be glad he didn't give you any diseases and your free now to find a better man. Lotsa love from DC.

If the govt puts you in jail, WE WILL RIOT! This is the funniest shit I've read in months!

Obviously your mother's affection for romance novels and extraterrestrials and illicit drugs, combined with your father's disappearing act, have created in you a narcissism that can only be undone with months of intensive therapy under the care and guidance of a trained professional. You indeed have self-esteem and so-called "daddy issues," and you will find no relief until you address that you have been damaged by parents serving their own selfish ends. Your entries read like a desperate call for help, and even more so if you published them for the whole world to see. I fear what Mr. Dwayne Johnson would extract from your missives—this goes beyond fandom into you creating a vision of "The Rock" as your stand-in father or stand-in life partner, neither of which is healthy. I am concerned for your well-being.

I'm guessing this blog is either a funny fictional account of some made-up character's life, or you were seriously screwed over by someone and they posted all your secrets online—which if that's the case, I sorta feel bad for finishing a bottle of wine while I read through every last entry! Also, LONG LIVE THE ROCK! Can you smelllllll what The Roooooooock is COOOOOOOOOKIN'!

THIRTY-SEVEN

April 26, 2016

Dear Dwayne Johnson,
Wow. It's been a while since I've written to you like this, with an actual pen in my hand. (Forgive my penmanship.) All those years of correspondence, after the Jerky Jackie "hacking" incident back in high school—I thought my letters to you were safe online, locked up tight under the world's most ridiculous, seemingly unbreakable password. For what, fifteen years, they've been safe?
But that was before I messed with the wrong super-secret nameless, faceless she-devil hacker.
Geez, DJ, it's been a horrible and insane few weeks. I've spent so much time apologizing—emailing, calling, texting, faxing, eating into my savings to pay for bloody flowers and fruit baskets—trying to do damage control wherever I can. I'll pretty much never be able to show my face at Stage III again, considering some of the PRIVATE entries I had about other actors that weren't always 100 percent complimentary. While my sisters are at least talking to me, they're still pissed, even though I've offered over and

over to babysit so Georgie and Samuel can have a night out (and I swore I'd never give her kids Dimetapp again). Jackie had to have her lawyer draft a disclaimer to hand out to patients explaining the "tragic circumstances" surrounding the hack because you know the girl she gave the Ex-Lax cake to? Yeah . . . she was pissed. Fired Jackie and is taking her Botox needs elsewhere.

And Mommy said the only way I could make this up to her was to prune the three million overgrown rhododendrons in her yard (!!!) and mow and weed and get the back flowerbeds ready for her new garden. Of course, we've had a remarkably wet spring, so thanks to long hours spent in my mother's yard in the pouring rain and then continued damage-management efforts and gym days and visiting Howie at the hospital and the resultant lack of sleep, I managed to pick up a lingering cold. Last night was the first night in a week I haven't had to sleep with VapoRub smeared under my nostrils just to breathe.

The day after everything went down, I wrote a blanket-apology email and sent it to every single person in my address book, explaining what had happened and begging people to stop reading. But humans are natural voyeurs—judging by the number of comments on every single post, this whole situation has gone totally viral. It's like a global wildfire, and fifteen years' worth of my deepest secrets are the dry undergrowth feeding it. My most intimate thoughts splayed out there, dating back to middle school! Thoughts about boys I liked and girls I didn't and pranks I pulled and virginity lost and hangovers that almost killed me and mean things I did to my sisters and the meaner things they did in return and my anger at Gerald Robert Steele and my total annoyance with my batshit-crazy mother and my raging insecurities and my epic failures and my ongoing, never-ending love for you . . .

Because that's what people write about in their diaries. Everyone is seeing it, DJ. Like with a therapist—there's the assumption that if you go to great lengths to keep something safe and private, safe and private it shall remain.

Wrong.

And EVERYONE who's been reading has a fucking opinion. I've been called a narcissist more in the last fifteen days than I think there are stars in the heavens. Which is ironic in itself: I never wanted anyone to READ these posts. That's why it's called a diary. I'd been assured repeatedly that this UNpublished blog would be safe from hackers because of the password and two-step verification I had in place. Even Elliott the IT guy told me once that HE writes his dragon fantasy stories online but in a blog that he would never publish because it could hurt him professionally. Dude, if Elliott's dragon stories are safe . . .

Maybe that's my problem. No dragons.

God, Dwayne, I feel so cheated and naked and ridiculous.

Even worse than that—the email that the hacker sent to my entire address book, it, like, infiltrated the address books of all THOSE people too, so the link was sent to everyone in their address books, and so on. It's like an infection, only the pathogen happens to carry a link to my blog under the custom URL the hacker created.

THIS SHIT ONLY HAPPENS IN MOVIES THAT STAR CHRIS HEMSWORTH OR JOSEPH GORDON-LEVITT.

Only it doesn't. It's happening in real time, and every day this email bot sends more links out to more people. Agent Superman and his cronies still cannot figure out how to get the blog back under my control, nor can they stop this email-humping bot. He said, "It's like nothing we've ever seen before."

Great. Awesome. FANTASTIC.

Jesus, I swear to all the gods, if the Russians really DO hack the United States government—if Agent Supes and his numbskulls are in charge of disentangling that clusterfuck—we're all ghosts.

Anyway, with all this carnage, I haven't been able to bring myself to sit down and write to you . . .

There have been a few positive comments—people who've had parents bail who can relate to those entries written during the bad-poetry stage of adolescence; other adult children who are glad they're not alone in their own quiet parental issues; people who've laughed and complimented me on making light of difficult situations; people who don't believe this is real because no one's family is this much of a freak show; people who are embarking on their own fitness journeys.

I like those messages.

This has all become so surreal. I've tried to distance myself from the whole thing—sort of treating it like the Danielle Steele on that website is someone different. Someone who is not me. Well, I've tried to think of it that way, until I went back to work yesterday.

DJ, if you think the Arctic is frigid . . . Pretty much no one from work is talking to me, except Charlene, which is great because I had a trunk load of cat supplies for her from Minotaur, minus what I need for Aldous— Howie the Pop-Can Man's crazy tabby that I've inherited while he's in the hospital. I had to cover the top of Hobbs's fishbowl, but I think he's less depressed now that he has a buddy. Aldous sits for hours on the table and watches Hobbs swim, and Hobbs is either showing off or terrified she's going to eat him.

Poor Aldous. I can tell she misses her dad, but I've sorta fallen for her. And I think Charlene is secretly hoping I'll become a cat lady too so she's not the only weirdo. Howie isn't doing well . . . in a medically induced coma, but the doctor who finally agreed to talk to me doesn't think his prognosis is good. I'm sad—Howie's a brilliant, decent man who's had a rough go—but he has no family. If he comes out of this coma, his doctor expects there to be significant damage from the stroke. Howie will end up in a state-run nursing home . . . that'll kill him faster than anything.

Viv is still pregnant, which is good. But she's not offering much more than the occasional hello, which is not good. I miss her.

And Shithead Trevor is still threatening legal action. He got so obnoxious at the gym, Miraculously Beautiful Marco and Trish with Muscles booted him out. I'm SUPER appreciative of that. I cannot focus on training when Trevor is making pointed comments about the size of my ass, and how I'd better get used to living in Flex Kavana because he's going to sue me for all I'm worth, and just basically being a stalker-ish creep. I thought Minotaur was going to remove Trevor's lungs last week. Epic. It's so great to have friends there—especially friends who apparently know NOTHING about this hijacked-blog bullshit. And if they do, they're not sharing that info with me.

Speaking of the gym . . . and Marco . . . NO, nothing has happened. Except for the huge crush that's only gotten bigger since he promised he wouldn't read a single diary entry. (And he brought me pho. And cookies. And the gorgeous leather journal I'm now writing to you in. And he told me an adorable story about his childhood love.) When I walk into the gym and see him there, I'm a giddy teenager again. Seriously. And then I try to show off and lift more weight, which in turn means extra ibuprofen once I get home. Minotaur says ibuprofen is bad—"It ruins your gains, bro!"—but it's either that or I get stuck in my chair with no MedicAlert button in sight.

Yup. I'm an idiot.

Otherwise . . . Marco and I have started running through Forest Park with backpacks full of sandbags, and I haven't been hospitalized nor have I passed out lately—and that's saying something because the trails in Forest Park are nuts. I'm down almost fifteen pounds from the start of this grand experiment, and although it doesn't seem like much, my clothes fit differently, and Marco says I'm replacing fat with muscle. This is good, right?

Can't wait to show Jerky Jackie my fancy new LDL cholesterol. *fist bump*

Marco is confident that if I continue to work as hard as I have been, that walk-on role is within reach. GET READY, DJ.

Hang on—phone call . . .

∽

Lady Macbeth. She knows about the hack, but given her own self-described "salacious" background of seducing her married director, she said, "Blow it off, Dani. People love drama, and thank the deities for that—it's how I make a living!" Audition tomorrow, but I can't go. Not on my third day back at work. I wonder how long I'm going to be on Joan the Crone's shit list.

Probably until Agent Superman gets that damn blog taken down. Or until they decide what to do with me now that I've involuntarily violated the terms of their nondisclosure agreement.

Is this guy in charge of national security? Good thing I ordered that parka for Port-aux-Français. I'm going to look adorable in all that faux fur. I'll send you a photo of me next to a penguin. I hear Antarctica is beautiful this time of year.

Gotta go. Aldous just made an epic poo, but she doesn't understand that she has to bury it, so now the entire apartment stinks.

Devotedly yours,
Danielle Public-Enemy #1 Steele

P.S. GYM UPDATE: The other night, I hit a few new personal records— Miraculously Beautiful Marco says we call those PRs—I moved up to 8 lb. dumbbells AND I added 5 lb. plates on the bench press AND I squatted more than just the bar—I think he put 10 lb. plates on? I felt like The Hulk when we were done. BOOYAH. Ain't no candy-asses 'round here, DJ.

THIRTY-EIGHT

"Hello, this is Alison Klein from Emanuel—I'm the nurse who's been taking care of your friend Howard Nash? I know this is against hospital protocol, but I think . . . it might be a good time for you to come in and see your friend. As soon as possible. Thanks, Danielle. Sorry to interrupt you at work."

THIRTY-NINE

I don't know if there is anything more depressing in this whole world than watching someone die.

My mother's mother wasn't much of a part of our childhoods—she never did approve of Mommy's eccentricities or her terrible taste in husbands, and she wasn't in love with the idea of being called "Grandma Wilma," so naturally we called her the Wicked Wilma of the West. (Not always to her face.)

Wilma went from being a vibrant, well-positioned real estate agent with gel nails and a poufy bleached bob to a sickly, emaciated shell in a matter of weeks. Pancreatic cancer that metastasized, quickly, right alongside her denial that she was really sick. We visited her at the end, but the bag of bones lying in the bed wasn't the Wicked Wilma I remember flitting in and out of our house once a year for enforced holiday bonding, her overwhelming perfume stealing the taste of the Thanksgiving turkey right off your tongue.

Howie looks like Wicked Wilma did. Paper-thin skin, sunken eyes, thin white hair greasy against the sides of his head. He's aged a hundred years since we scooped him off the pavement behind the high school that night. At least someone gave him a nice shave.

I've visited every other day since it happened, hoping that he'd just wake up and wink at me and give me more unsolicited life advice or tell me another story about his teaching days. I hoped that somehow my voice would trigger something in his head that would pull him back from the brink—I finished reading *Brave New World* out loud to him; I've updated him on Aldous's continued plots to entertain (read: *maim*) Hobbs, complete with photographic evidence on my phone, even though Howie's eyes are very much closed.

But today . . . today I know that no amount of fine literature or interesting discourse about ongoing feline-fish interpersonal relations will lure him back from wherever he is.

Midafternoon, Alison the nurse brings me coffee. When she goes on her dinner break, she returns with a chicken salad sandwich and a banana for me. "I would've given you one of the extra patient meals, but not even I'm that mean," she said.

And she sits with me when she gets off shift at midnight. Just after 2:00 a.m., we watch Howie breathe his last.

Alison leaves me alone for a little while, and I cry for a thousand different reasons, mostly selfish ones, but also because this man died here in this room, pretty much all by himself except for me and Alison. No kids, no wife, no friends, or colleagues. Not even his beloved cat.

Hospital staff give me an hour with Howie, but then things need to happen. Things that don't involve well-meaning nonrelatives.

I walk out of his room, sadness cloaking my shoulders. Alison is still at the nurses' station. "Thanks for waiting with me," I say, sniffing.

"I don't think it's right for people to die alone," she says. "It was nice that you were here for him, Danielle. I'm so sorry for your loss."

"Thanks."

"Before you go . . ." She turns and disappears into a locked room at the heart of this main hub. She comes back cradling a plastic bag labeled PATIENT PERSONAL EFFECTS. "We went through it when he first got here, looking for next of kin." Inside is the metal box Marco and I pulled from Howie's Whole Foods cart just before the ambulance took him away. "The only thing we found, other than his pictures, was a letter with detailed information for his lawyer. I made a copy for his chart—they'll call the lawyer when the sun comes up and make Mr. Nash's final arrangements. The original letter is still in the box, in case you need to talk to the lawyer for any reason. Maybe he knows of family we weren't able to find."

Howie had a lawyer? And documents? How could he afford that? Maybe from his professor days—it would have to be that.

I accept the bag from Alison, and she comes around the counter to give me a hug. "It was really nice meeting you, Danielle. Thank you for being Howard's friend."

I can't speak anymore. I'm exhausted and heartbroken and I just want to curl up with that crazy now-orphaned kitten and sleep for a year.

When I slide into the driver's seat of my car, I dig my phone out of my bag and power on. In Howie's room, I had turned it off out of respect—not even the nearly dead want to hear the constant digital chime of someone else's life imploding. Trevor won't stop harassing me. Jacqueline texts regularly to find out the status of Agent Superman's handiwork, even though technically I'm not supposed to be talking to her about any of it.

Waiting, though, are two missed texts from Marco.

Got your message about Howie. Let me know how he is.

And the second: Guessing the evening hasn't gone so well. Missed you at the gym. See you tomorrow if you're up for it. Be well, Dani.

Of course, that makes me sob even harder. By the time I get back to my apartment, I'm a snotty, stuffed-up, swollen mess. I'm still in my work clothes, as I left the office just after eleven this morning, as soon as I got Alison's call. Joan the Crone wasn't happy about me leaving given the thin ice I'm still skating on, but when I told her it was for Howie, a softness came over her face that rarely shows itself.

I slide Howie's photo box onto the kitchen table, change into jammies, and shuffle into the kitchen to put the kettle on for tea.

"Merrrrrrowwwww." I turn around, empty teacup in hand, to find Aldous sitting on the table, atop Howie's box, digging at the plastic.

"Yeah, sweetie, looks like you're stuck with me." I pluck her off the plastic bag and pull out the box. Lid open, I pull out the stack of photos, the letter Alison referred to, the other small keepsakes Howie thought enough of to store in here. As per the Rule of Cats, Aldous takes the opportunity to plant herself in the emptied container, curling her tail around her tabby body and purring like an idling freight train.

It's three thirty in the morning, and I need to be up for work in four hours, but I can't not look through these cracked, aging photos that have probably had too much exposure to the elements. A young, vibrant version of Howie wearing the gown and sashes they give people when they graduate from important university programs; Howie at the beach with a beautiful young woman with brownish hair in a blown-out seventies sculpt; a few pictures of a chubby black-and-white cat in the arms of that same woman, her radiant smile involuntarily teasing a smile from my own face, the back of the photo etched with the names "Clarence and Deanna"; that woman—must be Deanna—holding a newborn baby, her face exultant but exhausted; a few more photos of Deanna and a towheaded toddler, then little boy.

And then the picture that explains it all: a headstone with the names Deanna Mullins Nash and Tristan Andrew Mullins Nash, listing respective birth dates and the date of death they shared.

Jesus. Howie was married. And he had a kid. And the wife and child died on the same day.

He never once mentioned this.

I sift through the stack of keepsakes and find the hospital bracelet that must've been Tristan's when he was born, as well as a small sandwich bag with a lock of curled baby hair.

And then an obituary on fragile newsprint that has been opened and closed a million times, the print now rubbed clean at the folds in the paper. A car accident. Drunk driver.

I think of the Limping Lady at the gym, the drunk driver who killed her son and ruined her body . . . and of all my other gym friends who have tragic stories.

This is just too much. My heart physically aches in my chest.

Gently, I slide Howie's treasures into a bigger Ziploc bag so Aldous won't get to anything, and then I open my laptop. A quick email to Joan the Crone about what's happened, that I need the day off, that I will contact the lawyer about Howie's arrangements.

Aldous squeaks a little when I hoist her out of the box, but as soon as she's tucked under the covers with me, she settles right in.

Howie, wherever you are, don't worry. I'm gonna take good care of your girl. I promise.

FORTY

"You look awful," Thomas says, the first words he utters after finishing the last line from "Memory" off the *Cats* song list. Appropriate this morning, considering I woke up with a cat sleeping on my chest and now my nose is all stuffy. Or maybe it's stuffy because I cried enough calories last night to skip cardio today.

"Yeah. Howie died—the professor-slash-homeless-guy who collected our pop cans and gave me good books to read?"

"You have the oddest collection of friends," Thomas says.

"Yourself included?"

"Naturally." He reaches into the glass-front cooler case. "I'm sorry for your loss. You'll need food—these are oat bran and blueberry. No palm oil, no trans fats. In line with your training regimen, which, by the way, is definitely working." He gestures to me, head to foot. "On the house today. You look so sad, I'm about to start crying."

"Sorry. I was with him when he died late last night."

"Which is why you're here instead of at work? Or are you still suspended?"

"Suspension's over. I'm just exhausted. And I inherited a roommate who thinks it's funny to bite my nose at six in the morning when it's time to eat." I pull out my phone and show him a photo of Aldous being adorable, and at that very moment, I realize that I've become a certified cat lady.

"Male otters bite the noses of the females when they want to mate."

"Yeah, well, Aldous is a girl, and she doesn't want to mate. She wants a bowl of delicious, stinky wet food made of parts from other animals."

"That's it. We're having a sleepover so I can have a bowl of delicious, stinky animal parts."

As per usual when I come in for coffee, Thomas takes his fifteen and pulls me over to the corner table reserved for employees. I know what's going to come out of his mouth before he even sits.

"I received an email from you."

Told ya.

"Question is, did you click on the link?"

He hides his face behind his hands for a moment and then pinches the air between his fingers. "Just a tiny bit. Until I realized what it was." He stretches across the table and envelops my hand not wrapped around the coffee cup. He's a furnace next to my stress-chilled skin. "I know you don't want to hear this, but you should write comedy. That shit is funny."

"It's my *life*, Thomas. It's not supposed to be funny."

"You know as well as I do that tragedy is comedy. Does your mom seriously send you faxes?"

"Wow, you really did read."

"Sorry. But based on what you've told me about her, I so want to see those. If they're as far out as I think they are—and I mean that in the kindest I'm-sorry-your-mom-is-a-nutter way—you should compile and publish them. In fact, you should keep writing about *all* this stuff. It's great material, Dani."

I sigh and sip my coffee. I'm glad Thomas is amused, but this isn't material. This is my life. These are my *secrets*.

"The hacker who did this—she's obviously very good. So good that the alleged experts working on it can't figure out how to wrestle the blog back from her. My whole existence has been hijacked."

Thomas looks guilty for a moment, and I'm glad. I don't want him peeking into my private life.

"What are you going to do about it?"

"I've done all I can—now I have to wait until the so-called experts actually do their jobs."

I don't have much else to offer the conversation. Thomas updates me on gigs he has coming up, what I've missed the last few Sundays in our acting class, a potential new love interest he met at a greenroom mixer after a play he went to—oh, and he just happened to stop by Hollywood Fitness for a tour the other day so he could get a look at Miraculously Beautiful Marco.

"You're right. He does have great hair and nice knees and that British accent . . ."

"God, Thomas, how much did you really read?"

"Enough to know that your heart rate is raised by more than extra time on the elliptical?"

I blush.

"And . . . ?"

"And he's adorable. You should marry him immediately."

"Very funny."

"I mentioned that I knew you. His eyes got all sparkly when I said your name."

My heart skip-hops at this—but I'm not going to give Thomas anything more to tease me about. He has plenty for today. "Now you're just being mean."

"Nope. I think this is a match made in spandex. Mark my words. I come from a long line of soothsayers." *What I would give for him to be right . . .*

My phone buzzes against the tabletop, making us both jump. "That could be him right now, texting to profess his undying love." My stomach flutters at the thought.

"Or it could be Trevor again, threatening to sue me because I told the world about his curved penis."

"Trevor is a mutant, and not because of his curved appendage. That will probably make him famous. He should be thanking you, not suing you."

"Sadly, he does not agree."

"He will. Just wait—even Charles Manson has admirers. Trevor and his crooked cock will get their fifteen minutes of fame."

I slide my finger across the screen. It's not Trevor, or Marco declaring his undying love.

It's a brief email from Joan the Crone, requesting my presence at a meeting at four o'clock today.

Shit.

FORTY-ONE

I didn't expect the summons from the Crone to be awesome news, but walking into her office to see Agent Superman also present spikes heat into my ears and dampens my palms.

"Please have a seat," Joan directs me. I follow orders, tucking my nervous hands under my thighs to keep them from bouncing. "Danielle, I am sorry for the loss of your friend Howard. He was a colorful character. We'll all miss seeing him around the neighborhood." Joan sips from her nature-biscuit tea that makes her entire office smell like a postmarathon foot.

"Yeah, I guess you guys will have to pay for someone to wash the front windows again." I don't know why I'm being snarky. Maybe because everyone in this building has been a stuck-up asshole to Howie, and the last thing I want to hear is disingenuous condolences.

Agent Superman clears his throat and sits forward, adjusting the black folder on the table in front of him. "I'm limited on time here, so I'm going to cut to the chase. Your manager has called you in today as we have been in receipt of correspondence from the hacker, who we are now certain is the employee formerly known as Lisa Rogers."

That makes her sound so glamorous. I'm guessing she's chosen some esoteric symbol to represent her real name too.

"As I mentioned in my most recent voicemail to you, we—both the agency and your employer—are concerned about the violation of the nondisclosure agreement you signed when this investigation began."

"It wasn't as if I set out to tell the whole world what was going on. I was *hacked*. I'm a *victim* here."

"Yes, we understand that, which is why we are not going to pursue any further action against you in relation to this information. I cannot speak as to the actions of your employer—that is for your superiors to debate. With that said, however . . ." Agent Superman pulls a piece of paper from his folder. He slides it across to me and nods.

It's from The Hacker Formerly Known as Lisa. I read, and my heart drops into my stomach.

"So . . . she'll give us the blog back if you guys fire me?" I look up at Joan, and then at Agent Superman, and reread the dispatch. "Lisa" says she will revert full control of the blog back to my care, plus the designated website URL www.deardwaynewithlove.com, with the promise to never interfere in my future online activities in exchange for my termination from Imperial Health and Wellness, what she sees as "rightful and equitable punishment for the physical assault perpetrated against my person."

"Is this real? How do you know this is from her?"

"We have reason to believe it is. She communicates with a set of highly sophisticated crypto tools that the layperson would not likely understand or have access to. Plus, she knows specifics about the case that no one else would."

"Wow. So I'm basically being blackmailed out of a job."

"You can stand on your principles and keep the job—there's nothing more we can do for you at this juncture, however. Your hacked blog, while uncomfortable for you personally, is not the sole damage this person has accomplished. We're talking high-level corporate espionage. If 'Lisa' is ever caught and convicted, she'll be looking at significant prison time."

"What you're saying is I don't count because I'm just a person and not a corporation."

Agent Superman sighs. "What I'm saying is that she's hacked into government agencies, not just private companies—her actions are doing major damage on a scale that could be a threat to national security, and those issues are prioritized over wrestling your diary back from her. As such, I'd like to wrap this up today."

I sit back and pick at the calluses that have hardened along my palm from the weight lifting.

"Can't we just tell her I've quit? Is she spying on us?"

"We have no way of knowing that," the agent says.

Joan shakes her head no. "Danielle, there are managers above me who are pushing for your termination based on the violation of the NDA, especially after they allowed you to stay on despite the physical assault that occurred on company premises."

"But I served my suspension."

"Yes, and then the information contained in the leaked blog violated the terms of your agreement with the company."

"So I'm damned if I do and damned if I don't."

Agent Superman retrieves the dispatch from the tabletop and slides it back into his folder. He checks his phone; obviously, he's ready to leave.

"Best-case scenario, Danielle," Joan says, leaning forward on her elbows, "I will fire you quietly so you can apply for unemployment. That will give you some breathing room to find another job. When you start applying for future employment, I will provide a personal reference so that your potential employer understands that this was a unique and unfortunate situation."

"Is there another option?"

"You can resign. You won't qualify for unemployment that way, though."

Bottom line: I want the blog down.

"Fine. Yes. Fire me. Tell that vapid cow she's won. Just . . . just get the blog off the Internet and back to me, okay?"

Agent Superman pats the tabletop and stands, pushing his black-framed glasses up his long, thin nose. He really is Clark Kent. "I'll get to work on relaying the message immediately. Things should be back to normal by the time you're putting on your footie pajamas for bed."

"Thanks. I guess." Under my breath, "And I don't wear footie pajamas."

With that, he's gone, leaving only a hint of aftershave in his wake.

"If you want to wait until folks have started leaving the building before cleaning out your desk, I understand," Joan says, leaning forward on her crossed arms. Though she's not smiling at me, she's also not scowling. She isn't as intimidating without the scowl. I'm grateful. "I am sorry things have worked out this way, Danielle. But if it's just you and me being completely candid, you've never been happy here. I think there is something else out there that will be more aligned with your unique talents."

I guess that's as close as I'm going to get to a pep talk from the Crone. Hey, it wasn't the worst effort.

I shuffle back to my building, passing through the cafeteria where, on the counter, sits a telltale pink pastry box. The MotherCluckers must've had an impromptu meeting today, one I was not invited to.

Whatever. I can't eat that shit now anyway.

In the corner, the blue bags holding the recyclables are near full. My first thought is to tie them closed and leave them outside for Howie, followed swiftly by the second thought that he's dead so that's no longer necessary. And now with my leaving the employ of this fine establishment, I guess someone else will have to take over care of keeping recyclables out of the city dump.

At my desk, I start making piles: unfinished work, resource materials belonging to the company, all my Dwayne Johnson memorabilia that goes home with me, the best pens out of my desk, random office supplies I can pilfer just because I'm mad and a girl can never have too many staples.

I should be devastated about losing my job. I cannot pay rent or buy cat treats without actual employment.

Instead, though, this weird levity bubbles in my chest, and with every thumbtack and staple I pull out of my fabric cubicle wall, with every picture of The Rock and every collectible I put in the stack to go home, the desire to giggle tickles the back of my throat.

I might even be smiling.

"Hey." Viv leans against the cubicle's three-quarter wall.

"Hey yourself."

"What are you doing?"

"What's it look like?"

"Well, you're either redecorating to fill the space with more pictures of the Sexiest Man Alive, or you're leaving."

"Ding ding ding."

"Dani, you don't have to be nasty."

I stop moving and look at Viv. She's pale, the skin under her eyes a little more purple than usual. While she's still her buttoned-up professional self, her hair is a little lifeless. Looks like she's not feeling well.

"Morning sickness?"

She nods. "The worst. And it lasts all day." She scoots into the cubicle and perches on the edge of my desk. "That obvious, huh?"

"You look like you caught a bad batch of seafood salad."

Viv turns green. "Oh god, no food jokes."

"Sorry." I hate that my best friend and I have this prickly distance between us. "Viv . . . I am so sorry for everything. I didn't mean to hurt your feelings—I didn't mean to hurt anyone's feelings. It was my diary . . ." My eyes burn, the giddy feeling of just moments ago evaporating as reality slides back in front of me. "I don't want you to think you can't trust me. No one was ever supposed to see that stuff."

Viv nods and sips from the panda bear–decorated water bottle she's never without these days. When she exhales, I smell ginger. "I'm sorry I got mad. I should've been there for you. I can only imagine how awful this has been. If anyone saw *my* diaries . . ."

I unpin another photo, eyes averted, so she doesn't see me tearing up.

"Everything has been really stressful, and I feel like crap most of the time, and it sorta seemed like you were saying in your blog that you're too good for us, that we all work here because we have nothing better to do with our lives."

I wasn't saying that. Although I was.

"I'm a world-class jerk, I know. I shouldn't have said those things about you guys. I'm just so scared of getting stuck—because you know the corporate world isn't for me—"

"Stop before you dig yourself deeper. We can agree you're a jerk," she says, a small smile crawling across her face.

When I see that maybe she's accepting my apology, I place a hand on her elbow. "I've really missed you, Viv. I'm sorry you've been so sick."

"Part of the fun, apparently. Ben says it'll all be worth it."

"Ben's a boy. He knows nothing."

She laughs.

"So you're leaving, then?"

"Yeah. It's time." I don't go into details.

"At least this will give you more availability to train for The Rock's fund-raiser, huh?"

I nod.

"What will you do next?"

"Dunno. Guess I have to figure that out."

"I'm really sorry about Howie too. He was lucky to have you as a friend."

"We were all lucky to have been Howie's friend." I pull out my phone and show her my most recent shot of Aldous.

"You have his kitten?"

"She needed a home. She's pretty great, and now Hobbs isn't so lonely. Mostly because he spends his days in a state of sheer panic."

"You're going to have to get some Xanax for your goldfish," she teases.

"I'll just sprinkle some of mine into his fishbowl when he's not looking."

As the clock has now passed five, other employees in our building start shuffling about, pulling on coats and logging out of their computers. A few give me a look as they pass, but no one says anything.

"I'm gonna miss you." Viv eyes sparkle with moisture.

"You won't. Because we can still hang out. Can I come to the baby shower?"

"As long as you promise to bring me one of your mother's magic space wands. Could come in handy during labor." She laughs and sniffs at the same time.

I stand and give her a hug, and when I pull away she's offering her pinky. "Let's be friends forever. Okay?"

I lock my pinky around hers. "Sounds like a solid plan."

Viv returns to her part of the building, leaving me to finish packing in peace. Soon the evening cleaners are the only company I have. It's amazing how much junk I've accumulated in six years.

I write a quick note on a Post-it and place it on Charlene's desk with the few gift cards I'd been saving to dole out over the coming months. At least her kitties will have a few extra bucks this month.

I walk out to my car, the cool air redolent with the scent of wet greenery from a late-spring downpour. My box of personal effects on the front seat, I pull out of the lot for the last time, feeling a little bit guilty that my most prominent emotion is relief.

I think back to my first day at this job—the uncertainty of starting something new, something I didn't really want to be doing, the voice in the back of my head harping at me that I'd sold out and given up on the dream, me reminding that little voice that dreams are expensive, and landlords don't take IOUs or pizza coupons to satisfy rent requirements.

INT. DANIELLE'S CAR - EVENING

          DWAYNE "THE ROCK" JOHNSON
   Is it time for me to tell you the
   story about that last seven bucks I
   had in my pocket . . .?

          DANIELLE
   No. I know the story.

          DWAYNE "THE ROCK" JOHNSON
   Look at this as an opportunity to
   reinvent yourself! Joan the Crone's
   right. You hated this job.

          DANIELLE
   Yeah. I did. But I like food and heat
   and electricity.

          DWAYNE "THE ROCK" JOHNSON
   Don't we all. So: reinvent! I'm awesome at reinventing myself. After
   the football dreams didn't work out,
   I decided to go into the family business. My first wrestling event was in
   front of, like, twenty, twenty-five

people, tops. I've been Flex Kavana,
Rocky Maivia, and finally, The Rock.
For a while, the crowds hated me --
"Die, Rocky, Die!" and "Rocky sucks!"
So those commenters on your blog who
are dissing you? I get it.

But you gotta reinvent, kid. You
gotta make yourself into something
bigger. I did, and look at me today.

DANIELLE
Top-grossing Hollywood movie star,
father, devoted partner, Disney
demigod, all-around good guy.

DWAYNE "THE ROCK" JOHNSON
Don't forget incredibly handsome
super-stud.

DANIELLE
You do smell particularly nice.

DWAYNE "THE ROCK" JOHNSON
Dani, my girl, you gotta get clear on
what it is you want. You're half-ass-
ing this whole life thing. How many
times do I have to tell you, sis-
ter--you gotta be the hardest worker
in the room. This is your MATRIX
blue pill/red pill moment. You gotta
choose what path to take.

227

DANIELLE
Did Neo take the red pill or the blue
pill? I can never remember.

DWAYNE "THE ROCK" JOHNSON
All I know is Keanu Reeves never
ages. I need to get in touch with his
skin-care team.

DANIELLE
I think Morpheus should've had more
options. Like green or yellow. I
would've chosen green, but only if
it wasn't lime. I hate lime.

DWAYNE "THE ROCK" JOHNSON
Limes go well with tequila, you gotta
admit . . .

DANIELLE
True, true . . .

DWAYNE "THE ROCK" JOHNSON
Speaking of green . . .

DJ points at the stoplight that has
changed.

DWAYNE "THE ROCK" JOHNSON (CONT'D)
Dani, pick yourself up, dust yourself off, get this show on the road.

Find the good in this mess. Silver
lining and all that jazz.

DJ digs through my box from the
office.

DWAYNE "THE ROCK" JOHNSON (CONT'D)
Maybe when you get home, though, we
should hang up these photos. Wouldn't
want my face to languish in a box,
now, would we?

DJ finds a shot with his legendary
eyebrow raised, holds the photo up,
and smiles next to it.

DWAYNE "THE ROCK" JOHNSON (CONT'D)
See how handsome I am?

DANIELLE
How is this relevant to my current
predicament?

DWAYNE "THE ROCK" JOHNSON
Oh. It's not. I was just trying to
make you feel better so maybe we can
stop for deep dish. I have coupons!

DJ grins, holds up coupons.

FORTY-TWO

Hi, Danielle,

I just wanted to write and tell you that the entry you wrote back when you were fifteen, the one where you were teasing that guy Steve White and he got mad and slammed you against a row of lockers—I had a situation like that, and it really damaged me. This mean girl who had it out for me because I liked the same boy as her put a can of half-opened tuna fish in the back of my locker, in a forgotten box of Kleenex so I wouldn't see it. I think I know how she got into my locker—all the popular kids worked their volunteer hours in the main office where there was a master list of locker combinations for our ancient locker setups. Anyway, the tuna smelled awful, naturally, and it made my coat and all my books stink—I seriously thought I was having some sort of physical reaction to puberty that made me stink. This is a real medical condition, which I'm sure you know because of your job! Anyway, everyone started calling me Fish Girl, and they would leave samples of soap on my chair, and they'd hang air fresheners on my locker handle and spray perfume at me in the locker rooms.

The point of all this: High school sucked, and your diary and mine sound a lot alike, even though you're ten years older than I am. Thanks for being a real person with real problems and for sharing those with us.

Signed,
No Longer Stinky in Seattle
[Message from user ORIGINALDIANAPRINCE1998]

FORTY-THREE

May 2, 2016

Dear Dwayne Johnson,
Happy birthday to my favorite superhero. I hope you get to spend some time with the people you love most. Thank you for being awesome for the WHOLE WORLD.
In honor of your special day, I have in front of me a delicious red velvet lava cupcake with whipped cream frosting (don't tell Miraculously Beautiful Marco). I've bought Aldous her own kitty-cat "cupcake," and we're about to sing to you.
Happy birthday, to you . . .
Happy birthday, to you . . .
Happy BIRTHDAY, dear Dwayne Douglas The Rock Johnsonnnnnnn,
Happy birthday tooooo youuuuuuuu!

All our love,
Danielle and Aldous Stuffin'-Cake-in-Our-Faces Steele + Hobbs the Goldfish

FORTY-FOUR

"Hey, Dani—Janice, here. It's Tuesday morning so you're probably at the gym. Listen, I know this blog thing is a real shit storm for you right now, but I think it's going to help. Like, I'm not even kidding—I've had four different casting directors from Portland and a writer/director of a small theater company down in Los Angeles call me in the last twenty-four hours because, of course, your little email infection reached all kinds of people— side effect of you having my email address in your address book.

"And get this—my cousin is an assistant at William Morris Entertainment, Dani—WME, in Los Angeles! She works for The Rock's agent. And she got an email from me with the link because of the email bot or whatever you called it . . . Dani, can you even imagine if somehow the folks at WME got wind of this?

"Anyway, these casting directors are calling to see if you're available to submit on projects, kid. This is such great news!

"And a theater director—Davina Gudbranson is her name—you've seen the Vagina Monologues, *right? She did her own version of this a few years back with her own theater company, and she wants to talk to you about the possibility of putting something together about your crazy-ass family. Every cloud has a silver lining, my friend! Call me!"*

FORTY-FIVE

Ding-[*staticky growl*]-dong.

The world's most pathetic doorbell alerts me to company. I wipe the slobber off my cheek and check my phone. It's 9:32 a.m. I launch forward, disturbing my fuzzy new bedmate, panicked that I've overslept and now I'm so late—

Except I don't have a job anymore.

Oh yeah. Right.

I wonder how many weekdays in a row I'm going to have this fun panic moment.

The doorbell tries to do its job again.

"Coming!" I throw on my fleece bathrobe—yes, the one with The Rock's face covering the entire back panel as well as stitched into the breast pocket—and scurry to the front door. A check through the peephole. FedEx?

"Hey," I say, cracking the door. Could be a ruse. Could be a guy in a stolen black-and-purple uniform come to deliver a dirty bomb on behalf of Lisa "Dick-Pic" Rogers. Just because she allegedly told Agent Superman it's over doesn't mean it's *really* over. Maybe she still wants to splatter my guts all over the beige walls.

I keep my foot behind the door like they show you in those self-defense classes.

"Envelope for Danielle Steele—hey, my mom loves your books," the FedEx guy says, smiling widely to reveal his upper teeth silver with braces. Is he old enough to have this job?

Okay. Dude's real. Maybe. I open the door wider. "If I were really her, do you think I'd be living in this dump?"

His smile melts a little. "Just need you to sign here."

"Who's this from?" I ask, taking the stylus to sign his little electronic-signature doohickey.

"Looks like a lawyer. That's what *esquire* means, right?" he says, reading the return label. I hand him back his device. "Great bathrobe, by the way. Love The Rock. Have a nice day!"

I close the door behind me, my path impeded by a wide-awake tabby cat who is making it very clear she's interested in breakfast *right this second*.

"Come on, little sweetie." Aldous bounds behind me into the kitchen, mewling like a rabid demon until I slide the bowl of wet food under her nose.

I can't think about anything involving lawyers until caffeine.

Once the pot is brewed, I pay homage to Saint Drogo, patron saint of coffee, and fill my mug bearing said saint's likeness to the brim. Aldous, having finished her breakfast, plants herself on top of the table next to Hobbs and scratches at the fishbowl. In response, Hobbs twitches his tail and darts back and forth like someone has electrified his water.

"You cannot eat your new brother, Aldous." I throw a catnip-filled mousie into the living room, and she chases after it, much to the relief of my stressed-out goldfish.

The FedEx envelope isn't very thick—certainly not thick enough to be an improvised explosive device—but I'm assuming it's stuffed with important papers. Papers from lawyers are always important.

God, is someone suing me over the blog?

I unzip the FedEx envelope, my heart pounding in my chest. If someone is suing me, if this is a subpoena, they would've sent a process server, right? Someone to knock on the door or come up to me at the market while I'm hiding the box of cookies under the huge bundle of spinach and say, *Are you Danielle Elizabeth Steele?*, to which I'd naively reply, *Why, yes, do you know me from television?*, which is crazy because I've never been on television in any capacity that anyone would remember me. And then that someone, likely dressed in a shoddy Salvation Army suit and a tie with yesterday's coffee spilled on it, would say, *Here, you've been served,* and hand me a fat envelope. I would start crying in the cookie aisle, and another someone, a kind, caring woman who looks just like Julia Roberts, would feel sorry for me, so she'd stand there among all those delicious cookies and we'd open a bag of Oreos and she'd tell me everything is going to be okay, even though Oreos are terrible for us and they are made with palm oil, the farming of which is killing orangutans in Indonesia, and I shouldn't cry because the sun always rises—

"*Stop stalling*, Danielle," I say to myself. Aldous meows at me.

I pull the papers all the way out of the envelope.

It's not a subpoena.

It's a copy of Howie's Last Will and Testament and an accompanying letter. Which is heartbreaking, but I'm so relieved that I'm not being sued, I kiss the envelope.

Hello, Danielle.

Here we go with one of those maudlin openings: "If you're reading this letter, then I must be dead." So be it. I'm dead. Please, don't tell me how I died. It's enough of a relief to know I won't have to find a warm and dry alcove tonight or that I no longer have to fret about a decent spot to piss without someone chasing me with their pitchfork. (You can laugh at that last part.)

You're probably wondering why in the hell I'm writing to you and not some long-lost relative or perhaps a jilted lover or forgotten ally from my days in academia. To be completely honest, any long-lost relatives have long forgotten about me; my lovers were never jilted because I am a tireless romantic; and allies in academia, well, that is a sad, sick joke unto itself. Those prattling bastards don't deserve the turtlenecks they swaddle themselves in.

Now if I could've written this letter to a nice bottle of Chateau Lafite . . . Then again, who has time for such luxuries as letter-writing? Let us drink the Lafite instead.

SO: This correspondence and all its included peripherals are meant to serve as a thank-you.

You were my friend when the rest of the world was not. As Cassius says to Brutus in Julius Caesar, "A friend should bear his friend's infirmities." You did this for me. Something as simple as bringing me warm clothes, hot food, the regular contribution via the recyclables—all well and good. But it was your humanity, your respect, your willingness to engage in discourse with someone who had chosen a different path from the rest. I thank you for your endless kindnesses.

I loved someone kind once. I loved her with everything I had. We had a son. Both were taken from me.

I didn't choose to live under a bush; the bush chose me.

Tristan would be about your age, and I think you two would've been friends. He would've been lucky in your friendship. I like to consider myself the stand-in for the friendship that was never given the chance to happen. I also believe that my pursuit of protecting his happiness would've given me a purpose in life that I haven't had since the day I buried them both.

Thus, it is in the spirit of friendship and in protection of your happiness that I say this:

Get out of here. Go back to your dreams.

You're languishing. I know you refer to yourself and your coworkers as hens, forced into cages day after day to meet your quotas and keep the "farmer" happy. Nothing makes me sadder than to think of your vibrant creative energies being wasted on something that brings you absolutely no joy.

(In your honor, I've sworn off eggs in protest. If Saint Peter tries to serve me eggs here, I'll tell him, "No, sir, toast only, if you please.")

But if you find your way out of the Imperial Henhouse, away from those utterly snobby snobs, don't look back. Send a message skyward that you've found yourself again—I'll watch for it eagerly as it'll mean I can resume eating eggs. I hear the western omelets served up here in this cloudless afterlife are divine. (Pun intended.)

The books from my cart—my lawyer has instructions to make sure they are delivered to you posthaste. Accept them with my gratitude. Read on! The answers you need are there, in those pages.

Life is tough. But remember, only those things that make you question your sanity are worth pursuing.

Never let those go. Bernard Marx learned this; so can you.

Wishing you all the best, my dear friend Danielle.

Howard G. Nash

The date on the letter is from a year ago. "Howie, you were so full of secrets, my friend."

I realize that whatever books were in his cart wouldn't be with the lawyer because they're here, with me—actually, still in the trunk of Flex Kavana. I totally forgot about them after Marco and I cleaned out his cart that night we found him.

"Thank you, Howie," I say as Aldous pushes herself in front of his letter. She smells it and rubs her face against the paper's edge. "You smell your dad, do ya?" Purring, she bites at it, trailing her tail against my face.

I'll let the lawyer know that I already have the books—I'm glad they're not headed to some generic, cold thrift store where the new owners wouldn't know what a remarkable human had owned and loved them before.

Reverently, I refold Howie's letter into its envelope before Aldous chews any more of the corner. I scoop her off the table and nuzzle against her fuzzy belly, suddenly choked up with gratitude that Aldous is with me and not alone on the mean streets of Portland. That would've been the worst. As sad as I am that Howie is gone, I am so, so grateful that fate landed Marco and me at Grant Park that night. The alternative is unimaginable.

"While I'd love to hang out with your beautiful little face all day, I gotta be a grown-up," I say to Aldous, curled in the crook of my arm as she gnaws playfully on my knuckles. My hands are covered with fine, scabbed-over scratches, and most of my conversations lately have been with a kitten. I've gone full Cat Lady. Charlene would be so proud.

I check the time on the microwave clock.

The unemployment office opened at nine. There'll be a line already. Ticktock.

FORTY-SIX

From: Agent F.P. Wilkins <email redacted>
To: Danielle E. Steele <DS.May21972@gmail.com>
Subject: Status update RE: Blogger account

May 5, 2016

Hello, Ms. Steele.

Your blog is off the Web. Took a little longer than I'd promised because communicating with the hacker is a technical nightmare, but it's done. It and the URL are returned to your care (instructions for URL attached). Go in and immediately change your passwords or maybe consider deleting the whole thing. Don't be surprised if cached pages haunt you for a little while—people do love their screenshots and saved pages. Check the Wayback Machine online for evidence of cached pages (https://archive.org/web/).

Good luck, Danielle. No offense, but I hope we never have occasion to meet again.

Agent F. P. Wilkins

FORTY-SEVEN

Marco jogs alongside me, gravel crackling under our shoes with each step. Forest Park is breathtakingly glorious today—the sun is out, warming the moist air, but it rained overnight, so the mosses and ferns and undergrowth have exploded in luminous greens not even an artist could duplicate.

I update him about the audition last night for the new theater group I'm hoping to join (this one actually *pays* its actors), now that Stage III is solid Trevor territory—and then I spend an embarrassing amount of time recounting the funny things Aldous has done in the interim since Marco and I last saw one another, approximately seventeen hours ago.

He's very patient, smiling politely as I regale him with the latest misdeeds of my new feline adoptee—i.e., how she now perches on the refrigerator and launches herself at me if I even think about putting food into my mouth. "One excellent perk of this new living arrangement: Aldous does *not* like the fax machine. She attacks my mother's pages as they're birthed from the feeder. Very satisfying to watch."

"And not at all passive-aggressive," he teases. He's so handsome when he jogs and his hair bounces with each step.

"She's still haranguing me about joining her magic healing-wand business, 'especially now that you're unemployed, Danielle.'"

"Think of the possibilities," Marco says, splaying his fingers theatrically in front of him. I smack his arm midstep.

"I let Aldous eat her most recent fax—another one reminding me of my terrible life choices and disappointing similarities to her ex-husband. And the blog. Of course."

"Blimey. The site's been down for two weeks. Time to move on," he says, stopping at a fork in the trail.

"At least Trevor has stopped threatening to sue me every twelve seconds."

"He's a wanker. Don't lose any more sleep over him." Marco points to the hardened dirt path that climbs at a steady grade. "Should we go up?" I'm already sweating, even just a few minutes into our warm-up. Probably from the twenty pounds of sandbags I have in my backpack.

We run in single file, me behind Marco, which isn't terrible because he's obviously in better shape than I am, and this way I get a nice view of his Miraculously Beautiful buns. (Seriously, whoever invented these running tights, *thank you!*)

By the time we get to the top, I'm not even self-conscious about the armpit sweat rings soaking through my jacket because I'm too busy gasping for air and sucking back my amino acid–infused water.

"How do you do that?" I ask.

"What?" he says, sipping from his own bottle.

"Barely break a sweat. I'm dying over here."

"You're not. And think how far you've come, darling."

I love it when he calls me darling.

We continue along the path, not as steep as before but still at enough of a pitch that my thighs are on fire when we hit the two-mile mark. Again, we stop for water; I bend down to retie my stubborn laces.

"So I had an idea," he says, twisting the lid back onto his bottle.

"I'm all ears."

"In light of your upcoming competition, perhaps we could do some sort of preliminary fund-raising event at the gym. For example, we could set up a fun obstacle course in the back parking lot and invite patrons to come try their luck. Charge them a few dollars, and that money would go into the Team Dani fund for you to donate to The Rock's charity. It would be a great way to raise cash while also introducing the neighborhood to Hollywood Fitness and its offerings."

"Are you serious?"

"Completely serious," he says.

This is too much. No one—no *guy*—has ever done what Marco does for me. Is he just a remarkably nice human, or . . . dare I hope that it's more than that?

"Marco, this is—I gotta stop you right there. You cannot keep being so nice to me. It's confusing."

He chuckles under his breath. "What possibly is there to be confused about?"

A cloud passes in front of the sun, darkening our spot in the wooded trail, mirroring my sudden mood shift. "You hardly know me, and you keep going out of your way to help me—at the gym, with Howie, with dinner and the journal after the blog hacking, now this . . ."

"It's called friendship, Danielle. People express friendship through small kindnesses. You did it for Howie. You do it for your work friends and even your sisters and mother. Why is it confusing if it's coming from me?"

Because you feel like more than a friend. I want you to be more *than just a friend.*

But my lips won't let the words out.

"Plus, I like you. You're good people. You have nothing to fear from me. I have no ulterior motives . . ." He pauses here, and I'm wanting him to say that his ulterior motives involve late nights and tangled sheets—but he doesn't.

We stare at each other for a sec until the corner of his mouth slides into a grin and he breaks the connection. "Dani, if it makes you uncomfortable, we don't have to do the course—"

"It's not that. It's a great idea . . ."

"After the accident with my mate, my friends showered me with kindness. No one left me alone for that first month after. They took turns sleeping at my house and bringing meals and driving me to the workplace investigator meetings and to the therapist the director insisted I go see. I was a mess—and they wanted me to know that they had my back, no matter what. The mistakes that caused David's death were terrible—not a day goes by where I don't wish I could go back to that morning—but my friends had my back. And I want you to know that you deserve the same. You don't have to be on the defensive with me. I'm not your mother or Trevor or your sisters or your father. I'm your *friend*." He steps closer and cups a warm hand around my upper arm. "Let me be your friend. Please."

I sniff and nod, soaking in the heat that radiates from his hand through the thin lining of my running jacket. When he drops his hand and steps back, I'm chilled by its absence. The cloud moves away from the sun, brightening the woods around us.

"And maybe I'm not doing it for you. Maybe I just really like obstacle courses," he teases, winking, and then bending over to stretch his hamstrings.

I laugh and clear my throat. "Sounds like a lot of work, though. Do you think people would really come to it?"

"Why not?" Marco turns and starts in the direction we've just jogged, his smile signaling me to come along.

"I don't even know what to say."

He stops again, faces me, and my heart races. For a fleeting second, I think I should just kiss him. Just throw myself at him and smooch those deliciously pink-red lips that are moist with water and sweat. He used the word *friend*, though. Is that all this is?

Before Irrational Dani moves, however, Marco unzips his light-weight running jacket. When he splits the jacket halves like Superman revealing his red-and-yellow *S*, my laugh echoes through the forest.

He's wearing a black T-shirt—across its front, it bears a red-and-white screen-printed logo that reads TEAM DANI. He twists, showing me the T-shirt's back: HARDEST WORKER IN THE ROOM.

"Are you kidding me?" I'm cackling like a freak to hide the blush in my cheeks, because I was just considering smooching him against his will, but mostly because I'm so stunned by his surprise that I'm afraid I'll start crying. Again.

"What is there to kid about? This competition is serious business. We must get you on that stage and in that movie so your every dream can come true. Right?"

"I'm speechless."

"Say yes, Dani."

I can't, though. My voice won't work and I can't stop grinning. So I nod vigorously and give him a thumbs-up.

Miraculously Beautiful Marco flashes the smile that has a significant weakening effect on my knees, offers his fist for a bump, and zips up his coat.

"I wish I had this on video. No one will believe I rendered *you* speechless," he says, jogging off.

I follow Marco into the gym, the warmth inside welcome as I've cooled off from our run. Seems the crafty crew of Hollywood Fitness—apparently under the direction of one Marco Turner—have designed this insane obstacle course to be built in under a day in the parking lot.

"How . . . ?"

"Are you questioning my most excellent skills in the field of organizational science?" Marco asks, unrolling an actual blueprint atop the office desk.

"I guess not?"

He grabs a pencil from a repurposed coffee mug, and with the eraser end, he points out all the cool stuff we're going to have at the "Team Dani's *Rockin'* Obstacle Smackdown."

"That name, though . . ."

"It conveys the message. You're welcome to come up with something better."

"No, no, by all means. Carry on." I smile.

"We weren't sure if Rock the Tots was trademarked. Last thing we need is to get shut down because we've stepped on toes."

"*Smackdown* might be trademarked."

"Really?"

"Probably not. The Rock invented it, though," I say.

"Like Shakespeare."

"Meaning?"

"Shakespeare was credited with adding over nineteen hundred words to the English language."

"Which makes sense. The Rock is awesome like Shakespeare," I say, smirking. "Don't you need permits to do this sort of thing?"

"Trish and I are looking into it. Primarily it will be making sure the insurance covers us. Don't want anyone taking a tumble off a rope and then suing us because they've sprained a pinky."

"Yes, that would be a shame," I say, looking over their awesome schematics.

"We were thinking we could offer smoothies, vegan and turkey hot dogs, Esther's famous cookies, protein bars—all sorts of tasty treats for the participants."

I giggle. "Say that again."

"Say what again?"

"The part about the treats . . ."

"All sorts of tasty treats?"

I giggle louder. "*Tasty treats.* You're so posh."

"You do know that if you misbehave, I will just add more push-ups to your regimen." That smile, man.

"I would gladly do those added push-ups—and you know how much I loathe push-ups—as long as you stood over me telling me more about these *tasty treats*."

Trish with Muscles pops her head in the door. "Hate to break up the fun, but your next client has arrived."

"Thanks. I'll be right out," Marco says.

"Right. I should go. You have victims besides just me."

"Yes, but few harass me the way you do," he says, rolling up the blueprints. "You think this will work for our purposes?"

"Marco, honestly, this is freaking amazing. I can't believe you want to go to so much trouble."

"It's not completely selfless, Dani. It's a win for the gym too. We'll do it in a month or so, when we're sure the weather will cooperate, invite folks in the neighborhood to have a go, sign up some new gym members—we raise a few shillings, and it goes into the Team Dani fund to get you your walk-on role with Mr. Rock."

"You do know that I don't win the competition by donating the most money, right?" No, I win the competition by beating athletes like Bionic Barbie.

"Indeed. Which is why the whole Smackdown weekend, you will be here, running this course," he gestures with the rolled course blueprint, "a hundred times if necessary, to get your arse in gear for what's coming at you in August."

"I knew there had to be a catch."

"We're benevolent, sure, but we're all sadists and opportunists here, remember? You'll have to work that much harder so when you win the competition, you can make us famous right alongside you." He offers his hand for a high five, but I want to do so much more than that.

For a beat, the twinkle in his eye suggests he might want more than that too.

"All right, then, go get some protein in your body. Lots of hydration. You did well today. Every time we go, you improve," he says.

"Because I have the best trainer in the city threatening me with push-ups."

Marco follows me out of the office, his hand gentle on my elbow as he wishes me goodbye. Chills sizzle up my arm.

"Dani, before you go . . ." Trish with Muscles summons me from behind the front counter. I hope she didn't just see me giving Marco's backside the googly eyes.

She leans on elbows and lowers her voice. "Not sure if you were aware, but Marco's birthday is this coming weekend."

"It is?"

She nods. "We're doing a thing for him over at the Moon and Sixpence on NE 42nd, around seven-ish on Friday? I'm sure he'd love it if you dropped by."

"I wouldn't miss it. Thank you so much for inviting me."

"You bet," she says, reaching for the ringing phone. "See you tomorrow?"

"With bells on my toes."

En route to my car, my brain sets to spinning. Marco's birthday. Gonna need a present that says, *Hey, I think you're awesome and I'd like to see you naked but you keep using the word* friend *so the present has to be like* Hey, cool, you're a great friend *and not* Hey, let's lick frosting off each other's body parts.

FORTY-EIGHT

I've taken no fewer than a hundred mirror selfies to send to Jacqueline for fashion advice. I'd ask Georgie, but given that her wardrobe consists mostly of elastic waistbands and breast milk–stained hoodies these days (or collars, whips, and studded garter belts) . . .

Frustrated by my nonstop texts, Jackie finally FaceTimes me. "I have three patients left to see before I can go home, Dani," she says, sighing, and slurping what I'm sure is some magical youth elixir that only plastic surgeons have access to. (You should see Jackie's pores. To die for.) "I'd go with the dark skinny jeans and boots and that cropped red cardigan with a tank underneath."

"Really? Isn't that too casual?"

"It's a pub, right?"

"Yeah . . ."

"And it's a birthday party?"

"Do you think I should wear a dress, though?"

"A dress says that you want to show him your boobs." She tosses a handful of dried edamame into her mouth. "And I know you do because I saw what you called him on your blog—wait, did he read it?"

"*No*. Marco is a gentleman. He *respects* me." He said he wouldn't read it, and I want to believe him. I guess I have no way of knowing if he did, unless he accidentally drops a tidbit from some entry. As it hasn't happened yet, I'd like to believe that he's a man of his word.

She snorts. "Whatever, genius. You shouldn't have beaten up that woman at work, and then she wouldn't have hacked you."

"No, she shouldn't be cyberstalking and ruining people's lives."

"Hold your phone up to your butt," she says. I do. "I love those jeans. Jake would love my butt in those jeans. Where'd you get 'em?"

"Nordstrom Rack." Which is a lie. I splurged. Bought them at the proper Nordstrom store, but I don't want her to know that because then she will lecture me about Spending Money While Unemployed. It's the new Steele family refrain when talking to me. My savings depletion and credit card debt—for these jeans and the apology gifts and the gym fees I pay for the delicious company of one Marco Turner—is none of their beeswax.

"Hey, how goes the job search? A friend of mine—a pediatrician— she needs an office manager."

"You mean, around kids and boogers and barf and screaming babies?"

"Your compassion is limitless," she says, talking with a mouthful. "It's a job, babe. She read your blog, so she knows who she'd be dealing with."

Awesome. That's terrific. But it's a lead, and I've had exactly two interview requests from the forty-two résumés I've sent out. Unemployment is covering the rent and not much else, and my savings account is lasting only because I cashed in my 401(k)—please do not tell Jackie this part.

"Send me her email."

"It's worth a shot, Dani. Plus, you get free shit from the drug reps," she says. "Okay, I really have to go. I hired a new nurse and the patients hate her and she's laying on the buzzer like she's having a seizure, and

I have to get out of here on time because Jake and I are interviewing a decorator for the man cave he absolutely will not stop harping about. Seriously, Dani, wear the jeans. Your ass looks hot."

"Thank you, Dr. Collins Steele."

"You can trust my professional opinion. I know asses. I install them regularly. And yours is looking pret-ty fine."

"Squats, squats, and more squats."

"Gotta go erase twenty years off a dude's face. Call me if you get laid." She disconnects before I can be fake-horrified.

"Real professional, doc," I say under my breath to Aldous and the mirror as I pivot back and forth, examining my reflection from all angles. She's right, though. Eight weeks into this gym training business, and my buns do have a certain lift that wasn't present before. Still more work to be done, of course—six years of secretary spread and too many MotherCluckers' meetings to undo—but I'll take any compliments my sister is willing to dish out right now. At least she's not yelling at me about the bloody blog. And a job lead isn't too shabby, even if it means walking into a fog of germs every day.

"What do you think, Aldous? Does my butt look good in these pants?" She twists her head, shows me her white belly, and engages the purr motor before chomping down on her catnip-stuffed fishie. "I'll take that as a yes."

⌒⌒

Trish with Muscles said seven-ish, which is a little vague, and I don't want to be the first person to show up, but if I'm *too* late it'll look like I didn't really want to show up in the first place. Obviously not the case. I opt for seven thirty—that seems about right. And I'm carrying one of my big purses so I can keep Marco's present in there, in case no one else brought presents. I don't want to look like a googly-eyed fangirl.

Sure enough, when I walk into the crowded pub, the Hollywood Fitness crew has basically taken over the whole front area parallel to the bar.

"Daniiiiii!" Minotaur hollers, standing to offer me a chair as everyone waves in greeting.

Marco is talking to a woman I don't recognize—she's pretty, young, straight flaxen hair draped over bare arms that reveal she spends time in the gym. She giggles and touches his hand when he says something funny, and my stomach drops. Oh my god, is that his girlfriend? He hasn't mentioned one . . . maybe it's a new relationship and they haven't started using official terms like *girlfriend*. The way she's looking at him, it's clear she's been bitten by the same bug I have.

He turns while her hand is still touching his wrist and rises from the bench against the wall down from where I'm standing. He squeezes through and opens his arms for a hug, which I gladly fold into, hugging him like I haven't seen him in a year. I also make a small note that the look on the pretty girl's face is no longer so smiley; I feel a little guilty, like I've interrupted something.

"Ms. Steele, you made it," he says against my head.

"Hey, someone said there'd be cake," I tease. He steps back, his right hand still on my shoulder, and gives the drink signal to his friend manning the pitchers lined up along the strip of tables. "Happy birthday!" I say. I consider giving him his present, but a quick scan of the table doesn't reveal any other festively wrapped packages. Maybe I should wait.

"Thanks. So pleased you could come out and play with us. Have a seat." He finally lets go so he can pull out a chair for me. But then he returns to his spot on the bench down the way—Pretty Girl looks smug as he resumes his earlier position, which does not endear her to me. If Marco is her man, cool. This isn't high school.

Introductions are made around the table, but I'm nervous enough that I will remember exactly zero names by the time the beer is drained from the glass they've slid in front of me.

The group is a mix of his gym life and outside friends, and an hour in, pints filled and refilled, the stories of shared histories have most of us in stitches. Seems Marco and his buddies are magnets for trouble when they're allowed out of doors—one story detailed an ill-fated camping trip near Mammoth Lakes, California, which ended when a food-seeking black bear tore apart the door and interior of Marco's truck; another story found the birthday boy and his crew trying to save the car of a young woman who got stuck in the surf at Grover Beach—when the car was too mired in wet sand, they had to watch as the Pacific Ocean ate it, tires and all. Beyond a wee bit of trouble with the authorities, the story had a happy ending; the girl who lost her car later married one of Marco's friends and is seated at the table to blush appropriately as they razz her about driving on wet sand.

Pretty Girl doesn't have any interesting stories, but I smile into my glass every time she touches his arm or elbow and he slyly shifts away. Poor thing.

It becomes clear that a few of these folks are Los Angeles transplants, show-business friends of Marco's when they were all down south. When one among his LA crew segues into a conversation about the absolute best stunts in Hollywood history—from Tom Cruise in *Mission Impossible* to Daniel Craig in *Casino Royale*, and the king of the original Hollywood stunt, Buster Keaton—this friend talks about what a master Marco is, how he intuitively knows how to make a stunt look seamless. When he tells a crazy stunt story that involved David, the friend who died, the change in Marco's face is subtle, but still present. The conversation lulls for a moment before an astute Trish picks up the ball and changes course.

"So, Dani, tell these guys about the thing The Rock is doing in town in August." I feel weird, talking about myself when this party is about Marco, but the tone of the conversation has cooled—I can see in Trish's face that we need a diversion.

I launch into my cheeriest explanation about Rock the Tots, at once selfishly hoping that the very fit women sitting around the table won't join up and obliterate my chances even further. "Of course, the only way I'm going to be able to get through this whole thing is if the World's Greatest Trainer keeps yelling at me to stop whining," I say, lifting my beer. "Three cheers for the World's Greatest Trainer!"

The group livens up again, lifting their glasses to their *hip-hip-hoorays*. The blush that paints Marco's cheeks looks good on him; the wink he offers in thanks staggers my resting heart rate.

With my one-beer limit reached, I excuse myself to the restroom. As I pass the last two stools at the bar's end, a very red-faced man yells at his girlfriend, threatening to shut her up if she doesn't watch her mouth. The woman looks right at me, her eyes wide and bloodshot and haunted—for a beat, I consider asking her if she'd like to come with me to the bathroom. Before I have the chance, though, the bartender slides over and asks "Rusty" if maybe he'd like to switch to coffee.

My bladder is relieved to find no line for a stall. I finish my business, wash up, and refresh my lipstick, ogling my butt in these jeans one more time. Money well spent.

As I open the bathroom door, it's obvious that Rusty hasn't switched to coffee, and the words being exchanged with the bartender, and possibly other patrons, are no longer friendly. I try to scoot by, but just as I'm passing the woman, Rusty launches himself at her, shoving her into me, and we both fly backward onto the floor, her body on mine as Rusty straddles her and continues yelling, a beer bottle still clutched in his right hand.

Before I know it, the bartender is over the counter trying to pull us free, helped by Marco, Minotaur, Alex the Vet, and various others.

Minotaur wrestles the guy from behind and shoves him backward into the bar. Rusty slams the bottle against the counter's edge, handily weaponizing the glass. He lunges, but Marco has his hands outstretched to stop the guy from getting near Minotaur or the woman, who is still screaming and writhing on top of me.

And then there's blood. A lot of blood, streaming from Marco's palm.

Minotaur, Alex, two other friends of Marco, and the bartender disarm and slam the now-shrieking Rusty to the floor. Marco helps the woman and me off the floor with his uninjured hand, blood rapidly draining down his middle three fingers of the other and soaking into the carpet.

"Are you all right?" he asks me.

Firmly but gently, I grab his elbow. "You're not. Let me see." The wound looks like the one Georgette sustained on the outside of her left hand from an unfinished metal edge on a playground slide. She fainted the second she saw the blood, so Jackie and I had to carry her home between us, trailing blood on the gray sidewalk like some sort of sick Hansel and Gretel.

Once the woman is on her feet, sobbing uncontrollably, Trish and two other party members pull her aside; the waitress behind the counter has the phone against her ear, feeding details to who I hope is a police dispatcher; she tosses me a clean bar towel.

Marco offers me his hand, splayed atop the scratchy white cloth. As soon as he looks down at the frightening wound, his face blanches.

"Okay, head up. Look at me," I say. He obliges, brown eyes earnest. "We're going to get you some stitches."

"Yes. Right. Seems that might be necessary."

"Does it hurt? Do you need to sit?"

"It does hurt a bit."

Trish rushes up beside me. "Dani, Jesus, are you okay—" She stops midsentence, her attention drawn to the bloody mess lying across my open palms. "Shit. We need to take him to Providence, over on Glisan. That's the closest ER."

"Ladies, I'm fine," Marco says.

"Sure, you are. And I have some superglue in my purse. We'll just glue you back together so you can finish your pint."

"Your British accent needs work, Steele."

"Well, we'll have plenty of time sitting in the ER for you to correct my lilt and brogue." I look to Trish. Pretty Girl is still sitting behind the table, eyes wide, her face a little green. Guessing she's not a fan of blood. Her loss is my gain.

"I'll take him. I've only had the one beer."

Without having to be asked, Trish hustles to the table and grabs my purse and Marco's jacket.

"We should wait until the police arrive, shouldn't we?" Marco asks.

"If we do, you're going to bleed through all the restaurant's towels," I say, wrapping the terry cloth snug around his wounded hand.

"Is there ever a dull moment when you're around?" he asks, digging through his coat pocket for his keys.

"We can take my car. I'm in charge."

"I don't want to bleed all over Flex Kavana."

"He's seen worse," I say.

FORTY-NINE

Seems that not even a lot of blood makes folks move faster in an ER. I should've told Marco to faint so he could move to the front of the line.

At the admissions desk, he hands me his wallet. "My insurance card is on the right side. Help a fellow out?"

I find the card, pausing just long enough to confirm it's the right one. "Your real name is Marcellus?" I ask, trying not to smile.

"Roman mythology, after Mars, the god of war." I swear he's blushing. Miraculously Beautiful *Marcellus* . . . has a nice ring to it.

The admissions clerk, a carbon copy of Tyler Perry's Madea character, looks over the wire-rimmed glasses barely balanced on the end of her nose. "Is that what you were doin' tonight, sweetie? Engaging in some war?" She nods at the very blood-soaked towel wrapped around his hand.

"Actually," I interject, "he was defending two women from a mean drunk dude with a broken beer bottle. *Marcellus* here stepped in to help—and on his birthday, no less."

"Noble. Happy birthday," she says, typing in his info so slowly, I fear he will need a transfusion by the time he sees a doctor.

When he finally has his hospital bracelet on, the wide door swings open to transport him into the hubbub of the sick and wounded.

"Come inside with me?" he asks.

"Are you sure? I can just wait out here."

He smiles widely. "I hate needles."

The nurse who escorts us to a curtained-off bed—a petite thing named Lexie with eighties throwback bangs and what I think might be a perm—sets to asking all the requisite questions, though her Texan accent is so thick, I fear that the quizzical look on Marco's face means he can't understand what she's saying. I give her my summation of events from the pub, making sure she knows that Marco is a bit of a hero and should be given the highest standard of care.

When she steps away to retrieve a kit to clean the wound, I lean over onto the bed. "She sounds Texan. Texas and Oregon are about as opposite as you can get. Oregonians are like, 'I'll have an egg white omelet made with eggs laid by free-range chickens topped with sheep's milk cheese but only if the sheep was well loved, and please add roasted, non-GMO veggies and the tears of woodland sprites.' Lexie the Texan is probably like, 'I'll have beef. No need to slaughter it first, pardner. Just bring it to the table whole.'" Marco laughs, shaking his head. Seeing that she's heading back our way, I whisper, "Quick! I'll give you five bucks if you ask her if she had an armadillo as a pet when she was a kid."

Marco is still chuckling.

"So glaaaaad to see our birthday boy still has his sense of huu-mor."

I wink conspiratorially.

Lexie positions Marco supine on the bed with his injured left hand palm up across a rolling side table draped in sterile blue paper. He stretches out his right hand to me where I sit in the chair adjacent; I gladly take it, concerned that he's injured but selfishly flipping out on the inside because I'm holding his hand, and he's holding mine right back. I don't let go, even as he hisses lightly behind his teeth when

Lexie really digs in to make sure there's no residual glass in the two-inch-plus slash that runs from the callus below his middle finger and curves into the meaty part where the thumb attaches.

"Sorry about that, sweetheart. Gotta git it nice and clean for the doc to stitch up. Also gotta make sure there's no damage to the tendons."

"Hey, tough guy, just don't look at what Lexie's doing," I say. "Holy smokers, is that a real nun?" An old woman in a plain navy-blue skirt-and-jacket uniform walks by, her head covered in a white-and-blue coif and veil. "I haven't seen a real nun in years."

"They work with the chaplain here in the hospital," Lexie offers.

"Is it true that nuns are married to Jesus? Like, how would you ever get your honey-do list done? You'd ask him to do stuff, and he'd be all, *I can't, I'm performing miracles all weekend.* Jesus seems like he'd be a terrible husband." Marco's grinning, despite the obvious pain. "I suppose, though, if he didn't clean the gutters or get the snow tires put on the car, you'd be like, *Jesus, I'm gonna call your dad if I don't get some help around here!*" Marco loses it; Lexie gives me a tight smile as she pulls her necklace bearing a gold cross pendant out from under her teddy-bear scrub top.

I give Marco the uh-oh-I-said-the-wrong-thing-again look, and we try to control our immaturity.

"So where are you frooooooom, Mr. Turner, with that pretty accent?"

Marco smiles politely. "Greenwich. It's a borough—like a suburb—in London, England."

"That sounds fascinatin'. I've never been to England."

"Yes, I've never been to Jolly Old England, either, Mr. Turner. Grace us with a story," I add.

"Hmmm . . . Let's see . . ." Marco leans his head back against the pillow and closes his eyes for a moment. I grin with anticipation. I'm finding I love Marco's stories. "All right, here's one. When I was in high school, one of my mates was very much in love with a girl he'd met at an interschool dance. We went to a posh private school my parents had to mortgage their house to pay for, and this girl was from an all-girl high school, so these dances were a big deal for hormonal young people. My friend, Leo, he was head over heels—and I knew the feeling, given I'd lost my heart over my unrequited feelings for dear Nicola when I was a youngster," he says to me, "so I wanted to do whatever I could to help Leo win over the object of his undying affection.

"We decided that for Valentine's Day, we would skip class and go to her school and he could present her with flowers and chocolates. Only it couldn't just be him walking up to the front door and demanding entry. Leo needed to make a big entrance, and he knew that I was just the coconspirator he required.

"The night before, we sneaked to her school's rooftop, where we installed a rig that I had designed that would lower Leo in a harness hidden under his school uniform, which was a proper blazer and tie and this ridiculous boater hat, down the front of the building to the window where he knew she would be at the given time of day, in the science department.

"The morning of Valentine's Day, Leo was a mess, but a few shots of my gran's precious Irish whiskey sorted him right out. We stole away from our school, got to the roof of the girls' school without notice, and attached him to the rig." Marco winces as Lexie pulls the wound apart and looks at it with a lamp.

"Eyes on me," I say as his face pales and his grip on my hand tightens.

He focuses on me so intently, I swear we're the only people left on the planet. "Slowly, two other mates and I lowered Leo down the building's facade, his arms laden with a dozen of the reddest roses and a box of the sweetest Belgian chocolates. He swayed forward and knocked on the window, and when the girls in the class saw what was going on, they, of course threw up the sash, and our smitten Leo broke into song."

"What did he sing?" Lexie the Texan asks.

"You know, I don't recall. But Leo was quite the crooner. The instructor for the class ran out in a panic, shrieking for the headmaster, but Leo finished his song and then reached across and gave the now-crying girl the flowers and chocolates. Just as he leaned in for a kiss, the headmaster pushed the girl aside and slammed the window shut. At the same time, an administrator trapped us on the roof—we were escorted down to the front office so we couldn't lower Leo to the ground. They made Leo hang there for the duration so the entire school could get a good look. Had a terrific fit of rain that day too. Poor Leo was blue-lipped and soaked to the bone when they finally released him."

"Is this real? Are you making this up?" I ask.

"One hundred percent true," Marco says, grinning. "Me and the other fellows spent the rest of the day engaged in whatever chores the headmaster needed doing."

"What happened once they cut poor Leo loose?" Lexie asks.

"They gave him a towel to dry off, and then he, as well as the rest of us, were given in-school suspensions and banned from future inter-school events."

"No!" Lexie says at the same time I ask, "And the girl? Did he ever get that kiss?"

"Indeed, he did. They fell head over heels in love, went to the same university, and are now happily married with a gaggle of kids some-where in London."

"Now *that* is just so romaaaaaaantic." Lexie returns her attention to Marco's wound. "That's why I just love British leading men, don't you? I wouldn't let *this* one outta yer sight, honey," she says to me. My face ignites as she cleans up the wrappers from her medical supplies. "Okay, you two just sit tight. The doc will be right in. And thanks so muuuuch for that great story, darlin'!" She looks right at me, and her sugary grin melts a little. "For you, I will say a little prayer. Jesus is very forgivin'."

As soon as the curtain swooshes closed after her, I lean my elbows on the bedside, Marco's hand still wrapped in mine. "You didn't ask her about the armadillo," I scold.

"I would have, but she had sharp instruments poking about my lacerated flesh. And seeing how she reacted to your attempt at comedy . . ."

"Some people need to get out more."

The curtain moves aside and the doctor steps in—and I about pee my pants. "Dani?"

"Oh! Jake. I thought you worked in Beaverton."

Marco looks back and forth between the doctor and me, question marks all over his face.

"Good to see you! Though not under the best circumstances. Small world, huh?" the doc says.

"Marco Turner, this is Dr. Jake Halvorsen—he's my sister Jackie's boyfriend."

"Fiancé," Jake corrects. "And I did work in Beaverton, but Providence is closer to our new place, so I transferred. Hey, did Jackie tell you about my man cave?" Before waiting for me to answer, he offers a hand to Marco, which means I have to let it go. "So nice to meet a friend of Dani's. Wait—" Jake squints at Marco, then looks back at me and, oh shit, I know what's coming, and even though my eyes widen to saucer dimensions, I can't stop him in time. "Daaaaani, is this *the* Marco you swooned about in your—"

"*Okay*, Jake, thank you so much. Can you just not talk, and maybe stitch up Marco's hand sometime tonight?"

Jake laughs heartily and angles himself closer to Marco, whose face is now awash in amusement. "Dude, the Steele sisters are insane. Hold on for a wild ride."

"So I'm learning," Marco says, laughing as he turns and lifts an eyebrow at me.

"Jake. Seriously. *Shut up.*"

Marco laughs louder.

Dr. Halvorsen winks, and then pulls a rolling stool over to the side table supporting Marco's hand. He thankfully sets to work, numbing the incision and poking and prodding, all while making small talk about his dumb man cave so that Marco doesn't focus too heavily on the pain he's surely enduring. As obnoxious as Jake can be sometimes, his bedside manner is commendable.

When the last stitch is in and Jake is confident there is no tendon damage, he pulls off his gloves and pushes the lamp away. "The nurse will come in and bandage you up and give you some prescriptions to get filled. Keep the hand elevated if you can, and see your family doctor for a recheck in about ten days, sooner if there are any signs of infection, yeah?" Marco nods. Jake reaches for another handshake "I hope I get to see you again, though not for medical intervention—maybe at Dani's thing with The Rock? I seriously love that dude."

"Who doesn't?" Marco says. "Thanks so much for your expert assistance this evening. Hardly felt a thing."

Jake turns to me. "And you, stay off the Internet. Doctor's orders."

"Smart-ass." I smack his arm as he slips out.

"Everyone really did read that blog, didn't they . . . ?" Marco says.

I snort. "Whatever. Losers, every one of them."

"Did you really swoon about me?" he says, the devil in his smile.

"Another word about it and I'll reopen those stitches."

He laughs loudly, the sound a pleasing contrast to the moaning coming from the next bed over, but my face is burning so hot, I fear the cotton privacy curtains will catch fire.

I pull my phone out to check the time and avoid eye contact for a moment, but as I plop it back into my purse's zippered pocket, I realize I still have Marco's birthday present.

"Hey, almost forgot," I say, pulling it out.

"For me?"

"I would've given it to you at the pub, but then I felt dumb because no one else seemed to have brought presents, and then you went and played hero . . ."

"You really shouldn't have. Especially since you've sacrificed your whole evening here. Sorry about that."

"You were saving *me,* remember?"

He blushes. "Should I open it now?"

"Please do."

He sits forward and wedges the package between his knees, tearing at the birthday cake–decorated paper with his right hand.

"Are you even kidding me?" he says, cracking up, holding the aluminum water bottle printed all over with thumbnail-size John Cena faces. "This is perfect."

"You're still a blasphemer. But at least you'll stay hydrated."

"I'm so bringing this to the competition. Maybe I can get The Rock to autograph it for me," he teases as I wad the discarded wrapping paper into a ball. "Thank you so much, Dani." He pulls me up by my wrist and hugs me with his good arm. He smells so good . . . I never want to let go. I resist the urge to climb onto the bed next to him and curl against his side.

When he releases, our faces are so close together, but I don't know what to do, so I again sit in the hard plastic chair, my pulse pounding in my ears.

"Thank you for a fantastic birthday," he says, grinning.

I meet his smile with one of my own, so wide my cheeks ache. "Next time I'll just bring cupcakes."

FIFTY

May 20, 2016

Dear Dwayne Johnson,
   I AM NOT FALLING FOR MY TRAINER. That is so cliché.
   NO I'M NOT.
   NO. NO. NO.
   Shit. Yes, I am.
   YES I AM IT'S A DONE DEAL OH GOD HE'S SO DREAMY.

   Hopelessly a goner,
   Danielle Sucker-Punched-by-Cupid Steele

FIFTY-ONE

The next few weeks dissolve into a blissful blur—happily predictable, which is the way I like it. Get up, eat protein, go to the gym, come home, eat more protein, play with Aldous, go to auditions where far too many casting assistants and directors have read my blog and have all sorts of witty, unsolicited opinions, go to acting class, apply for new jobs I will probably hate, but food is expensive and unemployment benefits don't last forever, not get the jobs I do apply for (including the pediatrician's office manager job), and then go to the gym for a second workout, because staying away from Marcellus Turner and his gorgeous knees is impossible.

Three days a week, Marco and I meet up to run in Forest Park; three days a week I get a new story about his beloved younger brother (an accountant in London), his Irish gran, or his hardworking parents who aren't at all adventurous or crazy; about how he does miss his LA life now and again, agreeing wholeheartedly as we reminisce about the family-like atmosphere on movies and projects that pulls you back again and again, even when the hours are long and the shoots are grueling; about the nutty things he and his mates did growing up, from lying about their ages so they could go skydiving to streaking at football (soccer) games to helping arrange outlandish marriage propos-als for the smitten among their tribe. His stories repeatedly cement for me that not only is Marco nuts, but he cares—deeply—for his friends and family, and he will do anything for them.

Which I'm certain makes his friend David's death so much harder to bear.

Today, however, I won't be graced with a story. We're skipping trail running in Forest Park in favor of spreading sand and building the course for the upcoming "Team Dani's *Rockin'* Obstacle Smackdown."

When I arrive at Hollywood Fitness, I head around to the back of the building, where I'm met with cheers and high fives from all my buddies—Minotaur, the Limping Lady, Alex the Vet, Handstand Man, Trish with Muscles, the rest of the regulars—all of them wearing Team Dani T-shirts, all of them with shovels in hand as we wait for the ginormous dump truck to drop its load of sand.

I knew Marco's plans were awesome, but this . . . I'm completely floored. We've spent so much time training in these last weeks—and when Marco is being the trainer, he's tough—but in his softer moments, I'm desperate for clues that maybe he's feeling the same stir-rings that I am. Like how I cannot wait to get to the gym and see his face, how there is a literal spring in my step in those last few feet before I pull the front door handle and the gym atmosphere rushes at me; how when he smiles or even frowns at his clients, I experience a squeeze in my chest—the good kind, not the I'm-going-into-cardiac-arrest kind, although sometimes it feels like a heart attack when I go too many days without seeing him. He's told me the stories of the crazy things he's done for friends and his brother and even the thirtieth-wedding-anniversary surprise he coordinated for his parents when he hired a skywriter to fly above their house: JAMES LOVES FIONA FOREVER.

Looking around at all these people, at all this stuff, at this abso-lutely herculean effort, his words from that day in the woods echo in my head—*Let me be your friend*—but, dear man, aren't we more? Have

I misread this, because the signs are all there, Marcellus . . . I know for a fact that you don't look at your other clients the way you look at me. You don't spend the same unpaid time with them that you do with me—and if you do, how do you pay your mortgage?

Are you ever going to ask me out, or are we going to dance around each other for the rest of our natural lives?

Marco, hand still bandaged, though he reports he's mostly healed, flattens the blueprints over a plywood-and-sawhorse table. He points out where we're going to build the hurdles, rope climbs against the building's outer brick wall, the military-style crawl under chicken wire through the sand, the tire course, the 4x4-post carry, monkey bars, the sandbag up-and-over wall, the kettlebell relay, even hula hoops.

Once the dump truck rolls out, Marco delegates tasks, and we set to work. When I see him pick up a shovel, I step in. "Excuse me, young man, but you're not using that hand yet."

"Nurse Ratched, I can scoop some sand."

"I'm sorry, but as your resident high-maintenance pain in the ass, I'm going to have to insist that you let those of us who have not undergone thirty-odd stitches in the last month to handle this bit."

He leans on the shovel. "Does that mean I get to boss people around?"

"Isn't that what you do best?"

He snickers and hands me his shovel. "I'm known for other unique talents, but this will do for now."

"One of these days, I'd like to see those unique talents," I say, because why not? I'm going for it.

Our eyes lock for a beat, and he lifts a brow. "I'll have to take that under advisement."

⁓

Over the subsequent two days, we finish the course, hang up the huge vinyl signs Marco had printed, and distribute flyers throughout the local neighborhood businesses. Marco and I hit Costco for loads of fruit for smoothies, to be made with the borrowed blenders of at least five gym members; Alex the Vet brings a fancy barbecue for the multiple coolers packed with meatless and turkey hot dogs and buns donated by Minotaur's Target managers; Limping Lady brings in many dozens of *healthy* cookies that she's baked over the past week because "who doesn't like cookies"; Trish with Muscles has cartons of protein bars and fresh fruit and energy snacks donated by local health-friendly grocery stores. Even Lady Macbeth and her crazy-hyper nine-year-old son get in on the action by bringing boxes of dollar-store pencils and participation ribbons for the kids running the course.

It's an unrivaled team effort that catches the attention of local news and social media streams. Saturday afternoon, the sun showing off what she's got planned for us in the last few days before summer officially arrives, we have local TV personalities interviewing folks standing in the line that stretches up the block. People love a good cause, and what better cause than a children's hospital that The Rock himself supports? It's a perfect example of grassroots viral marketing, where people hear about an event and then come by because they want to donate a few bucks to run through our course while their friends take hilarious photos as they face-plant into the sand.

It's a total blast. The most fun I have had in *months*. Years, maybe. And not a single person brings up the blog.

As the weekend progresses, I gladly collect the congratulatory full-body hugs that Miraculously Beautiful Marco offers every time I complete another set of fifteen runs of the course. On breaks, his arm lingers around my shoulders for longer intervals, even though I'm sweaty and stinky and whining about sore muscles. We both seem to find excuses to touch one another's arms or place a hand on a lower back; I've checked his healing hand no fewer than five times "for dirt and pulled skin from overdoing it," but truly for no other reason than to have an excuse to touch him. He doesn't pull away until my inspection is complete.

If he doesn't make a move in the next week, I will. I'd have to be numb not to notice that the thumping in my chest has nothing to do with exertion, and everything to do with the way he smiles at me.

Sunday night, when the last racer has finished and the last smoothie has been poured, the obstacles torn down and the sand scooped back into the hulking truck it came in, Hollywood Fitness has a bunch of new members; Team Dani has raised more than $5,000; Marco has rubbed out the terrible knot in my calf a half dozen times, laughing as I squeal in pain but not really (it's all I can do to not tear his clothes off right there in front of everyone); and I've run the course—not even exaggerating—one hundred and one times as per the gauntlet thrown down by Marco.

Who's the candy-ass now, DJ? *Not this girl.*

Best weekend ever.

FIFTY-TWO

Dear Danielle,

I was a fan of your hilarious blog, but now it's gone. Do you have any plans to put it back up? I appreciate all the stuff where you talked about your crazy family and your fitness goals. My family is super crazy too (and some of them not in a good way!).

After years of struggling with a food addiction, I've recently lost almost a hundred pounds with the help of a trainer, a psycho-analyst, and modifications in my diet and exercise. I found your blog right at the time when I needed a good chuckle—one of my friends emailed me the link—and I was so happy to see that you are on a fitness journey of your own.

I totally understand why you wrote all these letters to The Rock. He's such an inspiration, isn't he? From that troubled kid who had nothing to who he is today. I had problems with shoplifting and getting into trouble for stupid stuff when I was in high school, and I know now that it was because I was trying to deal with my dad bailing and my mom being a drunk who dated losers. I don't blame my lame parents for the dumb crap I did, but I know that my actions were motivated by my anger toward them. I know stuff has been hard for you too, so I just wanted you to know that you're not alone.

I recently turned twenty-two, and I'm in college studying to be an occupational therapist so I can work with handicapped kids. I just wanted you to know that your blog inspired me to keep going with my diet and exercise routine. I'm sad that it's not up anymore, but if you decide to publish it again, or maybe start a new blog, I'd love to see more funny, inspiring stories, especially about you winning that big competition coming up! You should let your readers know if there's a place they can donate money to your fund-raising team.

Good luck, Danielle! If you meet The Rock in person, tell him I said hello!

Sincerely,
Tamara J.
Tucson, Arizona
[Message from user TAMMYJ94]

FIFTY-THREE

From: Georgette H. Steele-Preston <pupperspaintwithGeorgie@ gmail.com>
To: Danielle E. Steele <DS.May21972@gmail.com>
Subject: Proud of you . . . but st*ll mad

Hey, Dan*,

    *'ve been mean*ng to ema*l and thank you for help*ng Samuel w*th that awful back hedge—and then for the fru*t and w*ne basket last week? D*d you put that together yourself? So cute! You d*dn't have to d*ng-dong-d*tch l*ke a th*rd grader, though, Dan*. *'m not go*ng to throw crabapples at you. (Remember when we used to do that to that k*d down the block who would d*ng-dong-d*tch because he loved Jack*e? Good t*mes . . .) My anger at your r*d*culous blog has been suff*c*ently soothed by the W*llamette Valley P*not * almost d*dn't share w*th Sam—and the body chocolate—n*ce touch, smart-ass. JUST STOP WR*T*NG ABOUT MY SEX L*FE ON YOUR BLOG, you b*g jerk. (* shared the body choco-

late w*th Samuel. He says thank you very, very much. Ha ha ha, that's what you get, pervert.)

Anyway, * saw you on the news! That obstacle course—that's for the b*g compet*t*on you're do*ng w*th The Rock? W*ll you really get to meet h*m? * hope so. * know how *mportant he's been *n your l*fe, sort of a stand-*n for Gerald Robert Steele.

Sorry about the m*ss*ng vowel. * freak*ng need f*ve ch*ld-free m*nutes to get to the Apple Store. NO YOU CANNOT BABYS*T FOR ME.

As a s*de note, *'ve res*gned from my PTA pres*dency because *'m so hum*l*ated about the photos of my sex toys, even though a few of my fr*ends have laughed because they've got the same stuff we do . . . What can * say? Parents of k*ndergartners are horny?

And *'ve been talk*ng to Mommy so she lays off a l*ttle. We know you were hacked so we forg*ve you. Just so you know, * d*dn't read past the last few weeks of entr*es. *'m even sorry * read that much.

But *f you're ever go*ng to babys*t my k*ds aga*n, you absolutely have to prom*se you won't feed them synthet*c cough med*c*nes OR that sh*tty p*zza. SER*OULSY. Mary May pooped for a week, and *t was the nast*st poop ever. * should've saved *t for YOU to clean up.

Jack*e and * talked and we're go*ng to come root for you at The Rock's compet*t*on. Mommy *s st*ll try*ng to f*gure out how to get to her UFO th*ng, but Jack*e and * want to come support you. Also—that hot Br*t*sh dude you were stand*ng w*th dur*ng the news *nterv*ew—THAT'S M*RACULOUSLY BEAUT*FUL MARCO, *SN'T *T??? TELL ME HE'S S*NGLE AND YOU ARE BON*NG THAT! Jack*e sa*d Jake st*tched h*s hand back together after he beat up some dude at a pub? *f you don't tap that, there *s someth*ng terr*bly wrong w*th your bra*n and maybe your vag*na, Dan*elle.

See *f you can get us some of those awesome Team Dan* T-sh*rts, okay?

Love you, even though you're a huge d*ck . . .
Georg*e

FIFTY-FOUR

FAX
From: PENELOPE "MOMMY" STEELE

Hello, Danielle,

This is your mother. As you were unable to come for dinner last Saturday night because of "having to train"—honestly, are you competing in the Olympics here, or are you just avoiding me on purpose? Regardless, your sisters showed up, and we sat down and had an excellent discussion about this whole catastrophe of late, and both girls made me understand that this hacking incident was not your fault at all, and that I should not be angry with you about exposing our family's dirty laundry to the entire world. Even though I am still quite miffed, Jacqueline and Jake are concerned about my blood pressure so I have instead refocused my energies elsewhere to keep myself calm and out of the kerfuffle.

Georgette says I should thank you: My healing-wand business has taken off. Seems people have read your blog and then contacted me for more information. Apparently not everyone is as cynical as my own daughters. Why I even reproduced is still a question I ask myself on a weekly basis—just wait until you have your own daughters, Danielle, although if you don't hurry up, your eggs will drain out of your body, no good to anyone. Even though I must admit, I do love you all.

Jacqueline and Jake and Georgette and Samuel are helping me apply to become a certified grower of medical-grade marijuana for the state of Oregon. (You remember that Georgette's husband is a lawyer, don't you? Maybe he could've helped you with your hacking problem?) That way I won't have the federal government knocking on my door and arresting me for the few plants I had that I was using to help my friends. Just wait until you get older and things start to hurt, Danielle. Marijuana is nature's most perfect medicine.

Lastly, I did want to thank you for the package you left on the porch. I must've been at my Greys (Alien) Anatomy meeting when you stopped by, so I am sorry I missed you. The signed first edition from Mary Balogh is one I did not have—wherever did you find it? Even though I am disappointed that you are not able to accompany me to the UFO convention, I am grateful for your gift of the three nights' stay at the Best Western. It looks like a lovely hotel, not far from the conference venue. That was very generous of you, especially given that you are unemployed.

Speaking of, have you started looking for a job yet? Have you considered returning to school to finish your studies so you might find a higher-paying job? I would never turn you away if you found yourself homeless, but your old bedroom has been repurposed into the headquarters for my wand business.

Best of luck with your competition event. Georgette said you have been training very hard for it? I am still flabbergasted that you'd rather spend the weekend doing sports instead of with me at the beach where you might find a nice young man. Try not to pull any muscles—your body doesn't heal as fast as it did when you were a kid, and thanks to you, I am out of medicinal herb. I have half a mind to send you a wand to keep in your purse, just in case you do get injured.

I have to tell you, it was embarrassing to read that your former boyfriend Travis has a curved penis—you sure write some strange things in your diary, Danielle. But FYI, that isn't such an abnormal thing. Gerald Robert Steele also had a peculiar anatomy, though your sisters both said that was information they did not need to know. I'm going to assume the same is true for you.

Okay, I have to run. I have a planning meeting for the UFO group. Dante told me about those flying drone devices, so our group is building a papier-mâché spaceship that will fit over a drone so we can fly it at the beach. Doesn't that sound like a hoot? That Dante is so clever for a five-year-old, although he stole a Twix candy bar last week when I took him shopping at Target. Georgette said this is your fault he loves Twix?

Thank you again for the hotel gift certificate.

Love and light,
Mommy

FIFTY-FIVE

"Steele with an *e*, get off your phone!"

Marco hollers at me from across the gym—I'm supposed to be doing my cardio warm-up, but when this call came in, I had to take it.

I hold up a finger to my lips and walk over to a quieter corner. Davina Gudbranson—a colleague of Janice's who found my blog when the email bot was doing its nefarious deeds—runs a small theater in Los Angeles, and she's on the phone talking with me about her ideas for putting together an original three-act play about my insane family.

". . . I know that having that diary up for the whole world to read was probably not how you imagined things working out for you," Davina says, "but I have to tell you that I loved how real it was."

"Diaries usually are. I'm so embarrassed."

"Janice and I had a good chuckle over some of your entries. I got the email from her, and I thought it was something she wanted me to see."

"Yeah, the emails—that was part of the hacking. Long story involving terrifying technology."

"Janice says you used to live in LA? Whereabouts?"

"All over the Valley. Last in North Hollywood, off Magnolia. Wherever I could find a cheap couch or room to rent."

"Yeah, I remember those days," Davina says, laughing under her breath. "So what I was thinking—we're just off Cahuenga—near Barham, in the Universal Studios neck of the woods. Do you know it?"

"Yes." I can hardly keep the excitement out of my voice. I know this theater! I've had two friends do shows there, and they run a top-notch company.

"I was talking to my assistant director, Jayda—she also read your blog—and we're interested in writing a show based on the Steele sisters, and Mommy, of course—we love strong women and the families that made them who they are—plus, we could mix in some of your undying love for Dwayne Johnson, because who doesn't love that guy?"

"Seriously, he's pretty much the greatest." My thoughts are aflutter with the idea of being involved with a production in Los Angeles— here I thought my family was fodder for Jerry Springer, but no! We're going onstage, ladies!

She chuckles. "We'll need to option the rights first, get permissions in place from you and your family members, so I'll talk to Janice about putting together a deal. If we can come to an agreement on that, we were hoping you might be available via Skype or otherwise as a consultant during the writing process. Beyond just the rights deal, we'd pay you for your time to come down to LA, offer comp tickets, what have you. I know Janice will have your best interests at heart."

"Wow, absolutely, yeah, I'm totally interested," I say, a little flag of concern waving in the background. "When you say rights, does that mean I would lose control over this material forever?"

"No, absolutely not. We can work out a limited rights deal so that we could use just what you grant permission for."

"Okay, cool. I just don't want to sign away my life, you know?"

Eliza Gordon

"Totally, I get it," Davina says. "Our initial thoughts were to write a one-woman gig, but then we got to talking, and the cast of characters could be so incredibly colorful."

"You do know I'm an actress, right? Janice told you?"

"I'm glad you mentioned it—we'd love to have you read for us on tape."

"I can have Janice send my reel."

"Perfect. Okay, cool—if we have a spot for you, would relocating for this show be doable?"

My voice echoes inside my head: *Yes, yes, yes!* But the practical side of things . . . "I'd love to be offered the opportunity to figure it out," I say, hoping she can hear my smile in my words. Although, would I have to audition for a role in a show about *my* life?

"Excellent. Let me talk to Janice about that too."

I jump up and down on the spot as quietly as I can, earning curious smiles from my gym family.

"Either way, if you're just collaborating long distance, we'll definitely get you down here for opening night. We'd love to have you be as involved as you're able and willing to be, given that it's your life, and your humor is really what drew us in."

If I could scream out loud, I would.

And I can hear DJ in my head: *Find the good in this mess. Silver lining and all that jazz.*

Davina continues talking, telling me how they're a small production company, but they're covered by all the local theater trades, that reviewers are always interested in seeing what the Three Ring Players are up to because they push the boundaries of "safe" theater, but their most popular shows are comedies, of which they try to mount at least one original production a year. I let her give me the spiel, even though I know so much about the Three Ring Players already, given that it's one of those troupes my friends and I admire and aspire to perform

282

with. Unfortunately, I left Los Angeles before I'd gathered the nerve to audition for them.

Davina explains that since it's now summertime, they'd like to get started working on the project in the next six weeks so they'll have something to put up for the first of the year when people are dying for something funny to get past the midwinter/postholiday blues.

"That's so fast. Can this even be done?"

"Missy, you'd be surprised how fast we work around these parts," she says. "We have a show already in rehearsals for January, so if this doesn't work out right now, we're not screwed. But the sooner we can put something together, the better. The really fascinating thing about all of this—it's greater than just your obsession with The Rock. It's about the cult of celebrity that has defined your entire existence. I mean, your mom named you and your sisters after romance novelists! You've had this famous name your whole life, and it's obviously shaped your personality and experiences. And so for you to have this undying affection for another celebrity, it makes a great story. It's like you've come full circle."

"But . . . what if Dwayne Johnson hears about this and thinks I'm a complete nutjob?"

"Part of the fun, Dani. You're crazy but lovable. And even if we can't get permission to use his name, it's easy enough to work around."

My heart deflates a little. I feel weirdly possessive of Dwayne Johnson—which is ridiculous, I know. He's not *mine*. But I loved him long before any of these bandwagon latecomers.

A phone rings in the background on Davina's end.

"I have to grab this other call, but take a day or two to think about this, and get back to me. We'd love to move forward as soon as possible!"

"Okay! Okay, wonderful, thank you!"

When she hangs up, I don't know if I should do a backflip or faint or maybe both.

I really do not need a day or two to think about it. I want to call her back immediately.

But before I do, and before Marco has a chance to holler at me again, I bound onto the treadmill and crank it up, energized by the possibility that: a) I could be actively participating in a theater production that doesn't involve opening the show by thanking a local hardware store for providing the evening's popcorn and Folgers Crystals; b) I could be involved in a theater production that does not include Shithead Trevor; c) I could be involved in a theater production that might get my foot back in the door that is Los Angeles—which could segue into a real life back where real auditions happen and real movie deals are made. What's keeping me here? My mother is healthy, my sisters can take care of her, I don't have a job anymore . . .

"What are you so giddy about? Good phone call?" Marco says, his voice startling me out of my euphoria.

I slow the treadmill down so I can talk without growing dizzy. "*Great* phone call," I say. "A theater company in LA wants to write and produce a show based on my blog and my crazy family and my Rock obsession, and they want me to consult—maybe even audition!"

"Whoa, hey, that is good news."

"Right? And it might be a way to get me back to LA. Now that I'm not tethered to the insurance company, there's nothing really keeping me here." I watch his face, not sure if it's just the naive romantic in me hoping Marco will endorse himself as a "thing keeping me here."

Please say it. Please say it.

"You are a free agent. We would certainly miss you, though."

I stop the treadmill. "Would *you* miss me?" I ask quietly.

He looks down at his feet for a second, and then back up. "You know I would," he says, his smile wistful, "but you have to do what's best for you. Not anyone else, Dani."

"Have you ever thought about it? Going back to LA?" I ask.

His eyes darken. "I have."

"You could be a trainer there . . . lots of LA bodies need hardening too." I slap my own ever-hardening butt.

He laughs under his breath. "There are as many trainers in Los Angeles as there are Subarus in Portland."

"Still . . ."

Marco's eyes, the deepest brown, like the bark on a Douglas fir, lock with mine for a beat. I don't know what else to say to him; in that moment, he looks genuinely sad, and now I feel like shit for bringing up the topic of him returning to his old life. His best friend *died* under Marco's watch. I can't imagine how hard it's been for all the people on that crew—when most people have a bad day at work, that means a mocha when you ordered a latte, or you're given bangs when you just asked for a trim.

"You and I have talked about that life before," Marco continues. "I do miss it at times." The melancholy on his face is evidence enough that it might be too soon for talk of LA.

And *really* too soon for me to be dreaming about a future where he follows me to chase my dreams.

"So, we're down to three weeks. Is there anything magical you're going to pull out of your trainer hat to make me the champion?" I restart the treadmill, desperate to erase that unsure look on his face.

His demeanor changes, back to professional-trainer Marco. He rubs his healing hand, the incision line now a pink scar. "Absolutely. Yes." He rolls his shoulders and leans over, cranking up the machine. "I was on the website, looking at the schedule of events for August 6th. The competition starts at ten sharp Saturday morning, so you'll need to be there no later than eight to sign in. Seven if you want to size up the competition and the course before everything gets too hectic."

"Seven. Wow. Okay. That's so early." My stomach knots.

"Hardest worker in the room, right?"

I nod, but it's not very convincing. "Um, you're going to be there?"

"Of course. I wouldn't let my star warrior go into battle without a lieutenant."

"I cannot believe it's already here. Time flies when you're crying through the Bengay."

"You've put in a great deal of effort over these past four months, and I do honestly believe you have a fighting chance," he says.

I'm winded again—damn treadmill. "Marco, what if I don't win?" Subtext: *Will you be disappointed in me? Will you stop being the one thing I look forward to every single morning when my eyes open, and the last bright spot I think about before I fall asleep?*

INT. HOLLYWOOD FITNESS - DAY

    DWAYNE "THE ROCK" JOHNSON
Someone's in love.

    DANIELLE
Shuddup. I'm on the treadmill here.
Don't distract me.

    DWAYNE "THE ROCK" JOHNSON
Dani and Marco, sittin' in a tree . . .
K-I-S-S-I-N-G . . .

"Well, if you don't win, then you know you gave it your best effort. You can only go into this experience with the expectation that you will give it everything you have. Victory is secondary, even though I know you desperately want to meet The Rock," Marco says.

"I cannot thank you enough for all the great things you guys have done." I wipe at the sweat pouring down my neck.

"Not a second has been wasted. Win-win all around, remember?" He rips off and hands me a paper towel from the towel station next to the treadmills.

"Thanks." I smile, blotting self-consciously. "I've taken up so much of your attention, though. I almost feel guilty about all the help and cheerleading you've had to do."

"You have been a bit of a handful," he says, smirking. "Never a dull moment. But that's why you pay me the big bucks."

Right. Except I don't. Trish has continued charging me per the great deal they gave Janice initially. So I've been paying Marco half of what he's worth, and even then, he's spending way more time with me than I'm paying him for.

This in itself ignites a sparkler of hope in my heart that he's working with me because he chooses to . . . because I'm more than just a client, or friend. And even *that* scares me, because hoping for someone like Marco, someone so positive and strong and selfless and beautiful, to love me back—I've had run-ins with hope before, and she can be unsteady on her best days.

"Ten more minutes. No talking," Marco says, and saunters away, stopping at another machine down the way where his next training client awaits—the beet-faced guy from the first night I was here, when I barfed in the trash. We've met once—Ken is his name? He offers a polite wave when he sees me looking. He's slimmed down nicely, and like me, not barfing, Ken no longer turns into an eggplant when he's been on the machine too long.

The whole place simmers with progress and positivity and productivity. The first night I stepped in here I was so nervous that everyone would point and stare and laugh and judge, but it's been absolutely the opposite. Minotaur is on the other side of the gym adding an insane amount of weight to the leg press; Limping Lady is working through her exercises assigned by her physical therapist with Trish with Muscles' patient help; Alex the Vet is teaching his new, very cute girlfriend how to use the bench press; Handstand Man just walked in and is chatting up the new girl working the check-in counter. Whereas I used to think that creepy, I know he's probably giving her a history lesson on how some Iroquois and other Native Americans living in New England fought alongside the colonists in the Revolutionary War.

These people, they are a weird, funny-shaped, sweaty family, and they've adopted me into their ranks.

Even if I don't win this competition, I will still have a home.

FIFTY-SIX

From: Jacqueline Collins Steele, MD, FACS <DoctorJacqueline@
JCSMed.com>
To: Danielle E. Steele <DS.May21972@gmail.com>
Subject: Your latest lab results, etc.

From the Desk of Jacqueline Collins Steele, MD, FACS

Hi, Dani,
Before we get into your bloodwork, I have to say again, I am
so glad your diary is off the Web. Because I'm now a medical doctor and established in my practice, it does not make me look very
good for the world to know about that SAT incident. You know
I suffer from debilitating test anxiety, and Adderall was the only
thing that saved me in college and medical school. Plus, this might
come as a shock to you, but some of my patients actually READ
that entry—how could they not, after I involuntarily sent them an
email with a direct link to the blog?—and I had to tell them that
you are an actress and it was all in the name of comedy. HONESTLY,
Danielle.

If I'd known snooping into your stupid diary all those years ago was going to lead to this mayhem . . . I'm almost afraid to email you now, in case that hacker person comes back around and publishes all your emails next! Have you even thought about that? What security do you have in place? Maybe you should talk to Samuel about what he can do through his law firm. One of my patients is a cybersecurity expert—I could connect you two. He's done very well for himself, which is why he's one of my patients. Even computer geeks love Botox.

Second, thank you so much for the help moving Jake's stuff into the Man Cave—I'm so glad it's finally done so maybe we can finally talk about something else—and for washing my car while I was seeing patients (you even put my favorite strawberry air freshener in—thank you!), and for baking so many loaves of your amazing banana bread. The staff nearly clawed one another to death over it. You did not have to do all that, even though I know you're sucking up to us because we're your beloved sisters and you can't live without us, so I want you to know I appreciate your efforts.

Finally, I got your lab work back. Thanks for agreeing to be my guinea pig—I was very interested to see how your numbers would change over these few months with the significant lifestyle changes you've made. And with these terrific results, I can now brag about my baby sister being such an inspiration! Your LDL cholesterol is way down, the HDL (or "good" cholesterol) is good, and your iron has stabilized. And your weight too—you're far below the BMI you were at previously.

You have done a remarkable job, Dani. I am very proud of you.

I have patients waiting, but I talked to Georgie about Mommy's convention thing. We've arranged for one of her other UFO buddies, a gentleman her age named Hubert, to do the driving with the offer we'd pay for his gas and lodging. Mommy says they're just friends, but it would be great if she would find someone else to pester instead of it always being us.

Jake was asking after Marco's hand. How is it looking? Did he ever see his family doctor? You can tell me to the moon and back that you're "just friends," but Jake said Marco looks at you like someone who wants to be "friends with benefits." DON'T BLOW IT, Dani. You're not getting any younger.

Did Georgie tell you we're coming to the event to cheer you on? Do you have any more of those Team Dani T-shirts? If you can secure two for us, call my secretary. Otherwise I will have her whip something together so we can show our support.

Your loving sister,
Jacqueline Steele, MD, FACS
Board Certified, American Board of Cosmetic Surgeons

P.S. I got your voicemail about Dr. Greenberg—I am SO PROUD OF YOU for finally making an appointment. Really, Dani. And don't argue with me—I'm going to pay for your visits until you get a job. YES. Don't argue. This is really important, little sis. OKAY? Good. Glad that's settled.

I know that Gerald Robert Steele's sudden departure from our lives hit you the hardest—but I think talking to Dr. Greenberg on a regular basis is going to be a very positive step forward. She's so kind—I've known her since college. This is going to be great.

Talk therapy works wonders, Dani Beth. Lord knows I've bought my therapist a cottage in Cannon Beach with all the talking I've done over the years.

Again, thank you for listening to your big sister . . . for once. I do love you.

FIFTY-SEVEN

"*Danielle Steele! Janice here. I just got off the phone with Davina, and she said you're in? This is awesome!*" [hoots into the phone] "*Before we pop the champagne, though, there are some things we need to go over in terms of writing up the contract—I think Davina talked to you about optioning the rights? You'll need to talk to your family for permissions, but I think we should specify that they change your names. This might make your sisters more willing to sign off on the whole thing.*

"*I also will stipulate that you have final say over the production draft so that they're not using stuff you absolutely don't want the world to see— and Davina is open to employing some artistic license, which I think is smart. That will add another layer of distance so that it's not completely biographical.*

"*I've sent down your reel for Davina and Jayda—I told her you're absolutely interested in auditioning and that we will work out the logistics if they think you'd be a good fit for their vision. Which is silly, duh—it's your life they're putting onstage!*

"*As soon as we have a contract hammered out, they're going to need copies of the blog entries that you took down so they can get started writing—I know the blog's off the Web, so we can email the entries to Dav. I know that blog thing was awful, but it's gonna open up doors for you, kid. This would be so much easier if you'd just answer your phone, but I know, you're probably on a treadmill right now—or maybe you're nekked with a hot trainer? Anything I should know?*

"Oh—my god, I almost forgot the next greatest reason for my call—I got you an audition for a tampon *commercial, Danielle! Can you believe it? Start interviewing pool boys, baby! It's a national ad, and the casting director, Natasha—you remember her? Yeah, she read your blog—she was the one who auditioned you for the all-natural shampoo when that baby crapped all over you? Same company, only this time for tampies, so no pooping babies! She wants to see you first thing tomorrow, so get off the treadmill and/or your trainer and* call me. *Byeeeee!"*

FIFTY-EIGHT

August 6, 2016

Dear Dwayne Johnson,
It's two o'clock in the morning. I cannot sleep. For a million different reasons. Should I list them? Lists are supposed to be calming. I read that on Facebook the other day. Maybe this list will be so long I'll fall asleep in a puddle of drool atop my journal with this baby cat sitting on my head. I think she got so used to sleeping in Howie's beard that she's not happy unless she's tangled in my hair.

REASONS I CANNOT SLEEP

1. I have to be at the competition location at Delta Park in T minus five hours. This means YOU WILL ALSO BE AT THE LOCATION WITHIN THE NEXT X NUMBER OF HOURS. GAHHHH, YOU ARE IN PORTLAND!!! We're breathing the same hops-infused, pollen-saturated air! What am I going to say to you if I win, and I end up on the stage standing next to you when I'm covered in grime and stinking to high heaven? WHAT ARE WE GOING TO TALK ABOUT? Oh god, please don't say we're going to talk about me getting a better brand of deodorant.

2. Actually, #1 basically sums up why I can't sleep. Bionic Barbie and a ton of other real athletes are going to be there. Am I nuts? I can do this . . . right? I'm down 26 lb., I'm stronger than I've ever been, AND I have very cute activewear that I've been saving just for this event. (You'll be glad to know I've gotten so much better at putting on sports bras.) Still, I'm absolutely terrified. What if I fall flat on my face? What if I break a bone? Hey—wait—that could work to my advantage. I break a bone, you come and rescue me, you hold my hand while the EMS guys wrap said broken bone to stabilize for transport, you feel so enamored by my charms that you wipe away my tears and ride along in the ambulance with me, we become best friends before the cast is applied to my injured appendage, you offer me a role in your upcoming film with WAY more lines than the role Bionic Barbie is probably going to win after she finishes in the top four. Although you know what would be even COOLER? If you brought a ukulele and we could sing a diss duet like you do at the WWE events. I could write us a ditty—a song about Bionic Barbie and how silicone implants don't make you bionic and perfect skin is so yesterday and how she probably kicks puppies and wears real-fur coats . . . THIS PLAN COULD WORK, DJ. Think it over.

3. Miraculously Beautiful Marco: I feel like I can't take a deep breath unless he's in the same room. He's been a little distant since I talked about maybe moving back to LA at some point . . . Do I just come out with it? Thomas the Singing Barista says I should tackle him on the bench press and tell him I can't live another day without him. He also suggested I do so while singing "Seize the Day" from Newsies. Luckily for Marco, I'm not a singer. And he bench-presses more than my body weight, so this sounds dangerous. But come on, he has to be into me—he's done so much in these last four months. Plus, I watch him with his other clients, and the way he treats me . . . it's different. But good different, the best kind of different. Maybe he's afraid. Maybe that's why he hasn't made a move. Maybe he's worried that if we fall in love, I'll give up on my dreams so I can stay here with him (he knows the stories about me giving up stuff for my family), but then one day, twenty years down the road, I'll wake up and resent him for it and he KNOWS that, so he's trying to be quiet. Or maybe it's just because I'm reading way too much into this, and I am, in fact, a daft idiot.

4. Viv called. THEY'RE HAVING A BABY BOY!!!! And she's bringing her pregnant belly and the MotherCluckers to the event this weekend. (When I took in the chocolate-with-buttercream-frosting apology cake and apologized to their faces, the Cluckers agreed to closet their spears.) I'm so excited to see everybody. Viv even promised to bring "healthy" cupcakes for after the race—I told her as long as they're not made with kale . . .

5. Remember when Agent Superman mentioned cached pages? Yeah. Those exist. A few have popped up—people somehow are still emailing me about the blog entries! But now that I have control of the URL, I've started putting together my own website with bits and pieces of stuff I've learned in the last four months, everything from the best brands of activewear for fluffier body types (me!), sports bras that won't maim you, how to work out when you're fighting with your uterus (seriously, we women have to be careful so that we don't leave a crime scene behind on the stationary bike), recipes from my gym buddies (including Limping Lady's INCREDIBLE high-protein cookies), the supplement and protein knowledge that Minotaur has schooled me in, and of course, all the stuff I've learned from Trish with Muscles and Miraculously Beautiful Marco about weight training and cardiovascular workouts—and YES, trivia and anecdotes about YOU. You're like the original motivational poster.

Even if I don't get to meet you tomorrow, thank you for being the man my father never was, and the man my boyfriends never are.

See you tomorrow, DJ.

Love,

Danielle Ain't-No-Candy-Ass-Comin'-to-KICK-Ass-Instead Steele

FIFTY-NINE

"I think I'm going to barf."

"Barf later. Concentrate now." Marco is in full Trainer Mode. We've signed in, I have my number safety-pinned onto my new tank top, matched with these adorable black compression-fit capris with little bulls all over them (The Rock's trademark is a bull), and now we're walking around the course's edge. I'm trying to listen to every scrap of advice Marco is offering about jumping high and climbing low and not expending energy making things more difficult than they already are, but it's hard to hear above the dull roar of terror in my ears . . .

A ton of other competitors had the same idea we did—show up early, scope out the course, size up the competition. High ponytails, messy buns, newly shorn heads, activewear from every major brand, water bottles filled with energy drinks and smoothies of all shades, lots of bouncing and stretching and pep-talking and course-assessing.

"No, I seriously think I'm gonna hurl—"

Marco grabs my chin and forces me to look right into his face. "If I did not vomit when I had to give a speech in front of Prince Charles and his not-yet-wife Camilla on our school's pro-environmental and organic community gardening initiatives, then you will not vomit in front of all these people who are just as freaked out as you are. Now, take a deep breath and pull yourself together."

As usual, Marco's right. I need to suck it up. The Rock would be disgusted if he saw me over here whimpering like a toddler. Oh god, he's not in a trailer somewhere watching us, is he? Is he in his trailer making awesome Instagram videos without me?

My resolve steadies as Marco runs me through a few easy drills and some basic stretches to make sure I don't pull anything, forces me to drink one of several bottles of amino acid–infused water so I don't dehydrate given the rising temperatures (of course, this means I must wait in line for one of the four outdoor Porta-Potties, twice. Wrestling up elastane pants in a poop-filled box hardly bigger than a broom closet without tipping the whole stinky thing over . . .).

And then I see her. Bionic Barbie, pinning her newly acquired number to the tank top that reveals toned, tanned arms I would kill for. The man with her is model handsome, as are the twin towheaded boys running about their impossibly tall parents. How she and I were EVER in the same audition waiting room at the same time, I will never know. She must've been there auditioning for a completely different project—probably something involving the next generation of genetically modified human beings. If she'd auditioned with baby Hazel, I think even that seven-month-old would've taken one look at Bionic Barbie and said, *Nope, can't poo on this perfect lady or I won't get into heaven.*

"Danielle . . . don't." Marco turns me around so I'm facing away from the arrivals area. "I see the wheels turning. You cannot let these other people get into your head. Remember, The Rock is *your* hero. No one else's. *Yours.*"

"Yeah. Right. Mine. Okay."

"Who's the hardest worker in the room?"

I smile. "Me."

Marco throws his head back and then cups his hand around his ear. "I'm sorry, are you a mouse? Because that sounds like the voice of a wee little mouse. *Me,* says the wee little mouse. I'll ask you again: *Who is the hardest worker in the room?"*

"Me!"

"Eh?"

"Meeeeee!" I yell, attracting curious looks from folks nearby. Doesn't matter. The ensuing laughter and high fives are exactly what I need to stop staring at Bionic Barbie's perfection and focus on my own badassery.

"No time for doubts. Doubts are for cat tattoos and dubious marriages. *You* are a warrior," Marco says, throwing his arm around my shoulders. When he pulls me against him and kisses the side of my head, I almost burn up from all the hope sparklers in my chest. Almost.

But not quite, because through the crowd I hear my name—the entire Hollywood Fitness crew is here, and they're outfitted in their Team Dani shirts, and Viv and her beautiful little tummy and her husband, Ben, and the MotherCluckers—Charlene and Shelly and Simone and the ever-elegant Lydia—and they've brought one of those magical pink pastry boxes full of cupcakes, "but for after the race, even if you don't win." Thomas the Singing Barista lifts me off the ground in a spinny hug and belts out a few lines from "My Shot" from *Hamilton.* Jackie and Dr. Jake and Georgie are here, wearing Team Dani T-shirts, and Georgie's little ones all have their own Team Dani T-shirts, even baby William Morris, and I scoop up Mary May and smooch her gorgeous cheeks, already flushed from the sun, and then little Dante shows me the picture he drew of me standing with who I assume is The Rock, and in that moment, he doesn't look like a future serial killer at all.

I honestly cannot believe it. The achy-lump-teary-eyeballs thing reasserts itself as I scan their smiling faces. Dumb emotions. Even after all those embarrassing secrets were pasted across the Internet walls for the world to see, my people still came out for me.

Pretty soon we're all bouncing around in a big, rowdy circle, chanting *Daaaa-ni, Daaaa-ni,* and I'm chanting too, even though it's my name, because these are my people, and with all this support and energy, I am going to dominate on that course.

When our chant dies down and *hellos* and *good lucks* and small talk are exchanged, the mic on the huge stage crackles to life, and volunteers in black T-shirts and tanks that read ROCK THE TOTS start urging people to their respective spots: spectators toward the bleachers set up on the east side of the course, competitors and one support person per participant toward the holding area where we'll be divided into our appropriate divisions.

My cheering section hugs me and Marco, and then hurries off to find seats while a young woman in a pencil skirt and heels, apparently the head organizer, launches into her spiel, detailing how the Greater Portland community has always been so supportive of their fundraising events in the past but how this year's campaign has exploded beyond even their wildest expectations, as there are people from twenty-one states and six other countries participating. She sounds like she's recently had a nose job and then followed it up by taking a hit from a helium tank. But then she mentions The Rock's name, and everyone within a two-mile radius loses their shit. Yes, Portlanders are passionate about their causes, but The Rock's magnetic pull continues to expand, given the demographic spread of contestants on the field today. It's awesome.

And when he bounds onto the stage, all six feet five, 252 pounds of beautiful brown, muscled god, my knees weaken. I freeze, earning the growl of the competitors behind us who are moving toward the area behind the massive stage, but I can't move.

He's here. *He's right there.*

"Marco . . ." I gasp, pointing at Dwayne Johnson, microphone dwarfed in his ginormous hand as he welcomes the huge crowd. I don't realize tears are streaming down my face until Marco hands me a tissue pulled from the zipped pocket of his Adidas track pants.

Eliza Gordon

Marco chuckles, his strong, glorious arm around my midsection, and I feel the burn of adrenaline start behind my chest. "Yes, Danielle, he's a real human being. Not a hologram or a figment of your imagination. Now let's get in the queue before we're trampled."

Reluctantly, I move my body, though I'd much rather just stand here and listen to Dwayne Johnson as he whips the crowd into a frenzy.

We hustle around to the area behind the massive stage. "Don't budge from this spot. I gotta find your division," Marco says, heading toward another black-shirted volunteer clutching a clipboard.

"Danielle." I jump. *No, no, no, not here.* Slowly, I turn around.

"Trevor." I leave off the Shithead part.

"You look good." He ogles me from head to toe, despite the female standing next to him. Thick brown braid draped over her shoulder, big brown eyes, makeup heavier than one would expect for an event such as this, a black mouth guard swelling her mouth region so that she looks like she's heading into the octagon and not an obstacle course, biceps and legs thicker than Trevor's, although that's not saying much. Maybe she's his bodyguard? She sort of reminds me of that scary Russian dude Rocky Balboa had to fight—what was his name again? Oh! Ivan Drago.

"What do you want? Here to serve me papers?" I know that's probably not the case even before my mouth says the words, given that both Trevor and his female companion have numbers pinned to their fronts. "Oh. Right. You're competing. I forgot."

"Dani, I want to put the past behind us. Bygones and all that, okay?" He pauses and shifts to his right. "This is Ingrid."

Ingrid—Ivan Drago's long-lost American sister?

Ingrid smiles but realizes she has the mouth guard in. She spits it into her left hand, a long line of slobber draining from the teeth grooves, and offers her right for a shake. I stare at it, not sure what to do, finally meeting her handshake, but fingertips only.

"Nice to meet you finally, Danielle. I've heard a lot about you."

"All terrible, I'm sure."

302

"Actually, no. I read your blog. Got a link through a friend of a friend of Trevor's—which is how Trevvy and I met."

Trevvy? "Awesome." I look around, desperate for Marco to return. I should be focusing on the task ahead of me, listening to the soothing sounds of DJ's voice, not exchanging saliva-laden handshakes with Trevor's new bed buddy.

"I just wanted to thank you, Dani. I'm not mad anymore," Trevor says. "The stuff you said in your blog—"

"No one was supposed to see that. Ever."

"Right, and even though I probably could sue you for defamation of character—"

"On behalf of your penis?"

Trevor's face flushes, but Ingrid laughs. "I knew you'd be funny in real life! That is actually what made me want to meet Trevor in the first place." She steps closer and lowers her voice. "I wondered if the curve would work with the G-spot, ya know?" [*jab jab with her elbow*] "Let's just say, luck-y me!"

Gulp. "Luck-y you." The nausea returns.

"Anyway, we should probably get moving to our lines," Trevor says, his arm around Ingrid's shoulders as she pushes the mouth guard back into her face. "I just wanted to wish you good luck."

"Thanks, Trevor. You too."

Ingrid mumbles something that might resemble *good luck*, but she has to wipe more spit off her chin when she smiles too widely, and then it's on her right hand and she's smearing it on her pants and I can't even deal with so much grossness this early in the day.

The happy couple hurries off, and I'm stretched on tiptoes to see if I can catch a glimpse of The Rock on the stage, but he's too far away and there are too many people. When a hand lands on my lower back, I spin around, expecting that Trevor will have actually remembered that he *is* suing me and—

"Whoa, careful, slugger," Marco says, hands up. "Did I just see Trevor?"

I nod. "He and his penis found love."

"I don't think I want to know what that means." He smiles quickly but then reasserts his business face. "Put him out of your head. Come, time to line up. Over here," he says, shuttling me around through the crowd, his hand still on my lower back, my heart beating a little faster given the warmth of his contact. "You're in the second group."

"Second? Is it not by alphabetical order?" I'm used to always going close to last, given *Steele* is at the tail end of the alphabet.

"No clue. This is where they put you, though."

The crowd is impossibly thick. Marco grabs my hand and steps a little ahead, clearing a path as he pulls me through. A million different smells waft from so many bodies buzzing with adrenaline and nervous excitement and the already impressive swelter of midmorning. I'm trying not to notice how fit and tight and strong all these people look. When I make eye contact with a woman who is wearing a CAN YOU SMELL WHAT THE ROCK IS COOKING T-shirt, I smile; she smiles back, but I see the terror in her eyes. Like looking in a mirror.

"What did we get ourselves into, huh?" I say as I pass her, offering my hand for a high five. She smiles and slaps me hard on the palm. I don't even know that woman, but I wish we were in the same group so we could talk about The Rock and not think about all these superhuman specimens.

"I thought they said this was for amateurs," I say under my breath as Marco continues to pull me forward.

When we get to my group, I line up on the competitors' side of the makeshift border, made by a series of tall pylons with CAUTION tape stretched between. Tape-and-pylon cattle chutes, but for humans.

Though we can't see what's going on in the front stage area, rock 'n' roll blasts out of the sound system, and the mic is back in the hands of the shrill-voiced event organizer. The competitors assembled in the chute in front of mine start moving forward, led by yet another series of volunteers in the matching black event T-shirts and hats.

When they're off and around the east side of the stage, a roar rises from the crowd. "Must be lining up for the course," I say. Marco nods.

"Move forward! Group Two, move forward, please!" More Rock the Tots staffers wave their arms to move us into the space just vacated by the first group. Though our clipboard-bearing event volunteer has a bullhorn, it's very hard to hear her instructions over the din of the crowd.

"Marco? What is she saying?"

He scoots forward, closer to the front, but quickly returns once Bullhorn Lady is done. "Just going over the rules. No sharp objects, no water bottles or recording devices of any kind on the course, no phones, no stopping along the course for selfies, and no cheating."

"Okay. I can handle those rules."

An air horn sounds on the course side—the first competitors are off! The crowd again erupts.

Marco plants himself next to me, on the noncompetitors' side of the tape, but he stands so close I can feel the shimmer of heat off his upper arm. He's sweating already—we all are—the underarm of his black Team Dani T-shirt damp, a sheen of sweat along his stubbled upper lip and under the brown curls along his forehead.

He turns and cups my face in his hands. I can look only at him. Which is not at all terrible.

It takes my breath away, and not just because I'm more nervous than I ever have been in my whole life, even more so than the time I had to go to the principal's office for duct-taping that fifth grader to a chair after he pushed Georgie off the bus and she tripped and chipped her front teeth. It wouldn't have been so bad, but this fifth grader had a *lot* of body hair, and when the tape came off, well, suffice it to say, he had less hair.

"Danielle Steele with an *e*: Remember what you're here for. You've been preparing for this day your entire life, not just for the last four months. You gave up doughnuts and ate broccoli on purpose. The stands are full of people who love you, people who want you to succeed. I will be alongside the course the whole time, cheering you on, and when it's over you will have accomplished something spectacular today. It's only a win. Do you hear me?"

Nervous tears threaten. I'm such a weenie when I'm freaked out.

"Hardest worker in the room, right?" he says.

I nod, and he drops his hands, though I don't want him to. I'd rather like to curl up inside them and vanish.

Bullhorn Lady waves her arms to get our attention. Marco offers his fist for a final bump.

Group Two is on the move. Thankfully, neither Trevor nor Ingrid Drago is in this group.

Focus, Danielle.

Hardest worker in the room.

SIXTY

It's impossible to hear anything out here—music blaring through speakers the size of my living room, thousands of spectators cheering and hollering for their favorite competitor, terror screaming through my ears like a hell-bound freight train. Good thing the event organizers took this into consideration. Few words are spoken; instead, the volunteers organizing us carry a red flag and a green flag. They herd us into position and line us up ten wide at the starting line, our shoulders bumping into one another as we jostle to put the strongest foot forward.

In my mind's eye, I hadn't imagined the noise and chaos of an event this size. It gives off its own surreal energy—I can see how people might get addicted. You can't not smile at the person next to you, even as you bump and nudge into position—all of us different sizes, shapes, and colors, and all of us delirious with excitement. A general giddiness permeates the entire realm, like nothing I've ever felt before.

And I really have to pee. I should not have finished that last forty ounces of amino acids.

An event volunteer, a painfully handsome black man with a smile as wide as the horizon, stands in front of our line of ten. He adjusts his earpiece, red flag in hand, arm stretched to the side. We wait.

And wait.

From this position, the course looks impossibly huge. *What the hell have I done* . . . I keep looking at the event volunteer, back to the course, back to his shiny face, hoping he won't drop the flag without me noticing and then everyone will run ahead and I will be left in the dust of my fellow competitors.

God, I wish I could see Marco from here.

I don't dare search the huge crowd for my people. I might miss the flag drop.

The massive obstacle course snakes back and forth, like an *S*, offering a fifteen-foot scaling wall first, followed by a wire on-your-belly-in-the-dirt army crawl, side-by-side balance beams, eight earth-and-log hurdles, wooden up-and-over stairs made with what look like railroad ties, a sandbag carry of maybe thirty feet, followed by a hundred-meter swim in a shallow man-made five-foot pool that is already tinged with the dirt from the first group. We're waiting for the last Group One runners to finish their two laps around the edge of the entire course.

When we were assessing the field upon our earlier arrival, Marco confirmed estimates that it looks to be about a half mile. I can do a half mile, no problem. We've been running four-plus miles three times a week over in Forest Park.

Man, I really should've gone to the Porta Potty again.

Hardest worker in the room Hardest worker in the room Hardest worker in the room.

The Rock is here, Dani . . .

A loud buzzer sounds far across the field, and our hottie holding the flag cups a hand over his earpiece. He turns toward the opposite end of the course, to the finish line, and offers a high thumbs-up to the volunteer signaling from a distance.

He spins back to us and trades his red flag for a green one, arm high above his head.

"Racers, on your mark . . ."

Oh god oh god oh god.

"Get set . . ."

Don't barf don't barf don't barf.

"*Go!*" An air horn blasts our ears and we're off, shoving and sprinting forward toward the first obstacle. So much for smiles. Now we're out for blood.

I'm moving, but my body and mind feel disconnected. Up and over the scaling wall, zoom through the wire crawl (yum, dirt!), fly across the balance beam, no problem with the earth-and-log hurdles, defeat the up-and-over stairs like they were made just for me—

I hazard a glance back and note that there are more people behind than in front of me, which brings another squirt of adrenaline.

Sandbag carry, no problem. Done and done.

I flop into the pool and swim my heart out, though I know I'm losing time here because I'm not an awesome swimmer and I'm out of breath and I gulp a mouthful of the gross water. The coughing fit that follows slows me down, and two swimmers pass me, but I spit hard and slam my body into overdrive, throwing myself onto that dirt track, running as fast as my feet will carry me, passing one, two, then three of the racers so that only one guy and one woman are in front of me, so far away that I don't think I can catch them.

I've trained so hard for this, and here I am doing it, and the crowd is going wild, and my body is cooperating, and I feel like I have wings.

Last lap. Running out of steam.

Hardest worker in the room.

I push whatever I have left into my legs, ignoring the searing burn of muscles forced to their limits, and I manage to catch up to the woman in front of me and I'm running running *running* because the finish line is just ahead and I see Marco there waiting for me, jumping up and down in his Team Dani T-shirt, and I have never felt more alive.

And when the dude in front of me takes the number one spot from our group, I collapse against Marco and I'm swarmed by my people and Minotaur throws me on his bulky shoulder and it's like I've just won the Super Bowl and we're all goin' to Disneyland. We hoot and holler our way to the side to make room for the rest of the competitors as they finish.

"Dani, that was so awesome!" / "You were on fire out there!" / "I cannot believe that was my baby sister!" / "Danielle, you made us so proud!"

So much love. And so much sweat.

Minotaur lowers me to the ground, and I give sloppy hugs to everyone within range. Marco shoves an event-provided water bottle into my hand. "Drink!"

"I did it! *I did it!*" I hoist my water bottle above my head like I'm raising the Stanley Cup.

The event organizers shoo us back toward the bleachers as they work to clear the finish zone for the third group.

Marco and I agree to meet up with our friends once I've caught my breath and had a bathroom break.

"I can't believe we did it, Marco," I say, bouncing more than walking toward the row of portable toilets.

"*You* did it," he says.

"No way. Don't give me that humble British-gent bullshit. I would not be here today if it weren't for you. And did you see? I finished second in my group! Can you even believe it? Does that mean I stand a chance? How does this even work?"

Marco points at the blue box. "Washroom first. Before you explode."

My legs are quaking so hard, I can hardly relax long enough to let my bladder do its work as I hover above the germy seat. I can't stop smiling like a Cheshire cat, even in the humid fog of this most disgusting rectangular shit pot.

I did it, DJ. I can't believe I did it. Oh man, I hope you saw.

When I'm again out in the free air, hands washed and breath caught, Marco explains that we have to watch the times for the competitors still running the track. He has my time in his phone. Even though I came in second in my group, I was the first female in that group of ten.

But there are many, many groups of ten.

As I realize this, my exultation dims.

"*Noooo*, don't get discouraged! Your time was very impressive. You were faster than the women in the group ahead of you, so keep your chin up, yes?" He taps under my chin with the side of his finger, and then hands me his John Cena water bottle. "Drink. Let's stretch and join your cheering section."

As the morning turns into a scorching early afternoon, my skin and clothes dry, but I'm coated in a thin sheen of dirt from the course and pool. Still, I'm so glad I was among the earlier groups. Selfishly, I'm grateful for the sun—heat makes people slower.

Just around two o'clock, we watch from the bleachers as the last group in the seniors' division takes the course. The crowd goes absolutely wild when these competitors finish. The emcee lowers the music long enough to tell us that the oldest competitor on the course today is eighty-four-year-old Ennis Dwight from Crescent Beach, California. He waves just before he flops into the murky pool, and by the time he gets to the last stroke in his 100 m, the entire vicinity is chanting, "*En-nis! En-nis! En-nis!*"

I'm out of words to describe how awesome it is to watch that old dude cross the line, and not even the last in his group!

With the final race run, The Rock returns to the stage to great fanfare and asks for fifteen minutes of patience while the judges confirm the final scores and make the winners' list, at which time the successful contestants will be hauled up and crowned the victors. Dwayne reminds us that there are food vendors throughout the venue, if anyone's hungry, but no one in the stands moves. We're too busy basking in the glory of his Royal Samoan Greatness.

He spends the fifteen minutes sharing a few stories about his two daughters, of the film he's most recently worked on, of his dreams of playing in the NFL and when those dreams went sideways, he called his dad from Calgary and headed back down south to "join the family business, the wrestling business," even though his dad said he would ruin his life if he did such a thing.

"I pushed forward anyway—seems things worked out all right in the end," he says, met with a roar of applause and cheers from the crowd.

I know all of his stories. I've read about them, watched every available interview and press junket, stalked every website created in his honor—and yet, none of it compares to actually hearing him *in real life*.

"If she smiles any harder, she might freeze like that," Minotaur says to Marco over my head.

Marco nudges his shoulder against mine, and I giggle like a drunken schoolgirl.

"I can't believe this is happening," I say. Minotaur's right: I think my face might be frozen like this forever, even as the muscles in my legs and arms threaten to revolt.

Totally worth it.

Just as The Rock is finishing the story about how, as a troubled teenager in Hawaii, he used to walk five miles to the gym every single day, and on the way, he'd always steal a Snickers bar for energy from the same convenience store because he had zero money, how he would eat the candy bar and it would give him terrible zits but he would go to the gym and work as hard as he could, that it was those really tough days that helped him learn to work as hard as he does now—the nasally event organizer from earlier returns to the stage, waving a clipboard above her head before she hands it to DJ.

Again, thunderous acclamation.

As everyone quiets down, I grab Marco's hand and wrap both mine around it. "Sorry, I'm sweaty. I cannot handle this."

He laughs, switches his hands, and wraps his left arm around my shoulders. "No matter what, you did amazing today." I melt into him. I can't help it.

"Drumroll, pleeeeeeeeeease!" The Rock yells, and a fake snare buzzes out of the speakers, fading out as he holds the clipboard in front of him.

He calls out the winners from the juvenile division. The crowd erupts after each winner's name.

Then the men from my age division. Same crowd reaction.

Marco squeezes my shoulder; friends and family sitting behind and around us pat my back and limbs and the top of my head.

"The winners from the women's age nineteen to fifty-four division . . ." The Rock reads one name. *Applause and cheers.*

Then the second name.

I wish they'd stop screaming so loud. What if he calls my name and we don't hear it because everyone is being so damn noisy?

The third name.

I can't breathe. I can't swallow.

Then the fourth name.

And it isn't mine.

SIXTY-ONE

We're standing in our big group alongside the parking lot, the course and event activities behind us. I've got my shoes off—the thick green grass just feels too good under my aching feet. The Rock is gone from the stage, disappeared to wherever demigods retire when they're done building mountains and throwing thunderbolts. Competitors and spectators wander about eating, drinking, dancing to the live music played by a cover band rocking out on another smaller stage. People shop at small booths set up by event sponsors; Georgie's kids have had their faces painted and played all the carnival games. Dante and Mary May are smeared and sticky with the remnants of an enormous pink plume of cotton candy—I raise an eyebrow at Georgie, shocked she would let them have what is basically kiddie cocaine. "What the hell . . . it's for a good cause," she says, her smile telling me that she's forgiven me for telling the world she's a sex goddess.

"Dani, you did so great today, even if you didn't win." / "You're still a winner to us!" / "Next week, I'm bringing the best brownies you've ever had. Every champion gets a cheat meal now and again." / "The Rock doesn't know what he's missing out on, kid." / "Just think how far ahead you are for next time!" / *"The sun'll come out . . . tomorrow! Bet your bottom dollar that tomorrowwwwww, there'll be sun . . ."* / "Mommy isn't going to believe you did sports on purpose. So glad I took video!" / "Auntie Dani, even though you lost, I really like your cow pants."

Everyone is so kind.

But my heart is still broken.

Most of our crew, my two sisters and wilting offspring/fiancé included, wave and fade off to the smoking-hot asphalt of the parking lot to return to their lives. I, however, flop down on the grass, pouring the last of my now warm amino-acid water down my throat.

"Come. Let's find food," Marco says. I can't look up at him. I don't want to cry. Again. "Danielle Steele with an *e*, I am your trainer, and I demand you get to your stinky feet so we can stuff protein into your body and replenish your muscles."

He nudges me with the toe of his shoe and offers a hand. I take it, and he yanks me up. "I think I saw a booth selling kale smoothies," he teases.

We wander through to see what's on offer in terms of sustenance. Marco—or rather, our noses—finds a Greek stand selling chicken gyros. He orders two, plus some sparkling water and cucumber salad, and we find a shaded spot under a tree.

I'm starving, but I'm also really goddamn sad. Every bite feels like failure. (Okay, that's a little melodramatic. Every bite is ridiculously tasty—I must know what magic they used on this chicken!) All this work, my hero so close and yet so far—like, literally feet away but surrounded by security. Who am I, though, but one among a bazillion crazed fans?

I don't know what I was thinking. Me with zero athletic prowess, dreaming I could beat all these other people who've probably been working on their jumping and running and swimming skills for their entire lives like goddamn Eastern Bloc Olympians.

And yeah . . . fucking Bionic Barbie. She was one of the four female winners.

315

Salt in the wound? Like that heavy, gritty salt we throw on icy pavement in winter.

"Stop."

"What?"

"The self-flagellation."

"No one's flagellating."

"Really?" Marco passes me a napkin and points to the corner of my mouth.

"A little flagellation never hurt anyone."

"Pretty sure that's the opposite of what flagellation is meant to accomplish. At least, in the religious sense. I suppose if you're flagellating for *another* purpose . . ."

"I should've asked Georgie to bring me her whip."

"Do I want to know what that means?" he asks, lifting a brow.

"Right. I forgot. You're one of three people in North America who didn't read my blog." I swallow a long gulp from the sweating sparkling water, wishing I could shrink and swim in its icy goodness. "My sister Georgette? With the three kids named after artists from the anti-Industrial Revolution Arts and Crafts movement? Yeah, she's a sex-toy maven. She has a whip and studded choke collar and a long chain leash. I found her stuff while babysitting, photographed it as evidence as per the Strategy of Sisterhood, and it was in my digital diary that the whole world saw."

"That little tiny strawberry-blond creature who was here cheering you on earlier is a dominatrix?"

"Apparently so."

"I don't think I will ever understand sisters."

"Me either."

"It was nice that they came out to support you, though. Jacqueline is very chatty."

"Did she tell you she's a plastic surgeon?"

"She did mention that once or twice, yes."

"Oh god, she didn't offer you a discount on Botox, did she?"

Marco points to his forehead. "Only here. Though I did hear a fair amount about Dr. Jake's new man cave." He winks and finishes his gyro, his napkin scraping against his dark stubble. "Still hungry? I can fetch you another."

"Nah . . . Do they have ice cream?"

He laughs. "You've got room for ice cream after those decadent cupcakes?"

"Is that a rhetorical question?"

We sit for a while longer, leaned back on our hands under the blissful shade of a generous maple tree, watching the crowd ebb and flow, catching a few passing conversations from other attendees who are still riding the high of seeing The Rock in person.

Marco sits forward. "Oh, before I forget . . ." He reaches for the zippered pocket of his long-discarded Hollywood Fitness windbreaker, now doubling as a picnic blanket under his tight buns. He pulls out an envelope and passes it over. The return address—it's from the Rock the Tots campaign.

"What's this?"

"Open it."

I do. Inside is a letter, thanking Hollywood Fitness and Danielle E. Steele for the "incredibly generous donation" of $7,850 for the Rock the Tots fund-raising event.

"We raised that much?"

"Close. The gym threw in a little extra. Keep looking," he says, pointing at the envelope.

Inside is a second folded paper. I pull it out, unfold, and two tickets drop into my lap. This letter reads:

Hello, Marco and Danielle!
We are so excited to extend our invitation for the VIP
Thank-You Dinner for ROCK THE TOTS, Sunday,

August 7, from seven o'clock in the evening, at the five-star Nines Hotel on SW Morrison, downtown Portland. Come spend an evening with everyone's favorite superstar, Dwayne "The Rock" Johnson, our host for a celebratory gala after an incredible fund-raising event. Mr. Johnson will be available for a meet-and-greet with our top donors, which includes you, so bring your best smiles and get ready to Rock! Formal attire requested.

See you there!

Sunday, August 7, 7:00 p.m. That's, like, tomorrow.

"Wait."

Marco's smile is blinding.

"Does this mean . . ." I pick up the tickets. ADMIT ONE, ROCK THE TOTS VIP GUEST. "Are we . . . are we going to this?"

Marco stands and brushes the crumbs off his pants. "Unless you're otherwise engaged."

I spring to my feet, not even caring that my muscles protest heavily against such sudden, ill-thought motion, and throw myself at Marco, bouncing and jumping and kissing his cheeks, even if it's inappropriate, because *I'm going to meet The Rock!*

"Oh my god oh my god oh my god oh my god!" Bouncing, jumping, more hugging, jumping in circles, some hooting, a little hollering, lots of people staring and smiling even though they have no idea why the crazy chick in the bull-print spandex is freaking the hell out.

I hug Marco so hard, he squeaks like a dog toy. I hold the letter in front of me again. "Are you totally serious? This isn't a prank, right? Because I will end you if this is a prank."

"I believe you would indeed end me if I were to prank you over so grave a matter." He shakes his head, his grin ripe with mischief. "My lady, unless you have a ball gown in your closet . . ."

I freeze. "Shit. You're right. We have to go." I scoop up my stuff from our informal picnic, throw my gym bag over my shoulder, and check my phone for the time. "It's so late—I gotta go! The stores are only open until nine on Saturdays."

"Stop at your house first."

"Why? Does Aldous have a gown I can borrow?"

"Just go home. Get a shower. We still have twenty-seven hours to come up with something."

"What does that even mean? Wait—do you have a tux?"

He nods.

"Marco, how long have you known about this? You shoulda told me so I'd have time to get a dress!"

"You need to stop fretting."

That's it. I can't. I don't even care if my breath smells like Greek food mixed with chocolate cupcakes.

I throw myself at him again, and this time I kiss him. On the lips. And he kisses me back.

We kiss, and we kiss, and I moan against his mouth because I have never, ever been this drunk on a man. Marco's hand is in my hair, and mine are in his, and his other arm and hand are pulling me against him, and I only stop because I feel him slow down and smile against my mouth.

"Woman, it took you long enough," he says.

I could fly right now. I could fly to the moon and back.

"We should probably behave ourselves. Family environment," he teases, kissing the corner of my mouth. He then lets me go, but not really, because he's holding my hand as he grabs his gym bag from the ground with his free hand.

We start toward the parking lot, fingers intertwined. "How long have you been waiting for me to kiss you?" I ask.

"Since the night we found Howie."

Eliza Gordon

"But . . . why didn't you say anything? Why didn't you make a move? Why did you wait for me?"

"Because. It wasn't my place—first, I'm your trainer, so that could be seen as inappropriate; second, I didn't want to step into whatever was going on with Trevor. I wanted it to be on *your* terms. Believe me—this has been brutal."

"Really? Because *I love hearing that.* I love hearing that so much, I want you to say it again."

We stop next to Flex Kavana, his face so close, his lips brushing against mine as he speaks. "It's been bruuuuuutal waiting for you," he says, smiling. He takes my keys and opens the trunk to throw my bag in for me. He then walks back to me, takes my face in his hands, and kisses me again.

When we come up for air—which feels impossible because I only want to breathe him—he smiles and tucks a few errant hairs behind my ear. "We can talk after we find you something to wear. You have a date with destiny tomorrow, remember?"

"I can't believe this is happening. All of this . . ."

"You made it happen, darling."

"*You* made it happen."

"I'll only take a little credit."

"I'm actually going to meet The Rock. What am I going to say? What kind of dress should I look for? Something sexy?"

"Yes, please." Marco smiles.

"But I don't want him to think I'm hitting on him. Although if I get something too conservative, he'll think I'm an old lady or that I'm uptight, and then maybe he won't tell me a joke 'cause he'll be afraid to offend me. Oh man, I have to remember to shut my mouth before it starts rambling about some random trivia that I've been carrying around since I was twelve. *Oh,* I should bring the trading card Handstand Man gave me! Do you think Dwayne would sign it?"

"Go home. More fluids," he instructs. "Ibuprofen if you need it. High protein for dinner. And get your beauty sleep."

"*Marcellus*, I have to find a dress."

"You will," he says. "You did terrifically today, Dani. I am unbearably proud of you." He wraps his arms around me, squeezes, and then kisses me again. It has quickly become my most favorite thing ever, the bristle of his five-o'clock shadow against my face, his full lips against mine, how he holds my head like I'm made of glass, but tempered glass—he's gentle, but there's power behind his grip.

"Are you sure you don't want to come home with me?" I whisper against his mouth.

"Good things come to those who wait." And then he backs away, our fingers stretched between us until they untangle, mischief written all over his face.

If Flex Kavana weren't holding me up, I'd be a puddle on the smoking asphalt.

⌒

I don't technically break any laws on the drive home—except for that silly speed limit thing, and really, isn't that more of a guideline?

Car parked, I fly upstairs, fumble with my keys, and curse at my stupid sticky front door that scrapes the floor as I shove it open.

"*Surpriiiiiise!*"

I about pee down my leg. My living room has humans in it: Jackie, Georgie and Mary May, Esther the Limping Lady, Trish with Muscles, Charlene, Shelly, Lydia, and Viv, who has Aldous resting atop her swelling tummy. Along the back of the couch and on a metal garment rack positioned in front of the bookcases—dresses. A whole bunch of dresses.

"How the hell . . . Did you *know*? Did you all know?" The collective laugh and squeals tell me everything I need to know. "How did you guys pull this off? And where are all these dresses from?"

"Marco got ahold of us ten days ago, and we went to work."

I cannot believe this. I cannot believe everything this man has done for me.

Woman, it took you long enough.

My knees wobble with the very recent memory of his lips against mine, and I brace myself on the surface of the sofa table in front of me.

Georgie hoists Mary May, her face now cleaned of pink sugar, onto her hip. I don't see my nephews here—I'm guessing this is a Girls' Only event.

"But . . . how?"

"We're very crafty people when we put our minds together, Danielle," Jackie says. "Don't look a gift horse in the mouth. Let's just play dress-up!" Jackie spins around, nearly whipping me with her chestnut ponytail. "Who's in charge of champagne?"

"Me!" Lydia glides into the kitchen. I almost warn her to duck, but she can't be *that* tall.

"Before I do anything, I MUST take a shower," I say.

"Yes. Please do. We can smell you from over here," Shelly teases.

Before I disappear into my room to cleanse myself of athletic stench, I remember to grab my journal, the one Marco gave me to write my letters to Dwayne Johnson, from the box of Howie's books on the kitchen table. I'd hidden it among the spines, but I don't want to take any chances. You'd think I'd have learned my lesson, leaving my personal missives out in the open. Then again, when I left here at the crack of dawn this morning, I had no way of knowing that when I returned home, my cozy apartment would've been transformed into the formal-wear department of Nordstrom.

I flip on the shower, hot as I can stand it despite the roasting temperatures still lingering outdoors. The first rinse of my hair darkens the shower bottom, more dirt than water. I wash quickly so I can lean against the tiled wall and let the hot water knead my muscles, unable and unwilling to wash the rapturous smile from my face as I replay the events of this day—in particular, the last hour. His hands on my face, my hair, my body, him telling me he's so proud of me, telling me he's been waiting for me to make the first move, him admitting that all these weeks, he's had feelings for me too . . .

Knock-knock. The bathroom door opens.

"Dani, you have a strapless bra, yeah? Do you have any Spanx?" Georgie says.

Still smiling, I turn off the faucet, wrap in a towel, and step out. "I do, but I've reshaped my bod so the stuff I have doesn't fit like it should."

"Yeah, your ass is smaller than mine now. I sort of hate you for that."

"But you've had three kids. You get a pass. Plus," I spin her around and examine her backside, "you still have a nice butt."

Georgie stands in front of me, her hands on my still-damp upper arms—she's shorter by a few inches. Just a tiny little thing, and I'm positive she's still smaller than I am in every way, despite being fifteen months older *and* the mother of three. We teasingly call her Elastigirl. She pops out a kid and springs right back to her prior size. Her fuzzy strawberry-blond hair is pulled back in a messy ponytail, escaped curls arcing toward her face, making her look all of fifteen.

"I was really proud of you out there today, sis," she says. "I had no idea what this whole thing entailed, so I'm still sort of in awe."

"Thanks, Georgie."

"The Rock—he is pretty awesome."

"I've been telling you that for a million years."

"I was never into wrestling, though. That was sort of between you and Gerald Robert Steele."

"Do you remember anything good about him?"

"He wasn't the same father to me and Jackie that he was to you, Dani. Maybe because you were the baby? He worked a lot when we were little. And he and Mommy fought a lot. He always felt like a visitor with us—and I know you were really sad when he left, but life was so much more peaceful, don't you think?"

"Yeah, I guess," I say, turning so she can run the comb through my wet hair.

"That's why you love The Rock, though, isn't it? Because Dad did?"

"No. I love him because he's nothing like Dad. The Rock would never leave his girls behind."

We're both quiet as she untangles a knot. "So . . ." She clears her throat, "anything you want to tell me? You know . . . about a certain hot British trainer?"

Heat prickles my cheeks, and I'm smiling again. "Marco."

"I thought his full name was Miraculously Beautiful Marco . . ." She pinches the back of my arm. "And I'm going to guess by the size of the shit-eating grin on your face that he might find you miraculously beautiful too."

I smile harder.

"Did he read the blog?"

"He says he didn't," I say.

"Probably for the best."

"Yeah, probably why he kissed me before I left Delta Park."

She spins me around, and I almost lose hold on my towel. *"Whaaaaaat?"*

"God, Georgie . . . I'm so in love. Like, this is serious."

She squishes my cheeks between her hands. "I knew that sparkle in your eye had nothing to do with The Rock."

"Don't tell the whole world yet, okay?"

"What, you're not going to blog about it?" she teases.

"I'm serious. I don't want to jinx anything."

"I saw the way he looked at you today, Dani. I don't think there's anything to jinx," she says, gently weaving my wet hair into a single braid.

"My blog is off the air, if you hadn't noticed. I'm all about the paper and pen these days," I say. *Yes, the paper that Marco brought me.*

"Your blog wasn't *that* bad," she says under her breath.

"Yeah, it was. You lost your PTA presidency because I outed you. I'll never be able to apologize enough."

"Oh, stop it. You've made amends. I told you how much Samuel liked that chocolate . . ." She waggles her eyebrows.

"Okay, gross."

"I'm buying some for you. You're gonna need it now, sounds like," she says, twisting a rubber band around the end of the braid. "And who cares anyway. Those PTA women were the worst. Most of them are cheating with each other's husbands over three-bean quinoa salad, so I'm not the most depraved among the kindergarten set."

"I really am sorry, Georgie."

She pats my shoulder. "Not another word. Now cover your tight ass so I'm not jealous that you have no stretch marks. We only have a few hours to get Cinderella ready for the ball."

"Love you, Georgie," I say.

"Yeah, yeah, you're a pretty good little sister," she says, winking and then slipping out of the bathroom.

As I rub moisturizer into skin pinked by ineffective sunscreen, I try to remember the last time she and I had had a conversation that didn't involve her nagging me about Mommy or telling me how tired she is or how frustrated she is that she's basically a single mother because Samuel works such long hours or how she can't believe she has so many kids and how she really, *really* misses painting that doesn't involve drooling, farting canines.

I've missed my sisters. I'm so glad they're here, rather than hunched over a cauldron planning my murder.

Panties and strapless bra in place, I wrap in a light robe and head into the living room. Someone has turned on music—so festive!

I have no idea where these dresses came from—a few still have tags attached—but I try everything from long to short, spaghetti straps to three-quarter length. Jackie can't stop touching my upper arms; she can't believe her little sister has biceps *and* triceps. "You're like a new body."

Yes. Yes, I am, Jacqueline.

By 9:00 p.m., those of us remaining, about half the crew we started out with, are exhausted—but we have a winner. A red strapless with an empire waist and a skirt that swooshes when I walk.

"The Rock will leave his wife when he sees you in this gown," Viv says.

"Technically, he's not married."

"Even better." Viv winks.

"Forget The Rock—did you see how her trainer fella looked at her today?" Charlene says. My face ignites, but I look down. Like I told Georgie, I'm not ready to spill any beans yet.

Aldous yawns and mewls in her sleep, curled up against Charlene's ample bosom. "Howie would be so happy to see how wonderful his girl is doing with you, Dani."

"She's a handful," I say, pointing to the recent snags in the curtains she has conquered. "Unzip me, will ya, Viv?"

She helps me out of the gown and rehangs it while I pop into my room to free my tired boobs from the suffocating bra. Though I still have champagne left in my glass, it's warm, and I'm thoroughly drained. As soon as my butt hits the couch, my eyelids feel like they weigh a thousand pounds each. I try to keep up with the conversation, but . . .

Next thing I know, Jackie is tucking a light throw under my chin, and my friends, one by one, say their goodbyes. I feel guilty that I zonked out on everyone, but the tank is empty. Once the front door clicks closed, Aldous insinuates herself under my chin, and we sleep the slumber of the sated dead.

SIXTY-TWO

"Hullo . . ."

"Dani, wake *up*. I've been calling you for an hour!"

"Who is this?" I didn't even look at the caller ID before I swiped to answer.

"Danielle, it's Janice. I need you to wake up." I slide Aldous off me and push myself to sitting—wincing because *dear god I am so sore*. "Are your eyeballs open?"

"Yes." *No.* "What's up?"

"In one hour, my friend Jericho will be knocking on your door."

"What time is it?"

"It's twelve thirty. You've been asleep forever. I thought I was going to have to send in the police to make sure you weren't dead."

"Wait—who's Jericho, and why is he knocking on my door?"

"He's a hair-and-makeup artist. Absolutely fantastic. He's coming over to get you ready for the grand fête tonight."

Tonight . . . the VIP event—I'm meeting Dwayne Johnson tonight!

I'm seeing Marco again tonight.

My stomach flip-flops.

I'm suddenly wide awake.

"Janice . . . seriously, thank you. You've done so much for me."

"Jericho owes me a favor. I got him a sweet gig with the Shakespeare Festival, and he happens to be in town this weekend visiting his grandma who just got back from climbing Everest, so he's happy to do me a solid and make you beautiful."

"Thank you. This is amazing."

"Jericho's great. You're going to love him, and when you look good enough for The Rock to eat, then you can thank me. You can be his cheat meal."

I have an hour to make myself presentable for Jericho. Because I neglected to give Miss Aldous her wet food at her usual breakfast time, she's helped herself to the dry food by chewing a hole in the bag. The kitchen floor is littered with the brown pellets she didn't stuff into her face.

"At least she didn't eat you, buddy," I say, sprinkling fish flakes into Hobbs's bowl.

My phone buzzes with a text.

Miraculously Beautiful Marco: Good morning—er—afternoon, Ms. Steele. Inquiring if it would be easier for us to take one car tonight. I can pick you up at 5:30 PM? Plenty of time for us to get downtown that way.

I am deliriously happy to hear from him.

[*fumbling fingers*] Me: Yes! That would be awesome. Thank you!

Miraculously Beautiful Marco: Did you find a dress? *wink*

Me: Well played. How???

Miraculously Beautiful Marco: Never ask a magician to reveal his secrets.

Me: Thank you. So much.

Miraculously Beautiful Marco: As much as I did appreciate your bull-print capris, I was concerned you might try to wear them to the event.

Me: You = no faith in my fashion sense.

Miraculously Beautiful Marco: With good reason. See you at 5:30. XO

I stare at his text, my brain on hyperloop as I review everything he's done for me since the night I walked into his gym and hurled in his garbage can.

He's the consummate gentleman—takes unrivaled care of his friends and family, doesn't send pictures of his dong to strangers, doesn't even read a girl's diary when it's up on the World Wide Web and everyone else in her close circle *did* read it.

And tonight, thanks to the money raised by the obstacle course *he* designed and organized, I will get to meet my lifelong hero, in the flesh, wearing a beautiful dress he also arranged to have brought to my house (I still cannot figure out how the hell he pulled this off).

This sort of thing doesn't happen to me.

And yet, here I am.

INT. DANIELLE'S APARTMENT - MIDDAY

DANIELLE
I have to be so careful not to screw this up. I don't want to say it too loud, DJ, but . . . I think he's the one.

DWAYNE "THE ROCK" JOHNSON
What would you do to screw it up? He's already seen you barf. He's already heard stories about and met most of your crazy-ass family. He's already seen you cry like a baby over having to do too many push-ups.

DANIELLE
I really hate push-ups, though.

DWAYNE "THE ROCK" JOHNSON
No one likes push-ups. But check out
those sweet triceps, Dani-girl. The
push-ups look good on you.

DANIELLE
(examines triceps in the mirror)

Yeah. You're right. They are pretty
sweet.

DWAYNE "THE ROCK" JOHNSON
(The Rock offers his fist for a bump)

Now, about tonight . . .

DANIELLE
My tummy hurts. I'm so nervous!

DWAYNE "THE ROCK" JOHNSON
About what? Didn't we already estab-
lish that you're not a candy-ass?
You've met a decent guy who sees the
good in you. What trouble could come
from that, except the fun, kinky kind
you should write about in your diary?

DANIELLE

He's such a good person. He does so
much for other people, whereas I just
write nasty things about them.

DWAYNE "THE ROCK" JOHNSON
Bullshit. You're letting fear whisper garbage to you. You and Marco are
perfect for each other--and as someone who's known you since you were
a kid, if I thought he wasn't good
enough for you, I'd let you know. His
mana is good. I can sense this stuff.

DANIELLE
Thanks, DJ.

DWAYNE "THE ROCK" JOHNSON
And you wrote some shit about a few
people. Who cares? It's not like
you're a serial killer, unlike your
sister's oldest kid. That boy's got
crazy eyes.

DANIELLE
I told you!

DWAYNE "THE ROCK" JOHNSON
Danielle, it seems to me Marco knows
a good thing when he sees one. Why
else would he go to so much trouble,
unless he was really interested in
making you happy?

DANIELLE
Maybe he's a crazy-stalker type.
Maybe that's why he doesn't have a
girlfriend. Like, he does nice stuff
for them, and then when she finally
says yes in response to his efforts,
he turns into one of those psycho
dudes who controls her every move.

DWAYNE "THE ROCK" JOHNSON
And maybe you watch too many movies.
(slaps my forehead) Wake up, Dani.
Not everyone is an asshole.

DANIELLE
Ow. (rubs forehead) He IS British.
Isn't there some rule about British
dudes? Like, if they're bad, we can
kick them out of the country because
we won the Revolutionary War?

DWAYNE "THE ROCK" JOHNSON
Maybe refrain from calling him a red-
coat tonight.

DJ's right. As usual. I'm gonna have to let my heart just go ahead
and fall totally and completely in love with Marco Turner, and if I'm
wrong, well, then, we'll deal with the fallout later.

(I don't think I'm wrong. Not this time.)

The growling doorbell assaults my ears.

Aldous comes running, more dog than cat, to see who has come
to visit her.

I open the door to a man with such a pretty face, he could be a doll. He extends a hand. "You must be Danielle," he says, wide smile of dental-ad-impressive teeth. "I, Jericho, am here to make you even more beautiful than you already are."

"Do come in. Flattery will get you everywhere."

⁓

Four hours later, I don't even look like me. I never want to wash my hair again; I want it to look this fantastic forever. I don't know how I'm going to pay Janice back for this.

After Jericho zips me into my dress, I'm able to scrounge up forty bucks and an unused Starbucks gift card for a tip—he tries to deny me, but I refuse to let him leave until he accepts my paltry offering. When I tell him I've never felt so beautiful, he relents and even offers to stick around until Marco arrives so he can take a few photos. It's like the prom!

"I'm so nervous," I say.

"You look sensational. Also, nerves make you shiny, and that little handbag won't have enough room for a powder compact," he says, pointing at the beaded bag Jackie left for me.

We talk about his work at the Shakespeare Festival, how he got into makeup and hair work, about his grandmother who really did just climb Mount Everest. Again.

When the doorbell snarls at exactly five thirty, my heart skips a beat.

"I do believe your Prince Charming has arrived," Jericho says, winking. "Shall I grant him entry?"

I nod. As Jericho pulls my front door open, all feeling leaves my body.

Marco extends his hand and introduces himself as he steps into the apartment. I feel light-headed, and not because of the tightness of the gown. In his opposite hand, he holds a gorgeous bouquet of long-stemmed white and red roses cradled in baby's breath and greenery.

I might swoon.

Marco looks . . . miraculously beautiful. His curly brown hair hangs in messy spirals; he hasn't shaved too close, instead sporting a fashionable shadow; and the tux. Dear lord, help me to breathe again.

He turns from Jericho, and his wide smile lessens to something . . . sweeter. "Danielle Steele with an *e*, you are a vision."

I'm completely drunk on the look in his eyes. I spin, the dress fanning around me and catching the attention of my spastic cat.

He presents me with the roses. "I thought of getting you a corsage, but that felt a little cliché, even for me."

"They're stunning, Marco. Thank you so much."

He steps back and looks at the dress again, his hands folded in front of him. "When I recruited those ladies to help find you a dress, I knew they would find something suitable."

"Did they? I mean, is it? Suitable?"

Marco closes the distance between us and takes my hand, kissing the back of it. I smile like a lunatic. I want him to do far more than kiss my hand, but Jericho is still here and I don't want to insult him by smearing my painted-on face all over Marco. "Honestly, the other women in attendance will run and hide in the coatroom."

Jericho poses us for a few photos, both serious and silly, to record this momentous evening on each of our cell phones. I'll need proof to show my sisters that I can act like a grownup female.

"Now that I know the prin-cess is in good hands, I shall take my leave." Jericho gives me an enthusiastic okay sign and bobs his head, lips pursed as he points at Marco's back. "Nice to meet you, Marco!"

I step around my date and thank Jericho again for his handiwork. His cases full of magic in hand, he disappears down the stairs. I lean against the closed door, trying to control my racing heart.

"You really do look exquisite, Dani."

I turn, at once unfamiliar with what to do with the arms and hands that have been attached to my body since I was little more than a blob of cells.

"Speak for yourself, Marcellus."

He pets his lapels and adjusts his tie. "I clean up all right?"

"You're pretty much the most amazing thing I've ever seen," I say, emotion tightening my throat.

Marco actually blushes, rubbing a hand over his stubble to hide the smile. "Be careful or you'll give me a big head."

"Too late," I tease.

"Ah, it's just the hair. Makes it look bigger."

"The hair is perfect," I say. For a moment, we stand ogling each other, him by the kitchen table and me still near the front door, crazy Aldous attacking the plastic ring from the almond milk container in between us—at least until she sees the flowers in my hand. Her pupils widen, and you can practically hear her kittenish thoughts: *What is that delightful creation? I could destroy those so good for her.*

"Is it hot in here?" I fan myself. "Can I get you something to drink?"

"Perhaps some water for the road? We should go soon." He smiles, but the spell between us is far from broken. In fact, I fear if you were to light a match, the entire room would combust. "Were you aware that you're only wearing one earring?"

I grab at my ears with my free hand. "Oh. Right. Thank you. It's in the bathroom. Lady Macbeth called in the middle of Jericho doing my hair—oh, I should get you water. There's Perrier from last night—"

"Let me take the flowers—I will water us both. Will I find a vase in the kitchen?"

"On top of the fridge." I start toward the kitchen, but Marco stops me, a hand light against my bare arm. Ever so gently he kisses the tip of my nose, his smoldering brown eyes locked on mine. Dear lord, if Dwayne Johnson weren't hanging out in a hotel downtown waiting for his esteemed guests, I'd tear every last stitch of clothing off our bodies and call it even.

"Dani, I can get the water. Go fix your ears." He smirks.

"Yes. Sorry. I'm a little nervous."

"You don't say." That glorious grin will never find its equal. I shiver as his hand slides down my arm, and he takes the flowers.

I retreat into the bathroom, holding the dress's full skirt so I don't trip and break my neck. Would be just my luck to get an evening like tonight but end up in the ER in a full-body cast because I forgot how to walk in heels.

Left earring reattached, I check for lipstick on my teeth, rinse with mouthwash again, and fold up a few Kleenexes to stuff in my impossibly small handbag.

As I emerge, Marco is again standing near my two-seater kitchen table, a sweating bottle of Perrier in one hand, one of Howie's books in the other.

"*A Farewell to Arms*? Howie was a Hemingway fan?" Marco sets the bottle down and cradles the book in his palm, opening the cover. "Have you looked through these?"

"Not really. I had my diary you gave me hidden in there earlier. Glad I remembered to pull it out before one of my nosy sisters found it."

Marco flips the front pages back and forth. "Dani—I think this is a first edition. And it's signed."

"What?" No way. I swish across the apartment, and he shows me the opened book. "You're kidding me . . . shit, it is."

He folds the book closed and turns to the box, pulling out yet another title. *Tortilla Flat*, by John Steinbeck. Not signed, but first edition from 1935. *The Hobbit*, by J. R. R. Tolkien, signed, "Second Impression, 1937."

There are ten more books besides these. All first or second editions, half of them signed.

In researching and gathering signed and first edition books for Mommy, I know this is more than just a friend gifting me some old keepsakes.

"These are worth something," Marco says, before I can get the words out.

"How . . . ? Why would he have these in a plastic bag in his shopping cart, and not in a bank vault somewhere?" I ask. "I can't believe they're in such good condition, either. This is insane."

"Whatever his rationale, he knew their value. And he gave them to you," Marco says, gently closing a copy of *Wise Blood*, by Flannery O'Connor. "You get what you give, Dani."

"But I didn't give him more than any other decent person would have. And he could've *sold* these. He could've had a better life, off the streets."

"Don't discount the important role you played in his life. Something happened to him at one point that led him to make the choices he did."

"He had a wife and young son . . . they were killed by a drunk driver," I say quietly.

Marco sets the book down onto the table behind him, and when he looks back at me, I swear his eyes are damp. "That day in the gym, when I told you how everyone there had a story—Howie was no different. Perhaps you look at it as though you only took him hot food or lent a patient ear, but it meant so much more to him than that. He saw something special in you. It's the same special *I* see in you."

My breath quickens. "Stop . . . you're gonna make me cry, and I'll melt all my makeup."

With gentle fingers, he traces the sides of my neck, down across the top of my shoulders. My skin erupts in goose bumps. "Let's save the makeup melting for later, shall we?" His lips twist in a roguish half smile.

I nod and swallow hard, resisting the urge to kiss him. "Should we go?" I squeak.

He slides the books back into the box and closes the lid. "To protect them from Aldous," he says, nodding at the crazed tabby cat hanging from my shredded curtains.

If those books really are worth something, my first stop will be the pet store to buy Howie's fur baby a proper cat tree. *Thank you, Howard Nash. Thank you.*

I move to the counter and pick up my beaded handbag, double-checking that the Miami Hurricanes trading card is safe inside in its plastic baggie.

"Do you have the tickets?"

Marco pats his breast pocket. Of course he has the tickets. "Dani, take a deep breath," he says. "You're shaking."

God, I am. But it's less about seeing DJ and more about the very visceral effect this tuxedoed man before me is having on my heart and other relevant anatomy.

Marco offers his bent arm. "Milady," he says, "let's go meet your hero."

SIXTY-THREE

I've driven past the Nines Hotel a thousand times since it opened in 2008; I've even longingly perused their website, promising myself that when I became a famous actress, I'd stay here when I flew into town to visit Mommy et al. Locals know it as the part of the repurposed Meier & Frank Building; to everyone else, it's the swankiest hotel Portland has to offer, the perfect blend of contemporary furniture and design with its bright colors and Tiffany-blue patterns and modern-day luxury with glassed-in meeting spaces and intimate gathering spots and a breathtaking atrium.

However, the website does not do it justice.

We park in a structure around the block, because getting anywhere near the front of the hotel is impossible—I didn't know Portland even had that many limousines.

There's even a red carpet!

The sidewalk and main entry are lined with enough tuxes and taffeta worthy of a state dinner or even the Oscars. Elevators take us up to the eighth floor to the front desk/lobby area in smaller groups so we do not plummet to our deaths from overloading. Once we step out, it is again a sea of gorgeous humanity, the air frenetic. While beautiful, shiny people greet friends and take selfies and exchange air-kisses, Portland's version of paparazzi snaps photos.

I'm squeezing Marco's arm so hard, he pats the top of my hand and reminds me that if I cut off his circulation, he'll have to charge me for the amputation.

We check in at an antique wrought iron-and-glass table set up to receive us and are directed to either the elevators or the "elegant bird-song stairs" down to the sixth-floor ballroom.

Sure, the elevator would be safer, but being the dramatic creature I am, I want to take the stairs so the whole world sees me descend in this dress.

By the fourth or fifth step, I'm regretting my vanity, forgetting how bloody sore my legs are from yesterday.

We make it to the bottom without incident, following our fellow revelers to the doors of the huge ballroom. Marco checks in yet again, and we're given our table assignment. I'm so glad his brain is screwed in right tonight—I am in numb shock that we're even here. This place is jaw-dropping.

The walls are covered in more of the trademark patterned wallpaper; massive white chandeliers with fluted glass sconces bathe the room in a soft, warm light; the plush gray, red, and blue carpet underneath looks more like a painting than a floor covering; round tables wear gray skirts, tasteful flower decorations at their centers, surrounded by padded red-and-gold chairs.

The human energy coming out of this place could power the entire city for a year.

Once we find our home for the evening, a waiter swoops in and takes drink orders. Marco orders red wine for us both; I am too distracted watching every possible entrance into the room, hoping for a glimpse of our guest of honor.

"Dani, have a sip," Marco says, handing me my glass. "We're here. Time to relax."

One by one, the other seats at our table are claimed. Marco holds my hand under the tablecloth, rubbing a thumb over the top of my knuckles. I'd say it's easing my jitters, but actually, it's hot. Every time he touches me, I feel like grabbing him by the lapels and doing unholy things to his person.

"They may ask you to leave. No one is supposed to look better than the guest of honor," I tease in his ear.

"Says the woman who is the envy of all who spy her." He releases my hand to squeeze my thigh, but I yelp. He laughs. "Oh, is that tender?"

I nudge him with my shoulder (also sore) and turn so the new people at the table can't hear me. "I must confess, this is the best first date I've ever been on. It's way better than getting my period at the miniature golf course."

He chuckles. "That happened?"

"Wearing white pants, no less."

"Well, for our second date, I've received confirmation from my mate Elon—you know, the fellow with SpaceX? We'll be heading to Mars for dinner next Thursday. If your schedule permits, of course."

"Mars? Again?" I feign an exasperated sigh. "But it's so hot. What ever shall I wear?"

"Maybe no white pants. They don't call it the *Red Planet* for nothing." Marco leans over and plants a light peck on my cheek, his arm around the back of my chair, his thumb rubbing the side of my shoulder.

What is air?

Once our table is filled to capacity, the usual small talk commences—what do you do, did you participate in the event yesterday, are you affiliated with the children's hospital, how much do you love The Rock . . . I let Marco do most of the talking, not only because his accent and charm has the women at the table—me included—held captive, but because I don't want to answer questions about what I do. *Uh, I was fired from my job of six years for inadvertently violating a nondisclosure agreement after my unpublished blog was hacked by a crazy person in an act of penile retribution, and also, I'm a struggling actress who is hoping a feminine hygiene national ad will save me from the streets.*

Promptly at seven o'clock, the perky organizer from Rock the Tots ascends the dais at the ballroom's front; she's been poured into a gorgeous emerald, slim-fitting gown that, despite its beauty, does little to soften the shrill of her voice.

When it comes time for her to bring out the Reason We're All Here Tonight, Marco grabs my clammy hand under the table.

And when The Rock bounds onto the dais and welcomes us to this fine evening amid cacophonous applause, I squeeze harder so Marco won't let go.

Dwayne again thanks us for our generous contributions and how we blew the top off donation expectations; he tells a few jokes and talks about his commitment to helping people after all the help he's had in his own life.

Lord, that man in a tux . . .

Followed by my next thought: *He's almost as pretty as Marco in a tux.*

⁓

The three-course meal—all organic, locally sourced farm-to-table fare—is serenaded by a string quartet. With the last plate cleared, I cannot eat another bite. Well, until they put a fluffy chocolate liqueur mousse topped with Belgian chocolate shavings right in front of my face.

"One hell of a cheat meal, huh? Please, don't tell my trainer," I say to Marco. The woman next to me tee-hees and agrees, mentioning that if her trainer knew she was eating this, she'd never be allowed off the treadmill.

"Yeah, mine too. He's a brute," I say. Marco nudges me under the table and leans close.

"You thought I was tough before . . ." Wink.

Heat surges in my chest.

Once dessert is finished and we're all fat and happy and half-drunk on the wine that flows like Jesus himself is in the back room replenishing the carafes, the event organizer invites us, one table at a time, to make our way to the photo area for the meet-and-greet portion of the evening. I hadn't noticed until she drew our attention to it, but in the southeastern corner of the ballroom, white paper has been mounted on backdrop stands; banquet staff are moving small studio lights into place. It's the ideal setup for attendees to have flawless photos taken with the One and Only.

My leg starts bouncing.

"Have you rehearsed what you're going to say?" Marco whispers in my ear.

"You mean my speech about how he is a god among men and how he's sort of been my best friend since I was twelve and I still have his autographed picture from fifth grade and that my depressed goldfish and his French bulldog would be BFFs because they have the same name and if it wouldn't be too much trouble could he just put me in every movie he makes for the rest of his life and it's no Iron Paradise but he should totally come work out with us at our gym?"

Marco laughs, "That'll do," and finishes the last of his wine.

At last, Table 22.

Oh my god that's our table.

Instead of racing to be first, I linger long enough to let our tablemates queue in front of us.

"Ever the strategist, Steele," Marco says, his lips so close to my ear, my left side erupts in goose bumps.

One by one, our fellow benefactors shake hands with The Rock, smile, exchange a few polite words, and pose for their photos. By the time the woman in front of us steps up for her turn, I'm afraid I might have a heart attack. My ears are overcome by that ominous roaring sound, my fingertips are tingling, I can't feel my legs, and the tunnel vision creeps in. Oh man, I should not have worn these shoes. And this dress is so *tight* . . .

Marco wraps his arm firmly around my waist. "Do not lose consciousness, Danielle. Come on, deep breaths." He lets go long enough to grab a glass of ice water from a refreshment table ten feet to our left. "Drink. It's almost our turn."

I sip the water and take deep breaths and do my best not to wither into a red puddle on this pretty ballroom carpet.

And then the lady in front of us is done, and we're still standing at the little tape line where we're meant to wait our turn, and the assistant is to my right, asking Marco if I'm unwell, and then, holy shit . . .

"Hey, you okay? That dress is something else. Would be a shame if I didn't get my picture taken with that," he says. Dear god, he is huge.

Dwayne "The Rock" Johnson just talked to me, and it wasn't even a conversation written by my overactive imagination.

"Yes. Wow. I am so sorry. I'm fine." I offer my shaking hand, so thankful that Marco is still propping me up. "I'm Dani. Danielle. Danielle Steele. That's my whole name. Well, not my whole name. My middle name is Elizabeth. Oh, and I'm not the romance novelist. My mom is just really weird, and she named all her daughters after romance novelists, all three of us. But I'm the only Danielle. The other two have different names."

Marco and DJ chuckle, and Marco offers his left hand for a fist bump because if he frees his right arm, I'll hit the deck.

"Well, Danielle Steele who is not the romance novelist, it's a pleasure to meet you. Thank you so much for being a part of Rock the Tots—you competed yesterday?"

"I did. But I didn't win my division. Which totally sucks. This is Marco—he's my trainer. And my . . . friend. He's awesome, so it's not his fault I didn't win. I was hoping to get to be in a movie with you."

"Are you an actress?"

"I am. Well, sort of."

"You live here in Portland?"

"Yeah, but I'd love to move back to LA. I used to live there."

"Danielle will be consulting on a production at a theater off Cahuenga she wrote the source material for and that, incidentally, is about you," Marco adds, his playful smile directed at me. Is that . . . pride?

Dwayne's eyes widen. "About me?" He laughs.

"Yeah. It's a long, weird, embarrassing, very true story involving an unpublished blog-slash-diary full of letters written to you called *Dear Dwayne, With Love* that was hacked and put up online, and the whole world read it, but yeah . . . You're kind of my idol."

He pauses for a second and looks at me with his head tilted ever so slightly.

Oh god, do I have a booger or lipstick on my teeth? Why is he looking at me like that . . .

And then the smile returns. "Well, I wish we had more time—and some tequila—because the long, weird, embarrassing, very true stories involving diaries are always my favorite." The assistant running the photo area mentions that we need to keep moving through the tables.

"Right. Sorry," I say, smiling at The Rock and Marco. "Can we get a picture?"

"Absolutely."

The three of us step onto the white paper—now that he's talked to me and I can see that, though he's definitely a demigod, he's not going to strike me down with the People's Elbow, I'm a little steadier on my feet. The assistant takes photos with our phones, and then a photographer snaps a few shots that I can order online at no charge starting tomorrow.

Marco and Dwayne shake hands, properly this time. "It was nice meeting you both. Dani, good luck with the play. You should have

Eliza Gordon

your director or PR person send my team the info. I'm in LA a lot, so maybe we can check it out."

"Are you serious? Okay, that would be incredible. I'll do that. Thank you so much."

"Thank *you* for being a part of our fund-raising event," he says, that thousand-watt smile dimming every last bulb in the room.

"Oh! Wait! One more thing—" I spin around like a kid who's forgotten to tell Santa she wants a puppy. I open my wee handbag and pull out the Miami Hurricanes card nestled in its plastic bag. "Will you sign this for me?"

Dwayne takes it and laughs as he extracts the card. "Ah, shit, where did you get this?"

"I told you. I'm a big fan."

The assistant pulls a Sharpie out of her pocket; Dwayne asks me to turn around, and he signs the card against my bare shoulder.

He's touching my bare shoulder.

"This is awesome—I don't think I even have this. The 1991 champs, baby. I think I might have the Warren Sapp card somewhere," he says, handing me the card and the Sharpie.

"Nahhhh, Warren Sapp is a chump."

His laugh bounces off the ceiling as he throws his hand up for a high five. He turns to the assistant. "Make sure this girl gets all the tequila she wants tonight."

We move back toward our table—or rather, I float.

Once everyone has had their turn hamming it up with Dwayne, he takes his leave to great applause. The string quartet is replaced by a DJ (of the turntable variety), and the photo setup is swiftly removed, giving way to a dance floor that soon is filled with bodies.

While my abused leg muscles are in no shape to break it down on a 20x20 floor crammed with half-drunk VIPs, Marco offers his hand. "One dance," he says. "It's a slow song. I'll hold you up."

Only a fool would say no to him.

He leads me onto the dance floor, pulling me tight against him, one arm around my midsection, the other at ninety degrees holding my hand aloft in a gentlemanly waltz position.

"Was he everything you'd imagined?"

"And more. Thank you so much, Marco. Thank you."

"Don't thank me. You did this. This is all you," he says, kissing me softly.

"I can't believe you told Dwayne about the show," I say, once our lips part.

"Can you imagine the publicity if he got behind it?"

"Only in my wildest dreams." He touches his cheek to mine. "But the play . . . if I go, will you miss me? Because I don't know if I can do it. I don't think I can leave you here."

"If I go with you, you wouldn't be leaving me anywhere," he says.

I look into his face, my eyes widening. "You'd go? Back to LA?"

"I could be convinced."

My heart thuds in my chest. Really? He'd go back, to be with *me*? "But . . . wouldn't it make you sad? To go back? Too many memories?"

"Portland's been very good to me. I've done a lot of healing——I'm learning to forgive myself, at least a little."

"Marco . . ." I feel bad that I brought this up, especially tonight.

"Spending time with you, around your infectious energy, makes me realize how much I really do miss my life and my friends there."

"No pressure from me. I swear. I'm sure your friends would be thrilled to have you back."

"You won't beg and plead for me to hitch my cart to yours?"

"Maybe a little begging and pleading," I tease.

We sway until the song fades and a faster beat takes its place. Marco leans close to my ear. "Shall we go find some fresh air?"

A plan I can get behind.

With one last, loving look at the ballroom, I follow Marco to the elevator to ascend to the hotel's top floor, which houses Departure, a very posh Asian fusion restaurant. Marco asks for a table on the patio, and given that it's just after eleven on a Sunday evening, there are plenty of seats to choose from.

Marco orders wine for me, an espresso for himself since he's our chauffeur, while I sneakily remove my shoes under the table, my aching feet grateful for the reprieve. He stands and moves to the glass railing overlooking Morrison Avenue, Pioneer Courthouse Square to the right, the shiny atriums on buildings up and across the way, the twinkly lights of a quiet downtown core, and east to the Willamette sleepily flowing northward to meet its big brother, the Columbia River.

He turns and gestures for me to join him; I do, trying not to focus on the fact that we're a million feet from the street below, and should there be a calamitous earthquake, we're in trouble because I think Dwayne Johnson has left the building, or at the very least retired to his suite to take off his supersuit.

"Did you have a pleasant evening?" Marco asks.

"Like a dream."

"Excellent."

Marco wraps his arm around my waist as we gaze at the beauty of nighttime Portland.

"I think this is possibly the best night of my entire life. No, not possibly. For sure. The best night," I say.

Marco turns, his bow tie loosened and the top two buttons of his shirt undone, revealing just the perfect amount of dark chest hair and skin that is olive by nature and a shade darker thanks to our recent sunny days. My wine-infused fingers long to touch it.

He leans on his left elbow so we're facing each other, his smile soft as he reaches for my hand.

A grin creeps across his face. "The night's not over yet. There's still time for you to cause trouble somewhere."

I punch his arm playfully.

"*Oww*, you're much stronger now than you were a few months ago."

"I've been under the tutelage of an excellent trainer."

"Is that right?" Marco moves even closer, his eyes on my lips. "Well, give him my compliments."

We're so close, we're breathing the same breath. I'm sure he and anyone within a one-mile radius can hear my heart pounding through my chest wall.

And then his hand moves from the railing to my cheek, and we're kissing, and he tastes like wine, and his lips are plump and delicious, and then his other hand is around my lower back, pulling me to him, and the cheek hand moves to my gorgeously coiffed hair, but I don't even care because it's just hair, and Miraculously Beautiful Marco is kissing me, *really* kissing me, not that sloppy, slobbery tonsil hockey Trevor was so good at, but a proper, sensual, teasing kiss that pretty much melts all the bones in my body—

"Your drinks, sir," the waiter interrupts. We pull apart and Marco nods at the young waiter, who is sporting a blush almost as dark as my Cabernet he's just delivered.

Once we're again alone, I can't look away from Marco's face, the way the twinkly lights reflect in his widened pupils or the soft crow's-feet around his eyes or the dark shadow that so desperately wants to be a beard but serves to turn me on with a simple brush against my neck or how he tucks his curls behind his ear like he's a kid.

"Is this real? Are you real? This kind of stuff doesn't happen to me. I don't follow through with stuff, I don't meet my childhood heroes, and I certainly don't kiss men who look like you," I say, my voice barely above a whisper.

Marco takes my hand in his and kisses my closed knuckles. "Four months ago, this seemingly timid young woman with hair the color of caramel and a lofty goal tucked in her pocket walked into my gym. This girl had allowed the people in her life to dictate her destiny to her, and yet there she was, taking the first step toward reclaiming the reins of her fate. Over the course of four months, she stopped whingeing long enough to recognize the power she has always had within herself, despite the obstacles thrown in her way, despite the efforts of others to dampen that sparkle that outsiders gravitate toward. She became part of an extended family; she showed me the meaning of true friendship and gave freely of her time, her resources, her trust. She showed me grace under fire. She showed me her humanity, even as the rest of the world laughed behind their hands or shot at her with their poison-tipped arrows. She showed me that she had what it takes to show up every day and get the job done, even when things hurt or when the entire world was in flames around her. She showed me that she can find silver linings, that she's a true phoenix who can rise from the ashes rather than paint herself in their soot."

I open my mouth to interrupt him, but he shushes me with a finger against my lips.

"You are the biggest handful I have ever trained. But you also have the biggest heart. You work harder than any of my other clients. When you come in, you give everything you have, and not just to your workout but to the humans around you. You *listen* to their stories and ask about their days and their kids and their pets and their jobs. You give them time, which is often all people need. Look what you did for Howie."

I hiccup against the emotion rising in my throat; tears sting the corners of my eyes, but his fingertips are there to catch them before they track down Jericho's paint job.

"When Danielle Steele with an *e* walks into the fitness center, the entire place lights up like sunshine has burned through the ceiling. You lost your job because that building couldn't contain you when you burn so brightly. *That* is why we're here tonight. It's because of you. Your friends wanted to give to you what you give to them every single day just by being you."

"You make it sound like I'm saving orphans or curing cancer," I say, giggling through a light sob. "I'm a huge selfish jerk. You'd know that if you'd read my blog."

"I would know no such thing. That blog—your diary—that's personal. And even if I were to read it, it would simply show me that you're exactly who you present yourself to be. A bit nutty, the butt of a lot of other people's misspent jokes, the unfortunate recipient of some questionable parenting. Who among us doesn't have skeletons in the closet?"

"At least my skeletons have cute activewear now," I say.

He grins and pushes his forehead against mine. "That's my girl."

That's my girl? I want to be your girl forever, Marco. If this is a dream, please never let me wake up.

He wraps his warm hands around my bare upper arms, and I shiver under the intoxicating feel of his skin against mine. When he kisses me again, the shudder is full body, helped along by the steady breeze that tickles the edges of the orange patio umbrellas.

Marco takes off his tux coat and wraps it around my shoulders. "Would you care for your wine?" he asks.

"I do have wine at my apartment . . . unless Aldous and Hobbs beat us to it."

He lifts a brow, his smile slow as he bends to my lips again. "Are you inviting me over for a nightcap?"

I whisper against his mouth, "I'm inviting you over for breakfast."

SIXTY-FOUR

I'm up against my front door, laughing like a hyena—which will surely earn me some angry Post-it notes on my mailbox from my neighbors in the coming week—but Marco is pressed against me, trying to get the key in while he bites my neck.

Aldous mewls on the opposite side. I finally take the keys from Marco so I can get us inside with more expedience, but as soon as my back is turned, he wraps his arms around my waist, his torso pressed against me, and proceeds to nibble from behind.

"Would you mind your manners? What would the queen think if she saw you?" I whisper, finally getting the right key in the lock and scraping the door open. Marco stumbles in behind me, his brown curls already mussed, even as he tries to tame and tuck them behind his ears.

My shoes off, Marco's borrowed tux jacket on the nearest chair, I hold up a finger to keep him at a distance, just long enough to disappear into the kitchen and get a cat treat for Aldous. I need her occupied for a little while so that I can be occupied myself.

When I come around the corner from the tiny kitchen, Marco is in the center of the living room, a teasing smile on his face, his eyes sparkling under the influence of low light.

Slowly, I tiptoe to him. He's easily six inches taller than I am, so I do have to look up once we're standing so close. Without a word, I pull off his untied bow tie, unbutton one, two, three buttons of his shirt, pull it out of his tux trousers, finish unbuttoning, and then slowly I ease it off his beautifully sculpted, olive shoulders. His breathing, faster than usual, matches mine, and my hand against his heart tells me he's feeling the same thing I am.

His skin under my hands breaks into gooseflesh as I touch the muscles I've only ogled from afar. I splay his left hand atop mine, palm up, and trace the fresh scar from his heroics at the bar.

"My hero . . . you are a remarkable specimen. I'm so glad naive young Nicola lives thousands of miles away," I whisper.

His hands move to my bare shoulders, up my neck. He cups my face and leans down to me, our lips again meeting, stained with wine and swollen with lust. Slowly, he reaches behind and finds my gown's zipper. The dress loosens and puddles around my feet. I tremble under the warmth of his touch.

Softly, he pulls away and pushes me back a half step. He examines me, head to toe. "I must say, I am quite good at my job." He reaches around and cups my butt cheeks; his hands then move up my back, kneading gently. "Still sore?"

"I was."

"And now?"

"Less sore."

He pauses and lifts my arm, looking at the ink along my left rib cage. "Your tattoo . . . I've not seen this before."

"I haven't spent much time at the gym in my skivvies."

"What a loss for me," he teases. "Is that a number? Ninety-four?"

"Promise you won't laugh."

His lips purse together, and he pretends to lock and throw away the key.

"It's Dwayne Johnson's jersey number from when he played for the Miami Hurricanes the year they won the national championship—in 1991."

Marco smiles and runs a finger over the tattoo. "Steele, when you dedicate yourself to something, you really are all in." He snickers and kisses my neck again, atop my shoulders, his breath light against my ear. My whole body feels like it's made of flames.

With a boldness I didn't know I had, I unbutton his trousers; his hands find the clasp on my strapless bra. Both garments fall to the floor.

We're both shivering, though it's far from cold in here. His smile is infectious as he traces the contours of my face. "You're beautiful . . . you do realize that, don't you?"

"Takes one to know one," I say. He kisses the tip of my nose, and when I look down, my breath catches in my throat—and not just because of his impressive physiological reaction to our closeness. My hands on his upper arms, I take a step back. "Oh. My. God. Are those—are those Rock boxers?"

Marco grins broadly as he pirouettes, complete with the required ass-wiggle, to show off his WWE-licensed undergarments. "After the John Cena water bottle, I had to step up my game."

I tackle him onto the couch, straddling his lap, both of us giggling like fools, laughter giving way to less childish fare as hands and lips and tongues express the mutual admiration we've been delaying.

"It did seem a bit odd to have met a man in person while my most sensitive bits were swaddled in fabric with his face printed all over it."

"I have a solution for that," I say against his lips.

"Do tell . . ."

"Let me unswaddle you."

Marco smiles, bites my lower lip, and in one smooth movement, he lifts me up, supporting my ass with both hands, my legs tightly wrapped around his waist, arms around his neck. I never want to let go.

He carries me into my bedroom; holding my body with one arm, he uses the other to sweep my discarded robe and the throw pillows onto the floor. Gently, he lowers me to the duvet. I scoot toward the headboard as he crawls on after me, his curls dangerously messy, his lips full and hungry, his eyes on fire.

When he's hovering over me, I rest a hand against his chest. "Thank you. Thank you for everything."

Tenderly, he bends to kiss me. "The night is still so young . . . Don't thank me yet."

SIXTY-FIVE

A rather annoyed feline sits on my belly, biting at the hair on Marco's arm where it rests just under my bare boobs. Morning sunlight streams through the break in my gauzy bedroom curtains. I hazard a look at my bedside clock . . . ten before eight.

"Is Aldous going to eat through my arm, or should we maybe feed her?" Marco asks sleepily.

I turn my head, inhaling and holding it so he doesn't get a noseful of my morning dragon breath. When his eyes creak open and he smiles, my heart skitters in my chest.

He pets Aldous before she really gets hold of skin, but instead of lavishing all his attentions on her soft fur, his hand pets my exposed fleshy bits, and he moves to lean over me.

"What are you doing?" I giggle under his weight. He buries his stubbled face in my neck, my breath quickening under his soft kisses along my shoulders.

"What do you think I'm doing? It's morning, isn't it?"

"It's *Monday* morning. Don't you have to be at work?"

"I can be a few minutes late."

An hour later—after an inconsolable Aldous has been fed because *come on you bad humans what are you doing can't you see I'm starving here*— I'm hogging the showerhead as Marco rubs out my muscles that are knotting up after a very physically active twenty-four hours. While I'm sad that Jericho's beautiful hair sculpture is now a sopping mess, it feels good to be free of pins and hairspray as Marco's fingers scrub the shampoo into my scalp.

"If I'd known barfing in a garbage can in front of you would've earned me this kind of specialized attention, I would've done it years ago."

He chuckles. "Well, let the record show that not all barfing beauties get this level of attention."

"What made my barfing event so unique?"

"Because you looked so completely pathetic when it was over."

I halfheartedly smack the side of his muscled thigh. It's the only thing I can reach with my back to him, and this scalp massage is too bloody good to interrupt.

"You know, my sweet Danielle, just because your competition is over does not mean you can fall back to old habits," he says.

"Sure . . . Yeah . . . Whatever."

He kneads a tight spot in the musculature around my shoulder blade, and my knees threaten to buckle. "We're going to get clean, get dressed, grab proper smoothies, and head to the gym."

My eyes pop open. "Really? Today? Can't we just be naked in my bed all day?"

"We will have time for nakedness after the gym."

I turn around, taking my turn with the soap. "Are you sure? I can give you all the workout you need, right here . . ."

He moans under my hands, but then stops me before I can work him into a real lather. "Gym first. Then dessert."

I push out my bottom lip in a feigned pout. "Promise?"

"Promise."

⁓

When he brings up a bag from the car with a complete set of clean gym clothes, I tease him about his forethought. He said that it was his evil plan all along to corrupt my virtue, and now that he's done it, he can return his tux, get his deposit, and escape to South America to start a new life.

While I finish getting ready, Marco busies himself by making breakfast smoothies, and then flops onto the living-room floor to entertain Aldous, who, by all accounts, is very much in love with Marco's wet curly hair.

We drink up and head to Hollywood Fitness, me whining the whole way about how tired and sore I am, Marco promising if I get through my workout without being a baby, he will give me a full-body massage at day's end to atone for his sins.

That is a deal any girl in her right mind would agree to.

The gym is quiet—just a few regulars. Handstand Man is upside down against the cinder block wall, as per usual, and offers a wave as Marco and I walk in, nearly unbalancing himself. Limping Lady is here with her physical therapist, and Minotaur is over in the corner stacking weights onto the barbell at the squat rack.

"You're going to have to buy more weights to keep him in your gym, ya know."

"Pretty soon we're going to bring in cars for him to lift. Cheaper that way," Marco says. "Warm up and I'll meet you on the bench press in ten, yes?"

"Fine. Meanie." He slaps my ass as I walk away. Limping Lady sees him and giggles behind her hand—and then gives me the okay sign.

Oh my god, they all know. I'm bedding my trainer.

I'm such a bad girl.

Then why am I smiling so hard?

I stash my stuff in the locker room and hit the treadmill. I'm slower than usual because I've very recently exercised those secret muscles that have not had a decent workout in a while. I can't even complain about doing cardio this morning, because with each pound of my feet I replay last night on the movie screen in my head. At least if anyone asks why I'm so flushed, I can blame the treadmill rather than the memory of Marco's mouth on parts usually hidden by clothing.

Ten minutes in and I've warmed up enough. Muscles are malleable. Armpits and underboobs are sweaty. Marco meets me at the bench press, loading each side with more weight than I'm used to.

"Uh-uh. Too heavy."

"I'll spot you. Remember: full-body massage."

I lean closer to him and lower my voice. "What, now that I've shown you my boobs, you get to boss me around at the gym?"

"I would've bossed you around at the gym even if you hadn't shown me your boobs. That was just a bonus." He smiles and kisses my cheek. "Now lie down."

"Say it again," I purr, "only with *please* this time."

This time, *he* blushes.

I take a deep breath and clear my head. As much as I like the banter, lifting ninety pounds above my head and chest requires concentration. Hands wrapped around the bar, I quickly glance back and forth to see just how much weight he's added. Yup. Forty for the bar, twenty-five plates on each side. That adds up to ninety pounds. If I can do it, it won't be the only personal record I've set this week. Wink wink.

"You can do it," Marco encourages, standing directly over me, his own hands at the ready in spotter position.

I uncradle the barbell. One, two, three, fouuuuuuuur presses . . .

"Help on the next one," I groan. His hands lightly support the bar so I can finish the fifth and sixth repetitions before he racks it.

"Well done! Okay, rest for a count of sixty, and then we do it again."

I stretch my arms out to my side and let the muscles hang loose. Eyes closed, I count to sixty . . .

"Okay, you ready for the next set?"

My eyes spring open. That's not Marco's voice.

"Holy. Shit." I start to get up, but The Rock puts his hand up.

"It's Dani, right?" He reaches over the bar for a handshake. "When you're done with this set, can I work in?"

"How? Why? What is going on?"

"Not too many gyms in Portland called Hollywood Fitness."

"But . . . how did you know . . ."

Last night flashes in my head—the funny look he gave me when I mentioned the *long, weird, embarrassing, very true story involving an unpublished blog-slash-diary full of letters written to you called* Dear Dwayne, With Love *that was hacked and put up online* . . .

"No. *No*, you did not see it."

"Hollywood is a small town, kid." His smile reaches the borders of the universe, and then he leans over the bar, his upside-down face right over mine. He really does have the most incredible skin.

"Are you gonna lift this bar, or are you gonna be a candy-ass about it and talk all day?"

Dwayne "The Rock" Johnson winks at me, trademark eyebrow hoisted.

[*Aaaaand scene.*]

SEVEN MONTHS LATER

From: Danielle E. Steele <DS.May21972@gmail.com>
To: Jacqueline Collins Steele, MD, FACS <DoctorJacqueline@ JCSMed.com>; Georgette H. Steele-Preston <pupperspaintwith-Georgie@gmail.com>; Penelope Steele <thegreyswalkamongus@ gmail.com>
Subject: LIFE!

Hello, Mommy, Jackie and Jake, Georgie, Samuel, Dante, Mary May, and William Morris . . .

Mommy! Thank you for finally getting an email account. My fax machine died so this is way better. (No, you won't get hacked. I know—famous last words.)

Now for NEWS: The show—PREVIEW NIGHT WAS SO INCREDIBLE!!! Everyone laughed at the right spots and people cried at the right spots and the part where we wrote in the father character actually coming back . . . the four of us know it didn't happen in real life, but it was some great therapy happening on that stage, you guys. Just wait until you see it. (Also: Bring Kleenex.)

Thank you for the huge bouquet. Aldous thanks you too—she managed to pull out a rose and cart it around the house for an hour before Marco cornered her and traded the flower for a fresh catnip mouse. That cat will do anything for him . . .

Can't say I blame her.

(*Ewwwww*, Dani's so gross when she's in loooooooooove. ← There, I said it so you don't have to.)

Every seat for the preview was filled, thanks to my VERY FAMOUS MUSCLED FRIEND, Mr. Dwayne "The Rock" Johnson, sharing our posters on his Instagram account. And you guys teased me all those years about my weird obsession . . . HA. Who's laughing now, Steele sisters? ☺ Not only have we sold out every show, we've extended the run into March. Davina is talking about maybe extending even longer . . . I can't believe this is happening! And I LOVE being back onstage again. God, I missed this so much. And no weird Trevor ogling me from the light booth. NICE.

Jackie and Georgie, I'll have tickets for you at will call. I cannot wait to see you guys again—TWO WEEKS!—and absolutely not, you are not taking a cab in from LAX. That's ridiculous. It's no trouble at all for us to come get you. I sold one of the books that Howie so generously left me and bought a new (used) car. I think Howie'd be okay with it, especially because it is the Aldous Mobile—she LOVES going for rides! You should see her at the beach on her little leash. We're the hit of the sands, I tell you. (But I do miss Flex Kavana. He was like family . . .)

The place we're renting is absolutely adorable—a three-bedroom in North Hollywood, which is perfect because it's close to everything for both of us. And since Marco is working all over the city, depending on locations for whatever film he's doing, we really couldn't have landed in a better place. I can't wait for you to see it. And absolutely, there is plenty of room for you and your plus-ones (yes, Georgie, and the kids!), so I don't want to hear another word about hotels. Tell Dante that we even have a pool, but he has to promise not to drown his siblings.

Jackie, remind me when you're here—I have this amazing parka that I ordered when I was considering moving to Antarctica. I forgot to leave it with you when we moved, and I think you can use it when the Oregon winter turns against you in the coming months.

Also, Georgie, tell the kids I've got the Disneyland passes. And remind them that I am a way cooler auntie than Jackie. ;)

Mommy, Marco says thanks for the wand, and the weed, although maybe don't mail it next time, just in case a postal employee opens the package. Even though pot is legal in California, the postal service is federal and I do think that is still illegal . . . ? Marco hopes you like the signed first-edition Daphne du Maurier—it belonged to his beloved grandmother and is worth a small fortune, so take care of it. Also, in your next email, I want to hear all about Hubert. Did he really propose? WHAT ARE YOU GOING TO TELL HIM? My sisters say they've never seen you smile so much. I think a fall wedding would be perfect—you guys could dress up like the Greys for the ceremony . . . food for thought.

Okay, I have to be at the theater in an hour. The reviews should be up in the local trades within a week, so I'll email as soon as I see them, and as long as they don't suck. FINGERS AND TOES CROSSED.

Love you all . . .
Dani (and Marco and Aldous)

P.S. Almost forgot! Keep your DVRs on standby because my tampon commercial is finished and set to start airing nationally—and you guys said I'd never amount to anything. Ha! Feminine hygiene is so important!

AUTHOR'S NOTE

A few years ago, I developed a weird tingling sensation in my lower leg—like cold water, or even a spider, was trickling down my left calf toward my ankle. I finally went to my very awesome doctor, and she diagnosed bilateral Baker's cysts.

"But . . . I'm not a baker," I said.

She smiled in the way only very awesome doctors-slash-surrogate-moms do and gave me a requisition for an ultrasound. As she exited the exam room, she stopped at the doorway. "Get some exercise, my dear. It will make them go away. You sit too much."

But the prospect of going to a proper gym scared me to *death*. Even after I joined a local club, because it was new and inexpensive and owned by a popular retired Vancouver Canucks hockey player, I paid my monthly membership for six months . . . and never went. Not once. The only other time I walked into the building was to cancel the membership I was too chicken to use.

When the cold spiders got worse, the excuses had to stop. So I bartered a portrait session (I used to do kids' photography) for a used, very squeaky elliptical. Slowly, I started using it. Five minutes the first day, and I thought my heart would explode; eventually, I worked up to thirty minutes at a go, which was a lot for me, considering I do sit most of the time. While I was an athletic kid and teenager, I've not taken great physical care of myself over the years of being a full-time working mom. (And I might have a wee addiction to sugar. And coffee. But mostly sugar.)

I bought a few light dumbbells and a yoga mat (that my tuxedo cat soon decided was hers). On top of my elliptical torture sessions, I added some strength-training exercises I found on YouTube.

And then for Mother's Day 2015, my family gave me three sessions with a personal trainer. "That way, you can learn the equipment and not be scared, Mom." Perfect.

On June 11, 2015, I had my first appointment with my new trainer, Shelly Fey—absolutely could not have asked for a better person to ease me into this intimidating world of iron and cable machines and sweat. A former rugby player, this kid is tough—she once finished a match with a broken jaw. While I knew she wasn't going to scream in my face that first day, as we got better acquainted, I learned she wasn't going to let me slide, either.

Slowly, Shelly helped me not be afraid of the gym. She gave me a journal to track my food intake and activities; she sent me emails with great meal ideas, healthy desserts, and motivational memes with The Rock's face on them; and she gives the *best* birthday presents.

The more training we did, and the more time I spent at the gym, sure, the healthier I felt—physically *and* emotionally. But beyond exchanging fat for muscle and improving my cardiovascular endurance, I became part of a bigger family—and they are always happy to see me.

My writerly life is solitary and sedentary. The gym has eased some of the loneliness. I found a connection to real humans outside the four walls of my office—not because we could lift weights and make sweat and flex in the mirrors (which we occasionally do), but because these people all have remarkably interesting *stories*. Every person who walks through those doors has a story.

And as a storyteller, well, that's music to my ears.

I may not have been named after a romance novelist, but Dani and I have one thing in common: When we obsess, *we're Olympic-level good at it*. As such, when I'm working on a book, I rely on actors and actresses to serve as my muses, and I obsess, i.e., I learn everything I can about that individual. For one such upcoming project, Dwayne "The Rock" Johnson played the muse role tremendously well. I'd spent so much time researching him for this other project, studying him via interviews, photographs, his huge online presence, magazines, websites, his filmography, even Wikipedia—that I felt I actually knew him. Everything about his journey inspired me—and he became one of the reasons I got my butt to the gym consistently. If he can do it, I can too, right?

One day when I'd broken a personal record at the gym, I joked to a friend, "I should write my buddy The Rock and tell him how awesome I'm doing. I think he'd be proud of me."

And then the little voice in my head said: "Maybe you should write a blog about it, and then people can follow and get inspired for their own personal health and self-improvement adventures."

Except I'm way too lazy to blog. Writing a novel sounded way more fun.

Which is how Danielle and her crazy family were born.

I love the quote "Be bold and mighty forces will come to your aid." Stepping into that gym the first day, a bundle of nerves, I had to be bold. And soon, the mighty forces did come to my aid, in the form of new friends who never cease to amaze me with their unending support, even when I miss weeks at a time because of book deadlines, sick kids, and life in general.

Like The Rock says, "Always be the hardest worker in the room . . ."

Challenge accepted.

ACKNOWLEDGMENTS

Ginormous, frosting-slathered, heartfelt thanks go to:

World's most darling, indefatigable agent Daniel Lazar—honestly, Dan, have you grown tired of me thanking you yet?—and his unrivaled assistant, Torie Doherty-Munro, who is such a cool kid, I still don't know why she talks to me.

Miriam Juskowicz and Danielle Marshall, THANK YOU times infinity for acquiring this book. I seriously jumped up and down when you shared your enormous excitement around bringing Dani's story to the world. I still jump up and down when I think about it, sometimes while holding weights, other times while holding chocolate-glazed, rainbow-sprinkle doughnuts. It's all about balance.

Tiffany Yates Martin, thank you for whipping the novel into top fighting shape—and I'm so sorry for all those bloody commas, sister. You would make a great trainer if this whole publishing thing doesn't work out. Also: you, me, Scotland. We're going.

Chris Werner, thank you for taking on this project and for your awesome enthusiasm every time we talked about it and for making me feel like a million bucks when you told me how much you laughed

AND for finalizing a title I love. So, basically, thanks for pretty much *everything*, sir.

Gabriella Dumpit, a writer couldn't ask for a nicer, more on-the-ball author relations manager. I'm so glad you're so organized, especially because I am not. (Side note: Your tiny human is so cute that if you ever get bored of him, feel free to send him to me.)

To the whole Lake Union/Amazon team: production editors Elise Marton, Catherine Bresner, and Nicole Pomeroy, as well as copyeditor Jennifer Blanksteen, thank you for giving this book the shape I imagined, especially with all my weird formatting requests required to tell the story in this style, and for tidying where I left messes. I know I ask a lot of questions.

Julie Trelstad, digital marketing guru of www.JulieInk.com, fellow scribe, and all-around great human who understands the technical things I do not, I love our chats. Red pandas + otters 4ever!

My gym family, thanks for always lifting me up, especially when I'm down. Honestly, you've all saved me, and I adore you: Shelly Fey—my fierce trainer—and Alexa, Stuart (a.k.a. "Minotaur"), Richard, Chris, Leslie, Justin, Lauren (her healthy pancakes Instagram is GOALS), Mo, Katey and Marc (the world's most adorable bodybuilder couple), Amir, Rachel, and Karen . . . plus, the folks who always smile and say hello, though we don't know each other's names. Even those few lovely women who have scolded me midworkout for building muscles because "women shouldn't have muscles; only the men should have muscles"—thanks for keeping my days colorful. (And ladies? *Lift!*)

Thank you Yolander Prinzel and Kendall Grey for beta reading and the brilliant feedback that always saves my butt. We've been friends a long time, and I rest easier knowing you've got my back.

Writer and comedienne Nicola Enright-Morin, thank you for making sure Marco's British-isms are spot-on. Is it time for gin yet?

Brodie Rogers and Taylor Hurley, thanks for taking such good care of Eliza Gordon during your bookstore tenure—and Brodie, thanks for introducing me to Ronda Rousey, another terrific, powerful icon of strength. Our girl rocks.

Victoria Harrison, Janet Lewis, Demian Lord, Jesse Minary, and the entire Indigo Chapters Coquitlam/Pinetree team (including the World's Cutest Bookseller, Yaunna Sommersby), thank you for shoving Eliza Gordon into the hands of eager readers and for all the awesome signing events. You guys sure know how to show a girl a good time.

My thanks also go to the family who shares this crazy life with me: GareBear, Blake (and Holly and Zoey the Superbaby!), Yaunna, Brennan, Kendon, and Nuit.

And of course, Dwayne Johnson, because you're eight months younger than I am and a million times tougher—so when something hurts at the gym, I visualize your beautiful face yelling at me about being a candy-ass—thanks to your legal team for letting this book move forward, and thank YOU for serving as my muse and the dude who screams louder than the other voices in my head. (Okay, now sing, "You're welcome." PERFECT!)

ABOUT THE AUTHOR

 A native of Portland, Oregon, Eliza Gordon (a.k.a. Jennifer Sommersby) has lived up and down the West Coast of the United States, but since 2002, home has been a suburb of Vancouver, British Columbia. Despite the occasional cougar and bear sightings in her neighborhood, there's no place she'd rather rest her webbed feet (except maybe Scotland).

When not lost in a writing project, Eliza is a copyeditor, mom, wife, and bibliophile, and the proud parent of one very spoiled tuxedo cat. Eliza writes stories to help you believe in happily ever after; Jennifer Sommersby, her other self, writes young-adult fiction. Both personalities are represented by Daniel Lazar at Writers House.

Printed in Poland
by Amazon Fulfillment
Poland Sp. z o.o., Wrocław